Who's your DADDY

USA Today and International Bestselling Author

Lauren Rowe

Published by SoCoRo Publishing

Cover design © Letitia Hasser, RBA Designs

1

MARNIE

"Fuck him."

"The audacity!"

"Where did all the loyal, faithful men go?"

I'm dining in a downtown Seattle restaurant with my four closest friends since college, as well as two delightful plus-ones for our monthly meal, and I've just revealed an embarrassing truth: the smooth-as-silk, silver-fox businessman who's been wining and dining me for the past six months—a man known to my friends as "Mr. BDE"—isn't divorced and single like he told me. On the contrary, he's happily married to "the great love of his life." At least, according to his recently discovered Facebook account.

"For six months," I say, "that lying bastard swore he's never felt a connection like ours." I roll my eyes. "I was such a fool."

My friends tell me not to blame myself. They say it's not my fault Mr. BDE lied to me. But it's hard not to kick myself when, in retrospect, it's clear I ignored several obvious red flags.

"Do you know how long he's been married?" my friend, Victoria, asks.

"Two or three years. I'm guessing she's not his first wife, since she wasn't even born when he graduated college, but who knows? Either way, he's been married throughout the entire time he dated me."

The table expresses another round of outrage.

"How young is she?" Selena asks.

"In her early thirties, based on her high school graduation date." I shake my head. "And here I've been thinking *I'm* a pretty-young-thing to him. When I saw those photos of her, I felt like I'd fallen off the big conveyor belt in the sky and straight into the old lady slush pile."

Everyone tells me that's ridiculous. That forty is the new thirty. That I'm in my prime and have never been hotter, sexier, more confident or alluring. But no matter what my friends say, I know the truth: since my mother's death a year ago, I've been a hot mess. I've been focusing all my energy on trying to be a good mother to my almost-three-year-old, Ripley, and a comfort to my grieving father, while also trying to keep my so-called career as a private chef from flaming out. The stark reality is that I'm a woman with an unhealthy knack for pretending to have it all together when I don't, especially when pretending to be a hot older man's carefree plaything.

Geraldine, the sweet, kind-hearted plus-one I invited to our monthly meal, smiles sympathetically at me. Given that I don't know Geraldine all that well, it crossed my mind to *uninvite* her after finding out this bombshell about Alexander last week. I'm not the best at being vulnerable, even with my longtime best friends, and I worried I'd clam up even more than usual with a new friend at the table. As it's turned out, however, every time I've looked at Geraldine tonight and seen the supportive, kind look in her eyes—a look that reminds me so much of the way my mother used to look at me in times of crisis—I've felt uncharacteristically safe to open up and spill my guts.

Geraldine says, "My husband cheated and lied about it during most of my thirties, so I spent that entire decade thinking I was paranoid and crazy. We've all been there, Marnie. Please, don't let him make you doubt your intelligence or make you feel like a cast-off old lady. I'm fifty-three, and I can honestly say I've never felt better or happier."

I met Geraldine three months ago at an expensive yoga studio I'd joined for networking purposes. Unfortunately, trekking to weekly yoga classes hasn't landed me a single new client, but if it turns out meeting Geraldine is the only good thing to come out of my failed networking idea, it'll be well worth it. Not only because Geraldine is *bona fide* friend material but also because I'm sure she'd make a fabulous girlfriend for my darling father. Since Mom passed, Dad hasn't gone out on a single date; but whenever he feels ready, he couldn't do better than this lovely woman. In fact, Geraldine's sweet, nurturing, easy-going energy reminds me so much of Mom's, I was instantly drawn to her at my first yoga class.

Selena says to Geraldine, "I was married to a textbook narcissist in my twenties and the first half of my thirties. But now, at thirty-nine, I finally know exactly who I am and what I want, and I think that makes me hotter than ever."

"Cheers to that," Victoria says, and we all raise our glasses and drink to aging like fine wine.

My very best friend in the group, Lucy, says, "I'm so glad I brought Frankie tonight. That's exactly the sort of messaging I wanted her to hear—that we only get better and better, the more we know ourselves." Frankie is Lucy's daughter—a college senior who's home for spring break. When Lucy got pregnant with Frankie during college, and then decided to have the baby, we all pitched in and raised Frankie, along with Lucy and her parents.

"Frankie," I say to our beloved college girl, "can you imagine, ten years from now, being married to a man who's fifty-five?"

Frankie shrieks comically at the thought, like she's been shot, and we all guffaw. "Is that the age gap between Mr. BDE and his trophy wife?" she asks. When I confirm it appears to be, Frankie says, "What is it with older men wanting women half their age? Old dudes constantly hit on me at the gym, and I prac-tically barf every time."

The group asks a thousand questions of Frankie and expresses outrage at her answers.

Our quietest friend, Jasmine, a pediatrician, chimes in to say, "When Antonio and I divorced, he immediately started dating a woman fifteen years younger. I was so pissed."

"He could only do that because he's wealthy," Victoria says. "If he'd been poor, no young woman would give him the time of day."

"She certainly wasn't with him for his wrinkled pee-pee," our college girl, Frankie, deadpans, and we all guffaw again. Frankie asks, "Would any of you date a much younger man?"

The table explodes with conversation, with every last one of us, other than Selena, revealing we've already tried that route, at one time or another, without much success.

Geraldine, my plus-one, chimes in to say, "Right after my divorce, I went to Cancun with my highly attractive—and much younger—personal trainer. The weekend was a bust, in terms of the guy himself. God, he turned out to be annoying. But it was a massive success in terms of me getting to post photos of the trip on Facebook for only my ex-husband to be able to see."

As the table laughs, Lucy asks, "You can post photos on Facebook for only one specific person to see?"

Geraldine nods. "From what my sons told me, my ex-husband's reaction to my Cancun photo shoot was exactly what I'd hoped. *Fury.*" She giggles. "Another good thing that came out of that trip? When I got home, I finally felt completely feeling ready to move on from my divorce, and I've never looked back since."

"Well, you know what they say," Jasmine offers with a wink. "The best way to get *over* one man is to . . ."

The entire group replies in unison: "Get *under* another one."

Victoria smirks wickedly. "Or on top of. Or in front of while on your hands and knees. Or sitting on the face of . . ."

"Oh my gosh," our young plus-one, Frankie, says, blushing, and we all laugh hysterically at her cute reaction.

"And, hey, if you can post photos of your shenanigans for only your ex to see, even better," Selena adds, grinning at Geraldine.

"God, I needed this dinner so much," I say, exhaling and leaning back in my chair. "Thanks so much, ladies. This week was a rough one, but I feel a thousand times better now."

Victoria pats my hand on the table. "Maybe you should take the age-old advice about getting over a man. Get yourself underneath a randy, young sex machine for a night and Mr. BDE will soon be a distant memory."

As the table agrees and goads me on, I bite my lip and try to decide if I should tell them the truth, especially in the presence of our two plus-ones. Finally, I decided to go for it: I am who I am. "I've already tried that strategy this past week—with *two* randy, young sex machines, as a matter of fact. And it was a total bust, unfortunately." Everyone demands further details, so I explain that I found the two hot guys on a dating app, immediately after finding out the truth about Alexander. "I thought it'd be fun to get some petty revenge," I explain with a shrug. "But it only felt empty and pointless."

"Did the two men already know each other?" Lucy asks, her eyes wide and blinking.

I laugh, realizing my best friend thinks I had sex with those two men at the same time. "No, honey. It was one guy at a time on two different nights."

Lucy's face falls. "Shoot. You know how I live vicariously through you."

I giggle. "You wouldn't have wanted to live through me this time. Trust me, I only felt worse afterwards, both times. Brace yourselves, ladies, but I think I've finally arrived at a place in my life where meaningless sex isn't my jam anymore. I think I'm ready to find my own version of Trevor." It's a reference to Lucy's husband, a wonderful guy she met when Frankie was ten.

Since the beginning, Trevor's always treated Lucy like the goddess she is and Frankie like his own daughter. "If a guy isn't at least serious boyfriend material," I say, "or preferably, husband material, then I don't think I'm even going to bother with him."

My friends express shock, and I'm not surprised. I'm the only one in the group who's never been married. The only one who's never even *wanted* to go the traditional route. My whole life, I've wanted nothing but adventure, travel, glamor, and glitz. In my twenties and thirties, I traveled the world, plying my trade as a private chef. I'd work for a wealthy family, or on a yacht, or in a luxury hotel, until I'd saved up enough to get me to my next glittering destination. And in every new city, I'd enjoy yet another exciting fling. Sometimes, a fellow crew member. Other times, the wealthy son of the old couple who'd hired me. Sometimes, a random stranger I'd met in a bar. And I always had a fun, fabulous, carefree adventure.

But when I got accidentally pregnant with Ripley at nearly thirty-seven—by a man I didn't even know how to track down—everything changed. I realized in that moment that I was ready for a whole new life. A stable one, where I raised my baby in my hometown of Seattle with the help of my parents—but, mostly, my amazing mother, who was over the moon when she learned of my pregnancy.

After getting that positive test result, I took the next flight home, moved in with my parents, and ultimately gave birth five weeks early with complications. A year after that, we found out Mom had stage four cancer and precious little time left. Looking back, it's no wonder I've been a train wreck since that chaotic, painful time.

"Okay, but what if a guy's *insanely* hot, even though he's not serious boyfriend material?" Victoria asks. "You're telling us you'd pass on the chance to smash a guy like that?" My best friends since college are well aware of my lifelong, high-powered libido and seize-the-day attitude when it comes to enjoying hot sex with hot men. Thankfully, they've always accepted me for who I am and have never looked down on me or shamed me in any way.

"I've already had sex with plenty of hot men," I reply. "I'm ready for something more, and I'm not going to find that if I keep wasting my time with sex that's obviously not going to lead anywhere."

We continue talking about my romantic aspirations for a few more minutes. But after a while, I suggest a change of topic, at which point Victoria nudges Selena next to her and says, "Speaking of younger men, tell everyone about your sexy little wrong-number text exchange with that adorable twenty-five-year-old today."

Laughing, Selena tells the group the whole story, which in a nutshell, is this: Earlier today, she received a lengthy, wrong-number text from an unknown number. In his text, a guy named Grayson invited someone named Katie out to dinner after meeting her last night at Captain's—a fancy bar that's right down the street from this very restaurant. Selena says, "I replied to the poor guy to let him know I'm not Katie, and that he should double-check the number she gave him last night. When he confirmed she'd definitely given him *my* number, I started dispensing dating advice to the poor kid. Well, one thing led to another and I said I *might* meet him at Captain's tonight for drinks after dinner with my friends, but only to give him some more dating advice, if so."

"Selena asked him for a selfie, and he sent *three*," Victoria interjects excitedly.

"For research purposes only," Selena insists. "I wanted to see what Grayson's working with, so I could give him the best possible advice."

"Did you give him your photo in return?" Lucy asks, waggling her eyebrows.

"Of course, not. I'm not interested in dating the boy. I was merely trying to help him figure out why he's not having any luck with women."

We all express skepticism. In fact, we're convinced Selena had to have felt some kind of spark with the young buck, or she never would have agreed to meet him in person. We ask to see the selfies Grayson sent, and when we do, we're pleasantly surprised at how cute he is. How gorgeous his smile. In fact, we're all surprised the poor guy is having any dating difficulties with women at all.

"It's rough out there for a shy, nerdy guy with very little experience and zero game," Selena explains. "Grayson said he was in a long-term relationship with his college girlfriend. This is his first time being single as an adult, and he's not very good at flirting."

We all agree Selena absolutely *must* go to Captain's tonight to meet up with Grayson.

"Only if you all come with me," Selena replies. "I don't want him misunderstanding and thinking I'm meeting him for an actual date."

Well, that's an easy one. At least, for our core friend group. Our two plus-ones both beg off—our college girl, Frankie, because she's already planning to meet some friends for drinks at another bar; and my yoga friend, Geraldine, because, she says, her "bar-hopping days are long over" and she needs to wake up early tomorrow for a sunrise hike with friends.

Our plan settled, Selena asks for the check and generously pays the whole thing, despite our group's protestations; and then, our entire group heads outside into the chilly Seattle night. After saying our goodbyes to our two plus-ones, the group, other than me, heads off toward Captain's down the street.

"I'll meet you there," I call to my friends, and they wave and keep walking. "Hey, Geraldine, wait up!" When I reach her, I muster the courage to ask, "Would you, by any chance, be open to being set up with a handsome, kind-hearted, fit and active, financially secure older man?"

Geraldine looks interested. "Maybe. Who is he?"

"My father. He's a young sixty-five. My mother died a year ago, and I think you two would hit it off."

Geraldine's face falls. "I'm so sorry for your loss, Marnie."

"Thank you."

She shifts her weight. "I'm honored you consider me worthy of your wonderful father, but I think maybe a year is too soon. Has he been dating?"

"Not yet. I think he'd consider it if he met the right person."

Geraldine smiles kindly. "I'm not sure it works that way, honey. I think he needs to be ready and *then* the right person will find him."

My heart sinks. "Yeah, that makes sense." I twist my mouth. "Do I have your permission to mention you to him, and if he seems interested, give him your number?"

Geraldine considers it. "Yes, but only if he says he truly feels ready. There's no rush when it comes to finding love. It happens exactly when it's meant to."

Unexpected emotion rises up inside me. God, I miss my mother. That's exactly the kind of thing she would have said. At fifty-three, Geraldine isn't old enough to be my mother, but she's got robust maternal energy—the same earthy, non-judgmental, free-spirited vibe as my wonderful mom.

"Thank you," I say. "I'll take your advice to heart, not only for my father, but for myself."

Geraldine hugs me. "Will I see you at yoga class on Monday?"

"I don't know," I say. "I might have a job that day." It's a lie. I have no job on Monday; my attempts to drum up business since Ripley came along and Mom died have been abysmal, at best. Also, the way-too-expensive three-month membership I got at that inconvenient, fancy yoga studio across town, solely for networking purposes, expired today. But I've already embarrassed myself enough tonight in front of this kind woman. I'm not willing to bare yet another fact to her that makes me look like an even bigger loser. After hugging her again, I say, "I'd better catch up with my friends. If I don't see you at class on Monday, let's try to meet up for coffee."

"I'd love that." She puts her hands on my shoulders and looks me in the eyes. "Now, don't get too down about Mr. BDE. You're an intelligent, drop-dead gorgeous woman with a lot to offer. He didn't deserve you."

My heart skips a beat. "Thanks, Geraldine. You're amazing."

"So are you."

With a little wave, Geraldine heads toward her car across the street, so I start walking down the sidewalk toward Captain's. As I walk, I place a call to my father, so I can wish my beating heart outside my body, my greatest love, the best thing that's ever happened to me—my beloved daughter, Ripley—goodnight and sweet dreams before her fast-approaching bedtime.

2

MAX

As I make my way on foot from my office building to Captain's a few blocks away, I contemplate removing my tie. I had to leave straight from work to make it on time for my last-minute meet-up with Grayson for drinks, and I didn't happen to have a casual change of clothes at the office today.

Nah. I drop my hand. Whenever I'm dressed in a full suit and tie at a bar, I tend to attract women in their thirties and forties—the ones I'd strongly prefer attracting. Older women are confident. They go after what and who they want, no holds barred. Oftentimes, they're busy with careers, friends, and maybe even a kid or two. They've been burned in the past, and now, they're expressly looking for nothing but fun. In other words, it's older women, by far, who always seem to be the best bet for a guy like me.

I didn't become the top biller at the best law firm in Seattle for the past five years by prioritizing my personal life over work. I've arrived at this juncture in my career—at the very precipice of achieving my long-term professional goals—by becoming an unstoppable, infallible, indisputable *machine*—a patent-and-business-law-dispensing juggernaut. Once I've made partner at my firm, and then, hopefully, landed that coveted assignment with a certain tech client's core team, I'll probably take my foot off the gas a bit at work and start looking around for a steady girlfriend. Maybe even a wife. But that's not on my radar screen yet. Not till I've achieved my long-term career goals. And in the meantime, I'll do what any thirty-year-old with a high sex drive would do: I'll have some fun whenever I can find the time. I'll hook up with women who've got extremely full lives without me. Women with no time or desire for a serious relationship. That way, nobody gets hurt. Everybody has fun. It's a win-win, every time.

I reach Captain's and step inside, where I'm immediately blasted with high levels of noise and activity. I scan the packed room and easily spot my nerdy work buddy, Grayson, by the bar, looking like he's contemplating elbowing his way to the bartender. Grayson's not a pushy dude by nature, which works well for him in the IT department of my law firm, but on the flip side, his go-with-the-flow attitude isn't going to get him close to the bartender in a crowded, chaotic hotspot like Captain's.

I call to Grayson from where I'm standing, but the place is too noisy for him to hear me. I move slowly toward him, navigating the packed crowd, and nudge his shoulder when I reach him. At my touch, Grayson turns to me, looking frazzled, and I chuckle at his overwhelmed facial expression. "Hey, buddy," I say. "Find us a table while I grab us some drinks." It's our usual arrangement whenever we go out drinking. We both know I make a shit-ton more money than him. No shade to him. I'm a fifth-year attorney, and he's a minion in the IT department at a law firm. It's the way of the world. Plus, I'm far more comfortable being assertive in a crowd, so it's only natural I should be the one tasked with getting our drinks on a crowded Friday night.

To my surprise, Grayson doesn't nod and walk away to secure a table like usual. Instead, he grabs my arm to stop my movement and insists drinks are on him this time.

I roll my eyes. "We've already talked about this, Gray. Find a table, and I'll get the drinks."

"Let me buy this once," Grayson insists. "And then I promise I won't annoy you about it again for a while. It's been my turn to buy the next round for a long time, Max."

He looks earnest and immovable, so I cave. "Okay, fine. Just this once, though. I'll take a Scotch on the rocks."

"You've got it."

"Don't get anything too expensive," I add. "The brand doesn't matter."

"I'll get what you always get."

"That's too expensive."

"Don't worry about it." With that, Grayson begins elbowing his way toward the bar, so I head in the opposite direction toward the tables in the back. As I move through the crowd, I survey the various faces surrounding me, looking to see if anyone catches my eye. There are certainly some beautiful older women here tonight, many of whom appear to be without a date. But there's nobody who instantly makes me think, "Oooh, I want to hit on *her.*"

When I spot an empty two-top in the back, I snag it and continue people-watching. A short time later, four older women settle into the larger table next to mine. All four women—a platinum blonde, a dirty blonde, and two brunettes—are coming off as elegant and confident. The kind who eat men for breakfast. In other words, they're exactly my type.

The woman who sits closest to my two-top is a brunette in a red, clingy dress. That dress ain't no Target brand, baby. That's a designer dress that probably cost a cool thousand bucks. I don't care if a woman is rich or poor, as a general matter, but for my purposes, I've noticed the wealthier a woman is, the less she's looking for a husband. Again, a very good thing.

After getting settled into her chair, the brunette in red happens to look my way. When our eyes meet, I don't hesitate to say hello to her.

"Hello," she throws back nonchalantly before looking around the bar again.

This time, I address the group as a whole. "Are you ladies celebrating a special occasion tonight?"

"Nope," the platinum blonde says curtly. "We're just here for drinks, little boy."

I chuckle. "Is that your way of telling me I'm too young to be of interest to you?"

The blonde's smile is absolutely deadly. "It is. But I'm not the only one sitting here, so feel free to take your best shot with someone else."

"I actually prefer older women," I confess. "Older women know who they are and what they want, you know? I like that they don't play games."

The brunette in red levels me with a look that practically screams, "In your dreams, honey." But what she says is a polite, "If you say so." She looks away again, and whatever her eyes have landed on makes her entire face light up like a goddamned Christmas tree. I track her gaze, and to my surprise, she's looking straight at my work buddy, Grayson, as he approaches our table with a surprisingly large tray of drinks. But how is that possible? Grayson is too shy to have made any kind of headway with the proverbial firewall sitting to my right. Especially this fast. And yet . . . it really does seem like she's staring straight at Grayson with palpable delight.

"Hey, Grayson," I call out. "What took you so long?"

Rather than answering me with words, Grayson puts down his tray before me, revealing it's covered in even more drinks than I'd realized: mine, Grayson's, a martini of some sort, and an absurd number of shots. It's far more alcohol than Grayson and I would ever want to consume on our own. So, what gives?

"What's up with all the shots?" I ask.

Grayson gestures to the adjacent table—the one filled with those four attractive older women. As he does, a fifth member joins their ranks—a smoking-hot redhead who physically takes my breath away with her sultry confidence. *Holy fuck*. She's a walking wet dream.

As the redhead takes a chair next to the brunette in red, she says something to her that makes both women laugh heartily. And that's it. I'm transfixed. Watching that woman let loose with a throaty laugh is the sexiest thing I've ever witnessed.

"They're for all these beautiful ladies," Grayson says.

"Huh?" I wrench my gaze off the redhead to find Grayson gesturing to the shot glasses on his tray. Oh yeah, I asked him about the extra drinks, didn't I?

Grayson flashes a huge, beaming smile at the women seated next to us. "It's packed tonight," he explains, raising his voice to be heard above the din, "and hard to get the bartender's attention. I figured I'd get a bunch of shots for you ladies, if you'd like them."

I'm thinking they're going to turn him down since it's Safety 101 for women to turn down drinks they haven't personally witnessed getting poured. But to my surprise, they all express nothing but enthusiastic gratitude for the free booze.

"My pleasure," Grayson replies. As the women grab shots off Grayson's tray, he holds out the martini glass to the brunette in red. "I got this vodka martini for you, if you'd like it. I noticed you sitting at the bar earlier, so I asked the bartender to make you another round."

The brunette looks thoroughly charmed. In fact, she's batting her eyelashes at him. "Thank you so much . . ." She smirks. "*Grayson*."

Grayson's face lights up. "I knew it!"

Wait. What? *Grayson actually knows this woman*? No wonder her group accepted drinks from him. Does the redhead know Grayson, too? If so, he'd damned well better introduce me, or I'll never forgive him.

Speaking of the redhead, I take a peek at her again, curious to see how she's reacting to Grayson's tray of drinks. And to my thrill, her eyes are already laser-focused on me. *Well, well, well. Hello, there, beautiful.*

I quirk an eyebrow, letting her know she's got my undivided attention. And, *hallelujah*, she returns the gesture without hesitation. Ha. Love it. This one is definitely no shrinking violet.

"Is this the little friend you told us about, Selena?" the platinum blonde asks the lady in red.

"This is him," the brunette confirms. "Isn't he darling?" I wrench my eyes from the staring contest I'm having with the hot redhead to find the brunette in red looking Grayson up and down. "But he's not so little, is he?" It's true. Grayson is six-two, I think. Only a couple inches shorter than me. With a laugh, the brunette rises, gives Grayson an enthusiastic hug, and purrs, "Hello, Grayson."

What's going on? If I'm a "little boy" at thirty in my designer suit, then what does that make Grayson at twenty-five in a pair of khakis? But whatever. It's all good. I've never had any trouble attracting women, while Grayson seems pretty hopeless and hapless at it, God love him. So, if tonight's his lucky night, then more power to him . . . just as long as he stays far, far away from the redhead who's got my full attention.

Speaking of the object of my lust, I return to her, eager to continue our nonverbal flirting match, but she's engaged in an animated conversation with one of her friends—the ice-cold blonde. As I'm watching the pair converse, I chuckle to myself at the redhead's animated storytelling. Whatever she's saying, she's gesticulating wildly while doing it. She's comfortable in her own skin, that one. Charismatic and magnetic to the extreme. In fact, I don't think I've ever laid eyes on anyone who's quite this compelling at first blush.

As I'm still watching the redhead gesticulating, movement at my table draws my attention. When I turn, I find the brunette in red taking a seat next to Grayson. Well, I'll be damned. Shy Grayson successfully made a move on the brunette, even before I've made a move on the redhead? Good for him.

"How on earth did you figure me out?" the brunette asks Grayson with a laugh. "There are plenty of women around my age at the bar tonight."

Grayson is smiling like a goofball—like he's been picked first on the playground for Dodgeball. "I recognized you the second I saw you," he declares. When the brunette rolls her eyes, he chuckles and adds, "Not physically, obviously. It was your energy. Your confidence. You were everything I imagined Hot Teacher would be, and then some."

"*Hot Teacher*?" I mumble, intrigued. But not surprisingly, nobody acknowledges my outburst. Fine with me. I return my attention to the redhead again, and this time, she's looking straight at me. Actually, more accurately, she's devouring me with hungry blue eyes.

We trade a few brazenly sexual smiles. Raise our drinks to each other. Trade a couple winks and chuckles of acknowledgement. And by the end of our nonverbal exchange, there's no doubt in my mind we're gonna fuck tonight. There's no rush, of course. In fact, when I'm flirting with a particularly attractive woman—the kind who's used to getting any man she wants—I generally find it works to my advantage to let her simmer a bit. Let her wonder. Let her *chase* a bit. And so, despite the magnetic pull I'm feeling to the knockout at the next table, I force myself to look away and eavesdrop on the conversation at my small table again.

"And you claim to be bad at flirting!" the brunette in red says to Grayson. Her tone is flirtatious. Warm. Enthusiastic. Nothing like it was with me earlier.

"I am," Grayson bellows happily, his face beet-red and lit up like a sky full of fireworks.

"He is," I deadpan under my breath. I'm talking to no one. This pair only has eyes for each other. But why not let the redhead see my mouth moving? Why not let her think I'm engaged in conversation over here, rather than feeling knocked onto my ass at the mere sight of her?

After a short while, I can't resist peeking at the redhead again, even though I know I should let her simmer a bit longer. Shit. She's not simmering. She's laughing breezily with her friend again. Well, fuck me. Is she playing it cool, like me, or did I misread the situation?

Either way, it's fine. This place is packed, so I've got plenty of other options. I glance around the bar and scan the crowd. But there's nobody who even vaguely interests me. Now that I've seen my walking fantasy, I'm ruined for anyone else. At least, for tonight.

Grayson and the brunette laugh together, drawing my attention back to them.

"Will you introduce me, Gray?" I ask, figuring I'll finagle an introduction to the redhead through her friend. For a split-second, Grayson and the brunette both look at me blankly, like they'd forgotten I'm still sitting here. With a smile, I say, "I take it you two already know each other?"

The brunette flashes a lovely smile at Grayson. "Yes, Grayson and I met online earlier today. He invited me for a drink, and I found him way too charming and handsome to refuse, even though I don't usually date men his age."

With an eyebrow quirked, I turn to Grayson. *Well, damn, boy. Looks like someone has a fighting chance this time.* If so, it couldn't happen to a sweeter guy.

Blushing, Grayson clears his throat and says, "Selena, this is Max."

"Hello, Max," the brunette says, before returning to Grayson. "Would you boys like to join our table? There's plenty of room."

The process of dragging chairs and grabbing Grayson's remaining drinks begins. Of course, I squeeze my chair next to the redhead, while Grayson sits next to the brunette. Introductions follow, with each woman supplying her first name, one at a time. The brunette in red is Selena. The middle three are Jasmine, Victoria, and Lucy. And the stunning redhead sitting next to me, the woman who's so fucking gorgeous she's making my skin feel physically hot is Marnie. I've never met a Marnie before. And I know, just this fast, I'll never *not* think of this gorgeous woman, at least fleetingly, any time I hear the name in the future.

"Hello there, Marnie," I say, shaking her hand. "It's a pleasure to meet you."

"You, too, Max. Wow, that's quite a grip. Big hands."

"Big hands. Big feet." I leave it at that. Surely, she knows the rest.

"What size shoe do you wear?"

"Thirteen."

"How tall are you?"

"Six-four. You?"

"Five-ten." She motions toward her feet. "Six foot in heels."

"I'm a sucker for a tall woman. The taller the better."

"That's rare. Most men like itty-bitty women."

"How would you know that? I'm sure you've never been turned down in your life."

Marnie blushes but doesn't deny it.

"Yeah, I figured," I say, chuckling. "I'm a lawyer, Marnie. My bullshit detector is pretty well honed."

She sips her drink to hide her smile. "What are your thoughts on redheads?"

I wink suggestively. "I'm a big fan."

"Now it's *my* bullshit detector going off."

"As of today. After seeing you."

She smirks. "Nice save. Very smooth."

"Perhaps. But it's true, nonetheless."

Marnie flashes me a skeptical look, but I'm not going to take the bait. If she wants me to compliment her further, to regale her with all the ways she's making my tongue drag on the floor, then she's out of luck. Surely, that's what every man does in her presence. They chase. They seduce. They beg. Well, that's simply not me, no matter how alluring I find her.

Marnie takes another sip of her drink. "Is Max short for Maxwell?"

"Maximillian."

"That's quite a name."

"My father and mother both share names with famous rulers from history, so they went with Holy Roman emperors for my brother and me. He's Augustus."

"Damn. In kindergarten, you two had to learn to spell Maximillian and Augustus, while the other kids were writing Kai and Leo? That hardly seems fair."

I chuckle. "We go by Max and Auggie. A lot less letters to learn that way. Plus, we both figured out pretty young it's better to under-promise and over-perform. Nobody expects all that much from a pair of guys named Max and Auggie. But when Maximillian and Augustus walk into a room, everyone assumes they've come to conquer the world."

Marnie giggles, making my heart rate increase. I'm not planning to see her beyond tonight, so if our senses of humor didn't mesh, it wouldn't have been the end of the world. But still, it's infinitely more fun to hook up with someone who laughs at your jokes. Not to mention, someone you can laugh with between rounds.

"Is Marnie short for something?" I ask.

She shakes her head. "There's a Hitchcock movie of the same name. That's where my parents got the idea."

"It's cute and elegant at the same time."

"Thanks. It'd be nice to have different options, though, like you and your brother have. How nice to be able to come across as an everyman or an emperor, depending on how you introduce yourself." She looks me up and down. "Although I'm not sure you could come off as an everyman, no matter what you call yourself. You've definitely got some emperor-sized swagger, Maximillian."

I'm tempted to say, "That's not the only emperor-sized thing about me." But it's probably too crude and basic a thing to say, so I bite my tongue.

Marnie smiles. Apparently, she's read my mind. Or at least, my facial expression. When I return her smile, she laughs, taps the side of my head, and asks, "Are you having a dirty thought in there, Max?"

"I'm having several of them," I admit.

"So am I. Good to know I'm not alone in that." With that, she grins wickedly and sips her drink.

Palpable sexual energy is coursing between us. As a matter of fact, I can't remember the last time I felt physical chemistry this intense with someone, if ever. It feels intoxicating to be *this* attracted to someone. If Marnie is feeling even half the attraction I am, then we're going to have explosive, unparalleled chemistry between the sheets.

Marnie glances at Grayson across the table where he's currently chatting happily with Selena and the other women. "Is Grayson as sweet, adorable, and uncomplicated as he seems? Or is he the most talented grifter the world has ever seen?"

I chuckle. "Grayson couldn't grift his way out of a paper bag. What you see is what you get with that one. He's a human Golden Retriever."

Marnie's blue eyes sparkle. "In contrast to you."

I shrug. "What you see is what you get with me, too. And I'm certainly no grifter. But, yeah, nobody would ever call me a Golden Retriever."

"That's clear enough."

"Is that a problem for you?"

"No, honey, that's a *solution*. At least, for tonight."

My eyebrows ride up, but before I've managed a reply to that spicy comment, the table erupts in laughter around us, and Marnie and I turn our attention to the group. As we soon find out, the women are peppering Grayson with questions, and his earnest answers are charming every last one of them. Marnie and I join the conversation, and the opportunity to respond to Marnie's intriguing comment passes. For now, anyway. At my first opportunity, when Selena and Grayson slide into a one-on-one discussion that leads to the table breaking off into one-on-one conversations, I lean into Marnie and ask, "How might I be a solution for you tonight?" Marnie bites her sensuous lip but says nothing, so I add, "Do you have a problem that requires some solving tonight, Marnie? How can I be of service?"

Marnie takes a long sip of her drink. "The problem is my ex-boyfriend. A week ago, I found out he's been cheating on me throughout our six-month relationship with the wife I didn't know he had."

I grimace. "Sorry to hear that."

"Meh. I was an idiot to believe him. But, unfortunately, since I did, I'd now like to forget him through any means necessary."

"I think I can help you with that. Quite effectively."

"Oh, I'm certain you can. Over and over again, if you're game."

"I am. As long as we're talking about one night. Unfortunately, I don't have the time or bandwidth for anything beyond that. I hope you understand."

"I appreciate the honesty. I'm not interested in anything beyond that myself. I've just decided you're going to be my last hurrah before I start looking for Mr. Right in earnest."

I raise my glass. "Cheers to last hurrahs."

She doesn't clink my glass. "You wouldn't be cheating on someone to get with me tonight, right?"

"Nope. I'm single."

"How single, though? Is there someone out there who'd be shocked by that characterization?"

I shake my head. "I'm not even dating someone casually. I'm trying to make partner at my law firm, two years earlier than anyone has ever done it, and then get myself assigned to the core legal team for our biggest client. I've been working insane hours for years to make my goals a reality. I don't have time for a relationship. Not really even a regular fuck buddy."

"Sounds like we're a match made in heaven, then. At least, for tonight." She raises her glass, and I clink it. Marnie leans forward. "Heads up: When I tell my friends we're going outside to smoke in a minute, I'll be speaking in code."

"I don't smoke."

"Neither do I. It's a little inside joke. Since our sorority days at U Dub, whenever we've been at a party or in a bar, and one of us wants to leave with a hot guy to have sex with him, we say, 'Bye, ladies, we're going outside to smoke.' What that means is, 'Don't wait up for me, bitches. I'm leaving to fuck this man senseless.'"

I burst out laughing. I've never met a woman with this kind of sexual confidence. People often say they've got no fucks to give, but something tells me this woman could say it and genuinely mean it. "Let's do it," I say. "I'd be honored to be your smoking buddy tonight."

"You're hired. Do you live close?"

"I do. I live in the Fairmont Building. It's only about four blocks away."

"*Ooh la la.* I've always wanted to see one of the fancy condos inside that building." She flashes me side-eye. "Unless you're a serial killer who's planning to chop me up at your place."

"I'm not. I mean, yes, I'm a serial killer, but I ran out of tarps last week, and I'm meticulous about keeping my carpets clean."

"Not funny, Max."

"It's a little funny."

She shakes her head.

"Aw, come on. It's dark humor. Would a serial killer joke about being a serial killer?"

"Yes. That'd be a brilliant form of diversion."

I roll my eyes. "Ask Grayson about me. He'll vouch for me."

"I don't know Grayson from Adam. For all I know, he could be a serial killer, too."

I laugh. "Look at the boy. Do you really think he's capable of harming a fly—or even telling a lie, for that matter?"

Marnie looks at Grayson and mutters, "You've got a point." She calls to Grayson across the table and asks, "Is Max a serial killer or otherwise prone to psychopathic or violent tendencies? Please advise."

Grayson shakes his head. "Nope. He's a workaholic, though. Also, a womanizer, if you want to know the truth. But he's also the smartest person I've ever met in my life and a great friend."

"Perfect. Thanks." Marnie returns to me. "You've passed my extensive background check, Maximillian. Congratulations." She rises. "Are you ready to go outside for a smoke now?"

I rise alongside her. "I am. I'm greatly looking forward to it."

Marnie announces to her friends, "Hey, Max and I are going outside to smoke, ladies." And not surprisingly, given what Marnie told me earlier, her friends respond with snickers, smiles, and playful comments. I gesture to Marnie to walk ahead of me, and then follow her mesmerizing, swiveling hips toward the front door. Hopefully, we'll enjoy several "smokes" tonight. Highly memorable ones. And when it's all over, I'll kiss the hottest woman alive goodbye and happily never see her again.

3
MARNIE

Max's building, The Fairmont, is a few blocks away. And it's every bit as modern and luxurious as I'm expecting it to be. Based on the skyscraper's masculine vibe, I'm guessing the builder was hoping to attract rich, successful bachelors, people like Max, to live in their gleaming, glass dildo, as opposed to families and single women. The whole structure screams "bachelor pad" like nothing I've seen before.

When we reach Max's unit on a high floor, he opens his front door and motions for me to step inside. The minute I see Max's home, and the meticulous way he's chosen to decorate it, I can't help smiling to myself. It's exactly the living space I would have designed, if I'd been tasked to create one for a fictitious version of Max—the precise environment I'd expect a young, successful, smoking-hot patent attorney would choose for himself. The ceilings are high. The furnishings and décor, tasteful and sparse and every bit as modern and masculine as the building at large. Best of all, the living room we're standing in features spectacular views through floor-to-ceiling windows.

"This place is gorgeous," I whisper.

"Thanks."

I walk toward the large windows. "And this view is breathtaking. Wow."

"The view is the main reason I bought the place. Also, the location. It's only blocks from the office, so I can walk to work most days."

We stand together at the window and gaze at the twinkling skyline below, with Max pointing out various landmarks. As Max talks, I shift my gaze between his face and the view for the next several minutes, once again thinking about Alexander. Max reminds me of him. In fact, he looks like a younger, hotter version of the man who dented my heart. That's what drew me to Max the moment I saw him. The fact that he reminded me of Alexander. After that, his incredible confidence, charm, and raw sex appeal drew me in even further. And the rest is history. I simply couldn't resist, despite all my big talk at dinner about being done with meaningless sex. It's not completely my fault, though. I can't remember the last time I've felt *this* instantly, insanely, drawn to someone. In fact, standing here now, I'm not sure it's ever happened before. Not like this, anyway.

True, Max seems like a bit of a grump. A hardass. He's most certainly emotionally unavailable. Oh, and his confidence often veers into flat-out cockiness. But for me, all those things are positives, not negatives. As embarrassing as it is to admit, Max checks all my boxes in terms of the kind of man who turns me on the most. Physically, anyway. But since I'm not going to date or marry him, that's enough. Given what I came here to do, there's no harm in going for my usual, toxic type. Especially for a last hurrah. In fact, I think it's the smart thing to do. God help me, if Max were actually humble and overtly kind—the sort of man I'd want in Ripley's life—*and* he *also* got my ovaries vibrating like a weed whacker set to high, I'd be well and truly fucked. And not in a good way.

"Can I get you something?" Max asks. "A cocktail? Some water?"

"The only thing you can get me is a kiss, if you've got one to spare."

Max doesn't hesitate. With a smile on his face and his blue eyes blazing, he takes a step forward, slides his big palms to my cheeks, and plants a surprisingly tender kiss on my lips while cradling my face.

Jesus Christ.

He's good.

Max's lips on mine are tentative at first. Exploratory. Soft. Perfect. There's nothing worse than a man shoving his tongue down my throat and thinking it's a turn-on. Clearly, Max is letting my lips acclimate to his. He's taking my temperature. Or maybe he's simply teasing me. Waiting for my lips to nonverbally beg him for more. Whatever he's doing, it's working like a charm, because in two seconds flat, a pulsing has announced itself between my legs. A delicious ache that makes me yearn for a deeper, more passionate kiss. And then, whatever he's got for me behind those slacks.

I open my mouth slightly and slide my tongue gently against his lips, inviting him to deepen our kiss, and he does. My lips and tongue receive his new entreaties with enthusiasm, so he quickly takes things further. He slides his arms around me, presses his hardness against me, and devours my mouth like a starving man eating his favorite meal.

Yes.

From this perfect, masterful, passionate kiss alone, I know this hottie is going to be leagues apart from the two fools I slept with this week, both of whom I thoroughly regret now. Good lord, based on this kiss, I'm betting Max is going to be in my Hall of Fame. And I'm so here for it after the week I've had. Frankly, this fun little tryst couldn't have come at a better time.

The pulsing between my legs has morphed into a banging, clanging aching drumbeat. So much so, I can tell my arousal is beginning to soak the cotton crotch of my G-string.

After a gentle suck to my lower lip, Max leaves my mouth and kneels before me, his blue eyes ablaze. As I shudder with anticipation, he looks up at me and slowly unzips my pants.

I nod enthusiastically, letting him know I'm one thousand percent consenting to being eaten out by this talented kisser, and he flashes me a wicked grin in reply. Max quickly finishes the task of getting my bottom half naked, and once I'm bared to him, he grips my ass, leans into me, and dives into his hungry work.

"Oh, god," I blurt the instant Max's warm tongue touches the most sensitive spot on my body. It takes no time at all for Max to find the right rhythm with his swirling tongue, confident lips, and talented fingers—a rhythm that wobbles my knees and pulls deep moans of ecstasy from my throat. Within minutes, I'm physically jerking and spasming with pleasure—I'm gyrating into his mouth like I'm fucking his face as my pleasure hurtles toward what's surely going to be an insanely delicious orgasm.

I've got a nifty little sex toy at home that's supposed to mimic the sensation of oral sex being performed, but as effective as that feat of engineering is, it's now clear it doesn't even come close to the real thing when it's done well. Lord have mercy on my soul; this talented man is taking me to heaven on Earth. My idea of Nirvana.

I grip Max's close-cropped blonde hair as he licks and laps and becomes ever more enthusiastic and voracious. I'm not normally into blue-eyed blondes like Max; they generally lack a certain kind of intensity that gets me off. A certain kind of bad-boy, I'd-burn-the-world-down-for-you vibe I've always been a glutton for. With his silver hair, Alexander was one of the few exceptions to my usual affinity for dark-haired men. And now, the golden god between my legs is an exception, too. Based on Max's innate intensity, it turns out even blonde, blue-eyed hotties are capable of coming across as mafia hitmen under the right circumstances. Or at least, this one is—and the effect on my body is easy to surmise. I'm reeling. Feeling dizzy. So turned on I can barely stand.

I whimper loudly, suddenly feeling like I'm in the waiting room of The Promised Land. Standing right outside its doors, waiting for them to swing open at any second.

I groan at full volume this time, as my pleasure ramps up acutely. And then, wobble in place as my legs betray me. And all the while, Max grips my ass fiercely, keeping me in place, and methodically continues his masterful work with his tongue, lips, and fingers.

"Oh, fuck," I choke out. I grip the top of Max's head fiercely. "Don't stop anything. Just like that. Oh, God, baby. Yes. *Yes*."

Everything freezes inside me like my soul has been shot out of my body—and two seconds later when my soul abruptly reenters its container, I'm slammed with a forceful orgasm that sends my nerve endings through a proverbial paper shredder. The signals in my brain are screaming "pain!" and "pleasure!", all at once. And then, nothing but pleasure, pleasure, *pleasuuuuure*.

With my fingers clutching Max's head, I throw my head back and ride the wave. As I ride it, my body ripples and clenches fiercely, while Max keeps his fingers lodged inside me and groans along with me at whatever rippling sensation has overtaken his fingers. It's like my orgasm is giving him physical pleasure, too. *So fucking hot.*

When the rollercoaster subsides, Max rises to full standing. He looks beastly now. Like a starving lion. He licks his lips, lapping up some of the glistening evidence of my arousal on them. His chest heaving, he loosens his tie forcefully, like the damned thing has offended him. When he throws it to the ground, I lurch forward and unbutton his shirt as he hurriedly pulls off his jacket. We're both ravenous now. Intoxicated by our mutual desire.

Max pulls off his pants while I get my shirt and bra off, and a moment later, we're both fully naked, standing mere inches apart with Max's massive erection straining between us. Good lord,

Maximillian the Holy Roman Emperor is one glorious specimen of a man. All six-foot-four inches of him is spectacular. Mouth-watering. Sexual. Primal. God only knows what kind of a disappointment Max has been to whatever girlfriends he's had in real life, but for my purposes tonight, for the fantasy he's been hand-selected to fulfill for me, he's the perfect avatar. A blank slate for me to project my deepest fantasies and desires onto. The man is so fucking hot, I want nothing more than to lick up that pre-cum glistening on his gorgeous tip.

Damn.

I'm too late.

I don't know where the condom came from, but Max is covering his straining cock—and that glorious pre-cum— looking like he's barely able to breathe. When he's all wrapped up, Max steps forward until his covered tip nudges against my belly. As he did before, he slides his big palm against my cheek and kisses me deeply before lifting me up, grabbing my ass, pressing my back against his floor-to-ceiling window, and motherfucking impaling me.

I moan as his thick cock stretches my entrance, and then moan again, even more loudly, when his impressive girth fills me to the brim. As he fucks me against the window, we groan and grunt together with each beastly thrust. When we're not kissing, Max is muttering dirty talk in a hoarse, tight voice. He tells me I feel fucking incredible. Perfect. Like a fucking goddess. He tells me he's never been this turned on before. That I feel like heaven. Like a drug. And soon, to my shock, my eyes are rolling back into my head, and I'm being slammed with another intense orgasm. This time, with Max's cock buried deep, deep inside me.

Max yanks out of me abruptly, like he's saving himself from falling off a cliff. As my body continues rippling, he turns me around, instructs me to press my palms against the glass, and then proceeds to fuck me from behind while artfully massaging my clit. *Fucking hell.* I've never been fucked this well before.

This man is a virtuoso, and I'm his pricey violin. I'm delirious. Incapable of thinking coherently. I'm nothing but a jumble of nerve endings now, all of them craving nothing but this man's cock and voice and fingers.

"Oh, fuck," I blurt when it feels like I'm having yet another out of body experience. It can't be. But oh, God, it is. There's a pause. And then, my soul slams back into my body, like before. Followed by my entire body undulating with yet another orgasm, this one even more delicious than the last.

Max scoops up my slack body since I've become a rag doll by now, and he carries me to his couch. "Are you good to keep going?" he murmurs.

"All night," I whisper back. "Never stop."

He lays me down, sticks a pillow underneath my lower back and pushes my legs up next to my ears, and that's where he fucks me with such finesse, it's like I'm a video game, and he's cracked some secret code that tells players the secret to scoring maximum points. *How is he doing this to me?* I'm nothing but the man's puppet. And, oh, God, it feels good.

Max's body is glistening with sweat by now. His gorgeous muscles are slick and shiny in the moonlight. I don't know about the Holy Roman Emperor thing, but he definitely looks like a Nordic god. A superhero. I don't think I've ever been fucked by a man who's *this* handsome before, and I'm ashamed to admit how much fun it is. Getting fucked by someone so beautiful is like eating the finest gelato on an ancient Italian bridge in Venice and watching a gondolier pass and yell, "Ciao, bella!" It's like witnessing the most perfect sunset in Thailand while perfectly buzzed on mai tais after a day of visiting an elephant sanctuary with good friends. Really, it's one of the great pleasures every grown-ass woman should experience before she leaves Planet Earth: having sex all night with a gorgeous sex god and then never seeing his gorgeous ass again.

Out of nowhere, Max changes position. He sits on his couch and guides me on top of him—in reverse cowgirl position—and, of course, I'm happy to oblige. As I ride him, he holds my hips and enthusiastically grinds me into him, which then stimulates my clit in the most perfect way while the tip of his cock slams my G-spot, over and over again. I feel high. Drugged. Absolutely intoxicated. This is the best sex of my life, and that's saying a lot, considering all the amazing sex I've enjoyed since age seventeen.

When my orgasm comes, it's the biggest one yet. I slam myself down onto Max's cock and scream his name, and this time, finally, Max comes along with me. In fact, he comes so hard inside me, I can feel his large cock rippling forcefully against my most intimate muscles.

When our mutual release subsides, we both remain still for a moment, catching our breath. Trying not to die of simultaneous heart attacks. But, finally, Max mutters, "Jesus fucking Christ, Marnie."

"Well done, Maximillian," I reply. I slide off him, turn around, straddle him, and peck his lips. "That was exactly what I needed—some emperor-level sex, for sure. Thank you."

"I didn't over-promise?" he asks.

"If anything, you *under* promised. Which is hard to fathom, considering how cocky you were at the bar." When Max laughs, I laugh with him. "I knew it'd be good," I say. "But I never thought it'd be the best I've ever had." When I realize what I've said, what I've admitted, I quickly add, "I mean, it was right up there with the best of the best—good enough to get you nominated for my Hall of Fame."

Max scoffs. "Good enough to get *nominated*? Bullshit. I want the trophy, baby. Nominated, my ass."

I laugh. "It's an honor simply to get nominated."

"Pfft. After what we just did, it's an insult. Not to mention, a bald-faced lie."

"Why would I lie?"

"Because you've decided I'm an egomaniac who needs to be taken down a peg."

I purse my lips but say nothing. He's not wrong.

He snickers. "I can already read you like a book, babe."

"Impossible. I'm a highly complicated book, with lots of plot twists. Nobody can predict this plot line."

"I'm amazing at predicting crazy plot twists."

"You're calling me crazy now?" I say playfully.

He runs his fingers down my bare back, sending goosebumps erupting across my skin. "Crazy beautiful," he whispers. "Crazy sexy. Damn, I like reading this book. I like reading it a lot."

I lean down again and kiss him again. "That's great news, because I'm very much hoping you'll read this book at least twice more before I walk out of here, never to return."

A flicker of a scowl crosses Max's gorgeous features but it disappears as quickly as it came. "Only if you admit that was incredible and at least *tied* for your top spot, ever."

"I never denied it was incredible. I'm just saying it's not the first time I've had incredible sex. Maybe you blow the minds of the pretty little twenty-somethings you usually grace with your talents, but as fun as that was, I'm not willing to give you the title. At most, you're sharing the top spot on the podium." I'm a liar. He's easily the best I've ever had by a long mile. But there's no way I'm going to give this playboy the satisfaction. I stroke his gorgeous cheekbone. "That's going to have to be enough of an accolade for you. It's my final offer."

"I accept. As long as I'm *really* high on the list."

"You're way, way, *way* up there."

Max chuckles. "You're on my list, too. Way, way, *way* . . . at the bottom. But at least you've managed to squeak onto it."

I playfully punch his muscular shoulder and he laughs.

"I just rocked your world like nobody ever has," I tease.

"Why should I admit that, when you won't admit the same to me?"

"I'm ten years older than you. Plus, I used to travel the world for work, so I've been lucky enough to sample men from lots of different countries and cultures. Be happy you're on the list at

all, given that you grew up in America. Our idea of sex education is beyond pitiful. We're puritanical and shame-based. Not to
mention, as a culture, we don't care about female pleasure, if we
acknowledge its existence at all. Given the hurdles you had to
overcome growing up here, it's a miracle you're as talented as
you are."

Max bites his lip. "So, you admit I'm *miraculous*? I'll
take it."

I giggle. "Yes. I'll give you that. You're miraculous. Magical. Utterly spellbinding." I nuzzle his nose and whisper, "Thank
you."

"You made it easy, I assure you."

We kiss. There's no denying it. That felt supernatural. Like a
once-in-a-lifetime occurrence. Like a comet that only swings
past the Earth's orbit every eighty-thousand years. We have the
kind of chemistry people would kill to experience just once in
their lives. And we both know it.

"Can I get that cocktail now?" I purr.

"What's your pleasure? I've got a full bar."

As I place my order for a martini, Max gently slides me off
him, and as I curl up on his couch, he strides across his fancy
condo and into his kitchen. Once there, he throws away his
condom and washes his hands. And then, much to my delight, he
expertly makes us a couple of martinis, while I gawk at his
gorgeous, naked frame.

His task completed, Max returns to the couch with two
drinks and a bowl of salty snacks, and we sit and drink, chat and
nibble while our naked bodies recharge. To my surprise, our
conversation quickly veers from superficial, flirty topics, to ones
that feel far more real and meaningful. I don't tell him about
Ripley; there's no need to do that. But I do wind up telling him
about my mother, and he expresses what feels like genuine
sympathy.

At Max's urging, I also tell him a bit about my career as a
private chef, which leads to me telling him about the culinary

school I attended in Paris after college, which then leads me to telling him about the many places I've traveled while floating in the breeze from job to job.

After a while, I turn things around and ask Max some questions about himself, at which point I learn Max went to Stanford on a water polo scholarship and stayed to attend law school after that. When it came time to pick a law firm after graduation, Max chose one in his hometown rather than in Silicon Valley, like so many of his classmates from Stanford, because he figured the firm where he now works would be the surest path to achieving his top career goal: eventually landing an in-house legal position for some tech genius guru from Seattle.

At my prompting, Max tells me a bit about his chosen field of practice—patent law—and although he answers my questions, he doesn't go on and on about himself or his achievements, though I'm sure he's got plenty to dazzle me with. On the contrary, Max deftly turns the conversation back to me after only a short amount of time.

"Are you planning to stay in Seattle for the foreseeable future?" he asks. "Or is another round of globetrotting in your near future, Miss World Traveler?"

"I'm home to stay," I reply. "My father lives here. And now that I've been home for a while, I've realized it's time for me to settle down and spend quality time with my father and best friends. I'm ready for a whole new chapter in my life. A much more stable one, where I prioritize my personal relationships and try to build an actual, steady career, rather than living paycheck to paycheck, like I always have." Of course, taking care of Ripley and making sure she's thriving and that her various health concerns are properly addressed is the top reason I've decided to put down roots in Seattle. But that's a conversation I don't care to have with a one-night stand.

Max considers that. "Who are your target clients? Extremely wealthy people only, or do normal people hire private chefs, too?"

"Wealthy people are my target clients. Normal people always want you to work for the same price as it'd cost them to order from an online meal service, and that's not a price point I can do. Wealthy people, on the other hand, are usually clueless about how much things should cost. If something isn't crazy-expensive, they don't want it. If you land the right rich client, you can make three times the money for the same amount of work you'd put in for a normal person." I motion to Max's crumpled designer suit on the floor behind his couch. "I'm sure that suit cost three times what you could have paid for a perfectly attractive suit without the designer label sewn into it."

Max shrugs. "I like Armani."

"Exactly my point. I want to be the Armani of private chefs, so people don't think twice about paying a ridiculous price for me, instead of getting someone cheaper."

Max smiles and runs his palm across my naked thigh. "You want to work smarter, not harder."

"Exactly. So far, it's easier said than done. I'm a shit show when it comes to marketing and networking. The good news is my actual cooking skills are fantastic, so at least I've got that going for me."

Max runs his palm up my thigh again, giving me full-body tingles. "I have full faith in you, Marnie."

"Thank you, Maximillian."

He pauses briefly. Bites his lower lip. Finally, he says, "I bet some of the partners at my firm would hire you. They're all making more money than they know what to do with. They've all got closets full of Armani suits, not just a handful, like me. Maybe I could get you hired to cater one of their monthly dinners, so you could dazzle them and then pass out your cards."

I'm in shock—and also intensely turned on. Not only is Max's offer a surprisingly generous one, but it would also require us to stay in touch after tonight. I take a deep breath to regulate my racing heartbeat before managing to say, "Thank you. I'd be eternally grateful for your help."

"It wouldn't take much effort on my part. I'd give your card or marketing materials to the managing partner's secretary and tell her she'd be doing me a favor by giving you a chance."

"Do you think she'd do it?"

Max smirks. "She's got a big crush on me."

I roll my eyes. "I don't doubt that for a minute." I put down my drink and crawl over to Max on the couch. With my thighs planted on either side of his lap, I kiss his lips gently and then press my forehead against his. "You've made me horny and wet again. There's nothing like a man offering to be my knight in shining armor to turn me on."

"Well, let's not go that far. But I'm glad to help in this small way if I can."

"Thank you."

We kiss deeply, and soon, Max's hard, bare dick is nudging up against my wet entrance.

"I could mail you one of my cards, if you never want to see me in person again," I purr into Max's lips. "I mean, that's what we agreed at Captain's. One night only."

Max's tip is rubbing deliciously against my clit, driving me wild. "Why don't I take you to dinner one night this week and get the cards from you then?" he whispers. "Unless, of course, you want to stick with our initial agreement that this is a one-time thing. If so, I'll still give your card to the managing partner's secretary. It's up to you."

My heart is beating wildly. He's asking me out on an actual date—a real one, with dinner in a restaurant? It's not something I was angling for. But now that he's asked, I can't deny I'm thrilled. In fact, I suddenly feel like a blushing high schooler who's been asked to prom by her longtime crush.

"I suppose I could do dinner this week," I reply, trying to sound casual and not nearly as excited as I feel. "I'll have to let you know which night works for me. My work schedule is kind of unpredictable." In reality, I've barely got any clients at the moment. But since I have no idea which night my father could watch Ripley for me, I can't nail down a time for a date just yet.

"Yeah, my work schedule is crazy, too," Max says. "But we'll figure something out."

"Sounds good." I slide myself pointedly against the tip of his hard dick, inviting him to push inside. "I'm on the pill," I whisper. "So, if you feel comfortable going in, uncovered, feel free."

I don't need to ask him twice. Max grips my hips and slams me down, and we quickly begin moving and gyrating together, while our mouths devour and our tongues dance and swirl. Our movement quickly turns voracious. Furious. Frenzied. We're barreling to mutual bliss on a runaway train, and neither of us is doing a damned thing to slow things down. It's a stark contrast to the first go-around, when Max kept pulling out and doing whatever it took to last as long as possible. This time, when I come, he comes with me, while buried balls-deep inside me, gripping me for dear life as he loses control.

"Jesus," Max murmurs, after we're both quiet and still. "Sorry. I couldn't stop myself that time."

"What fun is a man who's always in full control of himself?"

Max chuckles. "The real question is whether I'm ever in full control around you? If I am, then I'm hanging on by a thread."

I press my forehead against his. "I feel the same way around you. You do crazy things to me."

Max kisses my cheek. "You want to take a shower with me? I feel like eating you in my shower."

I nuzzle his nose. "*Yes.*"

"From there, if you're feeling it, I'll take you to bed and fuck you there."

"*If I'm feeling it*? Have I not been clear? I'm putty in your hands, honey."

Max shrugs. "Still, there's only so much a body can handle in one night."

"If you're thinking your sex drive will outlast mine, think again. I promise you'll tap out long before I do."

"That's impossible."

I giggle. "Get ready to get broken, my sexy stallion."

Max smirks. "Break me, baby. Shatter me. *Destroy* me."

"Oh, I shall." I wink. "Get ready for total decimation, Maximillian. One broken stallion, coming right up."

4
MARNIE

"You're magic," Max murmurs. "Magic Marnie with her magic pussy. You're a drug. If I die, it was worth it."

It's late morning, and I'm riding Max's cock in his bed while he grips my hips and guides my movement and fills my ears with nonstop praise, compliments, and dirty talk. After fucking each other into the wee hours of the morning, we finally crashed for good in Max's bed in a twisted, tangled knot of satisfied limbs and flesh.

When sunlight hit my face, however, I woke up and dragged my tired ass into Max's bathroom. When I came back out and saw Max's naked, godlike form in the bed, I couldn't resist. Despite being sore and exhausted, I slithered back into bed and woke Max up with a blowjob and then mounted his hard cock.

When it comes to sex, Max just *gets* me. He knows when to tease. When to deny. When to keep it steady, slow down, or step on the gas. He's a mind reader, basically. A magic man. I can't wait to see him again later this week for our dinner date. And then, after dinner, to come back here and experience the sequel to what we did last night.

When I orgasm, Max lets out a roar and releases inside me.

When my body quiets down, I flop down next to him on the bed and snuggle into him, grinning and giggling like a fool.

Max strokes my back. "Do you have time for breakfast? I don't have any food in the fridge—I've been working like a maniac lately—but there's a great place down the street."

My heart leaps. Max asked me out to dinner last night, and today he's inviting me to breakfast? I'm not sure how to reconcile his invitations with the "one-night stand" conversation we had last night at Captain's, but I'm far too excited to spend more time with this hunk of a hottie to even try to figure out those inconsistencies now.

While flirting with Max at Captain's last night, I had the foresight to text my father and ask if it'd be okay for me to spend the night at Lucy's house. Dad replied that'd be fine and that I should take my time coming home today. But now, I'm not entirely sure if "taking my time" means I've got time for a leisurely brunch with Max.

"You need to eat, right?" Max says. Clearly, he's misinterpreting my silence as proof I'm vacillating on whether I want to spend more time with him; whereas, in reality, I want nothing more than to flit off to breakfast with him. The thing is, though, I don't know how or when I should tell this playboy I'm actually at the mercy of my father's schedule today, thanks to the cute little redhead at home who owns my heart.

"Breakfast sounds good," I say, figuring I'll backtrack on that if I text Dad and he asks me to come home now. "What's the name of the place down the street? I'll google it and check reviews."

Max smiles. "You don't trust my recommendation?"

"Food is my passion. I fully admit I'm a restaurant snob. I'll check out the menu and reviews, and if it isn't up to my standards, I'll find us another place."

Max chuckles. "Would you like to pick the restaurant for our dinner later this week?"

"No, I have faith in your selection for that. Breakfast is tricky."

Max tells me the name of the breakfast place and then leans in for a kiss—and when our kiss is done, he nuzzles his nose into mine and whispers, "I wasn't lying when I said I'm not looking for anything serious. I'm not trying to give you mixed messages here."

"You're not. Sometimes, a meal is just a meal."

Max sighs with relief. "Exactly."

"As long as we're both clear on what we want," I say, "and what we don't, then it's all good."

"Glad we're on the same page." His smile brightens, and yet again, my heart flutters. He strokes my thigh. "You wanna hop in the shower with me?"

"No, you go ahead. I'll join you after I've googled the restaurant."

Max chuckles. "Have fun."

"Do you have a coffee maker? I'd kill for a cup of coffee."

"In the kitchen. No killing required."

"I'll make a pot."

"Awesome."

Max slides out of bed, grabs his phone, and ambles naked toward his bathroom. As he walks, I admire his gorgeous backside. Once Max has disappeared into the bathroom, I grab my phone and swipe into my texts. Not surprisingly, my friends have been blowing up our group chat all morning with questions for Selena and me about Grayson and Max, respectively. Selena hasn't made an appearance in the chat yet, which is probably a great sign for Grayson. Selena is an early riser, and also prompt with her text replies, so if she hasn't gotten around to answering the group's demands for an update by now, it's probably because she's otherwise engaged.

Grinning, I tap out a reply to my friends, letting them know I just enjoyed the spiciest, hottest, most mind-blowingly fantastic night of my life, and instantly, I'm barraged with a cavalcade of

GIFs and texts. There's a splayed kitty cat fanning her nether regions in front of an oscillating fan. A woman eating a banana suggestively. A nuclear explosion. And so on. When I tell the group the further news that I'm going to breakfast with Max this morning and then to dinner with him later this week, the group chat explodes with another round of GIFs and comments.

Selena enters the chat to let us know she had a fabulous night with Grayson at a hotel and has invited him to spend tonight with her as well, since her son is spending the weekend with his father. We collectively cheer Selena on, since we know she rarely dates and never jumps straight to sex when she does, and Selena assures us it's nothing serious but a whole lot of fun.

As I'm saying goodbye to my friends, the shower turns on behind Max's bathroom door, so I press the button to call my father, slide out of bed, and pad on bare feet toward Max's kitchen.

"Hey, sweetie pie," Dad says.

"Hi, Daddy-o. Can I stay for breakfast with Lucy and Frankie?"

"Of course. Take your time. How was the slumber party?" Am I imagining it, or is Dad's tone a bit snarky? Does he suspect his wild child didn't actually sleep over at her best friend's house last night?

"It was fun. Just like old times." I take a seat at Max's kitchen table. "What are you and Ripley doing?"

"We're finishing breakfast now—chocolate chip pancakes, of course—and when we're done here, we're going to the park."

"How fun. Can I say hi to her?"

There's a shuffle, and then, the sweetest, most glorious squeaky voice fills my ears. I ask my sweet girl about breakfast. And then, we talk about her upcoming outing to the park. I tell her I love her to the moon and back and promise to come home soon, and she quickly gets off the phone, having lost interest. It's a relief. If Ripley had begged me to come home, I would have ditched breakfast with Max. But now that it's clear both Dad and

Ripley are perfectly happy without me there, I feel even more excited to get to spend a bit more time with my hot golden god.

Dad's voice returns, and we say our goodbyes. After disconnecting the call, I look around Max's kitchen for his coffee maker, which is when a couple of framed photos on a nearby shelf catch my eye. Curious, I walk over to them to get a better look and instantly have a heart attack.

No.

My hand shaking, I pick up one of the framed photos. In the shot, there are two smiling, blonde little boys with a man who's obviously their father. *And the father is Alexander.*

No.

This can't be.

But it is.

That's definitely Alexander. He's much younger in this shot by at least twenty years. His hair is blonde, instead of silver. *But still, that's him.* No wonder Max reminds me so much of Alexander. *Because Max has Alexander's DNA inside him!*

I feel sick.

Dizzy.

Like I'm going to pass out.

Oh, God. I fucked Alexander's son.

Panicking, I search "Max" and "Maximillian" and "patent attorney Seattle" on my phone, along with Alexander's last name of "Vaughn." *And there it is.* Max's gorgeous face on the website of his high-end law firm, with his name underneath his photo listed as "Maximillian Vaughn."

My heart crashes and I sprint with my phone into the hallway, praying Max is still in the shower. If so, I'll grab my clothes and throw them on in record speed, and then sprint away, never to be seen by Max again. Thankfully, Max and I haven't traded phone numbers or last names yet. So, I should be able to disappear without a trace.

Except that Selena is dating Grayson now, and Max knows Grayson.

Fuck!

I race into Max's room and freak out when I realize the shower isn't running anymore behind the closed bathroom door. Which means I'd better get moving.

I look around frantically for my clothes on Max's bedroom floor before remembering they're on the floor in the living room. Breathing hard, I race out of the bedroom and start furiously throwing on my clothes in the living room.

"Marnie?" Max says behind me.

Fuck.

I turn around, half dressed, to find Max standing before me with wet hair and a white towel around his trim waist. He takes in my frantic body language. My half-dressed frame. "Are you . . . *leaving*?"

It takes me a half-second to find my voice. But when I do, I'm able to choke out, "Yes. Sorry. Something came up and I have to go."

Max looks concerned. "Is everything okay? Is it something serious?"

"No, just time sensitive. For work. There's been a little snafu with some . . . ingredients. For a client." I can't fathom how or why a private chef who's not presently at a job would suddenly need to deal with ingredients on an otherwise languid Saturday morning, but it's all my panicked brain could come up with on the spot.

Max's jaw muscles pulse. "Glad to hear it's not a matter of life and death." His Adam's apple bobs. "Can I give you a ride home?"

"I'll grab an Uber."

"Let me drive you, Marnie."

"No," I bark out, far more sharply than intended. "I've already called an Uber. I'm good."

Max's nostrils flare. His shoulders tighten. "Are we still on for dinner this week?"

My heart sinks. Damn. I was really looking forward to that

dinner! Too much for my own good, probably. "Uh, no. The thing that came up is going to keep me busy every night this week."

Max looks like I've slapped him. "Yeah, dinner was probably a bad idea, anyway. On second thought, I'm too busy at work to take you out this week."

"Okay, great. This has been a lot of fun, Max. But let's not ruin what's going to be an amazing memory by pretending there's any real potential here, okay? Let's consider last night a fun one-off. A great memory. And that's about it." I pick up my bra and start putting it on, feeling like I'm going to keel over from stress.

"Did I do something to offend you?" he asks.

"No, no. You've been amazing. It's not you. It's me."

Max scoffs and crosses his arms over his chest. "That's my line, Marnie."

I pull my shirt over my head. "And now, it's mine. Thanks again for everything. Take care, Maximillian."

Anger flickers across his gorgeous face. "Yeah, you, too. Have a great life, I guess."

"Good luck making partner at your firm." I grab my purse, turn on my heel, and sprint out the front door without looking back. When I get downstairs and outside the building, I sprint a couple of blocks up the sidewalk, since I haven't really called an Uber and don't want to wait for one in front of Max's building.

After calling an Uber, I dial my mother's phone number while awaiting its arrival. At the sound of Mom's voice in her outgoing message, I clutch my heart, and then whisper after the beep, "I wish so badly I could tell you about the crazy thing that just happened. Is the universe punishing me for something or what? I love you." As I'm disconnecting the call, my Uber arrives, so I tumble into the backseat and quickly place a call to my bestie, Lucy.

"Why are you calling me, when you should be—" Lucy says in greeting.

"I just found out Max is Alexander's son!"

"*What*?"

In a long ramble, I tell Lucy about the photo in Max's kitchen and my subsequent google search that confirmed Max's last name is Vaughn. "Lucy, I just fucked Mr. BDE's son!"

She snorts. "Now, that's some petty revenge. Brava, Marnie Girl!"

"I didn't fuck Alexander's son intentionally. It was a crazy, awful coincidence."

"Did you tell Max?"

"Of course not. I flew out of there without explaining a thing. If I told him the truth, he'd never believe it was a coincidence. He'd think exactly what you just did: that I'm some kind of vengeful, diabolical ex-lover who was mad at the daddy, so I fucked the son."

"I was *joking*."

"Max wouldn't believe me, Lucy. He'd think I'm deranged."

"Oh my god," Lucy whispers. "You're right. He totally would."

"Of course, he would."

"Definitely."

"Fuck. I was so excited to go out to dinner with him, too."

"Why? He's not serious boyfriend material, honey. You have to know that."

I sigh. "Yeah, I do. But . . ." I whimper. "He's *so fucking* hot."

There's a long pause as my best friend processes the situation. She whispers, "What are the odds?" And then, true to form, my best friend bursts into snorting, hearty, wheezing laughter from the depths of her soul.

5

MAX

"Great tackle," my brother, Auggie, murmurs. He's sitting next to me on my couch. We're watching the Sunday night football game together. Normally, I'd bark at my brother to show some respect and get his dirty feet off my coffee table. But right now, I'm too distracted by endless thoughts about Marnie to care about my brother's shoes on my furniture.

It's been about thirty-six hours since Marnie left my place on Saturday morning. Plenty of time for me to get her out of my system and move on. To stop wondering, obsessively, what the fuck happened. And yet, sitting here with my brother, I can't stop thinking about her. Wondering. Trying, and failing, to solve the puzzle of what happened.

My lunch with Grayson today certainly didn't help to ease my anxiety and embarrassment about the situation. Grayson didn't mean to throw salt on my wounds; in fact, he had no idea he was doing it. But when he went on and on at lunch about his "magical, electrifying, once-in-a-lifetime" connection with Selena, I found myself thinking a truly shocking thought—one that made me feel even worse about the way things had ended with Marnie: *Yeah, that's exactly how I felt with Marnie.*

I was pissed at myself for having that thought. Marnie and I had had one night of fun. One night of sex. Granted, it was fantastic sex. Amazing sex. The best, ever. But, still, it wasn't that deep. Okay, fine, Marnie wasn't feeling it, after all? So be it. She doesn't want to see me again? Fine. Great. Fantastic. I've got enough on my plate without needing to make room in my busy schedule to wine and dine anyone, especially a woman with a fucking split personality. A woman who changes her mind with every shift of the breeze, apparently.

"Earth to Max," Auggie says. "Did you see that horrible call?"

"Huh? No."

"Watch it on replay. The refs are idiots."

I watch the replay. "Yeah, horrible call."

At lunch with Grayson, when he asked how things had gone with Marnie, I didn't tell him the embarrassing truth. Instead, I saved face. Played it cool. Told Grayson that sex with Marnie was fire, but, unfortunately, she bored me otherwise. When Grayson wouldn't let it go, I told him I'd *maybe* hook up with Marnie again, if we happened to bump into each other at a bar. But as far as going out on an actual date with her, I told Grayson, "I've decided I wasn't feeling enough chemistry for that." It was like saying a nuclear bomb doesn't have enough "oomph" for me. Like saying the ocean is a puddle. But I said it, and then changed the subject. I figured I'd stop thinking about Marnie by the end of my lunch with Grayson. But it wasn't meant to be.

If I hadn't walked into my living room at that precise moment, I'm positive Marnie would have walked out my front door without saying goodbye. That's the thing I can't wrap my head around. What happened between Marnie saying she'd google the breakfast place and Marnie throwing on her clothes to sprint away?

"There we go," Auggie says, clapping enthusiastically. "Great tackle. Now, hold 'em one more time."

"One more time," I echo. But it's no use. I'm fucking obsessed with The Marnie Conundrum.

Auggie sighs. "Okay, what's going on?"

I look at my brother blankly. "What?"

"We're on *offense*. I said that to test you. And you failed."

"Oh." I glance at the TV—and, yep, the Seahawks are on offense. Which means we're not actually tackling anyone at the moment.

"Sorry," I say. "I'm just thinking about work."

"You're always thinking about work, but you're not always distracted like this." Auggie tilts his head. "Are you worried about the partnership selection meeting in a couple weeks?"

He's given me an easy out since I am genuinely nervous about that. "Yeah, that's it," I say. "Nobody even came close to me on billable hours this year. Plus, I got some incredible results for my clients, too. My boss says he's gonna go to bat for me with the committee, but he said he's really got his work cut out for him to convince them to go with me."

"Because you're only a fifth year?"

"Yeah, that and also because I haven't done any work for the firm's biggest client. But I have no control over that. If they'd assign me to the guy's cases, like I keep asking them to do, then I'd kill it for him."

"Aren't you constantly picking up work for other associates, so they can take a vacation or go to their kid's game or dance recital?"

"Yep. I do that all the time. I'm hoping that'll help me with the committee. It's not why I do it. I do it because I like being a team player. But I feel like that's another thing working in my favor."

"They'd be stupid not to give it to you," Auggie says. "You're a beast."

"The good news is my boss, Scott, is firmly in my corner. I'm hoping he'll be able to convince the committee to give me the offer this time."

"How many associates make partner each year?"

"Usually, only one. Nobody's ever made it this fast before. It normally takes seven years. But when you consider the hours I've logged, I've basically worked the equivalent of seven years in only five."

Auggie whistles. "Damn. You need to slow down, brother. Nobody can keep up that pace."

"Once I reach both of my goals, I'll slow down. But not before then."

I don't need to explain further. My brother knows making partner is step one of my life plan. Step two is then getting myself assigned to the core team for our biggest client, Wayne Walters. His tech firm specializes in AI for the medical and education sectors, among other things, and they're killing it. Changing the world. Since day one of law school, I've wanted to work directly for Wayne Walters. In fact, I joined my law firm out of law school because I knew it's the one firm in Seattle used by Wayne Walters.

"Sorry if this is a stupid question," Auggie says, "but why not skip the partnership thing and get hired by that billionaire tech guy, directly?"

"He doesn't hire lawyers as in-house attorneys like that. He likes to pluck them from teams of attorneys who've worked for him at outside firms for years. That way, they prove themselves worthy before he takes them on."

Auggie looks at me like I'm crazy. "How many years, in total, are you expecting it to take to get yourself eventually hired by this guy?"

"Including my three years of law school?" I shrug. "Ten or eleven, I guess. Twelve, if you count the additional year it took to get my MBA."

Auggie looks at me like I'm crazy. "That seems like an awfully long time to invest in a master plan, when waking up tomorrow isn't guaranteed."

"Nothing worth having is easy to come by."

Auggie grimaces. "Just, you know, don't forget to get out there and live sometimes. I know you're a hard-working, goal-oriented person, and I respect that about you, but life isn't only about where you're headed. It's also about smelling the roses along the way."

"Okay, Mom."

"She's right, though. You can't always be waiting to be happy once such and such happens. What if it never does?"

"It will."

"Nothing is guaranteed."

"It will, Auggie. And don't worry about me. Knowing I'm doing everything in my power to make my lifelong professional goals a reality makes me happy. Very happy."

"Yeah, I can tell. The happiness is practically bursting off you like a rainbow."

I sip my beer. "New topic."

My brother snickers. "I've actually got some piping hot Ashley gossip. Apparently, she's starting to talk about wanting a baby."

My eyebrows ride up. From what I've been told, our father made it clear to his young third wife before marriage that he didn't want any more children, and she agreed that was acceptable to her. "How do you know?"

Auggie says, "One of my friends at school is best friends with Ashley's little sister. I told you about her, remember?" He's in his first year of veterinary school at the University of Washington. And somehow, despite how busy he is, he still manages to get all our family's best dirt.

"That's what happens when you marry a woman who's twenty-five years younger than you," I say. "I'm sure Ashley's biological clock is ticking."

"Meh. I'm sure Dad will simply throw more money at her expensive hobbies to distract her from the idea. More horseback riding lessons, perhaps? At Grandpa's birthday party she told me she wants to be in the Olympics."

"In what sport?"

"Horseback riding. It's called dressage."

"Huh?"

"That's when horses jump over stuff. At least, I think that's what she said at the party. I wasn't really listening."

"If she wants to be in the Olympics, she'd better get on that soon. Time's running out, babe."

"She's such an idiot," Auggie mutters. "The fact that Dad thought that airheaded gold digger was wife material is pure insanity."

"Dad cheated on Mom, Auggie. Obviously, Dad's idea of wife material is very different from ours, or else he would have thanked his lucky stars every fucking day of his life he'd somehow landed a woman of Mom's caliber."

My brother looks at me sympathetically, and we have an entire nonverbal conversation in the space of about five seconds. Auggie knows what I had to shoulder at age fifteen. He knows I had to make choices he didn't. And while my brother has expressed full support and gratitude for the decision I made—the decision to go to our mother with what I'd found out—I do wonder at times if Auggie wishes everything could go back to the way it was when we all thought, wrongly, we had the perfect family.

"I'm here for you, brother," Auggie says.

"Back at you. I'm good, though. Don't worry about me."

"Sorry, it's part of the job description." He smiles at me.

"Hey, Auggie?" When he looks at me, his eyebrows raised, clearly thinking I'm going to say something poignant, I tap his leg and bark, "Get your shoes off my coffee table, motherfucker. Show some fucking respect."

Auggie sits up and slides his feet down. "I think I liked you better when you were distracted."

Speaking of which . . . *Marnie.*

Shit.

Okay, that's it.

I'm now officially forbidding myself from wondering what happened with her, ever again. The world is full of unsolved mysteries, and for my mental health, I need to accept Marnie is one of them. Unsolved. A mystery. Batshit crazy. A woman with a split-personality. Starting now, she's banished from my brain, forevermore. *And that's that.*

6

MARNIE

I flop down next to Dad on his comfy couch. "Ripley's out like a light."

Dad chuckles. "She played extra-hard today."

Dad, Ripley, and I spent a lovely Sunday afternoon on the shores of Lake Washington. This house, Mom and Dad's dream home, is right near the water's edge, so the three of us go down to the lakeshore often to picnic and goof around. Whenever we have one of our family lakeshore days, Ripley and I crash here for the night rather than going back to my small apartment, since Ripley usually falls over at the dinner table and I enjoy spending some one-on-one time with Dad. That's especially true on Sundays during football season, when we can watch the Sunday night game together.

Dad offers me a bowl of popcorn, and we eat and chat while watching the game on TV. At half-time, though, Dad mutes the game, turns to me, and says, "Are you going to tell me what's been bothering you since you got home yesterday, or is it something you'd prefer to keep to yourself?"

I furrow my brow. "Nothing's bothering me."

"If you're going to lie to me, then do it well. Did you have an argument with one of your friends during your girls' night out?"

I snort. "Of course not. We had a great time."

Dad studies my face for a long moment. "Did something happen with that guy you were dating?"

I exhale. "Yeah, it's over with him. As it turns out, he's married."

Dad grimaces. "Sorry."

"I found out last week, and I was really upset about it. But I'm okay now. Looking back, I wasn't even my true self with him. I never even told him about Ripley, so how real could I have been?"

"Even so, it couldn't have felt good to find out he'd lied to you, all along."

I twist my mouth. "I think what's bothering me is that being with him—the fantasy of him, anyway—made me realize I'm ready to settle down. I'm ready to find the kind of guy I *would* want to introduce to Ripley. For a minute there, I felt like I'd lost my chance at that." I pat his leg. "But I'm okay now. Moving on."

He's not buying it. "It seemed like something was really bothering you when you got home yesterday. Was it the thing with the married guy, even though you found out about him last week?"

Shoot. Why'd I tell him the actual timeline? It would have been so much easier to blame yesterday's foul mood on Alexander and leave it at that. Suddenly, images of Max's forlorn face slam into me and cause my entire body to shudder in shame and regret. Since the moment I sprinted out of Max's apartment yesterday, I haven't been able to stop thinking about that moment and feeling horrendously guilty about it. I feel like I handled things horribly with him; but on the other hand, what else could I have done?

On a selfish note, I've also been feeling acute waves of disappointment since yesterday that I won't get to see Max again. That I missed out on yesterday's breakfast with him and that dinner date later this week. Even though I know Max isn't boyfriend material, I'd love to have sex with him again. Plus, I thoroughly enjoyed spending time with him. Chatting with him. He's an interesting, intelligent person, unlike anyone I've ever met—a fascinating blend of ambitious, intelligent, funny, and attentive. With all that going for him, I certainly wouldn't have minded making him my fuck buddy for a while, while I start looking for Mr. Right.

I smile at Dad. "You're right, Dad. The gloominess you sensed from me yesterday wasn't about the married guy. It was about someone else. I met a guy at a bar on Friday when I was out with my friends. Someone I liked a lot. But he's not boyfriend material, so the fact that I was super attracted to him, right on the heels of me being with that married guy, made me wonder what the hell is wrong with me. I've obviously got major issues when it comes to men, and I think maybe I should address them, rather than continuing to chase the wrong ones. I'm just so, I don't know, self-destructive. That was fine when I only had myself to take care of, but I want to be a great mother to Ripley. A role model." Tears prick my eyes. "And I also miss Mom. So much, it hurts. Sometimes, I just feel so alone and heartbroken. That's how I was feeling when I came home yesterday. Like I would have given anything to talk to Mom."

"Aw, baby, come here."

I dive into my father's arms, and he cuddles me like I'm fourteen again while I cry.

I sniffle. "When things didn't work out with the guy from the bar, I wanted so badly to call Mom and tell her the whole story. I even left her a voicemail."

"Aw, sweetheart."

"I called Lucy. She was amazing, but she isn't Mom. Nobody is."

"She was one of a kind."

I wipe my eyes. "I'm sorry to unload on you like this. I know you're dealing with your own grief."

"It helps me to feel less alone when you open up to me, honey. I've been struggling, too."

"Oh, Dad. I'm so sorry. I didn't want to burden you. That's why I've kept it to myself."

"You're not a burden, Marnie. Talking to you like this is a *blessing*."

I burst into tears again and cry on my father's shoulder for a solid twenty minutes. When I finally pull myself together, we talk and talk. About our mutual grief at the loss of my mother. About the fact that we're both stuck in our grief, feeling incapable of moving through it. We talk about my floundering business and the fact that it's a symbol of the fact that I can't seem to get my shit together in all aspects of my life. We talk about Ripley and how much we both love and adore her and want her to grow up happy, healthy, and safe—and with a mother who kicks ass and takes names and shows her the way, the same way Mom did for me.

"I'm always really worried about Ripley," I say. "It weighs on me, Dad. I can never relax." Dad knows what I mean. Our beautiful Ripley was born prematurely and with a congenital heart defect, and I've been a nervous wreck about her from day one. For a while there, every little cough and sneeze sent me racing with her to the hospital for a check-up. And then, we discovered she had some auditory processing issues and needed speech therapy. So, that made me worry, yet again. Frankly, when it comes to Ripley, there's never been a time when I've been able to sit back and relax, other than our family lakeshore days. But even then, I'm constantly wishing Mom were with us, so even those days aren't totally carefree. I say, "I think Ripley's having a problem with her eyesight lately. Have you noticed she's squinting hard to see things that aren't two inches in front of her face?"

"Now that you mention it, yeah, she has been squinting a lot. Let's take her to get her eyes checked this week."

I exhale. "Okay, yes, let's do that."

Dad pats my hand. "And let's also agree on a solid plan for you and me." When I look at him expectantly, Dad says, "I know how much you value your independence, but I think you and Ripley should move in here with me. You know Mrs. Leibowicz across the street? She told me there's an amazing preschool nearby. They have specialists that work there. People with expertise for kids with learning disabilities. If you lived here, it'd be convenient to take her there, whenever she's ready to start preschool."

"We're not ready for that yet. I don't think we'd do that for at least a year."

"Well, that's good because the place has a long wait list, apparently. But why wait till then? Move in here now, honey, and let's start working on ourselves together. We'll go to grief counseling. We'll support each other. Plus, I'll be able to watch Ripley for you, as you try to build your business."

My heart is racing. "How much does that preschool cost? Ripley's heart medications are so expensive, I'm not sure—"

"Honey, I'll pay for preschool and whatever else Ripley needs. That's yet another reason for you to move in here with me. The money you save on rent can go to other expenses. Even better, I'll pay for Ripley's expenses while you start a college fund for her with what you would have spent on rent every month."

It sounds like heaven. But still, I'm reluctant to be a burden to my father. I push back. Ask him if he's sure. And he replies that he'd love nothing more than to have Ripley and me here. He says, "Don't say yes because of this, okay? But I've been really lonely. I'd love to have you both here, all the time."

I hug him and thank him profusely for his generous offer. "I agree we should go to grief counseling together," I say. "I'd also like to start therapy for myself. To figure out why I'm always chasing emotionally unavailable men. I've got the best father in the world, so why am I attracted to men who don't want a future with me? I need to figure this out, so I'm attracted to the right kind of men when I start looking for a long-term partner. I don't want to expose Ripley to anyone who isn't going to be a wonderful daddy to her, in addition to being a wonderful partner to me. If I can't find that, I'd rather be alone."

He smiles. "That sounds good. I'm sure Mrs. Leibowicz will watch Ripley whenever we go to counseling together. And I'd be happy to watch her for you, so you can work on yourself." He winks. "Although, to me, you're already perfect."

I laugh. "Thanks, Dad. I'm far from it."

We talk some more and nail down some logistics and timing for my big move. And soon, it's settled. Ripley and I are moving in, and Dad and I are both going to work hard on ourselves.

"When it's time for Ripley to go to kindergarten, we'll reassess our living situation, okay?" I say. "By then, you might have a whole new life and your daughter and granddaughter might be cramping your style."

"Cramping my style?" Dad says, looking genuinely confused.

I nudge his arm. "You might be dating by then." When Dad scoffs, I add, "Anything is possible, especially a year or two from now." When Dad rolls his eyes, I ask, "You're not even tempted to get back out there?"

"God, no."

"If you're at all tempted, I recently met a lovely woman in a yoga class. I think you'd—"

"No, honey. Thank you for the thought. But I'm not even close to ready. Maybe someday. But not any time soon."

Mom made it clear she wanted Dad to find love again, as long as whatever woman he finds is kind-hearted and good to him, Ripley, and me. Surely, he remembers her saying that to him, so his current reluctance has nothing to do with some misplaced idea that he'd be betraying Mom by falling in love again. But, hey, if he's not ready, then introducing him to Geraldine would be pointless. She could be the perfect partner for him, but if his heart isn't open, then he won't see that.

"Okay, Daddy," I say, patting his arm. "Take your time."

He cringes. "Either way, I can't imagine myself dating one of my daughter's friends. I'd feel like a dirty old man."

I crack up. "My yoga friend is fifty-three."

He scoffs. "A child."

"Twelve years is a totally appropriate age gap at your age, Dad. Especially given how fit and active you are. Lots of men your age date women more than twenty years younger."

"*Why?*"

"Fuck if I know."

We share a laugh.

Dad says, "It's a moot point, because I'm not ready to date anyone of any age any time soon."

I smile. "There's no rush. I only mentioned my friend because she reminds me of Mom. She has the exact same kind of gentle, kind-hearted energy." I shrug. "In retrospect, the person I probably wanted to set her up with was *myself.*"

"Aw, my love." He kisses the side of my head. "Mom is looking down on both of us and telling us to get back out there and feel joy again. Especially you, Wild Child. You know it was her greatest pleasure to watch you taking the world by storm."

My heart is aching. That was Mom's nickname for me, not Dad's. This marks the first time anyone has called me that since Mom died, and hearing the nickname out loud is making me realize the truth about what's going on with me. I've been searching for comfort. To numb the pain. And to do that, I foolishly latched onto a walking red flag of a man. And then, onto Max, when it was clear he was hot as hell but not even remotely interested in a serious relationship. Where did my mother's fierce daughter—the one who always took the world by storm— go? In my present form, I can barely take the world by a slight mist.

"You know what?" I say, as full clarity descends upon me. "This former Wild Child is officially tamed. Or at least, for a while. Starting today, I'm going to delete all my dating apps and swear off men completely. I'm done chasing cheap dopamine hits for at least a full year while I work on myself. I'm going to become the best possible version of Marnie Long. The best possible mother and daughter and friend. And when I finally put myself back out there, I'll be healthy, so I'll attract a good man who wants a healthy relationship. Something wonderful for both Ripley and me." I smile. "With a little luck, I might even find the kind of true love you and Mom shared."

"And still do."

Oh, my heart. "And still do," I echo softly.

Dad smiles. "I'm excited about everything you just said. I think it's a great plan." He winks. "*Manifest* it, my love." It's another reference to Mom. That's what she always said and did. And I'll be damned, whenever Mom manifested something, it always came true.

"I'll start right now." I close my eyes dramatically, intending to model my amazing *manifestation* abilities, but the image that pops into my head, unbidden, is Max's handsome face. Followed by his gorgeous body. His straining, hard cock. And then, the look of complete bewilderment—and then, anger—on his face when I did him so fucking dirty without explanation. Dear God, the man must think I'm insane.

I open my eyes with a sigh. "It's too soon for manifestation, I'm afraid. I'm too messed up. I need to work on myself before I can be trusted with that particular superpower, or else I'm going to manifest the wrong thing for me."

The announcer in the football game announces the final score, which means we've been talking throughout the entire second half of the game. Dad grabs the remote and turns off the TV and we hug goodnight.

"Thank you for talking this through with me," I say. "I feel excited about the future for the first time in a long while."

"So do I."

I head to my bedroom and complete my nighttime routine. But despite all my big talk, I can't stop thinking about Max. I hate knowing he hates me now. That I'll never get to see him again. Never get to talk to him in the moonlight in his bed after enjoying another round of delicious sex. He's not in the market for a serious relationship, but he would have been a thoroughly delightful way to pass the time for a while.

No, Marnie. You're not going to do that anymore. You literally just finished telling Dad you're swearing off men for a year, at least.

Shit. I did, didn't I? And I meant it.

I look at myself in my bathroom mirror and promise myself, out loud, I'm going to do everything I said to my father mere minutes ago.

From my bathroom, I slide into bed and stare at the ceiling. I'm trying to expel the visions of Max that keep invading my brain. My heart. My soul. But I can't get rid of him. I need some closure. I need a *release*. I reach underneath the covers and touch myself to thoughts of Max—to memories of what we actually did, as well as some naughty fantasies we didn't get around to— and thankfully, my orgasm comes quickly and does the trick: At least for now, my mind is wiped clean—enough for me to finally drift off to sleep.

7

MARNIE

A year and a half later

"I can't believe you didn't go back for a second bite of that smoking-hot apple, girl. If it were me, I would have gone back for seconds, thirds, and fourths."

That's Victoria speaking. To me. And she's full of shit. Our darling Victoria doesn't trifle with younger men. And she certainly wouldn't stoop to dating a lowly patent attorney, even one who plies his trade at the best law firm in Seattle. Victoria's last romantic partner was a successful novelist. The one before that, a conductor for the Seattle Symphony. The one before that, a renowned plastic surgeon. The woman aims high, and rightly so, since she's a force to be reckoned with who heads up a big-time venture capitalist group.

And yet, despite Victoria's known preferences when it comes to men, she hasn't stopped making comments like that about Max, ever since he walked into this birthday party, looking like a casually dressed golden god. It didn't help that I lied and told the group I didn't see Max again after that one night because we didn't want the same things, and I decided to do the healthy, mature thing and leave him in the dust. Apparently, Victoria has sniffed out my lie, and now she's hell-bent on taunting me into divulging the truth. But that's not going to happen. To this day, only Lucy knows the truth about why I bolted out of Max's place the next morning. And since I can't tell Selena without risking the story getting to Grayson, and then to Max, I can't tell any of my other friends, either. If I'm not telling Selena, then I'm not telling any of them. Other than Lucy, of course; but they all know she's my extra-special bestie.

Along with Victoria, I'm sitting at a shaded table in Selena's spacious backyard with Lucy and Jasmine, while our hostess for today's birthday party, Selena, flits around the packed party with the sweet birthday boy—Selena's beloved boyfriend of a year and a half, Grayson McKnight.

True to form, Selena's gone all out for this Sunday afternoon birthday bash. She's got a DJ, catered barbeque, and a uniformed bartender dispensing all manner of delicious cocktails, including something called a "Grey Goose Grayson." Oh, and there's one more notable thing at this birthday party today. Notable to me, anyway. *Grayson's buddy, Max.*

It's the first time I'm seeing Max since our night together, and, man, I'd forgotten how smoking hot he is. Currently, Max is playing cornhole with the birthday boy across the party, and I don't think he's aware of my presence underneath this big umbrella. Or maybe he is, and he's been artfully avoiding eye contact with me, the same way I've been doing with him.

"If it were me," Victoria continues, her eyes trained on Max across the party, "I'd not only have taken a second bite of that apple, I'd have turned that hunk of a man into an apple fritter, and then, into an apple cobbler with extra crumbles on top, and eaten him for breakfast, lunch, and dinner for a full week."

I can't take it anymore. Victoria's taunting would have annoyed me, regardless, but it's especially annoying when I haven't had sex with anyone since Max, and the man is looking like a veritable smoke show across Selena's spacious lawn. "Would you stop already?" I snap, and everyone at the table, including Victoria, chuckles. "New topic, please. For fuck's sake, Vicky. Stop living through me and get your own boy toy if that's what you want."

Victoria's always loved getting a rise out of me. It's the reason our friends call us Fire and Ice. Yes, that's partly because I'm a redhead and Vicky's a platinum blonde. But I don't think the nicknames would have stuck since college based on hair color alone. In fact, they've stuck for so long because our resident ice queen's disposition is the polar opposite of my fiery one.

Thankfully, the conversation shifts. We find out the latest about Lucy's daughter, Frankie, whom we all adore. As Lucy's speaking, however, I can't resist sneaking a peek across the party at Mr. Smoke Show. When I look over at him, he's tossing a bean bag in his game with Grayson, and the second my eyes land on his tall, athletic frame, my blood flash-boils with lust. *Damn.* Max looked stunning in a designer suit at Captain's; he looked downright mouthwatering, naked and hard in the moonlight at his condo; and now, at this happy afternoon gathering, he looks like a runway model in those casual board shorts and a T-shirt.

"Hey, Marnie," Jasmine says, yanking my attention from Max. "Is your dad still seeing that woman he met at the grocery store?" A couple monthly dinners ago, I told my friends the exciting news about my father's encounter with a pretty lady at Whole Foods, which led to a sunset picnic at Kerry Park the next afternoon. Since that first bit of exciting news, my friends have regularly asked for updates on Dad's budding romance.

I never did introduce Dad to the wonderful lady I met at that expensive yoga studio. In fact, I haven't seen Geraldine since I moved in with Dad. For one thing, the yoga studio is way too expensive for me to keep my membership going. Plus, it's too far away from Dad's place to be practical. But even more than that, I realized I'd been so drawn to Geraldine because she'd reminded me of Mom, and that wasn't a healthy reason to pursue a friendship with her. All's well that ends well, though, because my father has been floating around the house like a schoolboy with a crush ever since he met his new crush, Gigi, at Whole Foods.

"Yep, Dad's still dating Grocery Store Lady," I say to the group, much to everyone's delight. "And increasingly over the moon about it. He's been taking it really slowly with her, but I feel like things have been noticeably picking up lately. He made Gigi dinner last week at the house, when Ripley and I were at Lucy's for dinner. And then, Dad and Gigi took Ripley to the zoo while I was auditioning for that new client referred by Victoria." I smile at Victoria. "Thank you again for that. I owe you big, even though you're presently annoying me."

Victoria laughs. "You're very welcome."

I return to the group, "And today, while Dad is watching Ripley for me, Gigi came over to join them at the lake for a little picnic on the shore."

As everyone expresses excitement about that, Jasmine asks, "You still haven't met her?"

"Not yet. Dad's thinking about having her over for dinner next week to meet me, but I don't want to pressure him. He'll introduce her when he's ready."

My friends ask a few questions about my fancy new client who was kindly referred by Victoria, but when that line of conversation runs its course, Jasmine, a pediatrician, tells the group a story about an adorable kid at work. As Jasmine talks, I find myself giving in to temptation and glancing toward Max's cornhole game again. But this time, Max isn't over there. *Damn.* Where'd he go?

"Hello, ladies. May I join you?"

"Why, hello, Max," Victoria says, her blue gaze fixed at a target above my head. "Yes, of course. *Sit.*" Victoria scoots over and a figure who smells delicious assumes the now-vacated chair next to me. *Fuck.*

"Hello, Marnie," a male voice says. It's a voice I'd know anywhere, despite the brief time I spent with the man and the lengthy passage of time.

I force myself to look to my right. "Hello, Max."

Oh, Jesus. Up close, the man is hotter than ever. A forest fire. In a flash, I see myself dragging Max into a guest room inside Selena's spacious house and fucking the living hell out of him. Quickly, I turn away, blushing, and sip my Grey Goose Grayson with a shaking hand.

Victoria asks Max how he's enjoying the party, and Max says he's having a great time. Jasmine asks Max if he won his corn-hole game earlier against the Birthday Boy, and Max tells the group the story of his epic battle to the death. Victoria asks Max how he met Grayson in the first place, and Max explains Grayson used to work in the IT Department at his law firm before Grayson took the plunge and went into business for himself.

And through it all, I never once look at Maximillian Vaughn again, even though I'm supremely aware of his body heat next to mine. His scent. His feral energy. Even though I can easily imagine every detail of the gorgeous, girthy cock that lies beneath those board shorts. Even though he's now resting his forearms on the table in my peripheral vision, and I can remember myself literally biting those forearms when he wrapped them around me from behind while fucking me senseless.

I don't have a choice, though. If I look at him again, this close up, my face will give me away. *He'll know I want him.* He might even figure out he's been my sexual fantasy for a year and a half. And I can't let him figure that out. If I do, one thing will lead to another, and I'll somehow wind up fucking him today. And, really, what kind of person *knowingly* fucks both a father and son? It was one thing when I didn't know that's what I was doing. But now that I do, I couldn't possibly do it again . . .

Could I?

No, Marnie. Absolutely not.

Although . . .

Isn't there some kind of statute of limitations in play here that wiped the slate clean regarding my brief and meaningless relationship with Alexander? I haven't even thought about that bastard over the past year and a half, except the few times I've mentioned him in therapy as a cautionary tale. And Max is the last man I had sex with, not Alexander, so it's sort of like Max's cock baptized me anew . . . Right?

No, Marnie. Wrong. You're so wrong, it's pitiful. Now stop trying to rationalize your way into fucking Max again. Why go through all that therapy if you're only going to jump into bed with him again?

Shoot. Before seeing Max today, I'd been proud of my progress in therapy. Proud of my progress in all aspects of my life. I've become a much better person than I was back then. I'm strong. Clear-headed. Healthy. These days, I know what I want in a man, and Maximillian Vaughn—Alexander's freaking son—ain't it, baby.

"What kind of law do you practice?" Jasmine asks.

Max says, "Patent and business law."

"Oh, that's right," Jasmine says. "I remember you mentioned that when we met you before. Back then, you were hoping to make partner at your firm at the end of the year, right? Did that happen?"

"No, not yet, unfortunately," Max says. "But it's okay. In retrospect, I was being a bit too ambitious to think I could get there in five years, when it normally takes seven. This year should be my year. The partnership selection meeting is happening in a few weeks, so hopefully I'll get some good news then."

The whole table, other than me, wishes him luck. But when I realize my silence has been weird and awkward, I murmur, "Yeah, best of luck to you." Unfortunately, I've made my comment a solid beat after everyone else, so my delay in wishing him well has come across as sarcastic, even though I meant the comment sincerely. It certainly didn't help that I didn't look at him when I said it.

"Gee, thanks, Marnie," Max murmurs stiffly. There's anger in that tone. Disdain. And I don't blame him. I'd hate me, too, if I were him.

The conversation shifts. Jasmine talks about her sister who's a family law attorney in San Diego. She says her sister opened her own small firm after failing to make partner at a big, national law firm. She assures Max that making partner isn't the only path to a successful law career, and he politely thanks her for the encouragement.

When Max is done speaking to Jasmine, I can feel his eyes on me. But I don't look at him. Deep down, I know he's a fire I simply can't play around with.

Suddenly, Max says, "Excuse me, ladies." He springs out of his chair and marches away, leaving his disdain for me floating in the air in his vacated spot. And that's that. He's gone.

"Jesus Christ, Marnie," Victoria barks. "Just because you're not interested in seeing him again, doesn't mean you need to be a fucking bitch to the poor guy."

"Leave her alone, Vicky," Lucy says. "That was awkward for her. She didn't know what to say or do."

"She didn't even look at the man!"

"Why do you care?" I shout. And when I realize I've raised my voice a little too much, I look around the party sheepishly.

"I care because he seems like he'd be good for you, actually," Victoria says. "And I care about you. I think you're self-sabotaging again, if you really want to know. I think you felt things with him you weren't ready to feel, and so—"

"Oh, for fuck's sake," I say. I get up. "Excuse me. I need a drink."

I start walking toward the bartender across the party, but when I notice Max talking to Grayson over there, I shift my trajectory and walk aimlessly in another direction. As I walk,

Max's eyes meet mine, and the smolder he flashes me zings me right between the legs like I've been zapped by a Taser gun aimed directly at my clit.

I stop walking and stare him down. And when Grayson unexpectedly walks away, and Max is suddenly standing on his own, I decide, fuck it. I'm a grown-ass woman. And Victoria was right. I was a bitch to Max for not even looking at him. I'm sure he thinks I'm a nut job from the way things ended before. And rightly so. All in all, the right thing to do is go over there and apologize for my behavior at the table just now. Yes. I'll wish him well and explain that I've been in therapy, and he caught me at a bad time in my life and I'm sorry if I've treated him badly. And then I'll walk away. Yep. I'll say all that to him, and that's it, simply to set his mind at ease about what happened a year and a half ago. I'll assure him he did nothing wrong and then walk away with my head held high; and after that, I'll never speak to, or think about, the sexiest man alive, Maximillian Vaughn, ever, ever again.

8

MAX

My heart stops.

Holy shit.

Marnie is walking straight toward me, her red hair practically glittering in the sunshine. At least, I *think* I'm where Marnie is headed. I glance behind me, thinking maybe Selena is standing there. But nope. There's nobody behind me or anywhere nearby. Even the uniformed bartender doling out "Grey Goose Graysons" is a solid thirty yards to my right—and that's not even close to Marnie's trajectory.

Marnie comes to a stop in front of me, and my heart jolts. My skin breaks out in goosebumps. Jesus. What is it about this goddamned woman?

"Hello, Max."

"Hello, Marnie." I fold my arms over my chest. "Did you come over here to chew me out for something I did over there? Perhaps because I had the audacity to sit down next to you?" Why, why, why does this woman have this crazy effect on me? I feel like a middle schooler around her. Butterflies exploding in my belly. Heat zapping across my skin. All this time, every time I jacked off to memories of my night with Marnie, I convinced myself I'd slowly turned her into a fictionalized character. One with far more sex appeal than the real thing. But now that she's standing before me, gazing at me with those big blue eyes of hers, I'm realizing my fantasies about her didn't do her justice. Not even close.

Marnie shifts her weight. "Would you like to hear what I came over here to say to you or would you like to keep putting words into my mouth?"

"Go ahead and speak."

"Gee, thanks." Her blue eyes narrow. "Actually, never mind. Now that I'm here, I'm realizing it's not worth it."

When she turns to leave, anger floods me. The woman unceremoniously ditched me after an amazing night over a year ago, *after* agreeing to breakfast and dinner with me, and then she *ignored* me at that table with her friends, and now *she's* the one acting like *I've* somehow done something offensive?

"Are you fucking kidding me?" I shout to her backside. "You fucked me like a goddamned sex addict for an entire night a year and a half ago and—"

Marnie whirls around, her eyes wide, and marches back to me. "*Quiet*," she hisses. "Selena's son is right over there in the pool!"

I take a deep breath. "What did I do? Explain it to me, so I can finally stop wondering and move on with my goddamned life."

Marnie rubs her forehead. "You didn't do anything, Max. It was a classic case of it's not you, it's me."

I scoff. "That's the thing I say when I'm not feeling it with someone. Which would be fine, of course, except that there's no way you weren't feeling it. A woman doesn't have *that* many orgasms with a guy when she's not feeling it with him. And she doesn't attack him the next morning like she's a junkie and his cock is crack cocaine!"

"Quiet!" she hisses, looking around frantically. "What the fuck, Max? Keep it down." She smiles at a couple strolling toward us on their way to the bar. As they pass, they say a polite hello to Marnie, and she engages them in small talk about the amazing sunshine, the lovely party, our fabulous hostess, Selena. When the couple finally continues on their merry way, Marnie glares at me and grits out, "Come with me. We can't talk out here. You're a goddamned loose cannon."

Without waiting for my reply, Marnie turns on her heel in a huff and marches toward the house, so I follow her with long strides—one for every two of Marnie's. In through a back door we go. Then down a hallway and up a grand staircase. Down another long hallway. And, finally, into a room that turns out to be an impressive home gym.

After slamming the door behind me, Marnie whirls around, her blue eyes blazing, and shouts, "Have you never been turned down before? Is that it? Am I the first woman who didn't fall madly in love with you after her first orgasm?"

"You're deflecting," I say, matching her gritted teeth. "You're trying to turn this around on me and make me the bad guy somehow, when you're the lunatic sadist with a fucking screw loose."

"A lunatic sadist with a screw loose?" she booms.

"Abso-fucking-lutely. One minute, you were agreeing to dinner and looking up the breakfast place I'd suggested, and the next you were hell-bent on sprinting out my front door, half dressed, without even doing me the courtesy of saying goodbye. If you weren't feeling it, fine. Trust me, I've been there more times than I can count. But I don't believe that's the case, or else you wouldn't have blown me the next morning before climbing aboard for another round. Obviously, you get off on mind-fucking a guy after fucking him. Which makes you a goddamned *sadist*, sweetheart. *With a fucking screw loose.*"

Marnie looks guilty as hell, as she should. If everything I've described—accurately, I might add—doesn't make this woman's hometown Crazy Town, USA, then I don't know what would.

When she doesn't speak, I throw up my hands in frustration and say, "Just tell me what I did that flipped your switch so suddenly that morning and also made you treat me like shit back there at the party. You wouldn't even look at me, Marnie. What the fuck?"

"I'm sorry about that," she mumbles. Her shoulders soften. "I actually came over to apologize to you for ignoring you at the table with my friends. That was totally uncalled for."

"Oh, wow. Another about-face from you? Surprise, surprise."

Anger sharpens her features. "Do you want to hear my apology or not, Max?"

I cross my arms over my chest. "Sure."

Marnie pauses like she's choosing her words. "You did nothing wrong. I had a blast with you. While you were in the shower, however, I realized I was in a terrible place in my life. Emotionally. Mentally. Remember how I told you I'd lost my mother? Well, for reasons I can't explain, I suddenly realized I hadn't dealt with my grief—that, in fact, I was trying to numb the pain with pleasure. I panicked. I had a panic attack, basically, and I didn't want to burden you with that or embarrass myself, so I left."

My heart is hammering. I wish I didn't feel sympathy for her, but I do. I wish my heart wasn't softening, ever so slightly, at the pained look on her gorgeous face. But it is. "I'm sorry to hear all that," I mutter reluctantly. "Grief can be a crazy thing. It can come up on you, suddenly, when you least expect it."

She nods. "And as far as me giving you the silent treatment down there with my friends . . ." Her chest heaves. "That was a stupid attempt at self-preservation, and I'm very sorry."

Aw, fuck. That same old heat is suddenly present in the air between us, despite how pissed I am at her. "Self-preservation in what way?"

Marnie twists her mouth. Her nostrils flare. "I knew if my eyes locked with yours for too long, especially when we were sitting so close, you'd be able to read me like a book. The night we got together, you said, 'I can already read you like a book.'

Remember that? And I . . . I was worried that might still hold true."

I do remember saying that to her. I remember everything about our night together, unfortunately. The details have been torturing me for the past year and a half.

I step forward, looking into Marnie's eyes, and I suddenly feel like I can read her the same way I did back then. *She wants me.* Is that what Marnie didn't want me to see in her eyes downstairs? I'm not sure how it's possible this crazy woman is still attracted to me, given the way she's treated me. If she wants me so fucking much, why hasn't she bothered to contact me for the past year and a half? She easily could have contacted me through Grayson. And yet, there it is. Written all over her stunning face. *Marnie wants me.* And fuck my life, I want her, too.

I take another step forward and whisper, "What were you afraid of me reading on your face, Marnie?" My breathing is shallow. "Spell it out for me. I don't have the time or energy to play your little mind games."

Marnie takes a deep breath and shifts her weight. And then murmurs something under her breath that I can't make out.

"Louder," I bark. "I can't hear you."

She's breathing hard now. Like she just finished running a hundred-yard dash. She tilts her head back and mutters a string of curses at the ceiling. And when she returns her face to mine, the look on her face says it all. The lust on her face is so brazen, in fact, it sends tingles straight into my dick.

"*Oh*," I say, my eyebrow raised. "Are you planning to do something about that, Marnie?"

It's all I need to say. In a flash, she's hurling herself at me and throwing her arms around my neck, and I'm sliding my arms around her waist and smashing my hungry lips to hers. Quickly, I open her lips with mine and slip my tongue inside her mouth. And when her body responds like she's gripping an electric fence, I deepen the kiss and devour her like she's oxygen, and I'm a drowning man.

As our tongues dance and collide, as our bodies cleave together in primal lust, I feel electrocuted by my desire for this enigmatic woman. For over a year now, I've wondered what happened that morning. I've fantasized about her while jerking off. I've thrown myself into work and stopped going to bars and completely ignored my sex drive in the hopes I'd somehow be able to rid myself of the confusion, the yearning, the fucking *hangover* I've felt since Marnie walked out my door. Now that she's here, and the reality of her tastes even better than my hottest memories and fantasies, all rationality is flying right out the window. In this moment, I don't care if she's a mind-fucker. A loose cannon. A sadist and a nut job. *I want her.* And, clearly, by the way she's clawing at my neck and moaning and kissing me back, she feels exactly the same way. At least, in this moment. God only knows what will happen next.

I shove Marnie's back against a nearby wall in a frenzy, pin her arms above her head, and urgently press my raging hard-on against her sweet spot. I'm shoving myself flush against her, right between her legs, as I furiously devour her mouth, and the result is a shudder of desperation from her that wobbles my knees.

Gasping for air, Marnie grinds herself into me and begs me to fuck her.

"You don't deserve it," I breathe against her lips, but my body is making it abundantly clear I'm going to do it, anyway. I wish I had the self-control to walk away. To leave her standing here with the same blue balls I've endured for a fucking year and a half. But I'm only human, and apparently, this woman is my crack.

In a matter of seconds, I've got Marnie's dress hiked up, her panties cast off, and my shorts and briefs down. I reach between her legs to find my target and moan at how soaking wet she is. How ready for me. When I touch her clit, she groans so loudly, I jolt, and when I swirl my finger around and around, she throws her head back, cracking the back of her skull against the wall.

"Are you okay?" I gasp out. But even as I'm saying it, she's gripping my shaft and begging me to impale her with it.

Marnie groans out, "You're hotter than my hottest fantasies about you," and my heart races, even more. She's fantasized about me since our night together? Good to know I haven't been the only one.

As my fingers work her wetness and she strokes and squeezes my dick, words begin hurtling out of me. Things I'd rather not say, since I don't like giving this she-devil the satisfaction. Stuff like, "You're the hottest woman alive" and "I've waited so long to do this to you again."

Marnie groans and orgasms against my fingers. As she shudders and growls with pleasure, I pick her up by her bare ass and plunge myself deep inside her, pinning her against the wall with my dick. As my body thrusts in and out, it's plain we're both in the throes of pure rapture here. Out of our heads with primal lust.

"Nobody else has ever felt this good inside you," I grit out.

"Nobody," she readily agrees.

I press my mouth to hers in reply, and we kiss deeply yet again, this time as I continue fucking her against the wall with everything I've got.

We're both insatiable at this point. Our mutual passion is so animalistic and intense, I feel perilously close to blacking out as my body hurtles toward climax. Reflexively, I slide my palm to Marnie's throat. I'm claiming her. Making it clear she's all mine. And Marnie growls her approval at the gesture.

While I'm balls-deep inside her and still clutching her neck for dear life, her innermost muscles ripple forcefully against my shaft. At the sensation, my eyelids flutter, and my eyeballs roll back. Bliss consumes every fiber and nerve ending of my body as my release barrels out of me like a runaway freight train. As my body jerks and shudders, Marnie wraps her thighs around me like a vise and bites my neck. *Hard.* If my palm on her neck was my way of claiming her, then she's clearly claiming me now with her teeth. She's a lioness marking her kill—and I'm most definitely her willing prey.

For a brief, glorious moment, pain and pleasure fuse inside me in a way that makes me feel like I'm tumbling through space while enveloped by blinding white light.

When my body finally stops bucking and quaking, I kiss Marnie's swollen mouth with a vengeance, and she returns my passion without holding back. After kissing her cheek, and then her jawline, I guide her down to her feet, pull her to me, and embrace her fiercely. I'm holding on for dear life. Too dizzy to trust my equilibrium without holding on tight.

Marnie rests her forehead against my chest and lets out a long, loud exhale. "That was even hotter than before," she whispers. "And that's saying a lot." She lifts her head and beams a glorious, red-cheeked smile at me—one that sends butterflies whooshing into my belly. "What is it about you that gets me off so hard, Maximillian Vaughn? Orgasms with you feel like an atomic bomb going off inside me."

I don't remember telling Marnie my last name. Did she ask Grayson for details about me at some point after storming out of my place, or did she simply google patent attorneys named Maximillian in the greater Seattle area? Either way, since she didn't bother to contact me, I guess the method she used to find out my last name doesn't really matter in the end.

"What's your last name?" I ask.

"Long."

I smirk. "Hello, Marnie Long."

"Hello." She returns my smirk. "Nice to meet you. Again."

I bite my lip. "When are we gonna do this again? Tomorrow at eight, my place?"

Marnie's smile fades. "I don't know if that'd be a good idea."

I start pulling up my pants and putting myself back together. "Sure, it would. As long as we're both clear this is gonna be about sex and nothing else. Lots and *lots* of sex."

Marnie begins putting her panties back on. "I've kind of sworn off casual sex since the last time we hooked up."

"You could have fooled me."

"This was a moment of weakness." She smooths down her dress. "I've been working really hard on myself. Despite this one little slip-up, I've been doing really well."

"I'm a slip-up?"

"A set-back. In terms of the goals I've set for myself. It's nothing personal. I realized after our night together it was time to forego the dopamine hit of casual sex in favor of something more meaningful. In favor of searching for a life partner. Someone stable and kind. Someone who wants a serious, lasting relationship with me."

I snort. "Good luck with that."

She looks deeply offended. "What the fuck is that supposed to mean?"

"It means you just fucked the living hell out of the guy you refused to even look at a mere fifteen minutes ago. It means whatever work you've been doing on yourself obviously isn't working all that well."

Anger flashes across her face. "It's been working. Like I said, this was a moment of weakness. Failure isn't falling down. It's not getting back up."

"Oh, so now I'm your failure? Nice, Marnie. You really know how to make a guy feel special."

"That came out wrong. I'm trying to tell you I'm not looking for something casual, that's all."

"Great. Fine. Good luck with that. As far as I'm concerned, however, you could look for something serious while fucking me, casually, now and again. I don't see the harm in an arrangement like that. Not when the sex is this fucking good." I've got her attention now. That much is clear. Not to mention, I've got my own pulse racing at the thought of getting to fuck this woman again, on a regular basis. "Look," I say. "My condolences about your mother and whatever panic attack you had at my place, out of nowhere. Glad you're working on yourself. More power to you. But the truth is I don't trust you as far as I can throw you and I don't particularly like you, either. You're obviously heartless. Probably, a sadist, like I said before. So, I promise you wouldn't have to worry about me catching feelings for you. That's literally impossible. Not only because you're a mind-fucker of epic proportions with a screw loose, but because I still don't have time to invest in a serious relationship. Not that I'd pick you, if I did. But that's beside the point."

"What's the point, again? I've lost track of it through all the insults you've been hurling at me like bullets from a machine gun."

"No bullets intended; I'm just being honest. For reasons I can't understand, you're the best sex I've ever had. Like, by a long mile. No pun intended, Marnie Long. So, I'd very much like to have sex with you again, whenever our schedules align. Keep looking for Mr. Right, if that's what you want. Good for you. Until you find him, however, or until one or both of us can't stand the sight of the other and the thrill is gone, then let's get together, now and again, and fuck each other's brains out."

She smirks. "You wouldn't mind having a fuck buddy who's a sadist?"

"Not if she fucks like you."

Marnie touches the spot on my neck where she bit me in the throes of passion a few minutes ago—and my traitorous skin electrifies at her touch. "Speaking of me being a sadist, I got you pretty good here. I broke the skin. Does it hurt?"

"No."

"I'm sorry."

"Don't be. It was hot as hell."

"I've never done that before. I don't know what came over me."

"Don't play blushing ingenue with me. Please, sweetheart, it doesn't suit you."

She narrows her eyes. "You truly can't stand me, huh?"

"Correct." I shrug. "Not sure what, exactly, there is to like about you."

In response to that, she steps forward and does something that shocks the hell out of me: she kisses me tenderly, and every neuron inside my brain, every nerve ending inside my body surges, all at once. Fucking hell. Am I that transparent? Does she know full well what she's doing to me, despite everything I've been barking at her?

"Okay, I'm in. As long as we both understand this is nothing but hedonism. And the minute I find Mr. Right, I'm gonna drop you like a bad habit. Which is exactly what you'll be."

"Great. Wouldn't want to be anything else."

Marnie curls her fingers around the back of my neck. "Why wait for tomorrow night to do this again? Let's leave the party and head to your place now."

"I would, if I could. Unfortunately, I have a family thing I have to go to after this." I look into her big blue eyes. "Although . . . I'm sure my family thing won't go too late tonight. We could meet at my place around ten or so."

She bites her lower lip. "Text me when you're on your way home, and if I can swing it, I'll come."

Before I've replied, my phone in my pocket rings, and I reach for it. I wouldn't normally take a call at a moment like this; I'd call whoever back. But I've been expecting a call from my mother regarding an urgent favor she might need from me before her big event this afternoon, and I don't want to leave her hanging, if this call is from her.

When I pull out my phone, Marnie audibly gasps. Her reaction baffles me, until I realize Marnie must think the vintage photo of my mom on my screen is a current shot of some gorgeous girlfriend in my life. I suppose it makes sense for Marnie to assume that, actually, since Mom is a radiant knockout in the shot. It was snapped the day she found out she was pregnant with me, I'm told. Hence, the reason I set the image as Mom's identifier on my phone.

"That's my mother," I say with a chuckle. "Not a girlfriend. It's an old shot of her. My favorite one. This will be quick. Don't go anywhere, fuck buddy." I connect the call with a wink at Marnie. "Hey, Momma. What's good?"

Mom tells me she does, indeed, need me to pick up a box of business cards at her place on my way to her event. Selena's house is pretty close to Mom's. Plus, Mom's at her new boyfriend's house across town right now, so it makes the most logistical sense for me to pick up the cards on my way to the gallery.

As Mom talks, I find myself distracted by the look of pure agony on Marnie's face. What the fuck? She looks pale. Like she's seen a ghost. As a matter of fact, Marnie looks every bit as shell-shocked as she did that fateful morning months ago, right before she ditched my ass. I'm sure she's skittish about unwittingly being the other woman again, given what happened with that married man she dated right before meeting me. But I told her the shot on my phone is my mother. Does she think I lied to her face about that?

As Mom continues chattering away in my ear, Marnie murmurs something in a panicked tone and sprints out of the room.

"What the fuck?" I blurt. "Marnie, wait!" But she's gone. "Gotta go, Mom," I bark at my mother, cutting her off mid-sentence. "I'll get the cards."

I end the call and fly out the door. When I get into the hall-way, Marnie's not there, but I can hear hasty footsteps descending the nearby staircase. I race to the top of the steps and shout, "Marnie, wait. Stop!" I fly down the stairs, just in time to see Marnie barreling toward the front door of the house. "You're ditching me *again*?" I shout, totally bewildered. "What the fuck is wrong with you?"

Marnie whirls around inside the front door, her face a bright shade of crimson. "I've changed my mind about meeting up with you again. I'm gonna stick to my plan and stay away from casual sex while looking for Mr. Right." With that, she turns and bolts out the front door.

"Are you fucking kidding me?" I roar. Does this nut job have a split-personality, or is mind-fucking hapless, unsuspecting men, immediately after voraciously fucking their bodies, Marnie's favorite hobby?

"You're insane, you know that?" I shout at Marnie's retreating frame from the porch of the house. "A total whack job!"

"I know!" she shouts back, not even bothering to stop running or turn around as she says it.

"You're not even going to say goodbye to the Birthday Boy? To your friends?"

"I'll text them!"

"If you leave now that's it for us!" I shout at her, even though I know it won't make a difference. "I'll never fuck you again, Marnie Fucking Long. *Never*. No matter how much you beg me!"

"Works for me!" Marnie screams. "Have a great life, Maximillian! Good luck making partner this time!"

I watch her hop into a car—a black SUV—and peel away from the curb like she's a firefighter speeding off to a five-alarm fire. "The photo on my phone is my mother!" I shout at full volume, but it's futile. She's gone. Dumbfounded, I watch Marnie's car turn a corner and disappear from sight.

What just happened? Is she a real-life Sybil? Did one of Marnie's many personalities fuck me like her life depended on it, and then another one took over a few minutes later and didn't know what the other had done? That's how it goes in movies, but is that even a real thing?

My phone rings, yanking me out of my stupor, and my mother's smiling face lights up my screen again.

"What?" I bark.

"Jeez," Mom says.

She's right to feel taken aback by my tone. She's not to

blame for this latest twist in The Marnie Saga. Surely, it was nothing but a coincidence Marnie turned sheet-white at the exact moment Mom called. "Sorry," I say on an exhale. "Yes, Mother?"

"I forgot to give you the new code for my front door. I didn't want to text it in case your phone gets stolen or hacked. I saw that on *60 Minutes*." She gives me the door code and tells me where I can find the box of business cards. She asks, "Do you have the address for the gallery?" She's been invited to display one of her paintings this afternoon as part of a local artists showcase and she's beyond thrilled about it.

"Yeah, I've got it," I murmur. "I'll be there soon."

"Auggie's coming, too. He's going to take a break from studying and pop down for a bit."

"Great."

"Henry's thinking about calling his daughter and inviting her down, last-minute. Now that you and Auggie can both come, he thought this might be a perfect opportunity to introduce our families. Would that be okay with you?"

I exhale. "Yeah, whatever. I'm not going to be able to stay long, though. I'll bring the box of cards, show my support and meet your boyfriend's family, but then I've got to get home and get some work done."

"However long you can stay, I'll be grateful for it. Thank you, honey. I'm really excited."

It's hard for me to give a shit about any of this right now. But I know it's important to Mom, so I say, "Yeah, I'm excited, too."

Grayson's amplified voice suddenly wafts from the backyard. "Hey, everyone," he says. "Thanks so much for coming today."

A collective cheer erupts from behind the backyard fence to my left. Voices shout, "Happy birthday, Grayson!" and "We love you, Grayson!"

"Gotta go, Mom," I say. "I think they're about to do the cake at my buddy's birthday party. I'll sing the song and say my goodbyes, and then head over to your place to get the cards."

"Thank you so much, love," Mom says. "I can't wait to introduce you to Henry."

I say a final goodbye to Mom and force myself to head back into Grayson's party, even though it's the last place I want to go. After experiencing Marnie's mental flagellation, yet again, I don't want to be around people. Especially not Grayson. No shade to him—I'm so fucking happy for the guy—but now that I've been given sadistic whiplash *twice* by Little Miss Changes Her Mind on a Dime, I'm not in the mood to witness his uncomplicated happiness with Selena. Frankly, I don't want to see any smiling, happy people right now; not even someone as awesome and deserving as Grayson.

9
MARNIE

I slow down to compare the address on the building outside my car window against the one in Dad's text, and when they're one and the same, I drive around the block and luckily find a convenient place to park. Parking in downtown Seattle is normally a hassle, but I guess Sunday afternoons aren't as crowded since all nearby offices are closed.

As I was driving home from Grayson's birthday party—after leaving Max looking bewildered on Selena's front porch—I received a call from Dad, extending a last-minute invitation. He said his new girlfriend, Gigi, is an amateur artist—a painter—who'd been invited to display one of her works in a local artists showcase this afternoon at a downtown gallery.

"Sorry for the late notice," Dad said during the call. "We're at the gallery now with Ripley, and I only just found out Gigi's sons are both coming down to support her. I was thinking this would be the perfect opportunity for me to introduce you to Gigi while getting our families together."

After spying the face of my old yoga friend, Geraldine, on Max's phone and discovering she's his mother, I wasn't in the mood to meet Dad's new crush this afternoon. If Geraldine is

Max's mother, then that means she's got to be Alexander's ex-wife, too. *Shudder.*

On the other hand, Dad's been playing his new romance close to the vest, so I'm not sure when I'll get another chance to meet her, my foul mood be damned. And so, despite my horror and embarrassment at finding out I've not only fucked Alexander's son, but my old friend Geraldine's, too, I told Dad I'd be delighted to come to his new girlfriend's art show. At the very least, I'd like to see how she interacts with Ripley, so I'll know for sure that my daughter is in good hands if ever Dad invites Gigi to babysit with him again.

My car parked, I turn off the engine and check my texts—and a message from Lucy prompts me to call her back immediately, rather than exiting my vehicle.

"Grayson proposed after I left?" I shriek. "*And Selena said yes?*"

"Yes!" Lucy shrieks, before filling me in on all the juicy details. In wrap-up, Lucy says, "Selena is over the moon. I've never seen her so happy."

"You're still at the party?"

"Yep."

"Hug her for me. I'll text her now to congratulate her and apologize for dipping out without saying goodbye, but please tell her I'll call her tomorrow to get the whole story."

"Will do. Why'd you leave so suddenly? Is Ripley okay?"

"Oh, girl. You're never going to believe this."

I tell Lucy the whole story of what I did with Max in Selena's house, and how I saw Geraldine's photo on Max's phone afterwards—and how I quickly deduced from the photo I'd fucked *both* my old yoga friend's ex-husband and son. And true to form, Lucy finds the entire situation hysterical.

"It's not funny, Lu," I say. "It's a total clusterfuck."

"Why? I understand why you might be feeling creeped out that you fucked your friend's son—"

"*And her ex!*"

"But it's not like Max is Geraldine's *teenage* son and you're his math tutor. He's a grown-ass man with a big dick who knows full well how to use it. Plus, you haven't seen Geraldine in over a year, right? So, it's not like you two are besties."

She's right about that. As much as I adored seeing Geraldine every week in yoga class, and also thoroughly enjoyed introducing her to my friends at that monthly dinner, we lost touch after Ripley and I moved in with Dad.

I palm my forehead. "When I talked about Mr. BDE during that dinner Geraldine joined, I was unwittingly talking to her the whole time about her fucking ex-husband, Lucy."

Lucy guffaws.

"It's not funny."

"It's hilarious."

"I feel sick."

"Why? You didn't know Geraldine's connection to Mr. BDE when you invited her to dinner. And you didn't know Max was Alexander's son when you fucked him after Captain's."

"I sure as hell knew Max was Alexander's son when I fucked him today at Selena's. That makes me a truly horrible person who's going to hell."

"Bah," Lucy says. "Mr. BDE is old news. You haven't seen or talked to him, even once, since you screwed Max, right?"

"True."

"It's not like the man's dick left a permanent mark on your vagina. You're allowed to fuck another grown man."

"But not his son."

Lucy giggles. "I can't believe you fucked Max again at the party. I knew the second you laid eyes on him today you wouldn't be able to resist him for long, but I didn't think you'd fuck him *today*. Girl, you got that dick inside you *fast*."

I can't help giggling. "You're not helping, Lu. I shouldn't be laughing. This is bad."

"Well, the good news is nobody will ever know. You're never going to see Geraldine again, right?"

"Probably not."

"And you're never going to see Max again, either."

"That's for fucking sure." I exhale. "Even if I wanted to see him, which I don't, he'd never give me the time of day again. He hated me before today, so I can't even imagine how much he despises me now."

"He didn't hate you too much to fuck you today."

I shudder. "Oh, God, it was so hot."

She laughs. "Why didn't you just tell the poor man you'd recognized the photo of his mother?"

"I panicked. It felt like a repeat of the thing with Alexander. Like *déjà vu*. When I saw Geraldine's face, I felt exactly how I felt when I saw that framed photo of Alexander in Max's kitchen. It was like the universe was screaming at me, once again, 'You've got no business messing around with this man!'" I run my palm down my face. "I can't believe I *knowingly* fucked Alexander's son this time. I really am going to hell if there is one. Please, write me postcards from heaven, so I don't get too lonely down there."

"Meh. If there's a hell, I'd rather hang out with you there than with all the boring goody-two shoes do-gooders upstairs. As long as you bring chocolate, graham crackers, and marshmallows for s'mores, count me in."

I giggle. "I love you so much."

"I love you back, Marnie Girl. Truly, the universe doesn't care if you screw Max, no matter who his parents might be. The universe has much more important things to think about than your sex life, as exciting as it might be."

"Exciting? Ha! Other than Max, I've screwed exactly zero people in the last year and a half. I haven't been living up to my billing as a *femme fatale* lately."

Lucy snickers. "Was Max as good as you remembered?"

"Better. *So much better.*"

"How is that possible? Last time, you said he was at the tippy-top of your Hall of Fame."

I flap my lips together. "Yeah, well, he somehow topped himself today. Anger and disdain can make it extra hot, I guess." I look at the clock on my car's dashboard. "I'd better go. I'm finally meeting Dad's new girlfriend. She's got a painting on display at an art gallery downtown as part of a local artists showcase."

"Aw, good for her. Keep me posted."

"Will do. Hey, don't tell the rest of the girls about what happened with Max and me today. I don't even want to think about what kind of snide comments Victoria would make."

"Oh, god. She'd be ruthless."

"I also don't want to risk Selena telling Grayson and the whole story somehow getting back to Max."

"My lips are sealed tight, baby."

"Thank you."

Lucy snorts. "Unlike your legs with Max today."

I snort-laugh. "I'm only human, girl. You saw him."

"I sure did. And I don't blame you one little bit."

"I'll call you tomorrow, babe."

"You'd better. Bye."

I disconnect the call, text Selena my effusive congratulations and sincerest apologies, and then exit the car and head off toward the gallery around the block, determined to put Maximillian Vaughn—and Alexander and Geraldine and the mess I've made because I can't control my hormones around Max—firmly behind me.

10

MARNIE

W hen I get to the front door of the art gallery, a sign announces today's showcase, while a smiling, elegant man in a suit welcomes me and hands me a pretty program.

Inside the gallery's airy space, there's a chic party going on with paintings and sculptures as its focal points. After surveying the large room, I spot my father standing in a short line at a bar, so I beeline over to him.

"Hey, Pops. Where's Ripley?"

"Hi, honey. Thanks for coming. She's with Gigi and one of Gigi's sons. Ripley has been stuck to Gigi like glue since we got here."

"Aw, I hope Gigi doesn't mind. I know how chatty and intense Ripley can be when she finds a new best friend."

Dad chuckles. "Gigi's in heaven. She's got two boys, both fully grown, and she said she's always wanted a little girl."

"I can't wait to meet her." I glance around, but I don't see a woman attached to my tiny doppelganger. "Where are they?"

Dad looks around. "They went over there somewhere with the gallery owner." He looks at me sheepishly. "Listen, I invited Gigi to come back to the house after the show and spend the night. Conditionally, of course. Assuming that'd be okay with you."

"Okay with *me*?" I chuckle. "It's your house and you're a big boy. You don't need to ask your daughter's permission to have your girlfriend sleep over."

"Well, it's not only my house. It's yours and Ripley's, too. I want you to be comfortable."

"Aw, Dad. Thank you for thinking of me. But, yes, that's great. The house is plenty big for all of us."

Dad looks equal parts thrilled and relieved. "This whole thing is so new. I don't have a clue what I'm doing."

"You're doing great."

"Gigi and I talked about maybe picking up some takeout on the way home and inviting her two sons to join us for dinner. We thought that'd be better than celebrating Gigi's first art show at a restaurant, since Ripley has school tomorrow. I know how much you like her to get a good night's sleep on a school night."

"Thank you so much for considering that. That sounds great."

"It was Gigi's idea. She figured this party would be highly stimulating for Ripley. Plus, she thought it'd be a more relaxed environment for both of our families to talk and get to know each other at home, instead of at a noisy restaurant."

"Gigi's already impressing me. I can tell we're going to get along great."

We reach the front of the line and Dad orders four wines and one apple juice. Drinks in hand, we make our way into the heart of the party to search for Gigi, Gigi's son, and Ripley. Quickly, we find Gigi and Ripley standing with their backs to us, alongside a young, fit man, in front of a painting.

Instantly, even from the back, I like Gigi's style and energy. Her dark hair is in a cute, chic bob. Her dress is casually glamorous. And best of all, she's holding Ripley's hand and gesticulating with the other as she explains something about the painting. As Gigi talks, her body language and voice are gentle. Comfortable. Nurturing. Indeed, just this fast, I'm certain Dad's made a fabulous choice in his first girlfriend since becoming a widower.

"Got our drinks and found Marnie, to boot," Dad says as we approach, at which point Gigi, Ripley, and the fit, young man turn around to face us.

"*Geraldine,*" I gasp, the moment Gigi's face is revealed to me. She's the woman I befriended in yoga class last year. The woman I'd wanted to introduce to my father. *And also the woman who gave birth to the man I screwed like a wild banshee about an hour ago.*

"Mommy!" Ripley shouts, hurling herself happily at my legs.

"*Marnie!*" Geraldine—Gigi—bellows. She throws her arms around me and embraces me warmly, as Ripley does the same to my legs.

"Dad always refers to you as Gigi," I stammer.

"That's how I introduced myself to him. It's my lifelong nickname and the name I like to use on dates." She bats her eyes at my father. "I think Gigi is flirtier and more fun than Geraldine. More alluring."

As Dad hands Gigi and her son their wine cups, he says, "Well, you could have called yourself Waldo and I would have found you alluring."

Geraldine giggles at Dad's joke before gesturing to the young man at her side. "Marnie, this is my younger son, Augustus. Auggie."

Augustus.

Shit. Being in the presence of one Holy Roman Emperor suddenly makes me realize the other one—*Maximillian*—is probably around here somewhere. Or at least, on his way. The thought sends panic surging into my bloodstream. I manage to stammer out a quick hello to Auggie, but I'm too freaked out about his big brother's whereabouts to say much more than that.

Gigi touches my father's arm. "Henry, Marnie and I have

already met. We met in a yoga class last year and really hit it off. I didn't recognize her in the photo you showed me." She smiles at me. "It's so wonderful to see you again, Marnie."

I'm a bit surprised Geraldine didn't recognize me in whatever photo Dad showed her, but I never wore makeup to yoga class, and my hair was always tied back, so maybe that's it. Or maybe I simply didn't make as big an impression on Geraldine as she made on me. Either way, I can't worry about that now. I'm too busy glancing around frantically, looking for Max. I manage to say, "Yes, uh, it's great to see you, too, Geraldine. Gigi. What a small world. I actually wanted to set you up with my father, remember?"

"That's right!" Geraldine says. "What a small world, indeed."

Dad palms his forehead and looks at me with wide eyes. "*Gigi* is the woman from yoga class you wanted to introduce me to? Well, that'll teach me not to listen to my brilliant daughter's advice, ever again."

I scan the exits, feeling like a trapped animal. I need to leave. *Right now.* What should I say that won't make Dad worry too much?

Auggie chuckles. "It sounds like you two were fated to meet, one way or another."

"It sure sounds like it," Dad agrees, beaming a heart-melting smile at Gigi.

Geraldine looks at me, and whatever panic she's seeing on my face causes her beaming smile to fade. "Well, maybe let's not call it *fate,* just yet" she says. "That remains to be seen. But it's most definitely a lovely coincidence."

My stomach tightens. Shit. Clearly, she's misinterpreted my anxiety about Max waltzing through that front door as anxiety about her dating my father. But that couldn't be further from the truth. I'm the one who wanted to get them together in the first place. I make a mental note to clear that up with Geraldine—

Gigi—later. Right now, however, I need to figure out an immediate exit strategy.

Before I've figured out an excuse to get me the hell out of here without making a scene, an amplified voice says, "Welcome!" When we turn to look, a well-heeled woman is speaking into a microphone. She thanks everyone for coming today and talks briefly about the importance of showcasing and encouraging local artists. And through it all, I'm on the cusp of a full-blown panic attack. Feeling like I'm going to barf, crap my pants, or faint. Surely, this is the "family event" Max mentioned at the party right after we fucked. This time, after I knew he was Alexander's son.

The crowd applauds. The speech is over. *Now's my chance.*

I open my mouth to say who-knows-what, but Geraldine beats me to the punch.

"Max!" she calls out. "Over here, honey!" Fuck, fuck, fuck! Geraldine waves her hand at a target behind me, and my entire body convulses with dread and shame.

"Hey, Mom," Max's voice calls out behind me.

"Oh, thank you for getting the cards."

"You bet."

"Everyone, this is my older son, Max. Max, this is Henry, his daughter, Marnie, and his granddaughter, Ripley."

Welp.

Here we go.

There's no avoiding it now.

I turn around to find Max dressed in different clothes than he wore at the party. He's freshly showered and wearing jeans with a long-sleeved knit shirt that clings deliciously to his muscular frame. The instant Max sees me, he murmurs, "*You gotta be fucking kidding me.*"

I look down at my shoes, feeling flushed. Sick. Trapped. If there's a God, then it's now undeniable I'm on God's shit list.

"What's wrong?" Gigi asks her son, not understanding the reason for his murmured outburst.

"Nothing," Max says. "My phone is buzzing. Another text from my boss, I'm sure. Hello, Henry, nice to meet you. Marnie. Ripley. You, too."

I force myself to look up. And when my eyes meet Max's, the homicidal glare he's shooting me makes my stomach twist.

Ripley hands me her apple juice, takes a step forward, and looks up at Max like she's taking in the full height of a towering redwood tree. "I'm four and a half," she says. "How old are you?"

When Max doesn't reply, but instead continues glaring at me, Auggie clears his throat and says, "He's thirty-one and I'm twenty-nine. We're brothers."

"I don't have a brudder," Ripley says. She looks at me. "Can I have a brudder, Mommy?"

Everyone chuckles except for Max and me.

"Do you two know each other?" Gigi asks tentatively. Apparently, our body language has tipped her off.

God only knows what Max might say about me, so I quickly reply, "Yes, we met once, briefly, a while back at a bar. We were both with our respective friends."

"And then, we ran into each other again today at a mutual friend's birthday party," Max adds.

"What a small world!" Gigi says. She turns to her older son. "I met Marnie about a year and a half ago, too—in a yoga class. I even went to dinner with Marnie and her friends once and really enjoyed it."

"I actually met Max that very same night," I say. "Remember how my friends and I went to Captain's after dinner, but you decided to go home?"

Gigi's eyes widen. Suddenly, I remember the salacious conversation we had at dinner. Specifically, the part where all my dinner companions, including Geraldine, encouraged me to find a hot guy at Captain's and get under him in order to get *over* Mr. BDE. Geraldine's ex-husband. Max's father. *Oh my god.*

Geraldine blushes. Is she putting two and two together and

realizing her handsome son might have served as my young amnesia-inducer of choice that night? "Yes, I remember that conversation," Geraldine says tightly. Blushing, she looks at me. "I remember it very well."

Whatever expression I'm wearing in this moment, Gigi's reaction to it tells me I've just given myself away. Nonverbally confessed I've fucked her son.

Quickly, Gigi looks away from me, blushing, while I fidget and shift my weight and rack my brain for an excuse to sprint out of here and never look back.

"What's that on your neck, Max?" Gigi asks. "Did you cut yourself shaving?"

Max touches the spot on his neck where I bit him an hour ago while he impaled me against a wall with his cock. "This? Oh. No. It's a bite mark."

I feel dizzy. He didn't have to admit that! His mother gave him a perfect cover story, for fuck's sake.

"*Max*," Gigi whisper-shouts. She looks at the rest of us apologetically.

"What?" Max says. "We're all practically family now, right? I think they can handle the truth."

Gigi looks hopeful. "Does this mean you finally have a girlfriend?"

"Nope." Max looks straight at me. "It means I stupidly did something completely forgettable and meaningless."

"*Maximillian*," Gigi gasps out. Clearly, the poor woman is beyond mortified. Practically having a heart attack about her son's brutal honesty in front of people she's trying to impress.

There's an awkward beat, during which all the adults are staring at each other, at a total loss regarding what to say or do next.

Finally, Dad motions to the nearest painting on the wall and says, "It looks great in an art gallery, honey. It's where it belongs." He addresses me. "This is Gigi's. She painted it. Isn't it amazing?"

"Oh, wow. Yes. It's really beautiful. Congratulations."

We all compliment the painting. As we do that, Ripley tugs on Max's pant leg, and he wrenches his blazing, angry eyes off me in order to look down at her. Figuratively and literally. Sweet little Ripley says, "We have a Max at my school. He's my friend."

"Cool."

"What's your big name?"

"My big name?"

"He's Maximillian," Auggie supplies. "But he goes by Max. Just like I'm Augustus and I go by Auggie."

Ripley doesn't give two shits about Auggie. That's plain enough. Even when Auggie was speaking directly to Ripley, her eyes remained fixed on Max. Not only that, both her pupils have now been replaced by little hearts.

"I like Maxy-Milly. Dat's pretty. I don't have a big and a small name. I'm always Ripley. Are you mad at my mommy, Maxy-Milly?"

Max looks at me briefly, like he wants to throttle me. But when he returns to Ripley, he smiles politely and says, "No, I'm not mad at your mommy. I feel nothing about her."

"Den why are you looking at Mommy like *dis*?" She puts her little hands on her hips and scowls comically.

"That's what my face always looks like, kid," Max says. "Even when I couldn't care less about something or someone."

Looking straight at Max, I scratch my nose with my middle finger, and he smirks in reply.

"Want to see me twirl, Maxy-Milly?" Ripley asks.

"Oh, I'd love to see that," Gigi interjects, still looking like she's on the verge of cardiac arrest.

"No, *him*." Ripley points at Max.

"Not really, to be honest," Max replies, and Ripley, for reasons I can't fathom, giggles with delight like he's the funniest human in the world. Either she's been watching too much *Sesame Street,* and Max reminds her of Oscar the Grouch, or my poor daughter is innately afflicted with the same worrisome condition as her mother: *she's hopelessly attracted to emotionally unavailable men.*

Ripley wastes no time. With her hands in the air, she abruptly spins, provoking her purple dress to fan out and everyone but Max to applaud riotously.

When my little girl is done twirling, she looks pointedly at Max and frowns at his lack of reaction. Clearly, she wants this handsome, scowling man's approval above everyone else's. And I suppose I can't blame her for that. Max is wildly attractive, and studies show even tiny babies respond to objectively gorgeous faces. Plus, Max and Auggie are the first male humans, other than Dad and some doctors, Ripley has ever met. Since Auggie's coming across as emotionally available, warm, and sincerely interested in her, it's no wonder Ripley's gravitating toward Max, the grumpy, nonchalant, brooding one, instead. She's my daughter, after all. Poor little thing.

"Why you not clapping for me?" Ripley asks Max.

"Because I don't believe in sugarcoating or giving false praise," Max says. "Your twirl was well done; I'll give you that. But that's to be expected, isn't it? You're four."

"And a half."

"So, you should be able to twirl. Show me something I'm *not* expecting you to do well, and I'll clap for you."

Ripley's nonplussed. She pushes up her thick glasses, trying to process Max's rebuke.

"I'm so sorry," Gigi blurts. "Please, forgive my cranky son. He's got an extremely dry sense of humor and zero experience with little kids."

Without warning, Ripley hurls her body onto the ground and then twists herself into a haphazard pretzel that causes her dress to fly up and her glasses to hurtle off her face.

"What the . . .?" I blurt, lurching toward my splayed daughter. "What are you doing, Ripley?"

From her crumpled spot on the floor, Ripley looks up at Max

with those same little hearts in her eyes and smiles. "What about dat?"

Max chuckles and slowly claps. "Now *that* was entertaining, kid," he says. "I don't know what it was, but it was definitely totally unexpected."

Thankfully, when I grab Ripley's glasses off the floor, both lenses are intact. In fact, there's miraculously not a single scratch on either of them. I hand them back to my daughter and pull her off the ground and dust her off, all the while glaring at Max's amused face.

"What were you trying to do?" I ask Ripley.

"Dance like a worm."

"A *worm*?" I ask, laughing. "That was you trying to do the worm?"

"Naomi's brudder showed me."

"Don't try that again, okay? Not till you're bigger. You could hurt yourself."

Gigi clears her throat. "Should we . . . check out some of the other artwork?"

"Absolutely," Dad says. When Auggie and I agree, off the group goes across the gallery, with Gigi taking Ripley's hand and Max and I hanging back to whisper caustically at each other.

"Be a dick to me all you like," I hiss. "But don't you dare treat my daughter with anything other than kindness and respect."

"Cool your jets, Sybil. That's how I speak to *all* children, on the rare occasions when I'm forced to interact with them. That's true whether I've been mind-fucked, repeatedly, by their mommies with split personalities or not. Also, if anyone deserves to be called a dick, it's *you*."

"Why? Because I had the audacity to walk away from your magic cock again today?"

"Thank you for admitting my cock is magic. Glad we both agree about that. But no, you're a dick for two other reasons. Actually, three. One, you're so fucking fickle and indecisive, you give me goddamned whiplash. Two, you're a sadist, like I said before. Mind-fuckery obviously gets you off. And that sucks ass, Sybil. And three, it's now clear you were never yourself with me. Not for one fucking minute. And that also sucks ass."

I roll my eyes. "What are you talking about?"

"You have a kid, Marnie. And you didn't think to mention that to me?"

I scoff. "During our one-night stand? No. Why would I tell you about that?"

"Because we talked a shit-ton that night, that's why. Because we talked about some real shit, that's why. And now, I come to find out you didn't even *mention* you have a kid?"

"I didn't think I'd ever see you again, so there was no point. If we'd gone to dinner and had a good time, I'm sure I would have mentioned her then."

"Bullshit." Max narrows his eyes. "I can see you clearly now, Marnie. And you know what I see? A bullshit artist. A chameleon. You morph into whatever fantasy you think a man wants, don't you, Sybil? That's your favorite game."

He's not wrong. Actually, no, correction. That's what I *used* to do. Quite well, too. But that very thing is something I've been working on, with extreme diligence, during my lengthy dating hiatus. I've been figuring out who I really am and what I want. I've been figuring out why I've always been so addicted to male validation, and I've been weaning myself off the drug. And now, after all that hard work, this asshole thinks he knows me and everything about my present state of being?

"Wrong," I say. "And stop calling me Sybil."

"Is the kid's father in the picture?" Max asks.

"No. I'm a single mother and always have been. Ripley's *de facto* sperm donor is some rando in Prague whose last name I never even asked."

"Lovely."

"Fuck you. I was single and traveling the world and the condom broke. You've never had a one-night stand?"

Max rolls his eyes. "You know very well I have."

"Then shut the fuck up." I gesture to my daughter as she bops along with Gigi and chatters away. "That little girl is the best thing that's ever happened to me and I'm not going to apologize for the way she got here. It was divine intervention, as far as I'm concerned."

Max's features soften. "I'm sorry. I shouldn't have said that."

"Damn right, you shouldn't have. It came off like you're slut-shaming me, and that's not something I'll tolerate from you or anyone else."

"Nor should you. Again, I apologize. I'm just . . ." He runs his hand through his hair. "I'm confused, I guess."

"About what?"

The group has stopped in front of a painting, so we hang back in order to talk without being overheard. Max sighs. "We talked about a lot of things that night, remember? Personal things. It felt like we made a genuine connection. A deep one."

"We did," I concede, my cheeks burning. "Regardless, there was no reason to mention Ripley to you because I knew I'd never see you again. There wasn't a chance in hell you'd ever want to become her daddy, so why tell you about her at all?"

He doesn't dispute me. In fact, he's nodding his agreement. "I see your point," he says. "But I still think it was weird."

"Think what you want. None of it matters now."

Max gestures to our parents ahead of us. "When did you find out about this?"

"When I got here. Although I found out my acquaintance, Geraldine, was your mother when her face popped up on your phone today."

Max furrows his brow. "*That's* why you ran out on me today? Because you realized you'd fucked your yoga pal's son?"

I look around. "Not so loud, Max. Please. Yes. It felt like a wakeup call that it was a mistake to fool around with you. Like the universe was telling me we're a bad idea."

The group in front of us walks to a sculpture, so Max and I amble behind, slowly, keeping our distance.

"Why is that, again?" Max says.

"Huh?"

"Why are we a bad idea?"

I look at him like he's got a horn growing out of his forehead. "Because we want very different things."

"Not in the short term. Seems like we both want exactly the same thing in the here and now. The best sex of both our lives."

Well, he's not wrong there. Before today, I would have sworn I'd left the feral side of me behind, thanks to all the hard work I've been doing on myself. But I can't deny I wanted to get railed by this man the nano-second I laid eyes on him at Grayson's party today. Nor can I deny he's the best I've ever had.

Max looks around and then whispers, "Who cares if you're semi-friendly with your fuck buddy's mother? It's irrelevant. By definition, fuck buddies aren't someone you'd ever take home to meet the parents."

"And thank God for that," I mutter, suddenly imagining the hellish scenario of Max taking me home to meet his father.

Max says, "You didn't need to bolt today—*again*—just because you saw your yoga pal's face on my phone. That was a massive overreaction, Marnie."

I glare at him. As a general rule, I don't like being told I'm overreacting—especially "massively"—and especially when the person saying it to me is a man. In this instance, however, I can't blame Max for thinking that, since he doesn't have the faintest idea about the overall context at play here. What Max doesn't know, and must never know, is that his mother's face on his phone felt like the universe screaming at me, "Didn't you hear me the last time, bitch? He's off-limits to you!"

"Oh!" Gigi says in front of us. "Would you all mind if we go back to my painting and take some photos in front of it? I totally forgot to do that."

The group says that's a great idea, and off we go across the gallery. When we get to Gigi's painting, everyone compliments her again, the same way we did before, and then we snap photos of her in front of her masterpiece.

"Let's get a group shot," Gigi says. "I want to commemorate all of us coming together for the first time." She asks a passerby to snap one of our whole group, and everyone huddles up for the photo.

As our photographer frames the shot, Max slides his arm around my shoulders and leans into my ear. "Actually, for the two of us, this isn't the first time we're *coming* together, is it?"

I snort-laugh, despite myself, which makes Max crack up, too.

"I have a feeling your mother's figured that out," I whisper back. "Much to my embarrassment and horror."

He scoffs. "She once screwed her personal trainer in Cabo. I think she can handle the shocking truth that her adult son isn't a virgin."

"Stop. Please. Let's pretend it never happened, okay?"

"Oh, but it did. And then again, mere minutes ago."

"Ssh. Our parents are dating. We could become step-siblings one day."

Max snorts. "Are you *trying* to turn me on?"

"Ew, Max."

He laughs.

Our photographer says, "Would someone pick up the little girl? The framing with the painting will be better that way."

I pick up Ripley, and she instantly leans her cheek onto Max's broad shoulder like she's been doing it all her life.

"Aw, that's so sweet," the woman says. "Hug your mommy and daddy, honey. That's so cute."

"I don't have a daddy!" Ripley calls out. "Only a mommy and a Grampy."

The photographer looks mortified. "Oh. Okay. That's great." Blushing, the woman hands the phone back to Gigi and mumbles to me, "Sorry. I didn't realize." And off she goes, as fast as her embarrassed legs will carry her.

When the photo shoot is over, I put Ripley down and she immediately takes Max's hand. "Come on, Maxy-Milly. Let's—"

"No, honey," I say, cutting her off at the pass. "Let's give Max some space now, okay? Hold my hand. Talk to me."

"But I want to hold Maxy's hand and talk to him."

When I look at Gigi for help, she looks every bit as uncomfortable and tongue-tied as I feel.

"Is everyone hungry?" Gigi finally asks.

"I am," Dad says cheerfully. "How about we all go back to my place and celebrate Gigi's world premiere as an artist together?"

"Sorry, I have to run," Auggie says. "Thanks for the invitation, Henry, but I've got a big test tomorrow. I wanted to come by to show Mom my support and meet all of you, but I really have to study."

"Auggie's in the veterinary program at the University of Washington," Gigi explains proudly. "He's working so hard." She smiles at Max. "Both my boys are extremely hard workers."

"What about you, Max?" Dad says. "Can you join us for dinner?"

To my shock, Max smiles at Dad and says, "Yeah, dinner sounds good. Thanks. I've got work to do, but I've got to eat, right?"

"Fabulous," Gigi says, sounding absolutely thrilled. "I'm so glad you can make it."

"I'll go into the office extra early tomorrow morning to make up for lost time," Max says to his mother.

"Thank you so much, honey," Gigi says. "This means the world to me."

Max smiles at me while speaking to his mother. "Happy to do it, Mom."

Ripley pulls on Max's arm, ultimately yanking him down to her face. When his ear is near her little mouth, she whispers something that causes Max to exhale and reply, "If I must."

"You must," Ripley deadpans. When she looks at me, my daughter flashes me a mega-watt smile and says, "Maxy is gonna sit next to *me* at dinner!"

11

MAX

Why has this little squeak of a sprite imprinted on *me* of all people—the least kid-friendly person at this dinner table?

We're back at Henry's house now. In the midst of dining on Greek takeout in celebration of my mother's first art show. And of course, I'm sitting next to Marnie's kid because she's been stuck to me like glue since I walked into the gallery. The only question is *why*?

I've got nothing against the kid. She's all right, as far as little kids go. In fact, she's kind of cute behind those thick glasses. Also, her silly little giggle is kind of infectious. But man, can this girl *talk*. In fact, she's a downright chatterbox. Which would be fine, I suppose, if every third sentence weren't a question requiring an active response from me. And not a one-word answer, either. If I try to get away with a "yes" or "no" or "cool," she bats her eyelashes and says, "Tell me *more*." Not sure where she learned that, but she says it like she's a forty-year-old therapist. Which, again, would be cute if I were watching her doing it to someone else.

Speaking of someone else, why isn't she giving my mother the time of day? Mom obviously worships the ground this kid walks on. Over and over again throughout this meal, Mom has tried to inject herself into the conversation the kid has been having with me, but, nope, my new stalker only has eyes for *me*.

Back at the gallery, she obviously favored me over Auggie, even though he was the one paying attention to her. It was bizarre, since creatures, big and small—whether kids or animals —always gravitate to my brother. Seriously, why didn't this tiny, bespectacled creature glom onto my brother, rather than me?

"Dat's why *purpole* is my favorite color," the kid says to me. God only knows what preceded the statement. She cocks her little head. "What's your favorite color, Maxy-Milly?"

"Red."

When it's clear that's all I'm going to say on the topic, the kid bats her eyelashes and dishes up her patented line: "*Tell me more.*"

I resist the urge to chuckle, simply because I don't want to encourage her. "There's nothing more to say. I like the color red."

She nods knowingly. "Your car is red. I saw it at da place with Gigi's painting."

Yeah, and not only that, when the kid saw me unlocking my red car outside the gallery, she waved goodbye to me, and then blew effusive kisses at me like I was standing on the deck of the Titanic as it pulled away from the dock, and she was waving a hanky at me and wishing me bon voyage. On top of all that, as I opened my red car's driver's side door, the kid shouted at the top of her lungs, "Don't forget to sit next to me at dinner!"

"My mommy's hair is red," the kid says. "So is mine."

"Yes, I can see that."

"It's really orange and red mixed togedder, doe. But it's called *redhead.*"

"Yep. That definitely tracks with my research."

"I wish my hair could be purpole. *Purpole* is my favorite color."

"Really? You haven't mentioned that."

The kid doesn't get sarcasm, obviously. She huffs out, "I told you dat!"

Despite my best efforts to keep the kid at arm's length and not encourage her chattiness, I can't help belly laughing at the indignation on her cute little face. As I'm laughing, I notice Marnie's face turning toward me in my peripheral vision. She's sitting on her daughter's other side, and it's the first time she's looked at me during our meal. In fact, every time I've peeked at Marnie over her kid's head, she's been engrossed in conversation with her father and my mother. Or at least, she's pretended to be. Who knows with that one. But, apparently, this time, the sound of my laughter has finally attracted Marnie's attention.

When my eyes meet Marnie's, she does something wholly unexpected: she beams a huge smile at me—a relaxed, authentic one—and whether I like it or not—spoiler alert: I emphatically do *not* like it—heat immediately spreads throughout my core in response.

"You know *why* purpole is my favorite color?" the kid says. "*Maxy-Milly.*" I wrench my eyes off Marnie's gorgeous face to look at her miniature doppelganger. When the kid has my full attention again, she repeats, "Do you know why *purpole* is my favorite color?"

I sigh from the depths of my soul, and Marnie chuckles. "No," I say. "But I'd bet a full year's salary you're gonna tell me, huh?" Again, Marnie laughs. In fact, the entire table does, which means everyone is now keyed into my conversation with the tiny human to my right.

As expected, the kid launches into explaining her love of purple to me. As far as I can tell, it's a story about some purple dragon in her favorite cartoon. As the kid rambles on, I glance across her carrot-top head at Marnie again. Same as the last time, she flashes me a smile that rattles me to my core, and I return the gesture.

Fucking hell.
What am I doing?

I quickly look away.

The last thing I need to be doing is exchanging goofy smiles with a woman who's made mind-fuckery an Olympic sport.

"So, dat's why we were all dressed like *purple* spiders!" Ripley concludes. It's the whiz-bang ending to her lengthy story, apparently, but I have no idea how she got there or what it means.

"Cool," I say, since she's clearly waiting for a reply. "Hey, you want to know a secret, kid?"

"Oh, yessss."

I beckon to her, and she leans in. I look around at the faces staring at us and then stage-whisper, "I sometimes dress like a spider, too. I find it relaxes me after a long day of work."

The adults at the table burst into laughter, so the kid dissolves into high-pitched giggles along with them—even though I'm quite certain she has no idea what's funny.

"Oh, Max," my mother says. "Don't do that to her. She thinks you're serious. Ripley, honey, Max is joking. He doesn't really dress like a spider."

Ripley looks disappointed. "Oh." She looks up at me hopefully through thick, smudged lenses. "Do you want to see my spider costume? It's in my closet."

"Maybe another time. How can you see anything?" I put out my palm. "Give me your glasses, kid. I'll show you a whole new world."

Ripley dutifully hands them over, and I get to work cleaning them on my shirt. As I'm working, I glance at Marnie again, and the look on her face sends heat skating across my skin. Marnie's not smiling at me this time. She's *smoldering.* Flashing me a sultry look that practically screams, "I want you to fuck me."

My cock begins tingling, which is the last thing I need happening while I'm seated next to a tiny human and across from my mother.

I take a deep breath and command my dick to read the room and pipe down.

"Here you go," I say, handing the glasses back to their owner. "Behold the world in all its glory."

Ripley slides her glasses back on and giggles. "Oh. Dat's better."

"Say thank you to Max," Marnie prompts. "That was very nice of him."

"Tank you."

"You're very welcome. Enjoy."

Soft music has been playing throughout our meal. A random playlist from a streaming platform. In this moment, a new song begins and Mom gushes, "Oh, I *love* this one. It's my current favorite."

Henry says he's never heard it and asks my mother about it, so Mom launches into explaining how she first discovered this particular artist after watching an episode of *Grey's Anatomy* that featured the song. Marnie pipes in to say she's obsessed with *Grey's Anatomy,* and the two women launch into a lively discussion about the show.

And . . . she's back. In the midst of the adult conversation gaining traction at the table, Ripley places her little hand on my forearm and says, "What's *your* favorite song, Maxy-Milly?"

"I'd have to think about that. What's yours?"

Ripley throws up her little hands in exasperation. "I told you. 'Da Itsy-Bitsy Spider.' That's why we were dressed like *purpole* spiders for da dance."

Again, I can't help laughing, despite myself. "Such a temper. I guess your hair isn't the only thing you inherited from your mother."

Marnie's head swivels toward me on a dime. "What was that?"

"She already told me her favorite song, apparently, but I didn't catch it amidst the many other bits of information she's told me. Apparently, she's frustrated with me for my lack of information retention."

"And rightly so," my mother says. "When a woman speaks, *listen carefully,* Maximillian."

Everyone laughs, even Marnie.

"I swear I'm trying, Mom," I say.

"She's being particularly chatty with you," Marnie says apologetically. She mouths over her kid's head, "*Sorry.*"

"No, no," I say. "She's a great conversationalist. Better than most lawyers I know."

Everyone chuckles again, even Ripley—who, once again, couldn't possibly have a clue what's funny.

"So, what's da answer?" the kid says.

"To what?"

"Your favorite song!"

"Oh. That." I pause to consider, and when the perfect answer pops into my head, I look at Marnie over the kid's hair and say, "'Barracuda.'"

Marnie's mouth twitches slightly, letting me know my message has been received, but it's her only visible reaction to my dig. My mother, on the other hand, who has no idea I've chosen the song to send a message to Marnie, sings out, "I didn't know you like Heart. I love them."

I address my mother. "I remember, as a kid, watching you singing along at full volume to one of their songs. It wasn't 'Barracuda,' but I can't remember which one."

"'Dog and Butterfly.'"

"That's right."

"That's one of my all-time favorites. I don't know why, but it always makes me want to cry."

"Me, too," Marnie says. "I don't even know what the song is about, but it hits me right here, for some reason." She places her hand on her heart.

When Mom agrees, Marnie pops up to find the song on the streaming platform, and we all listen to it together and talk about what we think it means and how amazing the lead singer's vocals are.

When the song is over, Ripley says, "Can we listen to barbe-quood now?"

Every adult at the table dies of laughter, including me. Fuck my life, the kid's a cutie. There's no denying it. As far as kids go, anyway.

Marnie turns on the song and then shows Ripley how to bang her head and put up her hands like she's at a rock concert. When Ripley gets it, the entire table rocks out to the song with her. Not surprisingly, when it's over, Ripley shouts, "Anudder one!"

Marnie shakes her head. "I'm glad you're having fun, but it's already past your bedtime, peanut. You've got school tomorrow."

"One more?"

"Nope. Say goodnight to everyone."

Ripley looks at me. "Will you read to me tonight?"

"No, peanut," Marnie says. "Let's let Max relax now and have some adult conversation with his mommy and Grampy."

Ripley gasps. "Gigi is Maxy's *mommy*?"

We all look at each other, grinning. I don't know how that fact has escaped Ripley before now, but, clearly, it's a revelation to her.

"Yes, Gigi is Max's mommy," Marnie says. "And Auggie's, too. Remember Auggie from the gallery? Max and Auggie are brothers."

"Naomi has a brudder."

"Yes, she does." Marnie looks at the table. "That's her best friend from pre-school." She returns to her daughter and begins guiding her from the table. "Say goodnight to everyone, sweetie."

Ripley heads straight to me and gives me a hug. During our awkward embrace, she whispers, "I love you so much." Not knowing what the fuck to say to that, I reply, "Thanks." From me, Ripley heads to my besotted mother and gives her a hug, at which point my mother buries her nose in Ripley's hair and says, "Aw, I love you, too, Ripley."

I sigh with relief. At least, the kid loves everyone. Not only me.

Mom says to Ripley, "Guess what? I'm sleeping here tonight, and I'm an early riser—so in the morning, I'd be happy to make you pancakes before you head off to school."

Ripley gasps with delight. "With smiley faces on dem?"

"Chocolate chip smiley faces, you mean?" After checking with Marnie and getting a nod, Mom returns to Ripley and says, "*Absolutely.*"

Ripley does a little happy dance before addressing me. "Are you sleeping here, too?"

"Nope. I'm heading back to my house now, as a matter of fact. I've got an early day at work tomorrow."

Ripley looks disappointed. "If you spend da night, you can take me to school tomorrow and *den* go to work. Dat's what Mommy does."

"No, honey," Marnie says before I've replied. "I'll be the one taking you to school in the morning, like always. Max is a busy guy. Let's be thankful for all the time he's spent with us today. He's been very, very kind."

"Tank you," Ripley says.

"You're welcome. I've had fun."

"Now, come on. Let's get those teeth brushed." With that, Marnie bustles her kid out of the dining room. But not before stealing one last look at me—a white-hot smolder that instantly sends tingles into my dick, yet again.

12

MARNIE

I leave my chatterbox's bedroom—after reading no less than *three* of her favorite books, all while parrying constant questions about why Max can't be her daddy like that pretty lady at the gallery said—thanks, lady—and head into my bedroom to change into pajamas, brush my teeth, and wash every trace of makeup off my skin. My bedtime routine complete, I head into the living room to see if Max is still here. But the room is empty. No Max. And no Dad or Gigi, either.

I hear laughter in the adjacent kitchen, so I head in there—and then stop short in the doorway. Dad and Gigi are standing, side by side at the sink, loading the dishwasher together, with Gigi happily rinsing plates and handing them to Dad, who then meticulously arranges them in the machine. It's a vignette I've seen before. Many times. Only with Mom standing where Gigi is standing now. For a moment, the sight of Gigi taking Mom's place is jarring to me.

When I first met Gigi—Geraldine—in yoga class, she reminded me so much of my mother, I had to fight the urge to throw my arms around her and sob. It wasn't a physical resemblance. Mom was a redhead, like me. It was Geraldine's energy.

Her kind smile. The easy, nurturing, non-judgmental way she has about her. All of it felt instantly recognizable to me. And I wanted to bask in the glow of it all. That's why I approached Geraldine after that first class and struck up a conversation. I'd joined the class for networking purposes only—I don't even like yoga all that much—and wound-up meeting someone who felt like a salve for my aching soul.

As I got to know Geraldine through weekly classes and post-yoga coffees, I only liked her more and more. Until one day, I realized she might be the perfect salve for my father's aching soul, too. When Dad said he wasn't ready, and I realized I was a hot mess who was constantly treating the symptoms of my distress, rather than digging down to the root of it, I let my friendship with Geraldine fade. And now, in a shocking twist, here she is. In Dad's house. Standing in Dad's kitchen. Taking Mom's usual spot. And I'm suddenly not sure how I feel about that. I wanted her here. This was my idea. And now, I'm not sure I can handle it.

"Hey there," I say to announce myself, and they both turn around, all beaming, bright smiles. I walk to the fridge and grab a bottle of white wine, and Dad and Gigi return to their task.

"Wine?" I ask the pair.

"I'd love some," Gigi says.

"I'm good," Dad says. "Why don't you two catch up for a bit? I'll head to my bedroom and read a few chapters of my book. It's just now getting good."

"Are you sure?" Gigi asks.

"Absolutely. I'm sure you two have plenty to catch up on." He pecks Gigi's cheek and then mine. "Goodnight, ladies." He smiles at Gigi. "Take your time." And off he goes with a skip in his step I haven't seen since Mom died.

I pour the wine and Gigi and I head into the living room where we settle onto the couch with our goblets and the rest of the bottle.

"I'm excited to get a chance to chat with you," Gigi says tentatively. She pauses to choose her words. "I'm wondering if maybe you're a little uncomfortable to discover me dating your father? Is it weird for you?"

"Not at all. I wanted to set you up with him, remember?"

"Yes, I know . . . but I think maybe wanting to do that, in theory, might be something different than actually seeing me with him and realizing we're really hitting it off."

She's a wise and observant woman. Which really shouldn't surprise me. Geraldine's empathy and emotional intelligence drew me to her in the first place.

I exhale. "Your Spidey-senses aren't wrong," I admit. "I think it's going to take a little getting used to. But that doesn't mean I'm not one hundred percent excited for you both. I am. My mother couldn't have been clearer she wanted my father to find love again, as long as it was with someone who'd be kind to him, Ripley, and me. And there's no doubt whatsoever you fit that bill, and then some."

Gigi sighs with relief. "Thank you. That means a lot to me. Your father is an incredible man. His heart is as big as the Grand Canyon."

"It sure is."

Gigi twists her mouth. "Did I do something to offend you or your friends at dinner that time? I had such a lovely time that night. I was sorry we lost touch after that."

"Oh, gosh, no. You did nothing wrong." I explain the whole thing to her as we drain our glasses of wine. I tell her the timing simply wasn't good for me to embark on a new friendship, especially with someone who reminded me so much of my mother. And Gigi expresses complete understanding and support. "I should have had the decency to explain all that to you back then," I concede. "I'm sorry. It never occurred to me you might think you'd done something wrong."

"You have nothing to apologize for," Gigi says. "I'm just

glad you've been able to get the counseling and support you needed."

"I have. I feel like a whole new person." The image of this woman's son fucking me against a wall today slams into me. With a smirk, I add, "Well, mostly. I'm still a work in progress."

"Aren't we all?"

I refill our wine glasses and she thanks me.

"As long as we're clearing the air," I say. "I do have one question. You expressed surprise when you saw me at the gallery today—like you didn't know I'd turn out to be my father's Marnie. But when we got back home, and I saw all the framed photos around, I realized you've been here before, right? So, you must have seen a bunch of photos of me at some point before today and realized you'd already met my father's daughter."

Gigi flushes. She looks sheepish. "Yes, that's true. I knew it from the very beginning, actually."

I'm flabbergasted. "Then why didn't you tell him before today you already knew me?"

Gigi runs her hand through her hair, looking flustered. "Oh, God, I've been feeling so guilty about this. Like I've been keeping a huge, horrible secret." She exhales. "I didn't meet your father, completely at random, Marnie, and I didn't want him to think I was some kind of deranged stalker. I figured you'd mentioned me to your father, way back when and I didn't want him thinking you and I had somehow ganged up on him—that we'd cleverly engineered our meet-cute at Whole Foods. So, when Henry showed me a photo of you and Ripley on our first date, I panicked and froze and didn't say anything. And once I'd made that initial mistake, I didn't know how to admit it later on. Ever since, I've been holding it in, and now I feel sick about it."

I cock my head. "What do you mean you didn't meet him completely at random?"

Gigi takes a deep breath. "After you told me about your father at dinner, and how wonderful he is, I was curious, so I did a little online digging and found a photo of him. I thought he was incredibly handsome—but that's no surprise, given that you have half his genes. And I also thought he had extremely kind eyes." She shrugs. "But then, you and I lost touch, and I never heard from you about setting me up with him, so I forgot all about it and went on with my life. I went on some horrible dates with men I'd met through dating apps. Went on a few more with men I'd met in my hiking club. Also, not great. And then, a few months ago, I happened to see your father standing in line at the deli counter at Whole Foods. I recognized him, instantly." She smiles. "He was gorgeous—even better looking in person than in his photo. And his aura was so gentle and sweet. So, I stood in line behind him, even though I didn't need a damned thing from the deli counter, and, luckily, he struck up a conversation with me. After that, I pretended it was pure happenstance I was standing there that day. So, how could I possibly tell him I'd recognized you in the photo he'd showed me on our first date? I was locked into my lies by then, and I've been feeling like I'm caught in a web of them, ever since."

Poor Gigi looks so forlorn, so apologetic and tortured, I can't help bursting out laughing. "Oh, Geraldine," I say. "You poor little thing. It's okay."

"It is?" she says, wiping a tear.

"Of course, it is. Come clean to my father. He'll understand."

"What if he doesn't? What if he thinks our relationship has been built on lies?"

"It was a tiny lie. A forgivable one. Come clean, and he'll forgive you. I'm sure he'll feel flattered to think you recognized him, after all that time had passed."

"How could I not? When I saw Henry's photo, I genuinely thought he's the handsomest man I've ever seen in my life."

Oh, my heart. "Is that why you introduced yourself as Gigi to him, instead of Geraldine?" I ask. "To keep your little lie from unraveling?"

"No, I swear I wasn't quite that diabolical. Gigi is my lifelong nickname, and I've always used it on dating apps and in my hiking club, etcetera. What I said at the gallery today was true: when it comes to dating, I feel like Gigi is much more flirtatious and enticing than Geraldine. Geraldine is someone's grandma, but Gigi is *fun*."

I laugh. "Yes, she is."

Gigi exhales from the depths of her soul. "I'm so glad we talked about this. This secret has been weighing me down."

"Tell him tonight, okay?"

She nods solemnly. "I will. I promise."

"Honesty is always the best policy."

"Absolutely."

Ha. I can't believe I just had the nerve to say that, while I'm sitting here keeping so many secrets of my own.

"Speaking of honesty," Gigi says, "let's talk about you and Max, shall we?"

Aw, fuck. Is she a mind-reader?

"What's going on there?" Gigi prompts, her eyebrow raised.

I look down at my empty wine glass. And then, at the empty wine bottle. "If you truly want honesty from me about this topic, I'll need to drink another glass of wine. I'll be right back." I head into the kitchen and grab a bottle of red off the counter this time, along with an opener, and then return to Gigi on the couch. I open the bottle, pour for both of us and then settle back into my comfy seat.

"Maximillian Vaughn," I begin on an exhale.

"That's his name," Gigi says. "I should know. I gave it to him."

I take a long sip of red wine. "Geraldine—Gigi—I say this to you as my friend, and not as Max's mother. I've had casual sex with Max a few times. And that's all there is to The Very Short Story of Max and Marnie."

Gigi smirks. "Judging by that fresh bite mark on Max's neck today, and the way he looked straight at you when I brought it up, I'm guessing you two added a page to your very short story recently?"

I blush. "Yes. At our mutual friend's birthday party today. It was the first time we'd seen each other since we first met at Captain's a long time ago—the same night you had dinner with my friends and me."

"I see." She sips her wine. "You two definitely have chemistry. That's pretty obvious."

"Well, we've had it in the past. There's nothing present tense about Max and me."

"You don't consider *today* to be in the present tense?"

"Today was a blip. I'm certain about what I'm looking for in a man. And while I'm sure your handsome son is going to be a perfect partner for someone, someday, he's not what I'm looking for, at all. I'm sure he'd agree with me on that. Especially now that he's met Ripley."

She chuckles. "Wasn't Max adorable with Ripley today? My heart melted at the way he interacted with her."

My heart skips a beat at the memory of Max belly laughing at something Ripley said. As much as I've always felt lust for Max, I've never felt it more acutely than I did in that precise moment. "Yeah, he was very cute with her today —begrudgingly."

Gigi studies me for a moment as I sip my wine. Finally, she says, "I hope you don't mind me saying this, but I wouldn't reach the conclusion there's no hope for Max and you, just yet. I know my son, and when he looked at you during dinner, I saw something more than physical attraction there."

I snort. "No, you didn't."

"I know him, Marnie. And I know what I saw. He's interested in you. As a person."

I laugh. "Gigi, I'm sorry, but that's not true. What you saw today was good old-fashioned lust. I'm sorry to be so blunt about that to the randy boy's mommy, but that's truly the only thing between Max and me."

She's not buying it, clearly. But she guzzles her wine and doesn't argue with me.

"That's especially true now that he knows about Ripley," I insist. "We both know your son isn't even close to ready to take on a package deal like me."

"I don't know about that. I think Max would be a fantastic father figure, even if he doesn't fully realize it. Ripley obviously likes him. And he couldn't resist her charms, despite his fervent efforts to do so."

I'm too stunned to speak for a long moment. "Okay, well," I finally murmur. "I'll let you delude yourself about that in the name of motherly love. But regardless, I think we can both agree that Max and I would be a total non-starter, regardless, now that you and my father are dating."

Gigi looks perplexed. "I don't think that matters. Do you really?"

I'm floored. "Of course, I do. Who knows what will happen with you and my father, but you and Dad have dibs here. If you two wind up in a serious relationship, Max and I would be kind of like step-siblings. Maybe even actual step-siblings one day. We couldn't possibly get together in that situation."

Gigi snorts. "You and Max are adults. No matter what happens, it's not like Henry and I would raise our children together under one roof, as one family. This isn't *The Brady Bunch*. I honestly think you're looking for reasons not to give Max a chance."

"Max doesn't want to be given a chance, Gigi. Trust me on that. Not in terms of what I'm looking for, which is something more than a casual fling. He literally told me today he doesn't like me."

Gigi looks shocked. "*Really*? How rude of him. Why on earth would Max say something like that to you?"

"It was well deserved."

"Well, that can't be true," she says. "You're a wonderful person."

"No, I'm not. I'm a terrible person, actually. The worst."

Gigi laughs. "In what way?"

I'm feeling drunk by now, which is probably why I'm feeling the thumping urge to confess my sins to Gigi, the way she confessed her sins to me.

"Have you robbed a bank?" Gigi asks.

I shake my head.

"Are you a bad mother to Ripley?"

"No. I'm a good mother. Not perfect, but very good."

"Well, I can plainly see you're a good daughter and friend, too. And from what your father's told me, you're an exceptionally gifted chef, as well."

I can't take it anymore. "Remember Mr. BDE?" I blurt. "The guy I was dating who turned out to be married?"

Gigi gasps. "You got involved with him again, even though you knew he was married?"

I lean back into the couch and pinch the bridge of my nose. "I figured out he's your ex-husband, Geraldine. Max's father. That's why I can't be with Max, ever, ever, ever. *Because I've slept with his fucking father.*"

When I dare to look at Gigi, her jaw is practically in her lap. "Mr. BDE is . . . Alexander?" When I nod, she processes that for a moment. "So . . . you were pissed to find out Alexander is married, so you befriended his ex-wife and had sex with his son as some kind of revenge?"

I burst into sloppy, drunken tears. "No, I promise it's all been one horrible coincidence after another—the universe's way of punishing me for being a horrible person. I saw a photo of Alexander in Max's kitchen the morning after I met him at Captain's. I swear on Ripley I had no idea he was Alexander's son before then. And I had no idea until today you were Alexander's first wife and Max's mother. I saw your photo pop up on Max's phone when you called him this afternoon, and I put two and two together then."

In a non-stop ramble of sloppy words, I tell Gigi everything about how I bolted on Max a year and a half ago without telling him about my discovery. And then, about how I did basically the same thing again today after seeing her face on Max's phone. And when I'm finally done talking, Geraldine does something that takes me by complete surprise. The same thing Lucy did when she first heard about all of this. She laughs. Heartily. The kind of belly laugh that has her throwing her head back and wiping tears.

"It's not funny," I insist. "It's evidence that I'm a horrible person."

"How?" Gigi asks. "It sounds like a comedy of errors to me."

"It was until I hooked up with Max again today *after* knowing Alexander is his father."

"Oh. Yeah. That was kind of bad of you."

"It was very, very bad of me."

Gigi ponders that. "Looks like we're both going to have to come clean, huh? Like you said, honesty is the best policy."

"But . . . I'm not dating Max, like you're dating my father. Do I really need to be honest with someone I've only casually messed around with?"

Gigi flashes me a motherly look of disappointment. "*Marnie.*"

"Maybe you could tell him for me?" I squeak out.

"No, you're going to have to do it," she declares. "I'm sure Max has been deeply confused this whole time about why you ran out on him. I don't think he's accustomed to that. I know he's my son, but I'm well aware he's a lady killer." She pats my hand. "Honey, I'm dating your father and things are going really well. The odds are high you're going to have to interact with Max in the future, if only at family events. You need to do the right thing by him and tell him the truth, the same way I need to do the right thing by Henry."

I flap my lips together. "Okay, I'll call him tomorrow and tell him the whole embarrassing truth."

"Good girl. The truth shall set you free. I promise I'll tell

Henry tonight, unless he's already asleep, in which case I'll tell him in the morning."

I lean over and hug her. "Thank you for being so amazing. I'm so glad you're dating my father."

"You're not mad that I sort of masterminded our meet cute?"

"Not at all. I think it's adorable."

Gigi sighs with relief. "Hopefully, your father will have a similar reaction." She grabs her phone and looks at the group photo we took today in front of her painting. "Henry is such a sweet man. I really enjoyed getting our families together today."

"I'm so glad you're the one dating him."

Still looking at the photo in her hand, Gigi says, "I have a crazy favor to ask, Marnie. Feel free to say no." She looks up from her phone. "Would you mind me posting our group photo from the gallery today onto Facebook for only Alexander to see? Now that I know your history with him, I think it'd be hilarious to post the photo with a caption that says, 'Congratulations to Max and Marnie on their engagement!'" She bursts out laughing at the very idea. "I promise I'll delete it after a few hours—once I'm sure Alexander has seen it. I'm sure he'll call me when he does, and I'll immediately tell him it was a prank. But the mere thought of Alexander seeing that photo and thinking Max is engaged to the woman he cheated on his current wife with . . ." She cracks up again. "The best part is Alexander couldn't tell me or anyone else about his history with you, without admitting he'd cheated on his wife. So, he'd have to sit there and pretend to be excited for Max, even though he'd surely be freaking out."

Maybe it's the wine, but I can't help laughing hysterically at Gigi's diabolical plan. "Are you sure Alexander won't call Max and tell him everything before I've had a chance to do it myself?"

"I'm sure," Gigi says. "Like I said, Alexander can't tell Max the truth without ratting himself out. Plus, even if Alexander called, Max wouldn't pick up his father's call, anyway. They're estranged these days."

"Why?"

"Max is the one who discovered Alexander cheating on me, and Alexander had the audacity to tell his son—his fifteen-year-old—to cover for him to keep our family together. Max rightly decided to tell me everything, but the whole situation was devastating to him."

"Oh my god. Alexander really is a monster."

"He's a piece of work."

I pause. "Okay, I'm down to help you inflict whatever pain you can on Alexander, through any means necessary. Post the photo for his eyes only. Let's give that cheating bastard a heart attack."

"Or at least, a panic attack."

We both cackle with laughter.

When we calm down, Gigi asks, "You promise you'll tell Max the truth tomorrow?"

"I promise. And you'll tell my father the truth, too?"

"I promise."

After we link pinkies to seal our promise, I run my fingertip over the rim of my wine glass. "Do you think I should have told Alexander's wife the truth about her husband cheating with me? I've been feeling guilty about not doing that."

Gigi scowls. "Absolutely not. Ashley knew Alexander was married to his second wife when she started dating him. If she thinks that man is miraculously going to remain faithful to her, even though he didn't manage the feat with his first two wives, then she's a fool."

"Oh, that makes me feel a whole lot better. Thank you for telling me that."

Gigi waggles her eyebrows mischievously. "And now . . . for our fun little prank." She taps on her screen, and when she shows it to me, the deed is done. The photo posted.

For a while, we sit and laugh about Alexander's reaction when he wakes up and discovers his son is engaged to me. After a while, though, I feel sleepy, so I rest my head on Gigi's comfy, warm lap and ask her to tell me about Max as a kid. As Gigi strokes my hair, she tells me stories about Max's innate tenacity. His protective nature. His generosity. His tenderness. His surprising goofiness. The moment feels so lovely and relaxing, I close my eyes. And soon, Gigi's pleasant voice and warm lap lull my mind and body into a pleasant, wine-induced sleep.

13
MAX

"Answer your fucking phone, Mom."

I'm shouting into the void of my empty car after my tenth call to my darling mother has once again gone straight to voicemail.

It's just before 7:00 am on Monday morning, and I'm driving to Henry's house, since my darling mother won't answer her fucking phone. She's normally up with the sun, so where the fuck is she?

I went into the office before dawn today to catch up on the work I didn't tackle over the weekend; but I'd barely sat down at my desk before my phone started blowing up with texts from family and friends on the East Coast. People in a time zone three hours ahead who woke up and scanned their Facebook accounts and then lost their minds to find out, at least according to a post by my mother, that the one guy they all expected to remain a bachelor for life has gotten engaged, out of the blue, to a woman nobody has heard of before. A woman with a kid, no less.

I don't have a Facebook account, so I called my mother immediately. No answer. I asked my cousin, one of the well-wishers blowing up my phone, to send me a screenshot. And when he did, I lost my fucking shit. What the fuck, Mom?

I tried Mom again.

No answer.

So, I called my brother and woke him up. When Auggie saw the post, he laughed and laughed, despite his grogginess. He figured Mom had pulled a prank on me, as she's been known to do. But that wasn't a prank if you ask me, because it wasn't the slightest bit funny.

As I take the exit off the freeway for Henry's house, I'm still cursing my mother out. I can't believe I have to take valuable time out of a Monday morning to drive to her boyfriend's house across town to demand she take the post down. Doesn't Mom realize the partnership selection committee meeting is in a matter of weeks? I told her about that, so she should understand that every billable hour counts right now. For fuck's sake, this is the home stretch.

As I turn onto Henry's street, my phone screen, which is on display on my car's dashboard, lights up with a text from my father.

> Saw the news about your engagement. Call me
> immediately to discuss.

I roll my eyes and mutter, "Fuck you, Dad." Even in the midst of my panic and anger, I can't deny I'm enjoying the idea that Dad thinks he's *this* out of the loop in my life. Even if it's only for this morning, I guess it's not the worst thing in the world to let him think I've met the great love of my life—a single mother with a cute kid—and didn't even bother to tell him I'd asked her to marry me.

As I pull into Henry's driveway, the display on my dashboard lights up with another text—this one from the last person

I'd ever want to see my mother's bizarre post. My immediate boss at the law firm, Scott Wagner. His text reads:

> Congratulations on your engagement! That's one adorable kid. I'm thrilled and thoroughly impressed you've decided to take on the role of husband and father, all at once. Come down to my office ASAP, so I can congratulate you in person.

"Fuck, fuck, fuck," I shout. "Thanks, Mom."

I don't think Scott is Facebook friends with Mom. But come to think of it, his wife knows Mom somehow, so she probably saw the post and told her husband about it. Fucking hell. This fiasco just keeps getting worse and worse.

I barrel out of my car and sprint to Henry's porch like a man possessed and then bang on his door like I'm trying to wake the dead. When nobody answers within two seconds, I ring the doorbell repeatedly. Until finally, the door swings open and Marnie appears, scowling at me. Her red hair is tousled. She's wearing pajama bottoms and a white tank top that does little to hide the exquisite shape of her breasts and hard nipples—the latter being the result of the cold morning air that's suddenly blasting her, no doubt. She looks just-rolled-out-of-bed sultry to me. Or at least, she would, if I weren't otherwise preoccupied by the need to strangle my mother.

"Is my mom still here?" I bark out. "She's not answering my calls or texts."

Marnie opens the door wider, inviting me inside. "Is everything okay?"

"No, it's not. But it will be." I stride into the house with Marnie. As we walk, she groans and touches her forehead like she's got a headache. "Rough night?" I ask.

Marnie nods. "Thanks to your hard-partying mother. We drank too much wine last night and passed out on the couch together."

"Well, that explains everything." I enter the living room and find my mother asleep on the couch. "Mom," I bark. "Wake up."

Mom's eyes jolt open. "What's wrong?"

Even if there weren't two empty wine bottles and goblets on the coffee table, I'd instantly know Mom was hungover. It's a rare occurrence; she rarely drinks. But give the woman more than two glasses of wine, and she always looks like this the next day.

"Is Auggie okay?" Mom asks, sitting up.

"He's fine. He's not the son you fucked over with your stupid little drunken prank last night."

Mom looks genuinely baffled.

"Your Facebook post," I spit out angrily. "You know, the one where you told the world I'm engaged to Marnie?"

Understanding washes over Mom's face. "Oh yeah." Mom glances at Marnie and snickers. "Your father congratulated you about that this morning?"

"Yeah, Dad and fifty other people. My phone's been blowing up all morning with congratulatory voicemails and texts. I need you to take it down now, Mom. Even my boss has seen it."

"What?" Mom says, turning pale. "*How*?"

"That's how social media works. When you post something for the whole world to see, then, surprise, the whole world sees it. Now I have to go back to work and explain to my boss I'm not actually engaged, but instead, I've got a mother with a truly bizarre sense of humor."

Mom's face is sheet-white. "But I set my post for only your father to see."

"No, you set if for everyone to see."

"That can't be." Her brow furrowed, Mom grabs her phone and taps on her screen for a moment. Suddenly, her face drops.

"Shoot." She looks up, her eyes wide. "I accidentally posted it for everyone to see."

"Yeah, no shit. Now, take it down."

"I'm so sorry, Max."

"Spare me your apologies. *Take it down*."

Mom taps furiously, and a second later announces with a weak smile that the post is gone.

"Gone but not forgotten. Why did you post it in the first place? Please, explain your drunken logic to me and why you specifically wanted Dad to see it."

Mom looks at Marnie, and they both look guilty as hell.

"Don't look at Marnie to bail you out of this," I say. "Even if she egged you on or dared you in a drunken game of Truth or Dare, it's still on you that you actually did it." When Mom looks at Marnie again, I bark out, "Eyes over here, Mother. Did you want to make Dad feel like a shitty father when he woke up and found out about my supposed engagement from a Facebook post? Was that your brilliant plan?"

Mom looks at Marnie a third time and swallows hard. "Um, I think maybe Marnie should answer those questions."

"No, I want to hear it from you. What, exactly, were you thinking? I know you love finding any way to make Dad feel like a loser—and normally, I'm all for it. But I don't appreciate you messing with my goddamned life in order to accomplish that otherwise lofty goal."

Mom twists her mouth. She looks deeply uncomfortable. Again, she looks at Marnie.

"Eyes here, Mom. She can't help you."

Mom returns to me and clears her throat. "What did your father say to you when you talked to him?"

"I haven't talked to him. He texted me, demanding that I call him immediately to talk about my engagement. But I've been too swamped with notifications to deal with him. Plus, I'm happy to let him stew and think he's the world's worst father for a bit longer. Which he is."

Marnie exhales. "I think I'll go and wake up Ripley for preschool, while you two finish talking."

Mom pops up. "No, I'll wake her while you answer Max's questions. I'll get her dressed and make her some breakfast."

"Marnie's not the one who should answer my questions," I insist.

"Actually, she is," Mom says. "Hear her out. If you have any further questions for me after you two talk, I'll be happy to answer them." She flashes Marnie a pointed look, and then begins walking out of the living room.

"Could you wake up my father, too?" Marnie calls after her. "I always wake him at the same time as Ripley. He hates alarms."

"Sure thing. There's something I need to talk to him about, anyway."

"Good luck."

When Mom is gone, I turn to Marnie. "Wow, you two are awfully chummy. Oh, what fun you had last night together, getting shitfaced and playing a prank on Max."

"The prank wasn't on you. Sit down. Please."

When I sit on the couch, Marnie sits on the other end of it, looking nervous and stiff. She clears her throat. Shifts her position. Wrings her hands. But before she says whatever bullshit excuse she's cooking up for me, my phone buzzes with an incoming call.

I look down at my screen. "Shit. It's my boss. I have to take this, so he doesn't start telling everyone at work about my supposed engagement." I connect the call. "Hey, Scott."

"I came to your office a minute ago, but you weren't there anymore. Where'd you go?"

"I had to step out unexpectedly. I'll be back shortly. Listen, about my mother's post—"

"That's why I'm calling. I happened to be on the phone with Wayne Walters when my wife texted me the good news, and in my shock, I couldn't help telling Wayne that the eternal bachelor of our firm, the last guy I'd ever expect to get engaged, has done exactly that—and to a single mother. Of course, Wayne was thrilled. I don't know if you know this, but his wife was a widowed mother of three small children when he met her, so he's got a real soft spot and deep respect for anyone who takes on a single mother. Right then and there, Wayne invited you and your new family to come to his ranch for the 'thank you retreat' he's hosting next week. You've heard about that, right? People at the firm jokingly call it 'family camp,' because it's so wholesome and Wayne encourages his invitees to bring their loved ones. Usually, he only invites people on his core team, so he's making a rare exception for you, Max. It's a golden opportunity for you to get in front of Wayne, and hopefully, *finally* persuade him to take my recommendation and let me add you to his legal team."

I'm paralyzed by my racing thoughts. This can't be happening. *Not like this.* I only joined this particular firm out of law school, even though I had other offers at higher starting salaries, because I knew the firm was the only one in Seattle used by Wayne Walters. He's one of the world's premiere tech inventors, a literal genius whose contributions to the world can't be overstated. My ultimate goal has always been to work for the man's main tech company directly. To be on the ground floor of patenting his many ideas and inventions and also get a front row seat to watch how he builds his sprawling empire. But since I also knew Mr. Walters never hires in-house attorneys until they've already been meticulously vetted through years of working for him on outside legal teams, the only path to my ultimate goal was to work my ass off at this firm, get myself assigned to his casework, and then do a stand-out job for him.

"Max?" Scott says. "Are you still there?"

I look at Marnie on the other side of the couch, feeling like I'm going to vomit from stress. "Uh, yes. I'm here."

"Have you heard about Wayne's dude ranch in Wyoming?

Shelby Kramer and her family went last year. Did she tell you about it?"

Again, I look at Marnie as panic threatens. "Yes, Shelby told me about it."

As a matter of fact, Shelby told me family camp was "mind-boggling." Like Scott said, Wayne Walters himself doesn't refer to his weeklong "thank you retreat" as family camp, since his invitees are welcome to attend solo or with an unrelated friend. But that's what we all call it. Last year, my colleague, Shelby, attended with her new wife and her wife's parents, and when she got back home, she was immediately offered partnership at the firm. Coincidence? I think not. Shelby deserved the promotion, to be clear. She's a brilliant, hardworking, kick-ass attorney who's impressed me many times. But given that I'd billed far more hours than Shelby last year, by a lot, and also had better results on the litigation cases I'd been assigned—none of them for Wayne Walters, unfortunately—I couldn't help thinking Shelby had been offered our firm's brass ring because she'd had the good fortune to spend a week rubbing elbows with our firm's biggest client. No matter the quality of legal services I might provide, I'm always going to lose out to someone who's been able to establish a personal relationship with the firm's biggest client.

"Your silence is a bit unnerving, Max," Scott says in my ear. "I don't know if you realize what a golden opportunity this is for you. Whatever you have to do to make it to Wyoming next week and bring your lovely fiancée and her cute little daughter with you, I'd strongly advise you to do it."

I glance at Marnie across the couch again to find her looking up at me with concern. "Uh, yes. I understand the situation perfectly."

"Excellent. We'll talk more when you get back to the office. We'll need to start reassigning your present workload, so you can give family camp your full attention next week. That way, when Mr. Walters invites you to his team at the end of the week, which I fully expect him to do, you'll be off and running on day one."

My heart leaps. "Sounds good. Thank you so much."

"Maxy-Milly!" a little voice shrieks. It's Ripley, of course, careening into the living room with my mother trailing apologetically behind her.

"Ah, I hear your little one in the background," Scott says, chuckling. "I'll let you go."

"Sorry," Mom murmurs, trailing after Ripley. "I mentioned Max being here to explain why we *couldn't* go into the living room right now, but my explanation only had the opposite effect than intended."

The phone line is dead now. Scott is gone. I slump back onto the couch and toss my phone onto the coffee table, and a second later, Ripley hurls herself onto my lap, grabs both my cheeks in her tiny palms and screams, "I knew you'd take me to school today! Mommy said you wouldn't, but I knew you would!"

I can't deal with this shrieking child right now. I only have the bandwidth to deal with one thing. One thought. One mission. Convincing Marnie Long to come to family camp with me next week. But how? I've been in enough negotiations to know everyone's got a price—something they want badly enough to do something distasteful to them. So, what does Marnie want that I could provide? Money? Or something else?

Ripley pinches my cheek. "I'm gonna show you my friends and my cubby and my sleeping mat and my art and my—"

"No, you're not," Marnie says. She gets up and pulls the kid off me. "Max isn't coming to school with you, honey. I'm sorry. He only came here this morning to talk to his mommy. Gigi is Max's mommy, remember?"

Mom asks hopefully, "Did you two have a good talk?"

"Not yet," Marnie says. "We didn't get the chance. Max got a call from his boss. Did you and my dad have a good talk?"

"We did," Mom says, beaming a smile at Marnie. "He laughed."

"Oh, I'm so glad," Marnie says. "And not surprised at all." Marnie addresses me. "Listen, Max, I know we still need to talk, but I have to get Ripley off to school now, so I'm not late to my client's house after that. Could we meet tonight after work and talk then?"

My heart is beating out of my chest. So hard I feel like my sternum is cracking. And yet, somehow, I manage to choke out the words, "Why don't I come with you to drop Ripley off at school? We could talk on the way or maybe over coffee after dropping her off, if you have enough time before work by then."

Marnie looks shocked. She looks at my mother, who nods, before returning to me. "Okay, yeah, that works." She puffs out her cheeks. "I need to get showered and dressed real quick. Ripley, why don't you get yourself a granola bar. We'll do pancakes with smiley faces tomorrow, okay? We ran out of time today."

"Dat's okay, Mommy." Ripley takes my hand. "Come on, Maxy-Milly. I'll show you where we keep da nola bars."

14

MARNIE

I pull my SUV out of the driveway with Max in my passenger seat and Ripley in her car seat in the back. Throughout my entire shower, and then while getting dressed, I've been trying to come up with the right wording to tell Max the reason his mother wanted to post that photo last night for only Alexander to see. But I'm still coming up short. At this point, I think maybe the only way to say it is to simply blurt it out. But I'm too big a coward to do that. Also, I can't very well say a word about any of that with Ripley and her big old ears in the backseat. And so, not knowing what to say, I've been silent and tongue-tied since I walked into the living room after my shower, other than saying to Ripley, "Time to go."

"Can you play Maxy-Milly's song, Mommy?" Ripley says behind me.

I look at my daughter in my rearview mirror. "What song, baby?"

"'Barbequood.'"

At any other time, I'd chuckle at her pronunciation of barracuda. But not now. Right now, I couldn't laugh if my life depended on it. "You know what, love?" I say, locking eyes with Ripley in the rearview mirror. "How about I let you watch a show on your iPad during the drive, instead of playing music, just this once?"

Ripley gasps in shock. "I'm not allowed to watch da iPad on da way to school. Only when we go somewhere far away like Auntie Leeloo's house."

"That's right, but I'm making an exception this once because I'd like to talk to Max and we might say a few things that aren't appropriate for little ears."

Ripley gasps again. Reverse psychology would dictate Ripley would *want* to overhear whatever "inappropriate" and mysterious things adults say to each other outside the presence of little ears. That's certainly what *I* wanted as a kid—to hear *all* the bad words and inappropriate things. But that's not how Ripley is wired. For reasons I'll never understand, the universe gifted me with a daughter who practically shudders at the mere thought of being exposed to something "inappropriate."

"Put on your headphones, love bug," I say. "The iPad is in the seat pocket."

"Max is still gonna come inside my school, doe, right?"

"I sure am," Max says. "I'll stay as long as you want."

"Don't promise that," I murmur. "They let parents stay all day to help, if they want."

"Oh. Yeah. No. I can't stay all day. But I'll definitely come in and see whatever you want to show me. How does that sound?"

Ripley cheers and claps while I frown and try to figure out what game Max is playing. Why is he suddenly being so nice to Ripley, when I know for a fact he wants nothing to do with her?

At a red light, I help Ripley get situated with the iPad and her headphones, and when she's all dialed in and her eyes are fixated on her screen, I say to Max, "So, about your mother's Facebook post."

"We don't need to waste time talking about that. I get it. You two got drunk and Mom got the brilliant idea to make my father feel like he's a shit father who's out of the loop in his son's life.

Which is true. There's actually something else I need to talk to you about, Marnie. Something important."

"Okay," I say tentatively. "Actually, no. I really do need to explain that Facebook post to you."

"Would you mind if I go first? My thing is kind of time-sensitive." He clears his throat. "What I'm about to say is batshit crazy and I know it. But I promise, if you do this huge favor for me, I'll make it worth your while. Remember how I was going to try to get you hired to cater the partnership dinners at my firm? I'll absolutely do that for you. In addition, I'll introduce you to my father. I don't speak to him anymore, but if you do this for me, I'll bite the bullet and call him to ask if he'll hire you to cater *his* firm's monthly board meeting. Everyone on the board is wealthy, so I'm sure—"

"I don't want you to introduce me to your father," I shriek, on the verge of having a panic attack.

"Oh. My mother's told you about him, huh?" Max says. "Okay, yeah, scratch that. If you do this favor for me, then I'll—"

"What's the favor?" I shout. I glance at Ripley in my rearview mirror to make sure my loud volume hasn't pierced my daughter's cartoon bubble, and when she looks blissfully unaware of my conversation with Max, I return to him and exhale. "Just spit it out, for fuck's sake. Please. You're freaking me out."

"Sorry. I wanted to dangle an adequate carrot before you heard my crazy request. Just, please, keep an open mind."

"Spit it out, Max. *Please*."

Max exhales and launches into his tale. He tells me about his firm's biggest client—some multi-billionaire tech mogul genius inventor wannabe cowboy philanthropist with a soft spot for kids who's been Max's dream employer and hero since his earliest days of law school.

"What does he have to do with me?" I ask.

"I'm getting there," Max says. He explains he took his

current job precisely because his firm is the only one the tech guru uses for legal services in Seattle. He says he's been trying to find ways to get assigned to the guy's legal team for years, to no avail, and that now, out of nowhere, thanks to his mother's drunken Facebook post, he's been invited to bring his "beautiful new family" to the tech mogul's sprawling ranch in Wyoming next week for a "thank you retreat" the tech guru hosts for a myriad of professional service providers—lawyers, engineers, accountants, etcetera. "The week has jokingly been dubbed 'family camp' by my firm," he says, "because everyone tends to show up with their families. The woman who went last year came back and was immediately made partner. This is my golden ticket, Marnie. My way in. *Finally.* All I have to do to cash in the golden ticket is bring my supposed fiancée and her kid to camp next week."

My jaw is hanging open. "You can't be serious," I say. "Tell me you're joking."

"I'm not. But don't say no yet. Think about how much fun Ripley will have riding ponies and mining for gold and doing arts and crafts. From what I've been told, the ranch itself is mind boggling and they spare no expense to make it an incredible experience for everyone. My friend, Shelby, said they have a country fair one night with rides for kids. You know, the kind you see at big country fairs, only it's a private party. And she said the food is incredible. And there are camp counselors to play games with the kids. Oh, and she said the accommodations are like staying in a fancy, rustic hotel."

Clearly, he's lost his damned mind. "Max," I say. "Have you thought about what happens *after* camp? When there's no more fiancée and kid? No wedding? How are you planning to explain that? Are Ripley and I going to get killed off or what?"

"I'll cross that bridge when I get there," Max says. "It shouldn't be too hard. My firm doesn't give a shit about anybody's family or personal life. They only pretend to care when it comes to Wayne Walters, since he's a big family man. I guess if I had to, I could hire actors at some point to come to the annual family picnic. Or maybe my wife could be visiting her grandparents out of state that particular weekend."

"You're insane. First of all, it would never work. Nobody's ever going to believe we're an actual couple and you give two shits about Ripley. Second of all, even if it did work, which it wouldn't, you'd be in the worse position of needing to supply a fake family for every family event for the rest of your professional life."

"Let me worry about that," Max says. "All I need from you is one week in Wyoming, during which you'll pretend to be my beloved fiancée. In exchange, I'll do everything in my power to get you more clients than you know what to do with. Plus, Ripley will have an unforgettable experience. The time of her life."

I'm gripping the steering wheel with white knuckles. "I can't do it. If it were me, on my own, I'd probably say yes, simply because I'm curious to see a multi-billionaire's ranch. But I can't drag my daughter into this. She's already head over heels in love with you. I can't risk you breaking Ripley's heart when we get home, and you drop her like a hot potato. I wouldn't risk Ripley's heart for all the clients in the world."

Max lets out a long exhale, but he says nothing.

In thick silence, I pull into the preschool's parking lot and find a spot. After turning off my engine, I peek at Ripley in the backseat and exhale with relief when she's still immersed in her show. She's so engrossed, in fact, she hasn't even realized we've arrived in the parking lot of her preschool.

"Okay, hear me out," Max says. "I think we could reduce the risk of harm to Ripley by inviting your father and my mother for the week, as well."

"How would that help anything?"

"Because the more people surrounding Ripley, the less she'll think we're a couple. If my mother is there, the same way she was yesterday, then Ripley will continue thinking of me as

Gigi's son and nothing more. Right now, my mother is the reason I'm in her life at all. Well, we'll take great pains to make sure she keeps thinking that."

I look into his pleading eyes. His idea is a good one, I must admit. But it's not enough of an insurance policy for me. "I'm sorry, Max. I really can't."

"Please, Marnie," he says. "I've worked myself to the bone to get ahead at this fucking firm for almost seven years, and this is the opportunity I've been waiting for to finally get what I've wanted since law school. I'll do literally anything you want. Name it, and I'll do it."

I press my lips together. "I'm sorry. I feel for you. And like I said, if I only had myself to think about, I'd do it for the sheer adventure of it. But I have to think about Ripley."

Max's deep sigh betrays his disappointment and frustration. But rather than push back or try to convince me further, he looks out the car window and says, "Okay. Thanks for hearing me out. I can't fault you for doing the right thing for your daughter. In fact, I admire you for doing that."

I touch his arm, causing him to look at me. "You're not going to want me to come, anyway, once I tell you the truth about why I left your apartment that morning. Once I tell you the truth about that, I'll be the last person you'd ever want to spend a week with, no matter what's at stake for your career."

Max turns pale. "What are you talking about?"

I take a deep breath. "Remember how I'd found out the guy I'd been dating was married?"

He nods.

"When I walked into your kitchen, I saw a framed photo of you and your father—"

"Oh, God."

"And I discovered—"

"No, Marnie."

"The married man was your father."

"Oh, God." Max covers his face with his palm. "I feel sick."

"Yeah, that's how I felt. That's why I ran away the next morning. Because I felt physically sick. I'm so sorry, Max. I should have told you the truth, then and there, but my fight or flight instinct took over and I chose flight."

Max drops his hand from his face and levels me with icy blue eyes. "You didn't think to mention this little fact before fucking me at Grayson's party?"

My stomach somersaults. "In my defense, my time with your father felt like a distant memory by then. I was in such a bad place when I dated him. I was grieving my mother and looking for an escape from the pain. I'm in a much better place now, in all aspects of my life. I stupidly thought when I saw you the other day that by-gone chapter of my life didn't matter anymore."

"Bullshit. You were horny, so you took what you wanted. You were fucking selfish."

My chest heaves. "You're absolutely right. I felt overwhelmed by my physical attraction to you, and I didn't want to ruin the excitement by telling you the truth about your father. I should have told you to give you the opportunity to turn me down if that's what you wanted to do. For that, I'm very, very sorry. It was disgusting and wrong of me and I'm so sorry."

Max looks out the passenger side window for a very long time.

When I can't take it anymore, I say, "Whatever you're thinking, please say it. Whatever it is, no matter how brutal, say it and don't hold back. I deserve your wrath." When he still won't look at me, I whisper, "See? I told you; you wouldn't want to go to family camp with me after hearing what I had to tell you."

"We're here!" Ripley shouts from the backseat. She rips off her headphones and begins exuberantly unbuckling the straps of her car seat. But even when she's untethered and bopping excitedly in her seat, Max and I don't move. "What are we waiting for?" Ripley shrieks. "Come on, guys. I want to show Maxy *everything*."

15
MAX

As Marnie helps her kid slide down from the back seat of the SUV, I exit my side of the vehicle in stunned silence, my limbs sabotaged by the images currently wracking my brain. I can't stop seeing my father railing Marnie to within an inch of her life. Marnie's orgasm face as he plows her from behind. Dad eating Marnie's magic pussy. It's all making me want to hurl. Either that or commit patricide. Maybe both.

As I'm standing stock-still and dazed next to the car, a little hand slides into mine, and a squeak of a voice chirps out, "Come on, Maxy-Milly. I can't wait to show you *everything*." The kid attached to the voice and the hand begins pulling on me with all her little might, so I somehow command my lead legs and move in the direction she's clearly intending to guide me.

As the kid and I close in on the bright yellow front door of the preschool, Marnie thankfully hangs back. Honestly, I need space from her right now. I don't think I could make eye contact with her in this moment, without flashing her a look of such disgust, I'd ruin all chances of convincing her to come to family camp with me. If that's what I still want. I'm honestly not sure anymore.

"My best friend is Naomi," the kid is saying happily, as she skips and bops alongside me with her hand in mine. "And my teacher is Miss Roberts. She's pretty. Oh! And my cubby is da one with da *purpole* stars on it, cuz dat's my favorite color and I'm a star. Did you know my favorite color is *purpole*? My cubby has my name at da top of it. R-I-P-L-E-Y. Dat's what spells Ripley, but my whole name is Ripley Amelia Long." On and on the kid rambles, despite my utter lack of any kind of verbal response. Unlike last night at dinner, I can't muster the energy or focus to offer her so much as a grunt.

Once inside the preschool, Ripley immediately sets about showing me everything she just told me about in the parking lot while I maintain my silence and let her pull me around the colorful room. Marnie is standing by the front door as Ripley gives me a guided tour, I can't help noticing. And again, I'm relieved she's giving me space to process.

"And dat's where we have story time," Ripley says proudly. "Miss Roberts rings da bell, and den we all sit on da story-time carpet!" She looks at me for a response, and when I don't give one to her, she pulls me toward the next exciting thing. Apparently, this happy little chatterbox has enough energy and enthusiasm for both of us today.

After dragging me to her cubby, Ripley pulls me toward a little girl—a dark-skinned cutie with gorgeous braids and a bright smile. When we reach the girl, I can't help noticing she's quite a bit taller than Ripley, which then makes me realize that's true of every kid milling about this classroom. As a matter of fact, almost everyone is a full head taller than tiny Ripley. What's up with that? Is Ripley a kid-genius who's enrolled in preschool way early?

"Maxy, dis is Naomi," Ripley says, after giving her friend a warm hug. "She's my best friend." After Naomi shyly greets me, Marnie suddenly appears at my side, just in time to hear her daughter explain to her friend, "Gigi is Maxy's mommy and Grampy loves Gigi, so Maxy is our friend now."

For the first time since we exited Marnie's car in the parking lot, I look at Marnie. And the second I see the look of agony on her face, I feel my body light up with the primal urge to protect her. To ease her pain. I lean toward her and whisper, "And you were so sure my presence in the kid's life would be confusing to her. Seems to me she understands the situation perfectly."

In one sense, it's a small thing for me to have teased Marnie. To have spoken to her in a calm yet snarky tone. In another sense, though, in context, it's a massive thing. I've let Marnie know there might be a possible path forward for me to treat her the same as before—to get past the bombshell she dropped on me in the parking lot. Hell, I think maybe, by breaking our awkward, uncomfortable silence this way, I've just now signaled the same thing to myself.

"The kid has a name," Marnie whispers, matching my snarky tone. "I've noticed you never use it."

I tilt my head. Is she right about that? If so, I've never noticed it myself.

I feel a tug on my pants. And then, the kid's voice. *Ripley's* voice. "Will you play dress-up with me and Naomi till Miss Roberts rings da bell?" She looks up at me through smudged lenses and smiles broadly. "All da tings for dress-up are over *dere*." Ripley points her little finger toward an area that's visibly bursting with colorful costumes, hats, and props.

"Nah. You and Naomi should dress up and give your mommy and me a fashion show," I say. My eyes drift to Marnie's, and it's obvious she's grateful I've expressly included her in my reply. Again, it's a small thing, but also an olive branch, in context. "But first," I say, interrupting Ripley's and Naomi's squealing delight, "let me clean your glasses, kid. *Ripley*. I don't know how you can see a dang thing through those smudges."

Ripley dutifully hands me her frames, and I clean them on my shirt while she hops from foot to foot and mutters, "Miss Roberts is gonna ring da bell soon."

"Hold your horses," I tease. "You wouldn't even be able to see the costumes without my help." Finally, I return the glasses, and Ripley slides them onto her face and gasps at the sudden clarity of her world.

"It's a beautiful world, right?" I say.

Ripley beams a huge smile at me. "*Beautiful*."

Aw, kid. I can't help returning her massive smile. "Okay, go on now. Find something cool to impress us with."

The girls sprint away with glee, and the minute they're out of earshot, I turn to Marnie. "You told my mother about you and my father last night after drinking a little too much wine, I presume? That's why my mother wanted to post that photo and caption for only him to see?"

Marnie nods, looking sheepish. "I guess I felt the need to unburden my guilty conscience. I've been dying to tell the truth for a very long time now."

"Not to me, though. Only to my mother."

Marnie grimaces. "Sorry." She rubs her forehead and takes a deep breath, but she doesn't say anything more than that.

Fuck. I'm feeling conflicting emotions. Anger. Disgust. And yet, sympathy for the look of remorse on Marnie's face. "Listen, I can understand you not immediately telling me you'd fucked my father that same morning. You were probably in shock and freaking out in that moment. Like you said, your fight or flight instinct took over."

"It did, and I chose *flight*. I went into a fugue state, I think."

"Fair enough. What I think is really shitty of you, though, is that you didn't get word to me later on. You could have easily gotten my number from Selena. But, nope. You chose, instead, to let me twist in the wind and rack my brain for a full year and a half about what happened between us."

"I genuinely didn't think you'd give me another thought. You'd talked a big game the night before about all your casual sexcapades. I figured I was just another notch in your belt."

"Okay, but I'm a human being. How could I not wonder

what the fuck happened? Everything was going great between us mere minutes before you bolted; and then, suddenly, you looked like you wanted to barf and couldn't get out of there fast enough. I thought I'd gravely offended you. I thought I'd done something horrible, and I couldn't figure out what. It's only natural that I'd wonder—and that my inability to come up with a logical explanation would begin to torture me."

"You felt *tortured*?" she asks incredulously. When I nod through my blush, she exhales and says, "Wow, I'm truly sorry about that, Max. I swear I thought you'd never even think about me again after that morning, let alone feel tortured."

"Okay, well, maybe it didn't rise to the level of torture. That's an overstatement. I was baffled. Let's not get it twisted, though. I didn't lose sleep over you or whatever."

Marnie pulls a face. "I feel like you're speaking out of both sides of your mouth. Should I have gotten word to you through Grayson or not? If it wasn't that big a deal to you, then maybe I was right to—"

"It would have been the courteous thing to do. The mature thing. That's all I'm saying."

Marnie's clearly resisting the urge to roll her eyes. But she says, "Fair enough. I'm sorry."

When she looks down, I study her for a moment. "Can you honestly say you never gave *me* another thought after that morning?"

Marnie looks up, her chest heaving. "I've already admitted I've fantasized about you since then. Honestly, you've been my go-to fantasy, every time I'm engaging in a bit of self-love. But I guess that makes sense, since you're the last man I've been with."

My heart lurches. "You haven't seen my father again?"

The question has angered her, obviously. But she manages a fairly calm tone when she replies. "No, I haven't seen, spoken to, or texted with him, Max. He's married. Not to mention, a lying sack of shit."

I run my palm down my face. "The bottom line is you mind-fucked me, Marnie. And I didn't appreciate it. I also don't like the fact that you fucked me at Grayson's party without telling me the truth about all this, and then ran out on me again, without explanation."

"I'm sorry about all of it. I don't know what else to say to you. *I'm sorry*. I was wrong. You deserved better." Marnie takes a deep, calming breath. Clearly, apologies aren't her forte. In fact, it's clear it's paining her to give me such an unequivocal one now. She huffs out, "By the way, please don't get it twisted and think my sexual fantasies about you this past year—or the fact that I haven't been with anyone else since you—mean that I've been pining for you. I haven't been. I decided to hold off on sex until I was ready to look for a serious relationship. You were a good fantasy because sex with you was objectively amazing, and you were my last sexual partner. It's as simple as that."

"I don't believe you."

She scowls. "Which part?"

"Ta da!" the girls shout. They've emerged from Dress-up Corner and are now standing in front of Marnie and me in costumes over their clothes. Marnie's kid is dressed as a doctor, which is easy to surmise based on her white lab coat and plastic stethoscope, while her cute friend is a construction worker, complete with yellow hard hat and a colorful tool belt with plastic tools.

"A carpenter and a doctor," Marnie says, replacing her scowl with a fake smile.

Ripley frowns. "No, Mommy, I'm a vet-ah-noomian, like Auggie. Gigi told me about dat. Dat's a doctor for animals."

"Now, that's a solid career choice," I say. "Animals are always honest with you. What you see is what you get with them, unlike with people."

As I say the word *people*, I glare at Marnie, letting her know, yeah, babe, I'm talking about you.

Marnie returns my glare before smiling at her daughter again. She says, "It's pronounced *veterinarian*, honey."

"Vet-ah . . .?"

"Narian."

The kid tries saying the word several times, and finally gets it. Sort of.

"Why don't you two put on another round of costumes?" I say. "The bell could ring at any minute."

The girls run off again, heading straight for Dress-Up Corner, and the second they're out of earshot, Marnie says, "What don't you believe?"

"That you haven't been pining for me."

She scoffs. "Why on earth would I *pine* for a thirty-year-old, emotionally unavailable man with zero interest in settling down?"

I shrug. "You know full well we connected that night beyond sex. Our conversations weren't the usual pablum. They were deep and interesting. We made a real connection. And ever since, you've been pining for me. Which is why you haven't had sex with anyone else since me."

Marnie snorts. "Sounds like *someone's* been pining. And it wasn't *me.*"

"Babe, I've been the opposite of pining. This whole time, I've been out there living my best life. Winning at the game of life."

"Yeah, you've been winning so much, you just now begged me to pretend to be your fiancée to get yourself a stupid promotion."

Anger vibrates through me, but I manage a calm tone. "The promotion isn't stupid. It's the only pathway I've been able to figure out to achieve my highest career goal. And I didn't *beg.* I asked. And you said no. So, whatever. Fine. I'll figure out another way."

"Good. Clearly, you wouldn't even want me to come now, anyway. So, it's all for the best I said no."

My stomach twists. Is that a true statement? Hearing Marnie say it out loud doesn't ring true, despite what I've learned about her and my father. As a matter of fact, I know in my gut if Marnie did yet another about-face and suddenly told me yes, I'd take her up on the offer. I'm not proud of that fact, but there it is.

My eyes drift to Dress-Up corner, where Marnie's kid and the other one are furiously getting themselves costumed. Suddenly, when Marnie's pint-sized doppelganger realizes I'm watching her, she waves enthusiastically at me and shouts, "*I love you!*"

"Jesus Christ," Marnie mutters. "Please don't let this be a preview of her future dating habits. Please, don't let my daughter grow up and be exactly like me."

"A coward, you mean?"

She glares at me. "A woman who throws herself at a handsome, disinterested, and emotionally unavailable man in a designer suit, only to realize he truly doesn't give a crap about her and never will."

"Would that be my father or me?"

"Both. And others, too. Although I admit you're the best example of my type I've ever run across, other than your age."

"Why are you so fixated on our age gap? Age is just a number."

"Not true. Age is related to timing. And finding the right person is often about timing, even more so than compatibility. In ten years, you'll be looking for a wife. I guarantee it."

I can't dispute her logic, even though I dispute her ultimate conclusion. I ask, "Does that mean you want to become someone's wife?"

"I think so, yes. But only if I met the right man. I'd rather be alone forever than hitch my wagon to anyone who isn't truly perfect for Ripley and me, and vice versa."

I consider that. "Did you want to marry my father?"

She rolls her eyes. "No. I hadn't even told him about Ripley. I was obviously playing a role with him. Pretending to be his version of perfect. I was a mere fantasy for him, and he was an escape from the pain for me. Looking back, I got what I deserved."

My heart pangs. "I wouldn't go that far, Marnie. Nobody deserves to be lied to like that. That's inexcusable."

Marnie looks at me with extreme surprise. "Thank you."

The moment feels meaningful. Like we've taken a massive step toward each other on some invisible path—a path toward redemption, perhaps. Forgiveness, maybe. Maybe even mutual respect.

"Hey, at least I can rest easy in the knowledge I fucked you way better than my father ever did, right?" I say. "Unless, of course, you were lying to me when you said I'm the best you've ever had. Something tells me you're a really good liar, so I wouldn't put it past you." Aw, fuck. Why did I do that? Sometimes, I'm my own worst enemy.

Marnie whips her head toward me, looking positively murderous, and my heart physically stops at the sight of her. She's exceedingly hot when she's laughing and smiling. But she's never hotter than when she's feeling inspired to commit homicide. "Okay, that's enough," she snaps. "I understand you're feeling angry and shocked and weirded out. And I recognize this whole situation feels like it's happening in present day to you, since you're only just now hearing this news. But to me, all of this is very old news. Something I've long since put behind me and moved on from. It was something that happened when I was in a very bad place in my life—a place I've worked hard to move on from. So, while I agree you're entitled to whatever emotions you're feeling, and I'm willing to let you take a few shots at me to release whatever anger you're feeling, I emphatically do *not* agree that your emotions entitle you to emotionally abuse, slut-shame, or otherwise disrespect me. Be angry with me all you want, Max, but let's not cross over into you being every bit as cruel and inhumane as your fucking father, okay?"

Damn. I feel like I've been slapped. But beautifully. Exquisitely. And justifiably. Not to mention, her enraged body language and lit-up facial expression is turning me on like crazy.

I suddenly realize she didn't correct my initial declaration that I was a better lover than my father ever was. And I can't help feeling massively relieved about that.

Suddenly, I'm slammed with another slew of images. The same kinds that hit me earlier in the parking lot. Only this time, it's not my father railing Marnie. It's *me*. I'm the one making her come. I'm the one pulling her hair and making her cry out. All of a sudden, Marnie's riding me with abandon in my bed . . . while my father looks on helplessly from the doorway. In my mind's eye, I flip my father off while Marnie continues fucking me and then smile at the tortured, angry expression my gesture provokes.

"Stop smirking like that and answer me," Marnie commands with a huff.

When I'm jerked back to reality, I realize I've missed something. "What was your question?"

Marnie scowls and says, "Would you rather keep it civil with me or catch an Uber back to your fucking car?"

"Oh. Uh. Yeah. I'll keep it civil."

Marnie exhales. "Thank you. So will I." She tilts her head. "Can I ask you a question? It's not to pick a fight, okay? I'm genuinely wondering about this." When I nod, Marnie says, "Tell me the truth. Really think about your answer."

"Spit it out, Marnie."

She bites her lower lip. "If I'd told you about my history with your father at Grayson's party, before we'd had sex, would you have walked away without fucking me, or would you have fucked me, regardless?"

In a heartbeat, I know my honest answer: I would have fucked her, regardless, to within an inch of her life, exactly the way I did. Maybe even more so, if that's even possible, because a) literally nothing would have stopped me in that moment from fucking this woman again. I was a runaway train of molten lust. And b) I'm quite certain, especially in that white-hot moment of unparalleled, hormonal intoxication, I would have relished the chance to fuck Marnie as a massive "fuck you" to my father. I'm sure I would have felt like I was pissing on the same fire hydrant as him, only doing it second—which all dogs know is the only way to actually mark any given territory.

Frankly, if it weren't for this new complication with Marnie's kid being totally obsessed with me, I'm sure I'd take Marnie back to my place now. I'm a competitive guy, in general, but especially when it comes to my father. I've also never met a woman who turns me on, quite like this one. Wild horses couldn't make me admit any of that to Marnie, though, no matter what honesty she's requested from me. I've only just figured this shit out for myself; I need some time to process it before I speak it into existence, if ever.

I pretend to consider Marnie's question for a long moment, and finally say what I'm quite certain is a bald-faced lie: "If I'd known in advance, I would have turned you down."

Marnie grimaces. "Well, in that case, then I'm a despicable person who owes you a massive apology. I coerced you into having sex with me through fraud, basically. Through lying to you by omission, which means you didn't give me informed consent."

I roll my eyes. "Let's not get carried away here. I genuinely enjoyed having sex with you at Grayson's party. I assure you; I was a very willing participant."

"No, because you didn't know something that would have made you walk away." She looks thoroughly remorseful. "I felt such raw physical attraction to you in that moment, I convinced myself what happened a year and a half ago didn't matter anymore. I convinced myself there was some kind of statute of limitations on what happened with Alexander."

"Well, I mean, it has been quite a while now. He's ancient history, really. He doesn't own you, any more than any of my past sex partners own me. I think you're being a bit too hard on yourself here."

She shakes her head. "No. In addition to everything else, I was selfishly scared to tell you the truth because I thought you'd maybe take that information straight to Alexander's wife. What if she came after me and accused me of being a homewrecker? What if she left a bunch of negative reviews about my business? In the end, my own self-interests were more important to me than your right to know, and that was wrong."

"Don't beat yourself up too hard, okay? And don't feel anxiety about my dad's wife. She was one of my father's many mistresses during his second marriage—and she, unlike you, knew full well my father was married." I shift my weight. "And who knows? Maybe I'm wrong and I wouldn't have cared all that much if you'd told me at Grayson's party. I don't even speak to my father, so maybe the news wouldn't have stopped me in that moment, after all. I was pretty overcome with lust for you, if I'm being honest. In fact, now that I think about it, wild horses couldn't have kept me away from you in that moment."

"You're saying that to be kind."

"No, I'm saying it because it's true. I realize that now. Nothing would have stopped me in that moment, other than you telling me no."

Marnie flashes me a look of brazen lust. A look of pure heat that sends arousal surging inside my veins and tingles skating across my skin and into my dick. Shit. I didn't intend to let her off the hook that easily. My intention was to torture her for as long as possible—to let her stew in her guilt and regret. But when she sounded so genuinely apologetic, instinct took over, I guess, and I felt the urge to protect her. To lessen her suffering.

Something passes between us. We're clearly reaching a truce of some kind here. A nonverbal agreement to lay down our swords. And the effect on my body is indisputable. *I want her.* More than ever. Physically, anyway. Every bit as much as I did in that home gym at Grayson's birthday party. But considering what she's clearly identified as her relationship goals, combined with the fact that I'm currently standing in her daughter's fucking pre-school, it's very clear to me she's off-limits to me now. But not because of her history with my fucking father. On second thought, that's not really as big a deal as it felt, when she first told me about it. No, it's because if I indulge myself in the pleasures of Marnie's body again, things are going to get messy and complicated in ways I'm not ready or willing to take on.

"Ta da!" Ripley shouts. This time, there are *four* little kids standing before Marnie and me—a ladybug, a cow, a clown, and a princess.

Marnie and I compliment the kids' costumes, and as they scurry away for another round, two more kids join their group in Dress-Up Corner, eager to join in the fun.

"Why is everyone so much bigger than Ripley?" I ask. "Is she a brainiac who started preschool way early?"

"No, she's the same age as everyone else," Marnie says. "Ripley was a preemie, so she was itty bitty right from the start. And then, it turned out my tiny preemie had a congenital heart defect that required immediate surgery. And then several more over the next two years."

"Oh, wow."

"Each time Ripley had another surgery, she lost out on some precious growing time. Her doctor says she'll catch up, eventually. But just in case she doesn't, I always tell her, 'The best things come in tiny packages.'"

My heart is squeezing. "Ripley definitely proves that in spades. The kid's a spitfire. Just like her mommy." Marnie's cheeks flush at my compliment. But before she's said anything in reply, I ask, "How's Ripley's ticker doing now? All good?"

"All good, thank God. She's a fighter, that one. A true inspiration."

A giggling group of costumed kids appears before us again. We compliment the kids, as before, and a moment later, the teacher rings a bell and calls the kids to the carpet for story time.

With a squeal of delight, Ripley races to me and grabs my hand. She leads me to a colorful carpet, where, suddenly, I'm swarmed like a sugar cube in an ant colony. The teacher approaches and asks me to kick things off by reading a book to the class.

"I should get to work," I stammer.

"I'll find a short one for you to read," the teacher says.

I look at Ripley's excited, expectant face. "Yeah, okay. Just one, though."

A cheer of triumph erupts from the kids—but nobody is cheering louder than little Ripley.

At the teacher's prompting, the kids sit "criss-cross apple-sauce" on the carpet, while I get myself situated in the world's smallest chair. As I open the book, I shoot Marnie a look that plainly says, "Fuck my life," and she chuckles in return.

After clearing my throat, I begin reading the book handed to me, much to the kids' delight. And much to my surprise, I actually start getting into it about midway through. So much so, I start experimenting with silly voices for the characters. One for the gopher. Another for the fish, and so on. And the kids simply can't get enough. By the time I reach the end of the short book, I feel like a rockstar, based on the kids' cheers and hoots.

Not surprisingly, my audience fervently demands another one. But luckily, the teacher shuts down the mob and thanks me for my valuable time.

"Be good, kids," I say in parting. "Stay in school."

"We can't leave," a random kid deadpans.

Another one adds, "We don't know how to drive."

Laughing, I head to Marnie at the edge of the colorful carpet, and we wave goodbye to Ripley and stride toward the front door together.

"That was quite a performance," Marnie says. "You made their day."

"It was actually pretty fun, once I got going."

As we step outside into the cool morning air together, Marnie says, "Sorry that took so long. I'm sure you're chomping at the bit to get back to your car and into the office."

"Not really," I admit. "When I get back, I'll have to tell my boss the truth about our so-called engagement."

"I'm sorry, Max."

"It's okay. You're protecting your kid. That's admirable."

Marnie opens her mouth like she's going to say something . . . but closes it sharply. *Is she feeling tempted to say yes to family camp?* That's how it feels. Although maybe that's only wishful thinking.

We load into Marnie's car and pull out of the preschool's parking lot. For several minutes, we drive in silence toward her father's house where my car is parked.

"Sorry to bring up my father again," I say after a long silence. "This will be the last time. But would it be okay with you if I don't tell him the truth about our engagement for a few days? He left a voicemail this morning demanding I call him back, and when I do, probably later this morning, I think it'd be fun to let him keep thinking we're engaged for a while. I'll tell him the truth in a few days or so, but I'd like to torture him for a bit first."

"Fine with me. But will he maybe find out the truth from your boss sooner than that?"

"I doubt it. They're acquaintances, but I don't think they're in regular contact."

"What will you say if you talk to your father and he says, 'Hey, son, guess what? I've fucked your fiancée'? Do you think you'll feel tempted to admit the truth to him then?"

I scoff. "My father can't admit that to me without risking me going straight to his wife. I'm the one who outed him with my mother, so why wouldn't I do it again, as far as he's concerned?"

Marnie looks sympathetic. "Your mom told me about that. She said your father wanted you to keep his secret, but you refused." She exhales. "I'm so sorry he put you in that position, Max. Especially as a child."

"It's pretty on-brand for him."

Marnie shakes her head while keeping her eyes on the road. "What a dick." She pauses. "Hey, would you be willing to call me after you speak with your father today? I'd love to know how it went."

"Yeah, sure. I don't have your number, though."

Marnie tells me her number, and I enter it into my phone.

"I just sent you a text," I report, "so you have my number now, too."

"Awesome. Thanks." She shifts her grip on the steering wheel. "When you talk to your father, will you say you already know about my history with him?"

"I don't know. I think I'll feel it out in the moment."

"You could tell him I've already told you everything, and you don't care." She chuckles. "You could also say you're going to rat him out to his wife, if he doesn't tell her first."

"That's what I said to him before I went to my mother and told her about his affairs. He thought I was bluffing that time. He wouldn't make the same mistake again." I snicker. "I'd never actually go to his wife, though. I only went to my mom because I love her so much. When it comes to Ashley, I don't owe her a damned thing." I look out the passenger side window. "The question is what will torture my father the most? Will it torture him to think I don't know anything . . . *yet* . . . but I might find out the truth at any moment and do God knows what with the information?"

Marnie giggles. "That sounds like a winner to me. Will you please call me right after you talk to him? I'm dying to know how it goes."

"Aren't you going to work after dropping me off?"

"My Monday client is never home when I cook for them. I can talk to you while I work."

"Okay, I'll call him on the way to the office and then call you right afterward."

Marnie squeals. "I can't wait to hear about how brilliantly you tortured him."

We reach Marnie's driveway, and she parks her car next to mine. After she turns off the engine, we sit and stare at each other, neither of us moving a muscle. It's like we've both got a thousand things we want to say, but neither of us is willing to go first.

Finally, I unbuckle my seatbelt and say, "Okay, well, I'll call you later—right after I talk to my dad."

"I can't wait."

"Bye, Marnie." With one last lingering look at her, I slide out of the car and walk to mine.

As I open my driver's side door, Marnie shouts my name. My heart crashing, I look over the roof of my car at her, but she shakes her head, exhales, and says, "Never mind. I'll talk to you later, Max. Sorry again. For everything."

16
MAX

I disconnect the call with my father and murmur, "Fuck you, asshole." But cursing him out isn't doing a damn thing to relieve the fury coursing through my veins.

I'm parked in the garage at my office building, feeling physically ill and enraged about the things my father just now said to me to save face. It's not that I believe his lies. It's that my father is willing to say such horrible things about Marnie—the woman he genuinely thinks is his son's fiancée—in order to protect himself from being unmasked as the serial cheater he is.

With a sigh, I scroll to Marnie's number but pause before pressing the button to call her. I promised to call her immediately after speaking with my father, but that was before I knew he'd stoop to such depths. When I told Marnie I'd call, I pictured us laughing at the masterful way I'd tortured my father during my phone call with him; but now that things didn't go as planned, the last thing I want to do is call Marnie and upset her.

As I'm still staring at my phone, waffling on making the call, a text from none other than Marnie lights up my screen.

Did you talk to Darling Daddy yet? Dying to
hear how it went!

Fuck. The woman's not only a mind-fucker—she's also a mind-reader.

With a deep sigh, I push the button to make the call, and Marnie picks up immediately.

"Hello there, Maximillian!" she chirps happily. To my surprise, her tone is jovial. Light as a feather.

"You sound happy."

"I am! Now that I've come clean to you and your mother, I feel like the weight of the world has been lifted off me. I didn't realize how much that secret has been weighing on me, but now that it's out in the open, I've been singing a happy tune all morning while cooking for my client."

"The truth shall set you free."

"Enough about me and *my* happy tune, though. Let's hear about yours. Have you spoken to your dad yet?"

"We just hung up."

Marnie squeals. "Tell me everything without leaving a single detail out. I bet you *really* made him squirm."

My heart is thundering. "Uh, actually, no, I didn't. He came out swinging in a way I hadn't anticipated, and I was too stunned to reply coherently."

"Shit," Marnie whispers. "He figured out our engagement is a hoax?"

"No, he bought my mother's post, hook, line, and sinker. That's why he came out swinging as hard as he did—because he genuinely believes we're engaged, which means he figured you'd already unburdened your soul to me, as one does with the person they're going to marry. Either that, or he figured you'd tell me soon. Either way, he wanted to protect himself, just in case I was thinking about doing the same thing I did when I found out he'd been cheating on my mother."

Her tone is apprehensive now. "What'd he say?"

I swallow hard. "He asked if I knew I was engaged to a sex worker."

"*What the fuck?*" Marnie shouts.

"He said he'd hired your services a few times about four years ago—which, conveniently, is right before he married Ashley—but he had to stop hiring you when you fell desperately in love with him and demanded to become his actual girlfriend."

Marnie mutters something indecipherable under her breath. And then, "Please, tell me you know he's lying his ass off, Max."

"Of course, I do."

"So, according to him, I was some kind of *Fatal Attraction* nut job? An obsessed, scorned sex worker who wouldn't take no for an answer?"

"That about sums it up. He went so far as to warn me you probably targeted me as revenge against him."

"*Excuse me?*"

"He rejected you and pissed you off, so you went after his son to get back at him."

Marnie lets out a scream of primal rage that makes me flinch and reflexively look around the empty parking garage. There's nobody near my car and my windows are rolled up. But my phone is transmitting through my car speakers, and that was quite the shriek.

"Motherfucker!" Marnie shouts, rounding out a long string of curse words. "So, I supposedly had a paid fling with him during the time I was massively pregnant with Ripley—or maybe right around the time I gave birth to her?"

"That's his story."

"Wow, does your dad have a pregnancy kink? Does he get off on fucking women with huge bellies and swollen ankles who can't stop craving cheese-covered pickles, because that's the state I was in when I supposedly banged him for money and then became hopelessly, psychotically obsessed with him." She scoffs. "Or wait, maybe I took his money for sex during the time I was visiting Ripley in the NICU every fucking day and crying my eyes out with worry and panic? Or maybe it was a bit later, when I found out my mother had stage four cancer and I started taking care of her, while trying to stay strong for my father and also caring for an infant? Wow, I'm one talented sex worker, huh? A woman with an astonishing ability to compartmentalize and multi-task!" She finishes her rant with a loud grunt . . . and then, to my horror, she bursts into tears.

"Fuck. I shouldn't have told you what he said."

Marnie sniffles. "Please, tell me you know it's all lies. There's not a shred of truth to any of it."

"Of course, I know that."

"I swear he pursued *me*. He was relentless."

"I don't doubt that for a minute. Who wouldn't pursue you? I certainly did. You're human cocaine."

Marnie sniffles again. "When I finally said yes to a date, he romanced me like crazy and swept me off my feet. It felt like a fairytale. But even then, the minute I found out he was married, I didn't hesitate to break it off, and I haven't seen him or been in contact with him, ever since."

"I know that, Marnie. He's a pathological dickhead. Don't let his lies get to you, okay? He's not worth your tears."

"I'm not only crying for myself. I'm crying for you, too. If he truly believes you're engaged to me, then that means he's willing to obliterate his own son's happiness to keep his infidelities from coming to light. What kind of father is willing to break up his own son's engagement in order to save his own ass?"

"A father named Alexander Vaughn. I found that out the hard way, a long time ago."

"Oh, Max. I'm so sorry."

"It's okay. I've known what he is for a long time."

"But still, having the point emphasized, italicized, and underlined during your conversation today must have been hard."

"It wasn't pleasant."

"My father would throw himself into a volcano to keep me or Ripley from getting a papercut. My mother was the same way. I wish so badly you knew what that kind of love feels like."

"I do. My mother is like that. That's why my brother and I are both so fiercely loyal to her. We'd do anything for her, and vice versa." I watch a colleague of mine walking across the parking lot for a moment before saying, "For what it's worth, I did manage to tell him my beloved fiancée had already told me the truth about her history with him, so at least he thinks our fake relationship is kick-ass and unbreakable."

"Good. Fuck him. Let him think you're my knight in shining armor." She sighs. "So, how'd the call end?"

"He blackmailed me, basically. He said, 'As long as you and your fiancée both keep your mouths shut, then I'll keep mine shut, too.'"

"*He's blackmailing us with a fucking lie?*" Marnie shouts at top volume.

"That was the implication."

"How, though? Who would he tell?"

"My boss, I guess. They're not good friends, but they do know each other. Or maybe he was thinking he'd spread his lies about you online. I don't know what he meant, exactly. All I know is he made it clear he'll do and say anything to keep us from going to Ashley and blowing up his third marriage."

"Why does he even care? If she finds out, wouldn't he simply move on to wife number four?"

"This one negotiated herself a pretty favorable prenup, apparently. He was convinced he'd turned over a new leaf this time. That, finally, he'd found The One."

Marnie is silent for a very long time—so long, in fact, when she finally speaks again, I was just about to say, "Well, I guess I'd better get into the office now." Marnie says, "Is this dude ranch family camp week in Wyoming really as spectacular for kids as you described it to me, or were you exaggerating to get me to say yes to your cockamamie plan?"

My heart jolts. *Is Marnie actually considering doing this batshit crazy thing for me?*

"I told you exactly what my colleague who went last year told me. She could have been exaggerating, but I didn't exaggerate anything she told me."

"There are pony rides and a country fair with rides and a creek where Ripley can mine for gold?"

My heart is thrumming in my ears. "From what I've been told, yes. Shelby said it was a hundred times better than Disneyland, not only for the kids but for the adults, too. She said it was magical. That's the exact word she used." I clamp my lips together and await Marnie's reply, feeling like I'm going to pass out with anticipation—like I'm holding a lottery ticket with five correct numbers, awaiting the announcement of the sixth.

Marnie exhales. "Okay, fuck it. Let's do it. Let's go to family camp and pretend we're engaged and deeply in love. We'll show your dad his threats not only haven't split us apart, they've made us stronger than ever."

"Oh my God, Marnie. Seriously? Thank—"

"But only if certain non-negotiable conditions are met."

My heart is beating in my throat now. "Whatever your conditions, my answer to all of them is yes."

"Not so fast. They're all hard lines in the sand, Max. You can't say yes now, and then not honor them when it counts."

"Marnie, I'm all-in. Whatever you want, I promise I'll deliver without fail."

She clears her throat. "For one thing, we're not going to use language in front of Ripley that makes her think we're actually a couple. Whenever we're in her presence, you're Gigi's son, and that's the reason we know you, and the reason we came to camp. That makes no sense, of course, but Ripley won't realize that."

"Done."

"You won't make any promises to Ripley, implied or explicitly, you don't fully intend to keep. Not even in front of important people in order to perpetuate the lie. Always choose your words carefully in her presence."

"I promise."

"She's already head over heels in love with you, Max. Don't break my baby's heart."

"I won't. I promise."

"Also, no mentioning your father to me, ever again. Not even in jest or to twist the knife about all the stupid mistakes I've made."

"He doesn't exist."

"I'm glad we're at a place where he's become our common enemy, but I feel physically ill even thinking about him. Please, I beg you, don't tease me about him or otherwise torture me with—"

"I won't, Marnie. He's dead to me. What's done is done. The past is over."

"Thank you. I really appreciate that." She takes a deep breath. "Our accommodations at family camp. We'll need a two bedroom, so Ripley and I can sleep in one room together, while you're in the other."

"I think each family gets their own little cabin."

"Actually, we'll need a cabin that's big enough for my father to come, too, and have his own bedroom. Gigi, too, if she can swing it. I liked your idea from before about having more people around Ripley. The more people Ripley is able to hang out with that week, the less attached she'll get to you. Plus, I'm sure we'll need a babysitter, now and again, so we can schmooze and all that; and my father is the only babysitter I trust with Ripley. Well, your mother now, too."

"I'm not saying no, but I think they supply camp counselors to entertain the kids all week, if that means anything to you."

"I won't feel comfortable going without my father, at least, and, hopefully, Gigi, too."

"Okay. Whatever you say. Let's call them now."

"We'll start with my father. I'll patch him in."

My stomach flip-flops as a ringing sound invades our call. My entire body ablaze with anticipation, I whisper, "Come on, Henry. Come through for me, man."

Marnie's father picks up the call and greets Marnie. When Marnie explains she's on a call with me and that we have an important question to ask him and my mother, Henry says he's with my mother now on his end of the line.

"Put the call on speaker phone, Dad," Marnie says, "so Gigi can hear, too."

There's a short pause, followed by Henry saying, "Okay, go ahead. We're both here."

"Hello!" Mom chirps.

Marnie and I say a quick hello to my mother, and then Marnie says, "I'll let Max explain the situation to you both."

I take a deep breath and launch into the whole thing, and Marnie's father and Mom both react with amusement and astonishment. In the end, they both say they'd be more than willing to come, except that Henry's just booked a little getaway for them to nearby wine country for next week.

"Could you change the dates for your getaway?" Marnie asks. "This would really mean a lot to Max. It's a huge opportunity for him."

Butterflies release into my stomach. Marnie didn't have to say that. But it feels amazing that she did.

"Uh, yeah, I'm sure I could," Henry says tentatively. "Is that okay with you, Gigi?"

"Absolutely," Mom says. "I'm always game to help Max with anything, and family camp actually sounds really fun."

After thanking them, I say, "I'll request you two have your own cabin right next to ours. My colleague brought her wife and her wife's parents to camp last year, and I think that was the set-up for them."

Our parents pepper us with a flurry of excited questions,

including asking us for the multi-billionaire's name so they can google the hell out of him, but I interrupt them fairly quickly to say, "We'll talk more later. Marnie and I need to iron out the rest of her conditions now." After we've said our goodbyes and disconnected the call, I ask Marnie, "Okay, what else?"

"You need to promise to move heaven and earth to get me a shit-ton of clients after camp."

"Easy peasy."

"I want to see you *hustling* for me, motherfucker, like your very life depends on it."

"It does. My professional life, anyway. I can't promise results, but I can certainly promise an all-out effort on my part. What else?"

Marnie doesn't hesitate. "Sex. It's off the table for us. I think it'd be too hard for me to play happy family with you by day and then bang you casually at night. I don't want to make myself vulnerable to getting hurt, and I think that's possible if we pretend to be in love while also having casual sex all week."

It's a bummer. A big one, considering we're going to be sleeping under the same roof for a full week. Why not enjoy ourselves after everyone else has gone to sleep? I'm well past the news Marnie told me earlier today about her and my father. She's a forty-year-old, well-traveled woman who's never been married; of course, she's had other dicks inside her besides mine —one of which happens to be attached to a man I know and loathe. I'm certainly no virgin myself and not entirely proud of every hook-up I've ever had. I get what she's saying, though. And I respect it. She knows she's looking for something more than orgasms these days, and, unfortunately, we both know I'm not the right guy to deliver that at this stage of my life.

"Okay, no sex," I say on an exhale, like it's not a big deal to me, even though it honestly pains me to say it. "What else?"

Marnie considers for a moment. "I think that's it."

"Are you sure?"

"I'm sure."

"Then it sounds like we've got ourselves a deal, Red. Hot damn."

Marnie giggles. "Should we meet to come up with some details about our amazing relationship? You know, basic stuff like how we met and how you proposed?"

"Great idea. We should probably learn some mundane things about each other, too. Stuff like how we take our coffee. It needs to be believable we know each other really well."

"Definitely."

"I could come over tonight after work."

"Perfect. I'll feed you. I'm cooking an extra batch to take home."

"I might be there later than dinnertime. I'll probably have to put in some long hours today, now that I'm going to Wyoming next week. My boss said something earlier today about reassigning all my workload to other associates, and I'm guessing I'll need to work late to ensure a smooth hand-off to everyone."

"Arrive whenever you can, and I'll feed you then."

"Awesome. I'm guessing around eight."

"Perfect."

"Thanks so much, Marnie."

"Meh. I'm getting some good stuff out of this, too."

"Yeah, but I'm getting the long end of the stick. This is the opportunity I've been waiting for—my chance to finally make my professional dreams a reality."

"I'm glad I can help. I'll see you tonight."

"See you then. Thank you again. I truly can't thank you enough."

17
MAX

I knock at Marnie's front door. When she opens it, my traitorous body involuntarily jolts at the sight of her. She's wearing pajama bottoms and a thin tank top with no bra underneath, which means I can easily make out the shape of her tits and nipples underneath the flimsy fabric. Which therefore means my brain is suddenly barraging me with a slew of uninvited images and memories, all of them involving me voraciously groping and/or devouring Marnie's naked tits.

I raise my eyes to hers and tell myself to look unimpressed and disinterested. You know, like a guy who's not imagining himself lurching through the doorway, pinning Marnie against the nearest wall, and doing exactly what we did at Grayson's party.

"Hey," I say flatly.

"Hey," Marnie echoes, matching my tone. She widens the door, and I walk past her into the house. As I stride into the living room, I catch the scent of Marnie's shampoo—the same one I buried my nose in the other day while fucking her senseless. And that's all it takes for my brain to supply yet another rapid-fire slide show, this one culminating in memories of Marnie coming with my cock buried deep inside her.

"Ripley is fast asleep," Marnie says softly, closing the gap between us. "Apparently, showing off her shiny new toy at school today tuckered her out."

I look around for any sign of her father. "And your dad?"

"He's staying at your mom's place tonight. He was able to change their reservation at the winery for tomorrow. There are lots of hiking trails over there, so they're getting an early start in the morning."

Damn. Knowing we're alone here tonight, other than Ripley being fast asleep on the other side of the house, makes Marnie's no-sex rule an even bigger bummer. I get why she doesn't want to play with fire when we're sleeping under the same roof for a week, but I'd posit, if asked, it'd be a good thing for us to smash it one last time tonight as a last hurrah—you know, simply to get each other out of our systems.

"Are you hungry?" she asks.

"I am. I was so busy pawning off my workload today, I barely ate a thing."

"You're in for a treat. What I made today is one of my top specialties." Marnie heads toward the kitchen, so I follow behind and try not to ogle her backside as she moves. It's a tall order, though. She's grace in motion. Sensual, even when simply moving from Point A to B.

In the kitchen, I ask if I can help, and Marnie suggests I open a bottle of red.

"I can do that."

I open a bottle, find some glasses, and pour, while Marnie gets to work pulling containers out of the fridge. When she heads to the counter next to the stove, I place a wine goblet next to her with a wink. "Here you go, my darling fiancée."

"Thanks, babe. You're always so good to me."

Chuckling, I take a seat at a small table with my wine and watch Marnie working like the pro she is at the stove. In short order, she places a beautifully presented meal in front of me. "*Bon appetit,* my darling fiancé."

At the sight of the plate before me, I can't remain in character. The food looks and smells too damned good. "This looks incredible," I say. "I didn't expect something so elaborate."

"I'm a professional chef, babe. I don't fuck around."

I laugh. "Clearly not. What is this?"

Marnie tells me a string of words, most of which I don't recognize. But the gist of it is that I'm about to feast on braised short ribs, truffle-infused mashed potatoes, and a medley of roasted vegetables.

Marnie takes a seat next to me at the table and watches with bated breath as I take my first bite. "Oh my god," I mumble as the incredible flavors envelop my taste buds. "This is fucking delicious."

Marnie looks genuinely excited. "I'm so glad you like it."

"No, I love it. It's the best meal I've had in a very long time." I take another bite and savor it, before murmuring, "No wonder I proposed to you."

Marnie giggles. "I hate to tell you but hiring me as a private chef to make this for you would have been a lot cheaper than proposing marriage to me."

I look up from my plate. "Oh, fuck. You need a ring for next week, don't you? A convincing one."

"I'm sure I've got something I can wear."

"No, it has to look the part. I make a lot of money, Marnie. I don't want to look like a cheapskate."

She laughs. "I'll show you what I've got after you eat. If nothing looks impressive enough, we can find a cheap fake online. We've still got plenty of time for it to be express-delivered before our trip."

I take another huge bite and compliment her again.

"Thank you," she says. She's flushed. Glowing. Clearly, feeding people well—and being appreciated for it—is a genuine passion of hers. She asks, "So, should we brainstorm some details of our relationship?"

"Let's do it."

"How and when did we meet?"

I shrug. "Why not say we met at Captain's a year and a half ago? The best lies are always based in truth. They're easier to remember that way."

Marnie flashes me side-eye. "Should I be concerned you've developed tips on how to lie most effectively?"

I chuckle. "I'm a lawyer. People lie all the time in my line of work. Not at my instruction, mind you. That would be unethical. But I suspect I've observed people lying too many times to count, and the best liars tend to keep it tethered to the truth."

Marnie twists her mouth. "Would it be okay if we said we met at a corporate event? We could say you attended, and I was hired to cater it. I'm the worst at networking and selling myself, so this would give me an easy opening to talk about my work."

"Sure thing." I take another bite. "I saw you, lost my shit, and immediately beelined over to you. We got to talking and instantly felt a mutual spark, and we've been inseparable, ever since."

"Perfect. It was instant chemistry, the likes of which neither of us had ever felt before."

"Like getting struck by lightning."

"Exactly."

My heartbeat is thrumming in my ears. My cheeks feel hot. Why does this suddenly feel like a confessional to me? I quickly break eye contact. Grab my wine glass and take a long swig.

We're both silent for a long moment. But finally, Marnie says, "Six months in, I introduced you to Ripley, exactly the way it happened in real life. You came for dinner and then helped me drop her off at preschool the next morning. And that sealed the deal for me. Once I saw how good you were with Ripley, and how much she instantly adored you, I was a goner. No turning back. You owned my heart."

"Cool." I clear my throat. "How long have we been together?"

She shrugs. "A year?"

"I like it. Do we live together?"

"Not officially. We're planning to move in together, officially, after the wedding."

"Such restraint. Am I moving in here?"

"I'd say so. Your place isn't very kid friendly."

"True. Okay. All good stuff." I motion to my plate. "Is this how you greet me whenever I come over after a long day at work?"

"Of course."

"Wow. I'm the lucky bastard whose fiancée feeds him a gourmet meal while looking like a goddamned wet dream? Talk about winning the lottery." What the fuck? *Why'd I say any of that*? Surely, it wasn't necessary to go that far.

Marnie looks down at her wine glass, blushing. "That's good. Definitely say something like that. It's a nice detail. Highly swoon-inducing." She takes a long sip of wine. She's still blushing. "Oh, here's something we'd better nail down. What will you say when people ask you about our age gap?"

I scoff. "Nobody will ask about that."

"Oh, yes, they will."

"You think?"

"One hundred percent. I'm a forty-one-year-old single mother and you're a gorgeous, successful thirty-one-year-old hot-shot attorney who could get literally any naïve twenty-four-year-old you wanted. They might find a clever way to ask you the question. Like maybe they'll ask if you're hoping to try for a kid of your own. But one way or another, someone will absolutely broach the topic."

I shake my head. "I can't imagine it. That'd be so fucking rude."

Marnie snorts. "I'll bet you a hundred bucks it comes up. Maybe they'll make it sound like teasing or ribbing, but *someone* will say it."

"You're on."

We shake on it. And as crazy as it sounds, when our hands touch, I feel a jolt of electricity skating across my skin—and judging by the sudden sparkle in Marnie's blue eyes, I'm guessing she's feeling something similar.

I release Marnie's hand and grab my wine glass. What is it about this woman that lights my fire like nobody else? It's annoying. No, infuriating. I don't *want* to feel helplessly, hopelessly attracted to her, but my body has a mind of its own.

"Practice your reply when someone asks if you want kids of your own," Marnie insists. "If you're not ready with an answer, it'll come across like you're being evasive or defensive. It has to seem like something we've already talked about at length."

I purse my lips, considering my answer. "I don't think we needed to talk about it at length. I saw you across the room and instantly wanted to put my baby inside you."

She laughs. "That's not a thing, Max."

"Oh, I beg to differ. When I finally convinced you I'm serious and in it for the long haul, we've been working diligently on it, ever since. Morning and night. Sometimes, during lunch breaks, too." Her chest rises and falls sharply, so I lean forward with my eyes locked onto hers and my heart pounding. "Oh my god, Marnie Long, how we fuck and fuck and fuck in the name of fun and love *and* possible procreation. The way we fucked after meeting at Captain's? Baby, that was nothing compared to the way we go at it as an engaged couple. We can't get enough of each other. Frankly, I think we've both got an addiction. It's a real problem." I smile. "A fucking awesome problem to have, though."

Sexual heat is coursing between us and ricocheting off the walls of the kitchen. My eyes drift down to Marnie's sensuous mouth, and she subtly drags her teeth across her lower lip.

Marnie shifts in her chair and breaks eye contact. "As much as I've thoroughly enjoyed that response, you can't say all that to someone at family camp."

"If they've got the audacity to ask such a personal question, then they're going to get a no-holds-barred personal response."

"If you're *that* baby crazy, nobody would believe you've settled on spending your most virile years with me. You'd have found yourself a much younger woman. A Fertile Myrtle."

"I don't want a baby with a Fertile Myrtle. I want a baby with *you*. If that's not in the cards, then I don't want one at all." I shrug. "We've got Ripley to raise together. I love her like my own. A baby on top of that would be icing on the cake, but not necessary. All that matters is that I'm with *you*."

Marnie looks like she's having a cardiac event. She grabs her wine and gulps down the rest. "Uh, yeah, I think that answer works." She takes a deep breath and motions to my plate. "Would you like more of anything?"

It's easy to see she's feeling turned on every bit as much as I am. For my part, I'm hard as a rock underneath this table. Is Marnie experiencing the female equivalent?

"I'm good on food," I say, maintaining eye contact. "It was incredible. Thank you."

"Glad you enjoyed it. Would you like a refill on wine?"

The wine bottle is on the counter, unfortunately. Which means someone needs to get up to refill our glasses. I'd normally tell her to stay put—that I'll refill both glasses. But I don't want Marnie seeing the massive bulge in my pants. "Thank you," I say. "Another glass of wine would be great."

Marnie grabs my empty plate and goblet, along with her own glass and practically sprints to the counter. When she gets there, she places the plate in the sink and puts down our glasses, but she doesn't immediately refill them. Instead, she grips the edge of the counter and bows her head. Her body language reminds me of someone who's just gotten off a brutal roller coaster with loop-de-loops and is now trying to chase away a horrific sensation of nausea.

"Are you okay over there?" I ask.

Marnie takes a deep breath. "Why don't you head to the

couch with our wine, and I'll clean up and meet you there. We'll look at my collection of rings, and if I don't already have something acceptable to you, we'll look for a cheap fake online."

18

MAX

By the time Marnie joins me on the couch in the living room, my hard-on has subsided, and I feel like I'm back in control of myself. She takes a seat next to me and opens a little box, which turns out to be a jewelry box filled with rings.

"Now, let's see," Marnie says, shifting the contents around. "Ah. How about this one?" She holds up her selection, and it's immediately clear to me we're not on the same page here. It's a woefully, thoroughly insufficient candidate for our purposes.

"I'd be embarrassed to propose to you with that," I say bluntly. "That's not even a diamond. What is that?"

"A garnet." When I scoff, Marnie adds, "There's no rule that says an engagement ring has to feature a diamond. Princess Diana had a sapphire engagement ring."

"Yeah, and it was probably worth millions. That ring looks like it's worth twenty bucks."

Marnie looks pained. "It was a gift from my father to my mother when they were really young. A promise ring, basically. That's her birthstone."

I feel my cheeks color. "Sorry. It's very pretty. Just not for our purposes."

After glaring at me, Marnie returns to her box and sifts its contents around again. She shows me a few more pathetic options, and I quickly nix them all.

"You're supposedly the great love of my life," I say. "The ring has to reflect that. I'd be an asshole to propose with any of those rings on my budget."

"Okay, well, what's your budget? Let's start there."

"I have no idea because I don't know what impressive engagement rings cost. All I know is my budget is astronomically more than whatever it'd cost to buy any of those rings."

Marnie grabs her nearby laptop and returns to the couch, and then proceeds to navigate to a high-end jewelry website—one featuring real diamond rings with astonishing price tags. "We'll get an idea of what real diamond rings cost, so we know what ring you'd actually buy in this situation, and then we'll find a fake that looks a lot like it."

"You're a genius." I peek over Marnie's shoulder at her computer screen. "Whatever fake we get, it has to look convincing. I'm sure some of the people at camp will know their diamonds."

"No worries. We'll get a ring that makes you look like a romantic baller who spared no expense to sweep your woman off her feet."

"Well, let's not go *too* far. I don't want to look like I went into bankruptcy to buy the ring. I don't want to look like a cheapskate, but I also don't want to look like a fool who doesn't know how to manage his money, either."

"Well, lucky you, there's plenty to choose from in lots of different price ranges." She stops scrolling and points. "How about this one? It's spectacular."

"Jesus Christ. Who spends that kind of money on a rock with zero functionality?"

Marnie snorts. "Says the guy with a top-of-the-line Ferrari."

"It's not merely a Ferrari, first of all. It's a Portofino M. Give the car its due. And second of all, you've only proved my point. A car is functional, unlike a diamond ring."

"A VW would serve the same function, and yet you were willing to spend some outlandish amount on a Ferrari—"

"Portofino M."

"Because you wanted to get from Point A to B in style. Because you wanted the world to see you in that car and think, 'Damn, he's *someone.*'" She shrugs. "It's the same thing with an engagement ring. Every time your fiancée looks down at the ring you got her, she's reminded how much you love her. She feels like she's living in a fairytale. You could buy a twenty-dollar silver band for the great love of your life, but you'd never do that because you're a man who drives a Portofino M, which means you understand exactly how a material possession can make a person feel *special.*"

"That's highly persuasive logic, counselor."

Marnie laughs. "Why don't we do it this way: whatever you spent on your Ferrari—sorry, your Portofino M—is your budget for Fake Marnie's engagement ring."

I grimace. "Yeesh. That's a lot of money. But I guess, if I loved you as much as I love that car, then I'd buy you a Ferrari for your finger."

Marnie rolls her eyes. "Well, I'd hope you love me *more* than a fucking car, if you want to spend the rest of your life with me. But okay, it's progress. How much was your fancy car?"

I tell Marnie the number and she practically does a spit-take with her wine, which then makes us both dissolve into cackling, wheezing, hysterical laughter. After a bit, however, we manage to pull ourselves together and return to the task at hand. "Damn, Max," Marnie murmurs after she's resumed scrolling through the jewelry website. "With your budget, I'm sure Fake Marnie wet the crotch of her G-string when she saw your engagement ring."

My body jolts at the imagery her comment provokes inside my head: Marnie wearing nothing but a G-string, looking aroused and tousled and eager to get fucked. Tingles shoot into my dick. My heart rate quickens. Is she *trying* to turn me on, or is she simply clueless about the effect she has on me?

Marnie points out an outrageously expensive ring. "Oh, can we pretend to get this one, Boo? I know it's a tad out of your budget, but it's my favorite, by far. *Pretty please, Boo*?"

I laugh. "Anything for you, Boo."

She squeals like I've actually agreed to buy the ring for her. "Thank you, Boo. You're the best fake fiancé, *ever*." With a cute little giggle, she navigates to a new website, this one featuring costume jewelry, and starts searching for a lookalike of the real one she's fallen madly in love with.

"Yikes," Marnie says after some scrolling. "I had no idea high-quality costume jewelry was this expensive. A fake copycat of the one we picked out is eight thousand bucks."

"That works for me," I say without hesitation. "Let's get it."

Marnie's jaw drops. "Absolutely not. I'm sure we can find something on another website for less than a thousand."

"But that one looks *exactly* like the ring you wanted. I literally can't tell the difference. I'm sure a much cheaper knockoff will look fake, and then we'll run the risk of someone at camp figuring us out."

Marnie shakes her head. "I can't let you spend eight thousand bucks on a fake diamond ring for me, Max."

"What if Wayne Walters is an expert in diamonds? I'm sure he's bought his wife several big, fat diamonds over the years. They're famously in love."

"It's too much."

"It's my money, Marnie. And my con. I'll decide the budget for the fake ring, okay?" I chuckle. "Not gonna lie, I'm also motivated by the thought of my father seeing that ring in photos and shitting his pants. I'd gladly pay eight grand to piss him off."

Marnie furrows her brow. "You're planning to post photos from camp?"

"No, but I'll text photos to Auggie, and he'll pass them along for me. He's not close to our father, but he stays in touch."

Marnie looks excited. "Okay, thank you. But only if you're one hundred percent sure you don't mind spending that much on a fake ring."

I wink. "I'm sure, Boo." I hand her my credit card, and she makes the purchase and thanks me again. As she hands the card back to me, I suddenly realize we're semi-entangled on the couch and my palm is resting comfortably on her thigh. How long has my hand been there? I jolt and yank my palm off Marnie's leg, muttering my apologies, which then causes Marnie to jolt and scramble to disentangle her legs from mine.

"Don't apologize," Marnie says. "It was my fault. I don't know how I got tangled up with you like that."

"We scooted close to be able to look at your screen together," I stammer. Even as I'm saying it, my eyes drift to Marnie's lips again. I've never wanted to kiss someone this badly in my life. Not even back in middle and high school when I got a hard-on with every breeze. Not even with Skylar in college, when I stupidly thought I'd found the great love of my life. I remember I couldn't wait to get back from whatever away-game to see Skylar again and kiss every inch of her. I felt addicted to that girl's lips, I remember. It felt like kissing her gave me life. And yet, looking back, that addiction pales in comparison to the one I feel whenever I think about Marnie. Physically, anyway, the craving I feel for her lips, body, and touch, blows everything else out of the water.

Marnie's eyes briefly flicker to my mouth and her cheeks catch fire. Am I crazy, or is she dying to kiss me, every bit as much as I'm dying to kiss her? When her eyes return to mine, I don't break contact. *Do it,* I think. *Fuck your no-sex rule, baby. Let your pulsing clit be your guide.*

Holy shit. I think Marnie is leaning toward me, ever so slowly, like she's going to kiss me. Holy fuck, she is—so I lean in, too. But just before our lips meet, Marnie's phone rings and she jerks back to answer it.

"Hey, Dad," she blurts, her face aglow and her features tight.

"Oh, thanks for doing that. No, she's got enough pills to last her. Thank you for double checking, though. Okay, have fun. I love you, too." She disconnects the call. "My father picked up a refill of Ripley's heart medication today and forgot to drop it off before heading to your mother's house for the night. He wanted to know if he should drop the bottle off in the morning before heading off to wine country." She's coming across as fidgety and adrenaline-fueled. Flustered as hell.

"Your father seems like a great guy," I say, feeling pretty flustered myself.

"He is. He's been my rock when it comes to Ripley. Both in terms of babysitting and helping me out with expenses. I don't know what I'd do without him. If left to my own devices, I couldn't afford her expensive medicine *and* the tuition for her amazing preschool. I'd have to pick her medicine, obviously; and even then, I'm not sure if I'd be able to cover it every month."

I ask how much the medicine costs, and when Marnie tells me, I'm outraged. "Nobody should have to pay that much for lifesaving medicine, especially for a child."

Marnie agrees and says, "Unfortunately, I'm too old to be on my father's medical insurance as a dependent. The only health insurance I can afford barely contributes to prescriptions. It's more like a safety net in case something catastrophic happens."

I shake my head, feeling disgusted. "What about the preschool? How much is tuition there?"

Marnie tells me the number, and I whistle. "Fucking hell. It's *pre-school.*"

"Yeah, but they're specialists. In the year Ripley's been going there, she's blossomed into the chatterbox you see now. She was practically nonverbal when she started a year ago. She's got some learning disabilities."

"She does? Oh. Wow."

"My dad is the one who found the place. And now that he's seen her results, he's every bit as sold as me. I know Ripley talks a lot; but I'm thrilled about that. Every time she chatters on, I remember where she was when she started school, and I want to cry with relief and joy."

"I . . . I had no idea."

Marnie smiles. "Don't worry about Ripley. She's doing great, thanks to my father. He not only helps me with all of her expenses, he also won't let me pay him rent. Thanks to him, I've been able to start a college fund for Ripley. My father plans to leave this house to me, so that's a huge help, but since my mother's illness wiped out a lot of Dad's savings, I'll definitely need to have some funds tucked away for Ripley's education. Also, her medications, if she still needs them as an adult, which I'm told will be the case."

I feel dizzy. Like I've been punched in the stomach. I had no idea little Ripley was such a fucking warrior—or that Marnie has had quite this much on her plate. No wonder she fell prey to my father. For so many reasons, Marnie was vulnerable as fuck—and Alexander Vaughn is a master manipulator.

"Please, don't worry about us," Marnie says. Clearly, she's reacting to my facial expression, whatever it is. "Ripley's doing great, and so am I. Work is starting to pick up for me, thanks to a great referral from Victoria. My plan is to impress my fancy new client so much, they can't resist referring me to all their wealthy friends."

The pit in my stomach is overwhelming me. "Can I ask a sincere question? Why do you think you haven't been more successful with your business? Given how good you are at the cooking end of things, I can only assume you've struggled because you're not so good at the business side of things—marketing, operations, networking."

"Correct. I'm honestly horrifically bad at that all stuff." She chuckles. "I'm an artsy-fartsy type. A creative soul. I love concocting new recipes and feeding people's souls, but the business stuff gives me hives. In my defense, being a single mom means I have to drop everything when Ripley gets sick. I've definitely lost a few clients that way."

I bite the inside of my check. My head is spinning. My heart panging. "I tell you what. I'll do some research into your industry and come up with a solid business plan for you. A step-by-step guide of what you should do to finally get your business off and running."

Marnie clutches her heart. "Oh my gosh, Max, thank you. My father has tried to help me, but he's an engineer, not an entrepreneur."

"This is something I do for a living. I help start-ups on a regular basis. Give me a couple days, and I'll figure out a game plan for you."

She throws her arms around my neck and kisses my cheek. "Thank you so, so much."

I can't handle her proximity. Her lips on my flesh. She smells too fucking good. My tongue is suddenly remembering how good she tastes. My cock is remembering how amazing she feels. I jolt up from the couch and cover my rising hard-on with my hands. "Thanks for the meal. It's been a long day. I'm gonna head out."

"Oh. Okay." She blushes and rises alongside me. "Do you need to work another long day tomorrow?"

I'm walking toward the door now, and Marnie is following. "No," I say, keeping my hands in front of me. "I successfully pawned off all my workload today in anticipation of camp next week and the mountain of work I'll hopefully get from Wayne Walters when we get back. For the first time since before law school, I'll wake up tomorrow with absolutely nothing stressful on my plate."

"How lovely."

I stop at the front door and pivot slightly, still keeping my hands in front of my crotch. "What about you? Are you working tomorrow?"

She nods. "I'm working for my big new client tomorrow while Ripley's at school."

"Awesome. Go get 'em, Boo."

She giggles. "Thanks, Boo."

"Thanks for agreeing to do this for me."

"No need to thank me. Like I said, I'm getting a lot out of it, too. Thanks for the amazing fake engagement ring and the offer to help me with my business. I'm ecstatic about both."

"You're very welcome. When do you want to talk about whatever business plan I've come up with? I'll spend at least part of tomorrow doing research, so I'll probably have some solid ideas for you by Wednesday afternoon."

"Awesome. I've got a client that morning while Ripley is in school, but I'm open after that. Would you like to come over? I'll feed you again."

"It's a date. I mean, an appointment. A plan." My eyes drift to her lips again, despite my best efforts to maintain eye contact. "Goodnight, Marnie."

"Goodnight, Max," she says. Her chest heaves. It's the only visible tell she might be feeling a surge of feral attraction, the same way I am. She smiles. "See you Wednesday."

"See you then."

I practically rip the front door off its hinges opening it, stride to my car in the driveway, and race back to my place. The second I'm home, I beeline to my bedroom, grab some tissue and lotion, and jerk one off to images of Marnie Long enthusiastically riding my cock.

19
MAX

"I swear, she's a drug," I lament to my brother. "The woman is human cocaine."

It's one o'clock on Tuesday, and I'm sitting next to my dork of a brother on a bench in a park-like setting in the middle of U Dub's beautiful campus. When I woke up this morning with nothing to do except some research for Marnie at some point, I called my buddy, Grayson, to see if he wanted to grab breakfast or lunch. When it turned out Grayson is out of the country with Selena, I called my brother and convinced him to ditch his morning class and meet me on campus for some hoops. We wound up playing two good games for about an hour before grabbing a couple Gatorades and this courtside bench.

"Well, I've never done cocaine, unlike you," Auggie says. "But I get the gist of your meaning. She's addictive and makes you act like a fucking idiot."

I exhale. "Do I *want* to feel addicted to her? Fuck no." I lean back on the bench. "What sane person *wants* to get a boner simply from looking at someone? I'm not a middle schooler."

"I think you should enjoy someone getting under your skin the way Marnie has," Auggie says. "It's a relief to know you're capable of feeling tormented by your attraction to someone again."

Again. He's referring to Skylar, obviously. Which pisses me off. Why bring her up?

"It's not enjoyable when that someone has dated your father," I snap. "Or when that someone has a four-year-old who's decided, for reasons unknown, she wants *you* to become her new best friend."

"I think Ripley's aiming a bit higher than her new best friend, brother." When I look at Auggie blankly, he says, "I think that little cutie is hoping to make you her new *daddy*." When I grimace like my brother has shoved a pile of dog shit under my nose, Auggie laughs and says, "Don't be so dramatic. You've dated MILFs before."

"I've never met their kids, though. And I've certainly never had a MILF's kid glom onto me the way Ripley has. She literally screamed 'I love you!' at me yesterday when I helped drop her off at school."

"Aw. She's so sweet."

"Why me, though? You were way nicer to her at the gallery, and Mom's the one who took her to the fucking zoo."

"To be honest, the way she only had eyes for you at the gallery kind of pissed me off. Children and animals usually love me."

"She takes after her shit show of a mommy. She likes bad boys."

Auggie scoffs. "You're not a bad boy. You're a grumpy workaholic with a high sex drive and commitment issues. But you've got a heart of gold."

I roll my eyes and take a swig from my Gatorade. "I'm not a workaholic."

"Of all the things I said about you, that's the one you're taking issue with?"

"I'm just saying I'm not innately *this* hardworking. I like to relax and have fun, but I set a goal for myself, so I'm doing whatever it takes to achieve it. Once I do that, I'll look around and smell the roses a lot more, I assure you."

"What's the point in living like that? Tomorrow isn't guaranteed, Max. Life is about the journey, not the destination."

"Mom? Is that you?"

He laughs.

"It's too late to give me that advice," I say. "I'm way too close to finally achieving my goal to even think about taking my foot off the gas now. It's full speed ahead, motherfucker. No one can stop me."

Auggie sips his Gatorade. "Just, please, promise you won't reach your goal and immediately set another one that requires you to continue working this hard. Please, stop and smell the roses at that point. Get yourself an actual life."

"I have a life. A good one."

My brother looks at me like I'm crazy. "If you say so."

"I do. So, shut the fuck up."

We watch the game in progress on the basketball court for a while. Finally, Auggie says, "I don't think it's a big deal Marnie has dated Dad, by the way. I mean, if you wanted to give it a go with her, that shouldn't stop you."

I don't disagree with him. After taking some time to process, I've come to the same conclusion. But since I'm quite certain I don't have room in my life to "give it a go" with Marnie, not in any serious sense, it's a moot point.

When I say nothing, Auggie adds, "Widows marry their dead husband's brother or best friend all the time. And it's not like Dad and Marnie were ever serious. Plus, you're not even close to Dad. I just don't think it'd be a major hurdle if you genuinely wanted to pursue her."

"I don't. I want to fuck her. Endlessly. That's what I've been trying to explain to you. I'm not sitting here weighing whether or not I want to give a serious relationship with Marnie a whirl; I'm sitting here lamenting the fact that she doesn't want something casual, which means fucking her isn't going to happen, which means my addiction isn't going to be fed. Don't get it twisted and assume I'm feeling something I'm not."

Auggie scoffs. "There are infinite women in the world to have sex with. At least, for you. If sex is really all you want, then go have sex with someone else and imagine she's Marnie. Problem solved."

I glare at my brother, poised to tell him he's an idiot, and the smirk on my brother's face tells me he knows his comment is ludicrous. Clearly, he only said it to get a rise out of me. To make *me* realize his comment is ludicrous.

Auggie grins at whatever he's seeing on my face. "Face it, Maximillian. The truth is you're catching feelings for this woman. Real feelings. Something a lot more than simple lust. That's why you're feeling so fucking tortured—because you genuinely *care* about her, and that's not according to plan."

"Fuck off. I barely know her. If there's one thing I'm clear about, it's that I don't have the bandwidth to seriously date anyone, especially not a single mother. I haven't had the time or energy for a serious relationship since I started law school."

Auggie frowns. "You haven't dated anyone seriously since Skylar?"

There he goes again. Why does he insist on bringing her up?

Luckily, my phone rings, saving me from needing to respond to my brother's annoying question. When I look down, it's Marnie's name on my screen.

"Marnie's ears must be ringing," I mumble before pressing the button to connect the call. "Hi, Boo. What's up?"

Marnie's labored breathing instantly tells me something's wrong. "I'm so sorry to bother you," she says. She explains she's in a pickle and panicking. She's been working hard for hours at her new client's house to complete all the prep work for a five-course meal for ten for a surprise birthday party the client is throwing for her husband tonight, which their maid is all lined up to serve in alignment with Marnie's meticulous instructions. But when Marnie was all finished with her work, she went to the bathroom before cleaning up, and that's when the family's two massive dogs barreled into the kitchen after a walk with their dog walker and proceeded to decimate the five sheet pans cooling on the countertops. "I have to run to the store for all new ingredients now," Marnie says. "And then come back and start all over. I don't know if I'll be able to get it all done again before the start of the party. I might have to stay and continue cooking the main course as the first ones come out."

"It's gonna be okay, sweetheart. I can come over there and help you. I'll be your *sous* chef. I'll slice and dice and we'll get it done in time. I've got you, Boo." I suddenly remember my brother sitting next to me on the bench. When I glance at him, it's clear he's noticed me using endearments for Marnie. And of course, he's assigning actual meaning to them since he doesn't know that's how Fake Max talks to his beloved fiancée.

"Actually, what I really need is for someone to pick up Ripley from school and watch her till I can get home," Marnie says. "She's never once stayed at school past three, and even that's a long day for her."

Fuck me. I didn't see that one coming.

"I'm so sorry to ask," Marnie says, filling the awkward silence. "But there's nobody else who can do it. My dad is out of town with your mom. Selena is in Costa Rica with Grayson. Lucy is in Portland on a work trip. I've already tried the mother of Ripley's best friend at school, but she can't do it today, due to a family funeral."

I take a deep breath. "Of course, I'll do it. Anything to help."

She exhales in relief. "Are you sure? I haven't called Victoria yet, since she's always so busy running her empire. But if this is too much to ask of you, then—"

"No, no. Don't call Victoria. She's working today, and I'm not. I've got you, Boo."

"Thank you so much from the bottom of my heart. I'll cook dinners for you for a month after we get back from Wyoming—

and you won't even need to see me. I'll drop the food off in a cooler on your doorstep every afternoon."

"I'm the one who owes you for agreeing to be my fake fiancée. Consider this part of my paltry attempt to pay you back."

"You paid your debt to me with an eight-thousand-dollar ring. At this point, I'm the one who owes you."

"I still owe you, and that's final." I look at my brother. He's smirking. "Now, tell me everything I need to know, so I don't mess this up."

Marnie takes a deep breath. "Pick her up by three, please. I'll email the school the form that gives you permission to get her. When you get home, make her macaroni and cheese. The box kind. Do you know how to make that?"

"I think I can handle it."

"And an apple, sliced up. She can have a cookie after her meal. But only one. They're big, and she's little."

"Got it."

"They have extra car seats at school for emergencies like this," Marnie says, "so you'll need to borrow one of theirs. Oh, fuck. There's no back seat in your stupid Ferrari, is there?"

"I'm sitting here with my brother, so I'll switch cars with him, and I'll be good to go. He's got an SUV. A perfect kid-mobile."

Auggie's eyebrows hike up. My brother has begged to borrow my beloved Portofino M several times to impress a date, and I've always said no. The most I've let him do is take over driving a leg when we drove to Vegas for a weekend. But even then, I was sitting right next to him, which is a very different thing than me swapping cars with him for who knows how long.

"Oh, that's great. Thank Auggie for me, please. I should be home in time for Ripley's bedtime, but if not, she goes to bed at seven-thirty. Lights out at seven forty-five, so she's asleep by eight."

Jesus Christ. How long am I going to be alone with the kid with nowhere to run or hide?

"Don't worry," Marnie says. "Ripley will tell you what to do for her bedtime routine if it comes to that. Don't worry about bath time, though. I'll bathe her in the morning."

"I've got this. Don't worry about a thing."

"Thank you so much. I'll bring you an amazing meal tonight as thanks."

"I'll look forward to that."

We say our goodbyes, and when the call is over, I plop my phone onto my lap, turn to my brother, and say, "Fuck my life."

Auggie chuckles. "I take back everything I said before. You're obviously not catching feelings for Marnie. *Clearly.*"

I roll my eyes. "Fuck you. She's my fake fiancée who's in a bind. Of course, I'm gonna help her out."

"By doing something you'd never normally do. Not for anyone. Not for all the money in the world."

"What I'm getting in exchange is even better than money. I've got my eye on the prize, son."

"Mmm hmm. Sure, Maxy-pad."

I look at my watch and motion to the basketball sitting on the bench next to my brother. "Grab your ball. We've got time to play one more game before I have to pick up my fake kid and try my damnedest to look fascinated when she tells me, again, all the reasons why *purpole* is her favorite color."

20

MARNIE

It's almost seven in the evening as I park my SUV alongside the one already sitting in Dad's driveway—the kid-friendly SUV Max kindly borrowed from his brother, so he could help me out of a stressful jam today. When Max shocked me by saying *yes* during that frantic call—and in a soothing tone that felt like a balm for my frazzled soul—I wanted to leap through the phone line and bear-hug him. Kiss him. And then feed him the best meal of his damned life and suck his dick for dessert, our "no-sex" agreement be damned. Or rather, *my* "no-sex" rule be damned. Why'd I insist on that again?

I check my reflection in the mirror in the pull-down sun visor, and scowl at my image. I look worn out. Which I am. But why do I care about that since I'm not even remotely interested in trying to impress or seduce Max after walking into the house? *Come on, Marnie. Pull yourself together. Let your smart brain, rather than your horny body, lead the way for once.*

With a determined sigh to keep my physical attraction to Max at bay, I get out of my car, intending to head straight to my trunk. I get distracted, however, when I peek into the backseat of Max's borrowed SUV and glimpse the school's emergency car seat strapped into it. Now, that's a sight I never thought I'd see when I met Mr. Smooth Playboy in an Armani suit at Captain's. *Ha*. I wish so badly I could have been a fly on the wall when Max picked Ripley up. I'm sure she nearly broke all the windows in the classroom with her shriek of pure ecstasy.

Ripley sounded like her brain was physically exploding with joy when Miss Roberts put her on the phone for me today, so I could tell her that Max would be picking her up and, yes, it's okay to go with him. But hearing that from me and actually seeing her crush waltzing through the front door are two different things. I can only imagine her ecstatic reaction when she first laid eyes on him.

I also wish I could have overheard the conversation between the pair during the drive home. Conversation probably isn't the right word, actually. Surely, my chatty, gleeful, excited baby girl unilaterally talked Max's ear off the entire drive, as she's prone to doing whenever she's over the moon about something. Did she ever calm down and let Max get a word in edgewise? For Max's sake, I hope so. Ripley is lovely to converse with when she calms down. I hope so badly Max eventually saw that relaxed version of her today. If not, hopefully, he'll get that chance during our week together in Wyoming.

Why do you care if Max gets to know the real Ripley, Marnie, since you're never going to see Max again after camp, except maybe at family events if Dad continues seeing Gigi? Now, knock it off and stop secretly hoping Max is feeling the same butterflies you started feeling around him last night.

Good talk.

My brain is absolutely right. I need to stop this shit right now.

I grab the extra food I made today out of my trunk and head into the house. Once inside, I immediately make out the faint sounds of Ripley's happy, excited voice wafting from the living room. She's talking nonstop, without stopping to breathe. Which means she's *especially* enthusiastic about something.

I creep toward the living room without making a sound. And

the minute I reach a spot where I can see what's going on unde-tected, my heart feels like it's exploding in my chest. Ripley is holding Max hostage in a chair while painstakingly beautifying him from head to toe. She's already applied loads of colorful makeup to Max's handsome, chiseled face—and not well, I might add. The poor man looks more like the clown from *It* than a beauty queen.

On his head, Max is wearing the plastic princess tiara Ripley picked out with glee during our recent trip to Disneyland. There's also an enormous amount of glitter in his short blonde hair, some of which has drifted down to his neck and the T-shirt covering his broad shoulders.

But that's not all. Max's fit torso is decorated in reams of zigzagging toilet paper. He's Ripley's Christmas tree and the toilet paper a string of lights or garlands. She's also wrapped Max's feet in fluffy towels for some reason. Did she give him a foot massage and pedicure, the same way I always do for her during our Mommy and Me Spa Days in my bathroom, and then wrap his feet in hot towels? If so, I sure hope the carpet under-neath those towels isn't soaking wet. When I do it, I always do it over a tile surface.

Last but not least, Ripley's holding Max's hand while care-fully painting his fingernails with a bottle of polish Max is holding for her in his free hand. Ripley knows full well she's not allowed to touch Mommy's nail polish without explicit permis-sion and supervision. And yet, I don't have the heart to feel anything but amusement about her rule breaking. Surely, she's been so drunk on dopamine since the minute Max waltzed into her preschool classroom this afternoon, she's utterly intoxicated at this point. Incapable of remembering rules even exist, let alone the specific one pertaining to Mommy's nail polish.

"Oh, you're going to have so much fun at da ball, Cinderel-la!" Ripley bellows in her little chirp of a voice.

"I can't wait," Max deadpans in his normal, deep voice.

Oh my god. Ripley's convinced Max to play princesses with

her, on top of convincing him to receive her head-to-toe makeover? Wonders never cease.

Ripley lets out a little giggle. "Dat's not how Cinderella talks, Maxy-Milly! Like dis!" She raises her voice a full octave, turning her little squeak of a voice into something only barely audible to the human ear. "Ooooh, Fairy Godmother!" she gushes, demonstrating how he's supposed to talk like a princess. "I can't wait to be so pretty and smart and funny and such a good dancer at da ball!"

A laugh threatens, so I slap my palm over my mouth to keep it from coming out and exposing my hiding place. Ever since Ripley was a toddler, I've infused little bits of feminism, as needed, into every princess book. When the prince falls in love in my version of a fairytale, he does so not only because the princess is physically beautiful, but also because of her brains, heart, and talents, too. Also, if the princess needs saving, then, somehow, by God, I figure out a way for her to save herself, rather than waiting around for the prince to do it for her. If I can't figure that plot twist out, then I come up with a way for the princess to at least save the prince in return. Hearing Ripley now, it's clear she's absorbed the lessons I've been teaching her through osmosis, and I couldn't be more thrilled to get confirmation of that fact.

"Now, you do it," Ripley commands.

Max frowns and pauses, so I'm fully expecting him to turn her down. But, once again, the man surprises me. After taking a moment to get into the right headspace, I guess, he delivers exactly the voice Ripley's demanded of him in the most heart-melting, ovary-melting way imaginable.

As Ripley squeals and applauds in response to Max's high-pitched imitation of her, I let out a deep and highly involuntary sigh of arousal. And that's it. I've given myself away.

"Mommy!" Ripley shouts happily when she notices me. "Look at how pretty I made Maxy!"

I force a smile and stride into the living room. "Yes, I see. He's very pretty, indeed."

"And smart."

"Yes, very, very smart. And kind and generous, too." I smile at Max. "Thank you again for picking her up. You're a life saver."

"I was happy to help."

"Yeah, you look really happy."

We share an amused chuckle that acknowledges Max's present misery.

I point to the bottle of nail polish in Max's hand and address my daughter. "Is that Mommy's nail polish?"

Ripley's face turns pale. "Oh. I forgot." Her little chest heaves. "Am I in trouble?"

I don't know where she got that verbiage. I've never once told Ripley she's in trouble or even that I'm mad at her. "No, you're not in trouble," I say. "You made a mistake. We all make them. But rules are there for good reasons, honey. You're not allowed to use my nail polish because you could spill it and make a mess on the carpet or furniture that won't ever come out."

"Maxy won't spill it, doe."

"He could. We all make mistakes. Even Maxy. Also, you need to respect other people's things and always ask permission before using them. That's what you'd want other people to do before using your things, right?"

Ripley nods and looks like she's holding back big, soggy tears. "I'm sorry, Mommy. I didn't forget. I wanted to make Max extra pretty, so I broke da rule." She bursts into tears.

I glance at Max and we share another smile. The kid would give up the nuclear codes if her interrogator said so much as, "It's not nice to withhold nuclear codes, Ripley."

"Well, I appreciate your honesty," I say, trying not to chuckle. I take the bottle from Max and reunite it with its applicator cap, and then sit on the couch and take my bawling daughter into my arms. "It's okay, love," I whisper while stroking her hair. "I did something naughty once, too, simply because I couldn't resist." I furtively glance at Max. "I get it. It's hard to resist temptation sometimes. But next time, remember how you're feeling right now, so you stop yourself from doing it again."

"I will, Mommy. I promise."

"I know you will, sweets. You're a very good girl."

I glance over Ripley's little head at Max again and the look on his face sends butterflies whooshing into my belly. He looks like he's feeling deeply moved over there. But maybe I'm wrong and he's simply relieved I'm finally here.

"Are those towels wet?" I ask, pointing to Max's feet.

"No," Ripley says sadly. "I wanted to wet dem, like you always do it, but Maxy said dat would be bad for da carpet, so we only pretended."

"Max made the right call," I say. "Thanks, Maxy. Excellent work."

"I didn't think twice about the nail polish, though."

"Bah. You did great. Are you hungry? I brought food."

"Awesome," Max says. "Thanks." He motions to his face and hair and hand—the makeup, nail polish, and glitter my daughter so lovingly applied. "Can I shower this stuff off?"

"Of course. Why don't you wash up in Dad's bathroom, while I get Ripley bathed and into bed? Feel free to borrow a T-shirt from my father's dresser while we throw that T-shirt into the washing machine. Otherwise, Auggie's going to find glitter all over his car when you return it to him."

"Good thinking." Max winks at Ripley. "We wouldn't want my brother thinking we picked up a hitchhiking unicorn in his car today."

Ripley's little features scrunch. "What's hitchhiking?"

I shoot Max a "thanks a lot" look for introducing this lovely concept to my daughter, and he responds with an "oops!" face that makes me laugh.

"Well, go on," I say. "Now that you've said it, explain it to her."

"Oh. Okay, well, hitchhiking is when a person gets a ride with someone they don't know."

Ripley gasps in horror. "Dat's not allowed. I can only drive with Mommy or Grampy or someone Mommy says. And only if it's Mommy who says so. Like today, when Mommy called and said it was okay to drive with you." Ripley doesn't stop there. She's energized by this topic, obviously. She begins excitedly explaining the concept of Stranger Danger to Max—the version she's been taught by me that was designed to be effective and make her wary without terrifying her so intensely she refuses to leave the house.

As Ripley embarks on her Ted Talk, Max flashes me a look that says, "help me," so I flash him a look in return that says, "You made your own bed, dumbass. Time to lie in it." As Ripley proselytizes, we continue exchanging several more looks and smiles, until, ultimately, by the end of Ripley's sermon, we're both holding back laughter.

When Ripley takes a breath, and there's a natural opening for me to cut her off, I say, "All of that is right, peanut. Great job. Now, let's let Max shower while we do our bedtime routine, okay? Now, tell Max goodnight and thank him for taking care of you today."

Ripley heads over to Max and hugs him. "Goodnight, Maxy. Tank you. I love you."

Max looks at me helplessly. But when I shrug, as if to say, "I can't help you," he pats Ripley's back and says, "Goodnight, Ripley. You're welcome. I had lots of fun with you today."

I guide her away and toss over my shoulder to Max, "My dad's bedroom is the one at the end of hallway. I'll set some nail polish remover on his dresser for you."

"Thanks."

I wink. "Meet you back here whenever you're done, Maxy. Open some wine for us if you're here first."

"Sorry to keep you waiting," I say to Max when I walk into the living room and find him sitting on the couch with two glasses of wine. He's freshly showered, the same as me. But since Max didn't have to put an excited, chatty daughter to bed in addition to washing up, he's the first to return to our designated meeting place.

"No problem at all. I was just sitting here, sipping my wine and enjoying the blessed silence."

I laugh. "I'm sure you were. You're a saint. She had a blast with you today. Thank you again."

"I had a surprising amount of fun with her, too." He grins. "Most of the time. When my brain wasn't short-circuiting at the onslaught of words coming out of her mouth."

As I laugh, Max rises and hands me a wine glass, which I clink with his before heading into the kitchen alongside him.

"Can I help with anything?" Max offers, and unlike last night, I accept his offer and give him a job—chopping veggies for a salad. While he gets to work at the counter, I head to the stovetop to boil some water for pasta and gently warm the batch of lamb ragu I've brought home for us to feast on.

As we work, Max asks me to walk him through my calamitous day, so I do. Luckily, now that I'm on the other side of it and catastrophe has been soundly averted, thanks to Max, I'm able to laugh my way through my storytelling. To my delight, Max belly laughs along with me, the same way he did when I told him funny stories during our long and delicious night together, all those months ago. I'd forgotten how attractive Max is when he laughs without holding back. When he's fully relaxed, like he is now, and his brow is smooth and not furrowed in the slightest and his blue eyes are twinkling. In this state of being, he's absolutely irresistible.

"All done here," Max says, motioning to the chopped veggies in front of him.

"Excellent work. You're hired."

Max whoops in celebration, making me chuckle.

"I'm almost done here, too," I say. I direct him to sit at the table while I finish up and plate everything, and he takes a seat, but not before refilling our wine glasses. A few minutes later, I set down two plates and take a seat next to him at the table. "*Bon appetit.*"

Max looks down at the meal I've served him in awe. "Fake Max is a lucky bastard. No wonder he put a ring on it. Damn." He looks up and flashes me a beaming, glorious smile that takes my breath away. "Thank you so much."

Butterflies are ravaging my belly, but I manage to calmly reply, "You're very welcome. I can't thank you enough for what you did for me today."

Max looks back down. "What am I about to eat here?"

I list off the menu, and when Max says he's duly impressed, I reply, "Cooking is my passion. I absolutely love doing it."

"Please, share your passion with me, any time."

My nerve endings jolt to life. I don't think Max meant anything sexual by that comment, but it's nonetheless making me remember the way he passionately impaled me against the wall with his cock mere days ago.

Max's blue eyes flicker with heat. I'm not sure if he's reacting to my body language, or suddenly seeing a similar movie inside his own head, but something's definitely come over him. In fact, the air between us is suddenly charged.

It takes a moment, but Max finally breaks eye contact and takes a bite, at which point he showers me with compliments.

As we eat our meal together, I ask for details about his afternoon with Ripley, and when he obliges me, I can't stop laughing, melting, purring, and cooing throughout his adorable—and hot as fuck—telling. Max is the only man I've ever slept with who's met Ripley; so before today, I had no idea it'd be such a massive turn-on to see a hot man being kind to my daughter. Now that I know about this newfound kink of mine, however, I'm having a hard time moving past it. In fact, I think I'm in very serious danger of throwing my "no-sex" rule out the window tonight.

"How'd she get you to play Cinderella with her?" I ask.

Max chuckles. "I honestly didn't understand what I was getting myself into when I said yes. We'd already played Chutes 'n' Ladders three times. Colored in her coloring books. We'd played Simon Says and danced to 'Barbequed-a.'"

"Oh, I wish I'd seen that."

"We also played Hide 'n' Seek. She's terrible at that game, by the way. I was hiding in plain sight, and she couldn't find me until I started making a bunch of noise."

I'm tempted to inform Max that I've never played Hide 'n' Seek with Ripley, for fear that she'd unwittingly hide somewhere dangerous, like the dryer, or maybe even run outside to hide, despite our firm rule that she's never allowed outside without Mommy's permission. But I figure I'll save that explanation for a day when Max hasn't been my knight in shining armor.

Max says, "By the time she pulled out that bag of makeup, I was so damned tired, I'd have said yes to anything she suggested."

"You gave her one of the best days of her life," I say. "And you really helped me out of a jam."

Max is looking at me intensely again. The same way he did in the living room, when Ripley was crying in my arms, and I was soothing her. "Fake Max is madly in love with you, remember?" he says. "He'd do anything for you."

"It was Real Max who came to my rescue today."

"They're one and the same for now, while we're creating our back story and finding ways to make our relationship feel authentic."

My heart is pounding. "I feel like we're doing a pretty good job with that."

"I do, too. A really, really good job."

I'm not sure which of us starts leaning in first. But the end result is we're both suddenly leaning in for a kiss.

"Mommy?" Ripley's little voice says behind me, just before Max's lips reach mine.

I jerk back from Max and leap out of my chair like it's on fire. "Yes!" I shout. "Yes, honey?"

Ripley's holding her teddy bear and her cheeks are stained with tears. "I had a nightmeero, Mommy." I've never corrected Ripley's pronunciation of nightmare because it's so cute. In this moment, however, I'm not finding it cute because I'm not feeling like a good and nurturing mommy. Mommy wants to get fucked on the kitchen table, Ripley! Mommy wants to get her pussy eaten out! Mommy wants to get railed by the sexiest man she's ever met in her life, by a goddamned country mile!

"Aw, poor baby," I squeeze out.

As I comfort Ripley and ask what she dreamed, Max gets up with his hands squarely in front of his crotch. "I'd better get going," he says stiffly.

Fuck my life.

"Do you want me to clean the dishes before I go?" he asks.

"No, that's okay," I reply, feeling my heart sink into my toes. Well, my vagina, anyway.

"Goodnight, Ripley," Max says. "Sorry you had a nightmare."

"Tank you. I love you."

"Thank you." Max flashes me a scorching look—one of such primal lust, it makes me whimper in return—and off he goes, striding out of the kitchen like his hair is on fire and he knows there's a big ol' trough of water on the other side of the door.

21

MAX

It's just past nine on Wednesday morning, and I'm on the treadmill in my home gym. Try as I might, however, even when running at top speed, I can't get this thumping, over-whelming, all-consuming craving for Marnie out of my system.

When I got home from swapping cars with Auggie last night, I headed straight into my home gym then, too, despite the late hour, and tried to sweat her out of my system by lifting weights. When that didn't do the trick, I took a long shower and tried getting her out of my system through an organ other than my skin. But that didn't work, either.

When I woke up today, I was hard as a rock and realized I'd been dreaming about Marnie, so I beat off to fantasies of her. But nothing changed.

Shit. I push the big, red button to stop the treadmill, suddenly having a horrible thought. What if it was only me who leaned in for that kiss last night, despite what I thought in the moment? What if I did that, unilaterally, in violation of Marnie's clearly stated no-sex rule, and now Marnie is sitting at her house, feeling pissed at me for not respecting her non-negotiable condition for attendance at camp? Did I fuck up everything last night because I momentarily let my pulsing dick think for me?

I grab my phone from the treadmill's cup holder and tap out a text to Marnie.

> I apologize for leaning in to kiss you last night. I got caught up in the moment, but I want you to know I genuinely respect your no-sex rule and promise it won't happen again.

I press send and wait.

And wait.

When Marnie doesn't reply, I head to a rack of dumbbells and continue my workout. An hour later, I check my phone before hopping into the shower. Still no reply. Fuck.

After showering, I make myself a sandwich and sit down on my couch with my food and laptop and start researching the private chef market. Marnie might decide to pull the plug on our fake engagement, thanks to my lack of impulse control last night, but a promise is a promise. I said I'd help get her business cooking with gas, and that's what I'm going to do, whether Marnie winds up coming to Wyoming with me in two days or not.

After several hours of research and analysis, I've managed to formulate some concrete business advice for Marnie. I check my phone again and curse in disappointment when she still hasn't responded to my earlier text. I don't want to send a second text before Marnie's replied to my first, but protecting my pride isn't as important as getting this information to Marnie, as promised.

> Hey, Marnie. I've spent the day researching your industry, as promised, and I've got quite a few suggestions for you. If you want the info, I'd be happy to meet with you to discuss. If you don't, that's fine, too. Have a great day.

This time, Marnie replies instantly.

> Marnie: Hello! So sorry I didn't reply earlier. I've been busy all day, volunteering in Ripley's classroom. Regarding our near-kiss last night, I think I leaned in first. Either way, I've been giving you mixed messages, and I'm sorry about that. My brain and body have been waging a tug of war when it comes to you. Yes, I'd love to hear your ideas for my business. Thank you. I'd suggest you come over tonight, but a) I promised to take Ripley to the movies tonight, and b) I don't completely trust myself to be alone with you. I don't think my brain and body are done battling it out. Why don't we meet at a coffee place tomorrow? I'm free all day.

Well, shit. If Marnie's brain and body are at loggerheads, then I vote she listens to her goddamned body. Life is short. Why can't we both agree explicitly that our physical relationship means nothing? That it's a no-strings bit of fun, just for the pleasure of it, and that's that? We're both adults, for fuck's sake. That's what I *want* to reply. But obviously, I can't.

> Me: I'm free all day tomorrow. Name the time and place, and I'll be there.

Marnie replies with a time and place and explains she'll be bringing Ripley along, since she doesn't have a job lined up tomorrow and doesn't take Ripley to school on days she's not working. "Don't worry, though," Marnie writes, "I'll give Ripley her iPad and headphones during our meeting, so we'll be able to talk without interruption."

Our *meeting*? Fuck me. I wasn't thinking of our meet-up as a date, *per se,* but the word *meeting* feels awfully formal and cold for the relaxed rapport we've built up these past few days.

I gaze out the floor-to-ceiling window on the far side of my living room and take in the gray Seattle sky while trying to decipher the intense feelings of disappointment inside me. The sense of loss. I should be thrilled with Marnie's suggestion, since it means she's for sure not cancelling family camp on me; and yet, my heart feels achy and heavy. My stomach tight.

I reply to Marnie, letting her know I'm down for the suggested ten o'clock "meeting" tomorrow and looking forward to it. And that's that. Our date—or, rather, our business meeting with Marnie's four-year-old in tow—has now been successfully calendared.

With no work to do today, and no Marnie to hang out with, I tap out a text to my buddy, Grayson, but delete it before sending when I remember he's in Costa Rica with his lady. I text my brother to see if he's free today. No dice. And then, I stare at my phone for an embarrassingly long amount of time. I've got several friends at work, but they're all working today. I suppose I could go to a bar or find an easy hook-up on Tinder. But neither activity appeals to me in the slightest.

I swipe into my text exchange with Marnie, feeling a thumping urge to ask Marnie what movie she's taking Ripley to see tonight and if she'd mind me tagging along. When the thought crosses my mind, however, I drop my phone like a hot potato. What the fuck? I can't do that! With a roll of my eyes, I grab the TV remote, flip on a show, and hunker down for what's surely going to be a long, boring—and, yes, extremely lonely —night.

22

MAX

I wake up on Thursday morning with a boner and the annoying realization that I was dreaming about Marnie again. Fucking hell. Make it stop. I sit up and run a palm down my face. What's wrong with me? I'm never obsessive like this. I'm an expert at moving on. Not giving a shit. I'm a machine. Why has she gotten under my skin like this?

I hop in the shower and deal with my boner, then slip on some workout clothes and head into my home gym, figuring I'll squeeze in a quick workout before meeting Marnie and Ripley at the coffee place later this morning. But as I'm getting onto my treadmill, my phone rings with a call from Marnie.

Shit.

I bet she's calling to cancel our meet-up this morning. Maybe after thinking about the situation overnight, Marnie decided our undeniable attraction is a forest fire, rather than a lit match—a flame she's not willing to ignite, after all. With a pit in my stomach, I step off the treadmill and connect the call. "Hey, Marnie."

In an excited voice, Marnie says, "I just dropped Ripley off at school, even though I don't have a job lined up today. I never do that. I always spend the day with her when I'm not working."

"Oh. Okay. Do you still want to meet me at the—"

"I did that because I think we should fuck today, Max. For as long and as hard as we can, until it's time for me to pick up Ripley at three."

My entire body jolts like I've been hit by lightning. "Count me in."

She's panting. "We need to get this *thing* out of our systems today, once and for all, so we're thoroughly bored with each other by the time we go to Wyoming."

Hallelujah, there is a God. "When and where?"

"Your place," Marnie says without hesitation. "Right fucking now."

"Get your ass over here as soon as—"

"I'm here. Standing in front of your building."

My dick jolts. "Get the fuck up here, Marnie Long. Run, don't walk."

"I'm coming now."

I sprint out my front door and down the hallway and then wait at the elevator. When the doors finally open and Marnie appears, her eyes are burning and her cheeks rosy. She hurtles through the steel elevator doors and into my arms, and I devour her mouth like I've waited a lifetime to kiss her. It certainly feels that way.

As we kiss, I grab Marnie's ass and pull her up, and she wraps her thighs around my waist and her arms around my neck, and I carry her down the hallway to my front door, kissing, groping, and attacking her as we go.

Somehow, I get my door open and our bodies inside without breaking our mouths' connection. Since I'm not sure I can make it all the way to my bedroom without physically exploding, I lay Marnie down on my couch. Breathing hard, I pull off both our clothes, roughly open her thighs, and stroke her pussy. She's already wet and swollen for me—as ripe and ready for me as can be. It's not typical for me to jump straight to fucking. Almost always, I'm gonna have myself an appetizer before the main course. But this time, getting inside this woman, right fucking now, is a matter of life and death.

I massage her clit, round and round, while my fingers inside her get her wetter and wetter, and when she's so wet she's making sloshing noises against my fingers, I turn her around, bend her over the couch, and plunge myself inside her from behind. At the sensation of my body stretching and filling hers all the way, Marnie growls and moans and digs her fingernails into my forearm.

I fuck her hard, gripping her neck with one hand while massaging her clit with the other.

I fuck her hard, until she's keening like a wild animal and releasing guttural groans with each beastly thrust. I fuck her hard, until I'm light-headed and tumbling through space on my way to unparalleled bliss. If my house were burning down around me, I wouldn't notice. I'm in a trance. A state of pure ecstasy—and I never want it to end.

With a loud gasp, followed by a growl, Marnie throws her head back, so I grope her extended neck, breasts, and nipples while continuing my circular, rhythmic assault on her clit. I pound her even harder, while whispering into her ear that she's a drug to me, a savage addiction.

Finally, when I'm reaching the bitter end of my ability to hang on, Marnie's most intimate muscles clench sharply around my cock and *squeeze*. For a brief, delicious moment, Marnie's body holds mine captive—a tell-tale sign she's on the bitter cusp of an intense release. She reaches up and grips my face behind her, and a moment later, her innermost muscles ripple so fiercely against my cock, I'm propelled forcefully into an orgasm that makes my vision blur.

As I come inside her, I feel like I'm being electrocuted by pleasure. Like I'm mainlining a powerful narcotic. Finally, when I come down, I crumple over Marnie's sweaty back, while she lies slack beneath me, both of us bent over the back of my couch.

When I've caught my breath, I straighten up and turn her around to face me, at which point she flashes me a satisfied grin that makes me chuckle.

"Did that do the trick?" I ask.

"You couldn't tell? I came so hard, I almost passed out."

"No, did that do the trick and get me out of your system, once and for all?"

Marnie snorts. "Not even close. But try, try again, I always say."

"And again and again and again."

"Yes, please."

I run my fingertips through her glorious hair. "It makes sense if you think about it. Feed an addict their drug of choice, and they're only going to want more of it. Not less."

"Shoot. Now you tell me."

I pull her to the couch and guide her to sit on top of me. She's facing me. Straddling my lap while I grip her ass and grin up at her stunning face. "I've never been happier for a plan to backfire in my life."

"Who says it backfired? We've still got time. Maybe this intense afterglow is part of the process. Maybe this is the kind of fire that burns crazy-hot and wild, right before it flames out for good."

"I guess there's only one way to find out." I pull her face to mine and kiss her passionately, and one thing quickly leads to another and we're making out on my couch. I throw her onto her back and forcefully part her thighs and eat her out, and by the time she's coming, I'm hard as a rock again and ready for round two.

This time, I carry Marnie to my bedroom and fuck her in my bed, with her on top, until she's creaming all over my cock. After that, we stop to fuel our spent bodies with a snack and some water and conversation. But the second we're both good to go again, we fuck on my kitchen table. And then, against the floor-to-ceiling window in my living room. I fuck her with everything I've got—with my cock, fingers, lips, tongue, and voice—until she's crying tears of euphoria and squirting like a geyser. I fuck her till she's screaming my name and babbling incoherently. I fuck her till she's ruined for any other cock, and I can't imagine wanting to fuck or taste or finger another woman's pussy as long as I live.

And yet, despite our best efforts, by the time two-thirty rolls around and it's time for Marnie to leave to pick up Ripley, I'm not feeling even close to done with her. Not even close to declaring her out of my system. On the contrary, I feel more addicted to her than ever.

Marnie hops into the shower, while I lie in my bed staring at the ceiling. Wishing I could stop time. When she comes out of my bathroom and starts putting on her clothes, I say, "Okay, hear me out, Red. Don't say no before you've thought about it, okay?" I sit up and Marnie stops what she's doing and gives me her undivided attention. "I respect what you said about being done with meaningless sex and ready for something serious. But what if we agree to have as much sex as possible between now and the end of family camp, simply for the fun of it, and when camp is over, our arrangement will be over, too? As long as we're both clear about the expiration date and the nature of—"

"Deal."

My eyebrows ride up. That was much easier than I thought it'd be. "Seriously?"

Marnie sits on the edge of my bed in her bra and undies. "We'd have to keep our fling a secret. I wouldn't want our parents knowing what we're doing behind closed doors and mistakenly thinking we've become a real couple. I don't want to have to explain it's only a sex thing to my father."

"God, no."

"And I wouldn't want either of them misunderstanding and saying the wrong thing in front of Ripley."

My heart is racing. This is a fantastic turn of events. "A

secret fling works for me," I say, trying to sound calm. "Secrecy will only make it hotter."

"And we'd have to be extra mindful of our body language in front of Ripley. She's not stupid, Max. She's a little sponge."

"She thinks I'm in her life because I'm Gigi's son, and we'll make sure she keeps on thinking that."

Marnie slides on her shirt and stands to put on her jeans. "I'm in. We'll have a family camp fling in the midst of our fake engagement. What could go wrong?"

I laugh. "Not a damned thing."

She slides on her sandals and grabs her purse. "What time is our flight tomorrow?"

"Eight. I've arranged a van to take all of us to the airport from your place."

"Good thinking. With five people, there will be a lot of luggage."

"My thoughts exactly."

Marnie smiles down at me on the bed. "I'll see you tomorrow, then."

My stomach clenches at the thought of Marnie walking out that door without me. And then, at the thought of me spending another lonely, aimless night on my couch, while Marnie and Ripley, and our parents, too, eat dinner together and chat about our parents' getaway to wine country.

"Hey, maybe it'd be easier in the morning, if I stay at your place tonight," I say. "There's a futon in your dad's office, right? I could sleep there. Or on the couch. Whatever."

Marnie's chest heaves. "That's a great idea. Our parents should be back by five. Why don't you come with me to pick up Ripley now, and we'll pick up takeout on our way home for all of us? We can have dinner and hear all about their trip."

Relief and excitement wash over me. "Great. Maybe after Ripley goes to sleep, we could sit down and talk about all the business stuff I was going to tell you today over coffee."

"Oh, yeah. Great." She tucks a lock of red hair behind her

ear and bites her lower lip. "After that, once everyone else has gone to bed tonight, maybe you could sneak into my room and get in one last practice run before our Secret Family Camp Fling officially begins."

I get out of bed and pull her to me. "You're a mind reader, Marnie Long. Hell yes. That sounds fucking amazing."

23
MARNIE

What in the *Modern Family* is going on here?

I'm sitting at the dinner table with Dad, Gigi, Ripley, and Max, enjoying the delicious spread Max and I brought home for our big family dinner. Currently, Dad and Gigi are in the throes of regaling the group with stories of their romantic getaway. They're freaking adorable together. Finishing each other's sentences. Laughing heartily at each other's jokes. However Gigi might have been holding back before, perhaps due to the guilt she felt about recognizing Dad in that deli line and not copping to it at the time, she's clearly not holding back anymore. And the result is obvious. They're closer than ever. Smitten. And absolutely lovely to behold. Not only for me, but for Max, too, which I know because we've been exchanging knowing, amused looks throughout the meal.

Speaking of Max, he's sitting next to Ripley again. But not because she begged him this time. But because *he* sat next to her after getting his food from our little buffet line in the kitchen. When Max took his seat, Ripley gasped and said, "Look, Mommy! Maxy is sitting next to me!" And what did Max say to that? "Of course, I am. Where else would I sit?"

"So, what did you all do while we were gone?" Gigi asks.

Reflexively, I look at Max, and the wicked smile he flashes me makes me blush and look down at my plate.

"Mommy and I went to da movies!" Ripley bellows happily.

"Oh, yeah? What movie did you see, pumpkin?" Gigi asks.

It's all the prompting Ripley needs to tell the group all about it.

As Ripley talks, I dare to peek at Max again, and this time, the radiant smile he flashes me stops my heart. That wasn't a suggestive smile. That wasn't a wicked smile that said, "We fucked all day, and nobody here knows it." No, that particular smile was sweet. Wholesome. The kind that overtakes a person's face, without their consent, whenever they're feeling pure joy.

"And what about you, Marnie?" Dad says.

I look at Dad, thinking he must be asking what I've been up to while he's been away. But he's standing and holding several empty plates . . . which means he must have asked if I'm going to get more food or if he can take my empty plate to the kitchen.

"I'm all done," I say. "Thank you. But I'll clean up, Dad. You and Gigi must be tired."

We go back and forth, but ultimately, it's decided I'll help Dad clean up while Gigi, at her request, gives Ripley a bath and Max finishes the business research he's doing for me.

In the kitchen, Dad and I get to work like a well-oiled machine, with me rinsing and Dad loading the racks like the meticulous engineer he is.

"It seems like you and Gigi had a blast together," I say.

Dad blushes. "We did. She's so much fun."

I stop what I'm doing and face him. "I hope you know I'm one thousand percent happy for you and not feeling conflicted at all. Mom wanted you to find love. So, if you're falling in love, or you're already there, you don't need to hide that from me."

Dad presses his lips together for a moment, apparently considering his next words, before his features soften and his eyes glint. "I'm head over heels in love with her, Marnie Girl," he confesses. "I told her so during our trip, and she said it back to me."

Tears prick my eyes. "Aw, Daddy. Congratulations."

I hug him, and he kisses the side of my head.

"She wants to honor your mother's memory, always," he says. "She likes hearing stories about her. She said she already loves her, through me."

I wipe my eyes. "That's so sweet. She's an amazing person."

Dad lists off a bunch of things he loves about Gigi, including, "I love how much she adores you and Ripley. I love how much she values family."

"Max says the nicest things about her. He's said, repeatedly, she's the world's best mom."

Dad raises an eyebrow. "You and Max seem to be getting along, better than ever."

"Yeah, we're getting along pretty well," I say evenly before returning to my work in the sink.

"How well?" Dad asks suggestively.

I blush. "Very well."

Dad laughs. "Okay, I get it. It's none of my business."

I hand Dad a plate for the dishwasher. "We're at different stages of our lives. We've both agreed there's no future that makes sense for us. But we're going to enjoy our time together, while it lasts."

One side of Dad's mouth quirks up. "How mature of you both."

"As you know, I'm nothing if not mature."

Dad laughs heartily.

"It's not *that* funny," I murmur.

Dad sighs and smiles. "Can I give you some unsolicited advice?"

"Something tells me you're going to, regardless."

"Give him a chance. Open your heart. The way he looks at you, I think there's a chance for a whole lot more than—"

"Dad, stop. Please. I'm not the one who needs this little speech."

"Oh." Looking disappointed, Dad puts out his palm and I hand him a plate. He asks, "Are you sure? By the way Max interacted with you and Ripley during dinner, I'd bet anything he's feeling something—"

"I'm sure, Dad. Max isn't looking for something serious. He's focused on his career right now, and I'm done wasting my precious time on fun that leads nowhere. When we get back from Wyoming, I'm excited to start looking for my person in earnest. And in the meantime, yes, Max and I are getting along great, precisely because we've both been clear and honest about what we want and what we don't."

Dad looks apologetic. "I'm sorry. I should have kept my big mouth shut."

My heart is racing. Dad's comments have made me realize I've been secretly hoping Max's happy, relaxed demeanor and smiles at dinner were signs his feelings are starting to match mine. But I don't want to think that way. In fact, that's precisely the kind of thinking I need to steadfastly avoid.

I force a smile. "It's okay. But, please, let's not talk about this again. I just want to live in the moment with him and enjoy myself, and not look for signs that aren't there. He's been clear about what he's willing to offer, and that it's not what I'm looking for at this stage of my life. The healthiest thing for me is to take him at his word."

"Sounds like a plan."

I kiss Dad's cheek. "I'll go see if Gigi needs help with Ripley."

24

MARNIE

After kissing Ripley's sleeping face, I head into the living room, where I find Max sitting on the couch studying his laptop screen. He's all business. Focused. And sexy as hell.

"Did Dad and Gigi go to bed?" I ask, looking toward the kitchen.

"Yeah, they decided to watch a movie in Henry's room, so we could talk out here." He's entranced by something on his laptop and therefore not at all noticing the sexy vibe I'm trying to lay down.

"Have a seat. I've got some ideas I'm excited to tell you about."

He's incredibly hot when he's got his lawyer cap on. What a pity he's genuinely wanting to talk business. I plop down next to Max on the couch and accept the wine he offers me and then sip and watch and wait while he finishes something on his computer.

"Okay," Max finally says on an exhale. He tilts his laptop screen toward me, displaying a graphic with "Marnie Long Meals" at the top. "You'll see here I've divided your business into various categories: actual services—which are universally praised as fantastic; marketing efforts—which seem pretty anemic, from what I can tell."

"Get the crash cart."

"And, lastly, we've got operations, which includes stuff like maximization of time and minimization of costs, as well as a few other things. Let's jump right into the second two categories, since it's clear you don't need to level-up on your services rendered."

"Thank you."

Max deftly explains his thoughts and advice. As he does so, he speaks in a way that's respectful, easily understandable, and non-judgmental. It's clear he only wants to help me. Also, that he knows his shit.

By the time Max has reached the end of his spiel, I'm electrified and grateful. I knew Max had to be good at what he does to work at a swanky firm like his, but I had no idea he was *this* good.

"Thank you for all of this, Max," I say, furiously tapping another note onto my phone. "You've given me some tangible things to work on."

"Report back to me once you've made some headway and we'll assess progress and figure out next steps."

My heart stops. We're leaving for family camp tomorrow morning, so Max must know I'm not going to put any of his advice into action until *after* we get back from our trip. Which means Max has just confirmed, without a doubt, he's fully expecting us to stay in contact after the trip. Perhaps, Max means only for business purposes, but it's hard not to think one thing might lead to another if we keep in touch.

No, Marnie. Don't think like that. Bad girl.

I finish my notetaking and put down my phone. "I'm honestly blown away."

"Why? This is precisely what I do for a living."

"Yeah, but not for free." I flash him a snarky look. "Wait. You're not going to charge me for this, right?"

Max returns my wicked smile. "Well, I'm not going to charge you money. But I'll definitely accept a swap of services."

I snicker. "Deal. I think it's fair to say I'm a deep-throat level of pleased with your services."

Max's eyes blaze at my saucy comment, but he somehow manages to keep his game face on. "Before we jump into my payment and leave this conversation, do you have any questions?"

"Actually, yeah. How quickly would you expect me to start seeing results? I think you might be disappointed in me, in terms of how long all this takes me. Something always comes up with Ripley that gets me off-track."

Max tilts his head. "What kinds of stuff?"

I give him a running list. The big and small stuff that comes along to thwart every working mother, especially when the child in question has lots of doctors and ongoing check-ups. "Another thing that slows me down," I say, "is that I'm only willing to work while Ripley's in preschool, unless it's a really special occasion. No nights and weekends if I can help it. That rule for myself kind of fucks me over, if I'm being honest, in terms of getting ahead. But I feel good about that choice."

Max scratches his chin. "Hmm."

"I used to work crazy hours," I say quickly, not wanting him to think I'm lazy or lacking a work ethic. "Before Ripley, I'd get hired by a family and travel with them, and then cook for them literally every day, from morning to night. I barely slept. But I can't do that kind of thing now. Ripley's my top priority. I'm not sorry about that, but I do recognize it limits my success in business."

Max looks at me for a very long time. "You know what?" he says. "Forget everything I just said. New strategy." After taking a long sip of wine, he closes his laptop, puts it onto the coffee table, and says, "What you need is a way to bring in money that's not dependent on services rendered or actual time spent. A line of products on your website, maybe? A cookbook. Cute oven mitts and aprons with funny sayings on them. Let's get you making money all day, every day, even when you're at the zoo with Ripley."

I'm buzzing. "That sounds like the ultimate dream. Literally. For twenty years, ever since culinary school, I've been jotting down all my crazy ideas for unique kitchen tools and gadgets in a notebook—stuff to make cooking easier and more fun."

Max's blue eyes light up. "Have you seen other people bringing your ideas to market?"

"No. Not the way I'd do it." I shrug. "Maybe I'm a weirdo. Some of my ideas are kind of out there."

Max palms his forehead. "Go get the notebook, Marnie. This is where we should have started our conversation."

My heart is thundering. "I've never shown my notebook to anyone."

"Well, I'm gonna be the first. Go get it."

"My notes are silly doodles, basically. It's not like I've sat down and designed something, in detail, the way an engineer would. I don't even know if any of my ideas would work the way I'm envisioning them."

Max leans forward. "I'm a patent attorney. I work with engineers who bring inventors' ideas to life in prototypes. It just so happens one of my greatest talents is spotting a great idea—the one to develop and invest in. Now, go get that motherfucking notebook."

I'm buzzing. Simultaneously electrified and terrified. With a trembling hand, I throw back the rest of my wine and then sprint on rubbery legs to my bedroom. When I return with the notebook, Max hands me a refilled glass of wine in return, and we settle onto the couch, our bodies entangled, while he slowly turns the pages of the book I've never shown to a single person besides my mother.

As Max peruses each page, he asks me pointed questions, which I do my best to answer. Watching Max's big hands turning the pages of my secret notebook is making me dizzy. Light-

headed. It's the most intimate thing I've ever done with any man
—far more intimate than letting one fuck me or eat me out.

Midway through the book, after my most recent explanation,
Max's body notably ignites. He asks me a flurry of questions,
and with each answer I give, his demeanor becomes more and
more energetic.

"This is it," Max declares. "Your Big Idea, baby. You're a
genius. This is the one we're going to focus on for
development."

We. We're going to focus on developing it—*together*? Max
and me? Mere minutes ago, when Max instructed me to report
back to him regarding my progress on the tasks he's given me
tonight, I felt excited to know, for sure, we'd be in contact after
family camp. But this comment from Max feels like an even
bigger deal than that. How long does it take to develop a doodle
into an actual, functioning thing? Weeks? Months? How long is
Max planning to work with me on this project?

"Okay, first things first," Max says. "We'll need to meet with
my engineer buddy to find out if he thinks this idea has legs, like
I do; and if so, the cost for creating a prototype."

My stomach sinks. "How much would a prototype cost?"

Max waves at the air. "Don't worry about that. I'll handle all
costs."

"It sounds expensive, though. Would this be a loan, or . . .?"

"If my buddy thinks this idea is as good as I do, then I'll pay
for the prototype as a gift to you. After that, we'll talk about next
steps and if it makes sense for us to create a formal partnership."

My heart is crashing. "A business partnership?"

"Yeah." Max considers. "If it comes to me investing more
than, say, twenty grand, we'll draw something up for me to
recoup my investment out of future proceeds. Until then,
however, we'll call whatever money I've spent a gift to you—a
thank you for everything you're doing for me."

Twenty grand? Max is willing to spend *twenty grand* to
develop one of my silly little doodles? And this, after already

having bought me a fake engagement ring for eight grand? "I don't know, Max. It feels like way too much to let you spend."

"It's not. I've got plenty in the bank. And if all goes well in Wyoming, I'll be making more money than I know what to do with in the near future. Let me do this, Marnie. I'm excited about it."

"Only if you're positive it's not too much," I murmur.

"It's not." He slides his palm on my cheek and kisses me softly. Reverently. I'm thinking our kiss is going to ramp up and become heated and passionate and desperate, like our kisses always do, but Max pulls away before that happens and leans his forehead against mine. "I meant it when I said you're a genius," he whispers. "That's not a figure of speech. I'm in awe of your incredible mind."

"I'm in awe of yours, too," I whisper. I'm trembling. "I knew you were smart, but . . . *Wow,* Max."

Something passes between us. A current that feels different than anything that's flowed between us before. Whatever it is, it's causing my heart to ache. No, to explode with adoration and affection for this incredible man. I jerk back suddenly, shocked by my sudden realization. *I'm falling in love with Maximillian Vaughn.* I don't want to be. God knows, I don't. But, alas, suddenly, I know that's exactly what's happening to me.

Max's chest heaves. His Adam's apple bobs. He runs his hand through his hair and stares at me for a long moment, looking flushed and out of sorts. Finally, he says, "Listen, I know we talked about going another round tonight, but we've got an early flight tomorrow. Maybe we should get a good sleep."

I force a smile. "Yeah, we need to be bright-eyed and bushy-tailed and ready to give a convincing performance tomorrow." What happened? Did my face give me away? Have I scared him off? "I was about to say the same thing," I add, rising from the couch. "Sleep well. Goodnight." With that, I turn on my heel and stride, red-faced, toward the hallway. Before I've made it out of the room, though, Max calls my name in a tight voice, so I stop and turn around, my heart pounding in my ears.

Max opens and closes his mouth. Shifts his weight. "Thanks again for everything you're doing for me," he finally says. "I hope you know I really appreciate it."

My heart sinks. "I'm getting plenty of upside out of our arrangement, too." With that, I stride down the hallway toward my bedroom. And this time, Max doesn't call my name or try to stop me.

25
MAX

"It's just like da house in *Cowboy Caillou*!" Ripley screams. She's clomping through our rustic two-bedroom cabin in the cowgirl boots and hat my mother bought her, shrieking with delight at every bit of "dude ranch" flavored decor. I look over at Marnie and not surprisingly, she's grinning from ear to ear as she watches her enthusiastic daughter. The second Marnie's eyes meet mine, however, her smile vanishes and that same nonchalant look she's been shooting me all day overtakes her features again.

I'm guessing Marnie felt offended by my sudden about-face on the sex thing last night. But I don't know that for sure since we've been around other people throughout our travel day with no chance to speak in private. I didn't mean to offend her, obviously. Things were feeling too intense for me, all of a sudden. Overwhelming. So, I decided to take some space to pull myself together. Which I did. But ever since then, from the moment we saw each other this morning until now, Marnie's been icy and distant toward me.

Case in point, when I catch Marnie's eye again and shoot her another amused grin, she quickly picks up a welcome packet off the coffee table. "Let's see what's in here," she says. She begins leafing through the pages. "Did you know the Walters' ranch is twenty *thousand* acres?"

"Now, that's a big ranch."

"It sure is."

I wait for her to look at me. When she doesn't, I add, "Hit me with some more factoids about this place. Dazzle me with information, Red."

My use of that nickname definitely hits its target: Marnie almost smiled just now when I said it, albeit while continuing to stare at the paper in her hand. "Well," she begins. "Did you know the Walters family is renowned for breeding champion racehorses on this ranch?"

"I did. But tell me more."

"They're quite prolific." She lists all the winning horses sired at this property and their notable achievements and wins, which prompts me to say I didn't realize the extent of their success. Marnie says, "They've also got an entire section of the ranch devoted to therapy horses for children with autism."

"That's so cool."

"Isn't it? That part of the ranch is open—*for free*—to charities tasked with bringing in children in need of therapy."

"That's amazing."

"Oh, wow, there are almost *two hundred* guest cabins on this side of the property, which the Walters bizarrely call 'The Guest Area.'"

I laugh. "That's a bizarre name for it, for sure. Weirdos."

Marnie can't help smiling. She looks up from her paper for the first time, her eyes twinkling. Is she thawing a bit? It sure seems that way. She says, "Do you think the family rents the cabins out, like a resort, for big groups? Maybe for conferences and company retreats and weddings?"

I shake my head. "My boss told me Mr. Walters and his family host lots of large groups here for free—mostly, groups from children's charities they support."

"They're sincerely passionate about philanthropy, huh? It's not only for show."

"It sure seems that way."

Our attention is pulled to Ripley when she clomps into the room holding a little book about horses she discovered on the nightstand in one of the bedrooms, and we gush over it with her before she runs out again to continue exploring.

When Ripley is gone, Marnie returns to the welcome packet. "Oh my gosh. There's an itinerary and list of activities for our week. Holy crap, Maxy! Listen to this." Well, that confirms it: Marnie is definitely thawing toward me. That's the first time she's called me Maxy, like Ripley does, when we're outside of Ripley's presence.

Paper in hand, Marnie lists off a dizzying array of activities and amenities available to us this week—some to be enjoyed at one's leisure, and others that have been arranged for the whole camp at a designated time. We're going to enjoy a barbeque with a "hoedown," whatever that is. If we're interested, there are classes all day, every day, in the arts and crafts tent and in the archery area. There are sports activities, games, and tournaments. A belly flopping contest at the pool, as well as a scavenger hunt. There's hiking, mountain biking, and horseback riding, all of it led by one of the ranch's many "camp counselors." And on and on.

"Ripley, come in here, honey!" Marnie shouts. "You're going to want to hear this!" When Ripley clomps into the room, red-cheeked and wide-eyed behind her thick glasses, Marnie says, "It says here they have a whole bunch of exciting activities planned especially for kids your age!"

Ripley squeals. "Like what?"

Marnie rattles them off. "And besides hanging out with Max and me and Grampy and Gigi, they've got a bunch of camp counselors to play with you, so you can run off and do fun stuff with the other kids, while the adults are relaxing or doing fun stuff, too."

Ripley shrieks with glee.

"Oh, honey, you're going to make so many friends this week and have so much fun."

"Will I get to ride a horse?" Ripley asks breathlessly.

"A pony. It says so right here."

Ripley screams with joy at the top of her lungs and hugs my legs. "Tank you, Maxy. Tank you."

As Ripley hugs my legs, Marnie says, "It says here they're gonna give you riding lessons this week, and then you'll get to show off your new skills in a pony parade for all the adults to watch at the end of the week."

"A pony parade!" Ripley shrieks. She looks at Marnie and me, gripping both cheeks with her little palms. "I've always wanted to be in a pony parade my whole entire life!"

I laugh, but Marnie tears up.

"I'm so happy for you, love," Marnie says, her voice breaking. She wipes her eyes and addresses me. "I had no idea this place would be *this* amazing. It's a little slice of heaven. Actually, no, a really big slice."

"I want to live here forever!" Ripley shouts. She runs to her mommy and embraces her legs, so Marnie crouches down and gives her a big hug. When Ripley pulls away from the hug, she's bopping in place. Ready to keep exploring. She says, "Can we go next door to see Grampy and Gigi's cabin and tell dem about da pony parade?"

"Why don't you go," I say. "We'll meet you there in a couple minutes." I've been dying to get Marnie alone all day, so we can clear the air about last night, or whatever caused the frost I've been detecting from Marnie all day.

"Can I, Mommy?"

Marnie smiles. "Go for it."

Clomp, clomp, clomp, and away little Ripley goes in her too-big cowgirl boots, shrieking happily as she goes. Our cabin shares a deck and wall with the one-bedroom cabin next door. In fact, Henry and Mom's front door for the week is literally ten feet from ours. But Marnie nonetheless stands in our doorway to observe her daughter's short journey. After a few seconds, I hear the sound of a door opening. My mother saying, "Well, hello there, cowgirl. Would you like to come inside?" I hear Ripley's voice, chattering away, along with the *clomp, clomp, clomp* of her too-big boots again, and the next thing I know, Marnie is turning away from the opened door, crossing her arms over her chest, and leveling me with an icy glare.

"I thought we should have a private conversation before the opening party," I explain.

Marnie folds her arms over her T-shirt. "About what?"

I sigh. "Whatever I did to make you barely look at me all day."

"I don't think that's what's been happening."

"Are you upset about last night—that I suggested we sleep instead of having sex?"

"Of course, not. It's your right and prerogative to decide what to do with your body. You didn't want to have sex with me? Great. No problem. Like I said, I was going to suggest the same thing. In fact, I think maybe we should go back to the no-sex rule for the whole week."

It feels like a gut punch. "Is that what you genuinely want?"

She thinks about it. "I don't know, to be honest. My head is spinning. This place is incredible. And Ripley's excitement is already making me want to weep tears of joy. I think I'm going to be highly emotional in this place." She chews the inside of her cheek. "Before we got here, I had a strong hunch I might have a hard time playing happy family by day and then having suppos-edly meaningless sex with you by night. And now that I'm here, I can see the risk is even bigger than I thought. This place feels like an alternate universe. A fantasy. A bubble. It's the kind of place that makes a person let down their guard. The kind that makes a person's heart believe what they're feeling is real, even though their brain knows they're in a little vacation bubble without a care in the world."

I try to process all that through the racing of my pulse. "Yeah, that makes sense. Now that I've come to care about Ripley so much, I definitely don't want to do anything to lead her on or confuse her. Same goes for you. I don't want to hurt you, Marnie. I hope you know that."

She exhales. "I do." She pauses. "If we get too cozy and comfortable with each other—for real—then we're bound to slip up and get too touchy-feely around Ripley. She might see that and assume we're like the rest of the families here at camp —*real*. And then she'll fall even more head over heels in love with you than she already has and expect the same level of attention when we get home. I can't stand thinking about the heartbreak she'll suffer when that doesn't happen."

I shift my weight. "I'd still like to be in Ripley's life after we get back. Like an uncle. I'm Gigi's son, so that wouldn't be weird, right?"

When I said the word uncle, the pain that flickered across Marnie's face, ever so briefly, was like I'd stabbed her in the heart. "No, that wouldn't be weird," she says. But her tone is distant and cold. She adds, "It would be lovely and most welcome."

She's pulled back again. Retreated. Put up her guard. For a second there, I felt like we were barreling toward that same feeling of intimacy we had when poring over her notebook together. But now, she's a million miles away.

"And we'll be seeing each other when we get back, too, remember?" I say.

"Mm hmm. Yep. For business stuff."

She said that last phrase without particular emphasis, but even so, it felt like a curse word to me. I suddenly feel like I'm standing on quicksand, like no matter what I do, I can't get myself out of this hole. I open my mouth to speak, but motion at the opened front door of the cabin draws our attention. It's Mom, Henry, and Ripley, enthusiastically breezing into our cabin.

"Did you check out the welcome packet?" Mom booms

excitedly, waving a piece of paper in the air. "This week is going to be amazing!"

Unlike me, Marnie looks grateful for the interruption. She replies with a comment about the itinerary, and the two women peruse it together for the next several minutes.

Finally, Henry says, "Are we ready to head to the opening party? I hear music, so I think it's starting."

"Yep," Mom says, pointing at the paper in her hand. "According to the itinerary, it's time." She looks tentatively between Marnie and me, and whatever tension or words left unsaid she's detecting prompts her to say, "If you two need to chat, Henry and I can take Ripley—"

"Nope, we're good," Marnie says, without looking at me. "Let's go." She grabs Ripley's hand. "Come on, cowgirl. Something tells me you're about to have the time of your four-year-old life."

"Four and a half."

26

MARNIE

oly crap.

And here I thought *I* was doing *Max* a favor by coming to this ranch.

Looking around at the astonishing opening party on this perfectly manicured, sprawling lawn, I can't believe I had the clueless audacity to dole out the terms and conditions of my attendance. Little did I know then, Max was offering a once-in-a-lifetime experience to my daughter and me. Something far more than a simple vacation. A week that's sure to create life-long memories for us both, as well as for Dad and Gigi, too. If I'd known what kind of Nirvana this place would turn out to be, if I'd only known about the incredible amenities and activities lined up for this week free of charge, I'd have begged Max to bring us here. True, it's now fairly certain this week with Max will ultimately lead to a broken heart for me. But that feels like a fair price to pay, all things considered. Broken hearts mend, but joyful family memories last a lifetime.

I continue surveying the opening party in unfettered awe. The Walters family has gone all out. There are games such as horseshoes, corn hole, and bocci ball in one area. Carnival games in another. Roaming rodeo clowns are making balloon animals for the kids while face painters turn them into horses, cows, and other barnyard animals.

In another area, there are several different obstacle courses to try, each with varying degrees of difficulty and each staffed with cheerful camp counselors in cowboy hats and brightly colored T-shirts. There's food, too. So much food. And a live band providing a soundtrack for all of it. And the best part? As we enjoy the party, we're surrounded by spectacular views of mountains, trees, blooming wildflowers, and endless, blue, late-afternoon Wyoming skies.

When I finish my turkey leg, Dad insists on playing me in a game of horseshoes, so we head over there with Gigi while Max and Ripley are off doing who-knows-what together. After our meal, Ripley grabbed Max's hand and physically dragged him to the roaming face painter. And that's the last we've seen or heard from the pair, ever since.

When my horseshoe game with Dad ends with him soundly beating me—no surprise there—I suggest Gigi take a crack at him.

"Please, Gigi," I say. "Humble him for me. He hasn't let me win at anything since age ten."

Laughing, Gigi says she'll do her best, while I set off to find my fake fiancé and very real daughter. I scan the packed crowd and, to my surprise, discover Max carrying Ripley on his broad shoulders while chatting with none other than Mr. and Mrs. Walters. Well, good for him. He's wasted no time infiltrating his target. I head over there, figuring I'll take Ripley off Max's hands, so he can schmooze his dream employer in peace. When I get over there, however, both Mr. and Mrs. Walters greet me with such warmth and enthusiasm, it's immediately clear grabbing Ripley and sneaking away isn't in the cards.

"I'm a pony, Mommy!" Ripley shouts from her perch atop Max's shoulders. She's pointing to her face paint with pride and excitement.

"I can see that, my love," I say. "You look mahvelous, dahling."

Ripley and the Walters laugh at my reply.

"I'm not a real pony, doe," Ripley assures me. "Don't worry."

"Oh, phew. That's a relief."

Everyone laughs again.

"Are you sure about that, Ripley?" Mrs. Walters teases gently. "You look like a real pony to me."

"No, it's paint. See?" Ripley opens her eyes wide, like that's somehow going to prove her identity to Mrs. Walters, and the kind woman gamely peers into my daughter's wide eyes and says, "Oh, yes. I see it now: you're definitely a little girl wearing a fabulous disguise."

It's an adorable exchange. One that makes me instantly like Mrs. Walters—and by extension, her husband, since it's my experience only lovely men have lovely wives. Well, Alexander excluded. How that man ever landed Gigi, God only knows.

I'm thinking this conversation with the Walters will likely turn to questions about Max and me and our recent engagement —a topic I don't want to discuss in front of Ripley—so I ask Max to let Ripley down, which he does. I prompt Ripley to thank the Walters for allowing us to enjoy their beautiful slice of heaven and then suggest she find Grampy and Gigi and show them her face paint.

Ripley expresses excitement at the idea, since I rarely let her run off anywhere alone. After she dutifully thanks the Walters, I point out the spot where Dad and Gigi are still playing horse-shoes across the massive lawn and then watch with eagle eyes as she bounds to her destination and immediately gets smothered with double bear-hugs and kisses.

"She's adorable," Mrs. Walters says, her eyes trained on Ripley across the lawn. "Which of your parents are they?"

Shit. Max and I didn't discuss how to handle this question.

"Actually, they're both our parents," Max says. "My mother

and Marnie's father." He chuckles. "It might sound a bit strange at first blush, but our parents were both single when Marnie and I met. We started having family dinners to get everyone together, and the next thing we knew, those two were inseparable."

"Oh my goodness," Mrs. Walters says. "How romantic!"

I sigh with relief. "We were definitely surprised," I say. "Not to mention, a little bit worried about people thinking that's weird. You know, for our parents to get together. But it's turned out to be an incredible blessing."

"I'm sure it's made it awfully easy to blend your families," Mrs. Walters says. She waves at the air. "Don't listen to naysayers. You're all unrelated adults. I think it's fabulous you've all found love. That's the whole point of life, isn't it? Giving and receiving love."

"Thank you, Mrs. Walters. That's a lovely way to put it."

"Call me Jenny, please. And he's Wayne." She smiles at her husband. "When I met Wayne twenty years ago, I was a young widow with three small children, and everyone said I fell in love with him too soon. But you know what? Their opinions didn't matter. I knew what I felt. I knew it was right for me. And I knew my first husband would have been nothing but happy for the kids and me to have found a man as wonderful as Wayne to love us all."

Wayne seems like a man of few words. But he's certainly nodding along with his wife's comments. Adorably, when his wife finishes talking, Wayne takes her hand and kisses the top of it, letting us all know he's elated she didn't listen to naysayers, but, instead, followed her heart.

"How did you come to be a single mother, Marnie?" Mrs. Walters asks. "Are you a widow like me?"

If she'd asked me this question right away, I'd have felt defensive. Worried my answer might somehow cast me in a bad light and hurt Max's chances to impress this family-oriented couple. But now that she's already established herself as a non-judgmental and kind person, I don't mind the question at all.

"No, I've never been married," I say. "I'm a private chef. Five years ago, I was working a job in Prague and enjoying everything the city had to offer during my time off, including dating a local guy. One day, I didn't feel right, so I took a pregnancy test and got the shock of my life." Yeah, I've fudged my story a bit. I wasn't dating Ripley's sperm donor; we'd had a simple one-night stand. But I don't think that detail is anyone's business.

Both Mr. and Mrs. Walters express empathy for my shocking discovery, but not judgment, so I forge ahead. "I was terrified to go it alone. But even more than that, I was excited. The minute I saw that plus symbol on the test, I felt like it was meant to be. I went back home to Seattle to have the baby and raise her with the help of my parents. And that's what I've done, except that my mother sadly passed of cancer right before Ripley's second birthday." When Mr. and Mrs. Walters express their condolences, I thank them and add, "I'm grateful my mother was able to be there for Ripley's birth and to get to know her granddaughter for as long as she did. Also, my father and I have become really close since her passing. My father and Ripley, too. So, that's a silver lining." I look at Max. "I wasn't even looking to date anyone when I met Max. I was too busy with Ripley and work. But I fell head over heels for him, against my will, basically."

The Walters laugh.

"How could I not?" I add. "He's got the kindest, most generous and beautiful soul imaginable. He doesn't open up easily, but when he opened up to me, I fell madly in love with what I saw, and there was no turning back. I was a goner." I look away from Max, feeling like I've bared too much to him. Made myself too vulnerable.

"That's exactly how it was with Wayne and me," Mrs. Walters says. "I wasn't looking for a relationship when I met him. I was simply trying to survive with three small children.

But he walked into the charity where I worked and it was like being struck by lightning for us both. *Bam.*"

Max clears his throat. "That's exactly how it felt when I saw Marnie for the first time. Like I'd been struck by lightning." He looks at me. "*Bam.*"

My heart skips a beat.

"Good for you for following your heart, Max," Mr. Walters pipes in to say. "My mother was a single mother, just like Marnie. Exact same sort of thing, so I never knew my father. When I was around Ripley's age, she married my stepfather, and that man has been a father to me, ever since. The best father imaginable."

"That's what Wayne has been to our kids. He's their daddy, along with their daddy in heaven."

Jesus Christ. Where did these tears come from? I suddenly can't hold them back.

As I wipe my eyes with one hand, Max grabs the other and kisses the top of it, the same way Mr. Walters did to his wife's hand a moment ago. And that's it. I'm no longer falling in love with Max. I'm there. I've fallen. My brain knows he's only putting on a show. Mirroring what Mr. Walters did to win favor with him. But my stupid heart doesn't know the difference between what's real and what's fake, and it's exploding with love at Max's gentle, affectionate gesture.

"Look at that engagement ring!" Mrs. Walters says. Max bringing my hand to his mouth has shown it off, apparently. Is that what Max was intending to do—show off the ring—rather than sincerely comfort me when I started crying?

I wipe my eyes again and smile. "Oh, yes, thank you. I couldn't believe my eyes when Max dropped to his knee and proposed to me with it. He really outdid himself."

Mrs. Walters gasps and places her hand on her chest, displaying an asteroid-sized diamond on her third finger. "How did Max propose? Tell me everything. I'm a sucker for proposal stories."

Fuck. Max and I never talked about this. I think we meant to do it. It was on our list of details to hash out. But somehow, we got distracted and never got around to it.

I look at Max for help, but he says, "You tell it, honey. I love hearing you tell it." He grins at me, but his blue eyes are screaming, "Shit! How could we overlook this detail?"

"With pleasure," I say smoothly. I return to the Walters. "It was perfect. Nothing elaborate. Just heartfelt. We were having a little barbeque at the house with our best friends and family to celebrate Max getting a big win for a client at work." Ha. Had to throw that in there. "And midway through the party, Max asked everyone to gather around for a toast, at which point he kneeled before me, ring in hand, and asked me to be his wife in front of everyone we love the most, including Ripley."

"*Awww*," Mrs. Walters says. "Perfect."

I smile at Max. "After kneeling before me, Max kneeled before Ripley, too, and asked her if he could be her daddy."

Mrs. Walters loses her goddamned mind. She looks at her husband with tears in her eyes and says, "Honey, are you hearing all this?"

"I am," he says.

"What a beautiful story!" she gushes. "What a beautiful family!"

"Thank God they both said yes," Max says. "I was sweating it."

"You were not," I tease. "You knew I'd say yes."

"No, I knew *Ripley* would say yes," Max counters, making the Walters laugh. "But I wasn't positive about you. You never even wanted to date me in the beginning. I was scared to death you'd turn me down."

I look at our audience. "I'm ten years older than Max and a single mother to boot. In the beginning, I was convinced we were at different stages of our life. I kept telling him he didn't know what he was getting himself into. But he was persistent. And convincing. And soon, I was powerless to resist him."

"When did the tide turn for you?" Mrs. Walters asks, her dark eyes blazing. "Do you remember when you realized you couldn't help falling in love with him, whether you wanted to do it or not?"

"I sure do. I remember the exact moment. I'd had an emergency at work one day, so Max picked up Ripley from preschool for me and took her back home. That evening, when I got home, I discovered Max bound to a chair by toilet paper, with makeup smudged all over his face and glitter in his hair and a tiara on his head. He'd let Ripley give him a princess makeover. She was his fairy godmother, and he was Cinderella." I look at Max. "That was the precise moment I knew he was the man of my dreams."

Max's chest heaves. "That day was a turning point for me, too. That was the day I knew I could do this. I could be a father. A good one. A husband and a father." His Adam's apple bobs. "I realized I wanted to be both, more than anything."

"Oh my goodness," Mrs. Walters breathes.

Fuck. If the Walters weren't here, I'd throw my arms around Max's neck and unwisely confess all the shocking feelings I've been having for him since that precise moment. But since they are here, thankfully, I clear my throat and say, "Max isn't telling you something important about that day. He's not telling you there was a dark side to it. A very, *very* dark side." When everyone staring at me looks adequately freaked out and fearful about what the fuck I could possibly be mean, I add ominously, "To this day, no matter how many times he showers, Max *still* has glitter in his hair from that day."

Everyone, including me, bursts out laughing.

"It's true," Max says, sighing with relief. He bows his head. "Look closely and I'm sure you'll find some pink and purple sparkles."

Mr. Walters laughs and says, "Thankfully, all our kids are out of the glitter stage. But there was a time when I kept finding glitter on every item of clothing in my closet, no matter how much they got washed."

We all commiserate with Mr. Walters' story and question the wisdom of glitter being invented at all.

Mrs. Walters asks, "Are you two hoping to have a baby of your own someday?" And the minute the words leave her mouth, it takes every bit of restraint for me not to punch Max in the shoulder and scream, "Pay up, motherfucker! You owe me a hundred bucks!"

Max smirks at me, letting me know he's well aware he just lost our bet. He says, "We're actively trying, as a matter of fact. But if we're not successful, we'll both be perfectly happy with that outcome. I'd consider my life full and complete, if I get to spend the rest of it as Marnie's husband and Ripley's daddy."

As I grab Max's forearm to keep myself from keeling over, Mrs. Walters does what I wish I could have done to Max a moment ago: she punches her husband's shoulder—although, granted, much more gently and playfully than I would have punched Max.

"Okay, honey. Calm down," Mr. Walters says, laughing. He lays a palm on Max's broad shoulder. "I'm told you specialize in patent law. Is that right?"

"Yes, sir. Both business and patent law. I've got both an MBA and JD from Stanford."

What the fuck? No wonder Max is such a smart cookie about business stuff—because he's got an MBA, along with his law degree. Why didn't Max tell me he's got *two* advanced degrees? That's damned impressive. Surely, most men in Max's shoes would have mentioned that fact within the first minute of meeting a woman in a bar.

With a beaming smile, Mr. Walters says to Max, "How would you feel about me telling Scott to assign you to work exclusively on my matters after camp? I think having someone around with your two areas of specialty, combined, would be invaluable to me."

"It'd be a dream come true."

"Consider it done, then."

Max looks like he's going to explode. "Thank you, sir. Mr. Walters. Wow. Thank you."

"Wayne, please."

"Wayne. Yes. I'll work very hard for you, Wayne."

"I don't doubt it. Although, please, not so hard that you don't spend quality time with your beautiful wife and little girl."

Mrs. Walters lays her cheek on her husband's shoulder and smiles at me. "Do you see why I love this man?"

"I sure do," I say. "Thank you so much, to both of you. This is a dream come true for all of us."

Mr. Walters inhales sharply, having a thought. "What are your feelings about relocating for work, Max? To Silicon Valley, specifically. Do you and Marnie want to stay in Seattle, no matter what, or are you open to a move like that?"

"We're very open to relocating," Max says excitedly.

"Absolutely," I chime in. "I'm a private chef, so I can work anywhere. And Ripley is so young, she can still move anywhere and make new friends without missing a beat."

"I've got a top team that works very closely with me in California," Wayne says. "You'd still be employed by your firm, but you'd work alongside my in-house attorneys on high priority matters."

Max looks like he's about to explode. But he manages a fairly calm voice when he says, "That sounds amazing. Yes."

Wayne explains the gist of the role he's envisioning for Max —and he also makes it clear he's offering this unique opportunity to Max, specifically, because he's so damned impressed with him, both as a professional and as a person. The men chat for a bit until Mrs. Walters tugs on her husband's sleeve and says they should probably tend to their hosting duties and sprinkle themselves around the party.

When they're gone, Max and I look at each other, slack-jawed and astonished.

"Did that just happen?" Max says. "Please, pinch me and tell me I'm not dreaming."

I pinch his muscular arm. "You're not dreaming, Boo," I say, laughing. "You did it. You're going to work for your hero—and on his top team in Silicon Valley."

Max palms his forehead. "I can't believe it. Thank you, Marnie. Oh my fucking god. *You did this.*"

I throw my arms around Max's neck and squeeze him tight as tears of joy—along with tears of sadness that Max will be moving away from Seattle—squirt out of my eyes and down my cheeks. "You deserve this," I whisper into his neck. "Congratulations, honey."

"They fell head over heels in love with you," he says, holding me tight. "Without you, this never would have happened." He leans back to look into my face, and when he sees me crying, his features melt. "Why are you crying?"

"They're happy tears," I insist. It's not a lie, really, even if it's only a partial truth.

"You're crying happy tears for *me*?" he asks, like that's a shocking thing to believe.

"Yes, for *you*. Who else?"

Max wipes a tear from my cheek with his thumb. "I'll never be able to thank you enough, Marnie Long. I'm forever in your debt."

My heart squeezes. Oh, how I'd love to hear Maximillian Vaughn saying the word "forever" to me in a totally different context. "You owe me nothing," I whisper. "Being here and watching you achieve your longtime dream is more than enough payment of whatever debt you might think you have."

Max winces. "I forgot to talk up your private chef services to them. Don't worry, though, now that—"

"Don't be silly. That wasn't the time. Frankly, this whole week isn't the time. Let's drop that condition completely, okay?"

"A promise is a promise."

"No. It'd be weird, at best, and insulting, at worst, for you to push my stupid little business after Wayne Walters has offered you a spot on his Dream Team."

"It's not a stupid little business. You're incredibly talented. A legit genius."

I wave at the air. "Please, let's enjoy the rest of the week and be present and in the moment and not think about the plan, or our business goals, or anything but having fun. If I'd known how spectacular this place was going to be, I never would have made that stupid list of conditions."

"Are you sure?"

"Positive. You've already helped me with my business beyond my wildest dreams." I gasp. "Oh my gosh. I just realized something, Max. When you move to California to work alongside Mr. Walters, what if they invite us to dinner?"

"Shit."

"I said I can work as a private chef anywhere. Mrs. Walters is so nice, I bet she's already planning to hire me or refer me to her friends."

"Fuck. You're right. She's nice like that."

My breathing is shallow. "It never occurred to me before we got here the Walters might actually *befriend* Fake Max and Marnie. But now, given the incredible connection we've already formed with them, I think that's a very real possibility."

"So do I," Max says. "Fuck. We really hit it off with them, didn't we?"

"Well, Fake Max and Marnie did, anyway."

"*Fuck.*" Max runs his hand through his hair. "Okay. Here's what we'll do. If they invite us to dinner in California, then I'll fly you in for a command performance. You'd be willing to do that, right—spend a weekend in California for free and enjoy a great meal with me and an exceptionally nice couple?"

I wring my hands. "I don't know, Max."

He looks panicked. "What? *Why?*"

"Because I can't promise I'll be available to continue to be your fake fiancée for the rest of my fucking life, that's why."

"Well, duh. At some point, you're going to become my fake *wife.*"

I glare at him. Is he fucking kidding me? "I don't think so, Max. I've been straight with you about my relationship goals. I'm going to start looking for a serious boyfriend when we get back, remember? At some point, I'm hoping to have a fiancé—a real one—who then becomes my very real husband who actually *wants* to spend his life with Ripley and me. I won't be able to fly off to California to play fake wife with you when I'm in a committed relationship with someone else."

Max looks shell-shocked. He mutters, "Yeah, I see what you mean."

What the hell? Did he think I'd come home from camp and then sit around waiting for him to start feeling for me what I'm feeling for him? If so, Max can fuck right off with that idea. When I get home, I'm first going to throw myself a brief, but necessary, pity party about Max not wanting me the way I want him. But after that, even if I'm still in love with Max, I'm going to move on. I'll upload profiles onto all the best dating apps, including that one for celebrities. I'll ask all my friends and clients to set me up with every eligible bachelor they know. I'll pursue what I want and not settle for less because that's what I fucking deserve, even if it breaks my heart in the short-term to do it.

Max looks pained, but he's not saying a word. And that only makes me angrier with him. Does Max look tortured because he can't stand the thought of me falling in love with another man . . . Or because he's freaking out about how he's going to continue the charade around Mr. and Mrs. Walters after he moves to California? If it's the former thing, then I'm glad. I hope the thought of me with another man makes Max feel like his very soul is being sliced apart by a thousand sharp knives, all at once. If it's the latter thing, then fuck him. I've done my part. The rest is up to him.

"Should we find the rest of our family and tell them your spectacular news?" I suggest.

"Uh, yeah." He's distracted. Deep in thought. Visibly stressed.

I pat Max's arm. "Don't worry too much about the future, okay? You just got your dream job. Let's focus on that and celebrate. The future is unknown. Anything can happen. One way or another, we'll figure it out."

Max looks hopeful. "Does that mean you'll help me again, if you can?"

Fuck. I'd love to leave him hanging and twist the knife; but unfortunately, I also love the man and dislike watching him suffer. "Yes, if I can. We're going into business together, remember? I'm sure I'll need to fly to meetings with my business partner now and again, right? And while I'm in California for business, I suppose I could go to dinner with you and the Walters, if that sort of invitation comes up. Which might never happen. We're probably getting ahead of ourselves on that stuff, anyway."

Max looks relieved. In fact, the sparkle is back in his blue eyes. "Yeah, we'll figure it out, right? No need to stress about it now."

"If worst came to worse, you could always kill Fake Marnie off," I suggest. "That'd be a perfect solution."

Max rolls his eyes. "So, instead of sending out fake wedding invitations, I'd be hosting a fake funeral?"

"Make sure it's somewhere pretty with lots of flowers, please. And don't worry, you'd only need to fake-grieve me for a year or two, and then you could hire an actress in California to play fiancée number two. That'd be much more convenient than constantly having to fly me in."

"That's an excellent point."

"Plus, California is positively teeming with professional actresses. I'm sure you'll find someone brilliantly talented to fill my shoes there."

"Nah. Nobody else could ever come close." Max beams me a wide smile, and despite the swirl of emotions I'm feeling, the anger, the yearning, the feelings of rejection because he's clearly not feeling what I am, I can't resist returning his smile in kind.

"I really can't thank you enough," Max says. "I can't believe he offered me a spot on his top team on Day *One* of camp, thanks to you. I didn't see that coming. Not in my wildest dreams."

"It takes the pressure off for the week, doesn't it? Now, all we have to do this week is relax and have a great time together."

Max nods. "And that won't even require acting. At least, not for me."

Fucking hell. Is he *trying* to torture me? "Not for me, either," I admit begrudgingly. "I always have a blast with you." My heart is thundering, and my cheeks turning hot, so I look around the party. "Do you see Ripley and our parents? We should find them."

We both survey the bustling party for a moment.

"Found 'em," Max says. He points across the lawn. "They're waiting in the sundae line."

And off we go.

"You owe me a hundred bucks, by the way," I murmur. "Mrs. Walters asked if you want a kid of your own. *On day one*. Told you so."

Max chuckles. "I should never have doubted you." He beams yet another glorious smile at me and takes my hand. "It'll never happen again. I'm now thoroughly convinced Marnie Long is a fucking genius, in more ways than one."

27
MAX

After beating off an hour ago, I've been lying in my lonely bed in our cabin, tossing and turning and trying every trick I know to fall asleep. But I can't make it happen. I'm too amped for a myriad of reasons. For one thing, I can't believe I'm finally going to be working for my longtime hero, Wayne Walters. And not as one of the many lawyers assigned to his matters at my law firm; no, in a shocking twist I never saw coming, Mr. Walters has offered me an unprecedented slot, working alongside his in-house lawyers in Silicon Valley. Coming here, the biggest I could dream was that I'd somehow ingratiate myself enough to Wayne Walters this week to secure myself a spot on his legal team back home at the firm, which might eventually lead to me proving myself enough to one day, possibly, get myself hired as part of Mr. Walters' in-house team of lawyers in California. I never in a million years thought he'd create a position, specifically for me, working alongside his in-house team while still working for my firm.

Of course, the man only did that because I've defrauded him. Because Wayne thinks I'm a guy who fell madly in love with a spitfire single mother and her daughter and moved heaven and earth to make them my own family.

Fuck.

The reality of what I've done is suddenly hitting me like a ton of bricks.

Shit.

I didn't imagine myself spewing lie after lie once we got here. I thought Marnie and Ripley would be my ticket to get here, but that's it. I thought I'd somehow manage to have a conversation or two with Mr. Walters over the course of the week. And that one thing might lead to another, and he'd remember my name when it came time to assign lawyers to his team, and I'd then be able to weasel my way into the slot. I never thought I'd actively dupe the man.

I turn on my other side and breathe deeply, trying to calm myself down. But I can't make it happen. This time, for another reason. God help me, when Marnie said that thing about maybe having a serious boyfriend in the future—and then, maybe even a husband—I felt a surge of jealousy inside me like nothing I've experienced before. It wasn't rational. Made no sense. But the mere thought of her falling in love and building a life with someone else made my blood flash-boil inside my veins. And now, thinking about it again, I'm having the exact same physical reaction.

I roll onto my other side.

Marnie was so sexy at the party today. So magnetic and confident. No wonder the Walters fell in love with her. Who wouldn't? She was a knockout. A genius. The way she so deftly handed me my dreams on a silver platter, I want nothing more than to thank her by making her come tonight.

I turn on my side. And then onto my back.

It's definitely not helping me fall asleep to know that Marnie is lying in a bed on the other side of that wall, and I can't knock on her door and invite her into my bed. If I could, I'd—

A soft knock on my bedroom door interrupts my thoughts. Did I imagine that? I get out of bed and creep across the room, past a painting of a cowboy on a horse herding cattle, and open the door a crack.

Marnie.

She's standing before me, breathing hard.

"I can keep things straight and compartmentalized, if you can," she whispers. "I propose we put sex back on the table this week. No strings. We're here together, sleeping under the same roof, so—"

"Hell yes."

I yank her into my room by her arm, close the door, and kiss her against it. And when we're both so horny, we're gasping for air, we rip our clothes off and hurtle onto the bed. Panting, I spread her legs wide open and devour the meal I've been craving like a drug all day—the one I can't get enough of, no matter how many times I've indulged my cravings. In no time at all, Marnie is writhing and groaning and, eventually, warping deliciously against my tongue, lips, and fingers.

My breathing is labored like I've sprinted around the block at full speed. Growling with anticipation, I place Marnie's legs on my shoulders and plow into her. As I push myself inside her, all the way, Marnie groans so loudly, I reflexively place my palm over her mouth to muffle the sound. I adore the chatterbox in the next room, but if she wakes up and calls for her mother in the next few minutes, I'll be hard-pressed not to drop-kick her across the twenty-thousand-acre ranch.

With one palm over Marnie's mouth and the other lightly gripping her neck, I deep-fuck my woman with everything I've got—and, holy fucking hell, she feels better than ever. Everything this woman does turns me on. Every sound she makes. Every smile and belly laugh and toss of her hair. And now, on top of everything else, this goddess somehow managed to make my dreams come true as easily as she cooks up a gourmet meal? She's magic. That's the only way to explain it. This woman is magic, and I'm most definitely under her spell.

"You feel so fucking good," I groan out, and she moans incoherently behind my palm. "You're so sexy, baby. Oh, fuck, I'm gonna come so hard."

Marnie lets out a tortured sound behind my hand, and I can feel her muscles tightening around my cock, like they're coiling and getting ready to release.

"That's it, baby," I growl. I gently squeeze the sides of her neck, and she moans even harder. "Come on, baby." My thrusts are becoming more and more enthusiastic. I *need* to come inside her. I *need* to claim her and ruin her for anybody else.

When Marnie releases, when I feel her muscles rippling, I let myself go, too. For a moment we're one. There's no Marnie and Max. There's only our nuclear fusion. Our combined energy. Our mutual bliss. But, finally, we both exhale and collapse into a tangled, sweaty heap of racing hearts and flopping limbs.

When my soul has reentered my body, I roll off Marnie and lie next to her, motionless. When I'm finally capable, I head to the bathroom to take a piss and grab some tissues for Marnie to wipe herself up. When I return to the bed and hand Marnie the tissues, she says, "I was worried you were gonna say no."

"To what?"

"Sex."

I laugh and slide into bed. "I would have come to your door myself if I didn't think suggesting sex would get me stabbed."

"My horniness would have won out over my urge to kill you. Actually, my urge to kill you would have made it even hotter."

"Hotter than what we just did? Impossible."

I pull her to me, thinking we'll cuddle for a bit and maybe even have sex again, but Marnie sits up and pats my arm. "I think I'll shower and get back into bed with Ripley. I don't want to risk falling asleep here with you. I wouldn't want Ripley to discover us sleeping together in the morning."

My heart sinks. She's right, obviously. But I can't help wishing she could stay. "Yeah, that's a good idea."

"Good night, Maxy-Milly," she whispers. "Sleep tight."

"You, too."

She pecks my lips and slides out of bed but stops walking when I whisper her name.

"You were incredible today," I say, when she turns to look at me. "I was in awe of you, Marnie."

"It was a team effort." With that, she blows me a kiss, winks, and slips quietly out of the room.

When she's gone, I lie back down and stare at the ceiling. Why does my stomach hurt right now? I should be feeling nothing but euphoria, and yet, I feel a pit in my stomach like I've fucked something up. Made a wrong turn. Am I incapable of feeling truly satisfied? If I can't feel full satisfaction now, after accomplishing the goal I set for myself in law school, then when will I ever feel it? Am I doomed to feel eternally incomplete?

I roll onto my side in a huff, but my new position doesn't fix the problem. *I've messed up.* Am I feeling guilty for lying to Mr. and Mrs. Walters today? Yeah, that's definitely part of it. A big part. It seemed like a great idea at the time, but now that I've looked into the man's eyes and told my lies and made him think I'm the kind of man who got down on bended knee before Marnie, the same way he got down on bended knee before his own wife, I'm feeling guilty about my little ruse. My *lies.* Let's call them what they were.

And yet . . .

As bad as I feel about that, I don't think the fraud I've perpetrated on Wayne Walters is the main source of this nagging feeling. I think it's more related to Marnie in this moment. I loved seeing that ring on her finger today and knowing it means she's all mine. At least, at family camp. I loved introducing her as my fiancée today. And, man, did I love watching Ripley racing around the opening party like the top of her head was going to pop clean off from glee.

But all of that is situational, right? I couldn't rationally expect those feelings to continue back home, especially now that I'm moving. I need to remember Marnie and Ripley will be living in Seattle when we get back, while I'll be living in California. Even if I wanted to try to be the man Marnie seriously dates when camp is over, how could I swing that? I couldn't. That's the only conceivable answer to that question. *It wouldn't work.* To suggest otherwise would be pure lunacy.

I lie awake with my racing thoughts for at least another hour. But finally, blessedly, at some point, sleep comes for me, and with it, the promise of a new day with a fresh start, and hopefully, the absence of the nagging thoughts currently swirling inside my head—the ones making me feel like a gigantic piece of shit.

28

MARNIE

As Max twirls me around the dance floor, I throw my head back and laugh from the depths of my soul. It's the last night of family camp, and we're having a blast at an old-fashioned country fair, complete with rides, games, and a live band that's been pumping out country-music standards for our dancing and listening pleasure. I'm not a big fan of country music, generally, but even I've been able to recognize and enjoy every smash hit on the band's play list.

As the song ends, Max dips me, making me giggle—and when he returns me to an upright position, I throw my arms around his neck, buzzing with the desire to kiss him. Max and I agreed not to lock lips whenever Ripley might see, but following that rule feels like a tall order in this euphoric moment. In fact, after a week of daily fun and nightly sex and all-around family bonding with Max, it feels like the most natural thing in the world to give him a smooch at a happy moment like this. Some-how, though, I force myself to give Max a peck on his cheek, same as always, before breaking free of his strong embrace.

"Impressive dancing, you two!" a female voice calls out nearby, and we both turn to find Mr. and Mrs. Walters in a clinch a few feet away on the dance floor.

"The band is great!" I call back. "We're having a blast."

"We can see that," Mr. Walters says with a wink. "You two are showing everyone how it's done."

Oh, my heart. It was one thing to impress our targets with our fake romance when we first got here. When that was the plan. But throughout this week, we've become genuine friends with these wonderful people, so I can't help feeling guilty about our continued deception. Even worse? I don't even feel like I'm deceiving them. I feel like I've been nothing but honest throughout this whole week because I've only been doing what comes naturally. Acting on what's in my heart. Namely, my undeniable, heart-rending, heart-melting love for one Maximillian Vaughn.

"Should we find Ripley and our parents?" I ask. "We've been dancing for a while."

"Yeah, let's see what they're up to," Max agrees. He grabs my hand, and we head into the heart of the party.

When we find our people, Ripley's waiting in line to run a three-legged race with another little girl while Grampy and Gigi stand nearby, ready to cheer the girls on. Ripley made friends with this little girl on the first full day of camp, and they've been inseparable, ever since.

When Ripley sees Max and me, she shouts, "Mommy! Maxy! Watch us race! If we win, we'll get a trophy!"

Max and I stop next to Dad and Gigi.

"Every team gets a trophy," Dad murmurs, and we all laugh.

A staffer goes down the line, tying each team's inner legs together, and when she gets to Ripley and her friend, Max says he's gonna head over there to give the girls a few pointers for the race. Curious, I follow him. And then smile when I overhear Max's advice to the girls.

As he crouches down before the kids, Max says, "Okay, girls, here's how you're gonna get that trophy. Ripley. Sweetie. Look at me, honey."

Sweetie? *Honey*? He's never called her either of those

endearments before. My heart can't bear it, especially knowing it's probably the one and only time he'll ever call Ripley those things, since we're leaving camp tomorrow and Max will be moving to California shortly thereafter. After this, when will Ripley get to spend quality time with her beloved Maxy-Milly, ever again? When will she ever get to hear him call her sweetie or honey? I'm guessing never.

Max grabs Ripley's glasses and cleans them on his shirt as he talks. "Here's the key to winning this race, girls," he says. "All you have to do is remain upright through the whole race. That means never falling down. That's it. Everyone else is going to sprint off the starting line way too fast and get caught up and fall over. So, as long as you go slow and steady from the start, and keep yourselves upright the whole time, I guarantee you'll make it to the podium. That means you'll come in first, second, or third place and win a trophy."

Ripley gasps. "I've wanted to win a trophy my whole life."

He hands Ripley her glasses. "Well, follow my advice and you will."

I snicker. "Or don't. And you will, regardless." Nobody can hear me back here. I'm merely amusing myself.

"Work as a team," Max continues. "That's the key. You're both too little for one of you to drag the other, so you have to work together. Got it?"

"Got it!" both girls shriek.

Max puts up his palm, and both girls high-five their coach with gleeful squeals. I look away, my heart aching. At this point, everything that man does only makes me want him more. It's excruciating.

"I'll stand on the sideline and coach you during the race, cutie pie," Max says to Ripley. "Henry, will you come be my assistant coach? There's a lot riding on this."

Dad laughs. "You bet."

As Dad and Max trot away toward the sideline, Gigi stands

next to me behind the starting line. "Wonders never cease," she murmurs.

"He's a competitive dude," I reply, figuring Gigi is talking about Max's surprising level of commitment to coaching the girls in the race.

"No, I mean, Max just called Ripley cutie pie. I haven't heard Max call anyone that, in any context, ever."

My heart stops. *Gigi caught that, too?*

I smile. "Max isn't one for terms of endearment?"

"Not really. At least, not that I've heard for quite some time."

"He calls me Boo, when we're being silly."

"Really?"

"When we're playing our parts." *And, lately, he calls me baby in bed, too.* As a matter of fact, Max whispers "baby" into my ear, like it's a sacred prayer, every time we make love. Or, rather, have sex. I'm making love these days. Max is still fucking me. But whatever. The point is, I happen to know Max uses terms of endearment quite liberally. At least during sex with me. And it always turns me on like crazy. But, of course, that's not something I'm going to tell his mother.

"On your marks, get set, go!" a staffer yells. And off the racers go. Immediately, after literally one step, our team topples over into a pile of rubble, causing Max to jump up and down like a lunatic on the sideline, cheering them on.

"Almost everyone else fell, too!" Max shouts at the girls. "You've still got this! Get up and keep going!" When the girls finally get up, we all cheer them on like crazy. And with each staggered step they manage to take as a unit, our cheering only intensifies until it's reached a fever pitch.

"That's it, sweetie!" Max shouts at Ripley. "You've got this, peanut! Go, Ripley, go!"

"Oh my goodness," Gigi whispers. She looks at me and it's like a lightbulb has gone off inside her head. "*Marnie*," she says, her eyes wide. "What on earth?"

Blushing, I turn away just as the girls reach the finish line

towards the back of the pack. We race over to them, along with
the other girl's parents, untie their legs, and celebrate. And
through it all, I can feel Gigi's eyes on me.

Max puts Ripley on his shoulders and off they go to collect
her plastic trophy. And when she has it in hand, Max runs around
with Ripley on his shoulders, alongside the other little girl and
her father, with each girl holding up her plastic trophy in
triumph.

"It's wonderful to see Max having so much fun with Ripley,"
Gigi says. "I haven't seen Max's goofy side in way too long."

"He's got a whole goofy *side*?" I joke. "And here I thought
he had a goofy streak, at most."

"Oh, no. As a kid, Max was my silly, affectionate little goofball. But it's been a long time since he's let down his walls and
shown that side of himself the way he's doing now."

"Are you referring to what happened with his father when he
was fifteen?" I ask.

Gigi nods. "He also suffered a terrible heartbreak in college
that changed him. I thought he'd bounce back after a while. But
he never did. Not fully, anyway."

My heart is racing. "What kind of heartbreak?"

Gigi presses her lips together. "Max would have to tell you
about that." She looks at me pointedly. "Ask him if he's ever
been in love, Marnie. See what he says to that."

I sigh. "What would be the point in doing that? He'll be
moving to California when we get back. There's no future for us,
so there's no need to push him into having a heart-to-heart with
me about his romantic past."

"Maybe a heart-to-heart is the exact thing that would make a
future possible."

"That's a pipe dream, Gigi."

She looks at me intently. "I haven't seen Max this happy in a
long time. He's lit up around you and Ripley. Calling her cutie
pie and honey and sweetie and peanut and gazing at you like you
walk on water. He's a new man." When I shake my head, Gigi

grabs my hand. "Don't let him fool you into thinking he doesn't want you, Marnie. I'd bet my life he does. Max has had his walls up for a very long time. So long, I don't think he knows how to take them down without a little help and encouragement from someone he trusts and loves. Someone who loves him back." She tilts her head. "Do I have that right? I can tell Max loves you. *Do you love him back*?"

I glance at Max across the lawn, where he's now talking with Dad, Ripley, the other little girl, and her parents. "Yes, I love him," I admit, even though it pains me to say it out loud. "But it doesn't matter because you're wrong about *him*. He doesn't love *me* back, Gigi."

She shakes her head. "His walls are up, that's all."

"If you think I'm the right person to show him how to take them down, then you're wrong about that. I've got my own walls up. *I'm* the one who needs help taking *my* walls down."

Gigi sighs. "One of you is going to have to be vulnerable first. I know it's scary, but since when do you back away from something that scares you?"

"Always. I always do that. At least, when it comes to being vulnerable with my feelings."

"Oh." She considers that. "Okay, well, you're turning over a new leaf, starting today."

I laugh. "I love you, Gigi."

"I love you, too. Maybe I'm being selfish, but I've loved watching Max's face light up around you and Ripley this week. I've loved watching him fall head over heels in love. I don't want that to end."

The comment slays me. But before I've replied, Dad appears with funnel cakes for Gigi and me, and we sit on a blanket and eat them while watching the next two three-legged races—both featuring kids older than Ripley.

"And now, it's time for an adult race!" the announcer says. "Adult teams of two report to the starting line!"

Gigi and Dad bound off enthusiastically to participate

without hesitation, and a moment later, Max plops down next to me on the blanket.

"They're seriously gonna race?" Max says.

"They seemed excited about it."

"They're so damned cute."

"Where's Ripley?"

Max points to my daughter across the lawn, where she's twirling with another little girl and a camp counselor.

The announcer says, "We've still got room at the starting line for the adult race. Are there any other teams of two? Come on over."

Max nudges my leg. "What do you say, Red? Should we try to beat our parents to a three-legged pulp?"

I giggle. "Let's do it. My father never let me win anything as a kid past the age of ten. I had to earn it, every time."

"Now, that's a good daddy. Exactly the kind I'm gonna be one day."

What the fuck? It's the first I've heard Max say anything that confirms he definitely plans to become a father one day. If he'd said, "That's the kind of father I'd be," I wouldn't feel quite as shocked, but that's not what he said. As Max pulls me up and off the blanket, I look around for Mr. Walters or his wife nearby, but they're nowhere to be found. So why the heck did Max make that shocking comment? Who was he trying to impress?

I don't have time to think about it. Suddenly I'm standing at the starting line with my leg tied to Max's, talking smack with Gigi and Dad next to us.

"On your marks!" the announcer booms. "Get set . . . Go!"

And we're off. Or at least, I am. Max has a different idea. Without warning, he leans to his side and lifts me up off the ground and onto his hip, at which point he sprints to the finish line with me on his hip, giggling my ass off without my feet ever touching the grass. Not surprisingly, by the time Max and I cross the finish line, we've left every other team in the dust, including Dad and Gigi, and we're both laughing hysterically.

When it's clear we've won the race, we tumble onto the grass in a mutual fit of laughter. One minute, he's on top of me laughing and I'm underneath him, giggling and feeling light-headed, and the next, we're kissing. Did Max lean down or did I lean up? I have no idea. All I know is I'm enjoying the most electrifying kiss of my life with the man I love, while the rest of the world melts away.

To my surprise, Max doesn't quickly pull away from our kiss like he's touched a hot stove. Even after he's had ample time to realize what we're doing, he deepens the kiss. Revels in it. *Savors it.* He brushes his fingertips against my cheek as his mouth devours mine. And then rakes his fingertips through my hair. And I let him do all of it because I'm weak and stupid and totally caught up in the moment.

"Mommy?" Ripley's little voice says. "Can Fantasia and I get cotton candy?"

Aw, fuck.

Max and I break apart and scramble to get disentangled. But since we're still bound together at the leg, we're not remotely successful. While Max unties our legs, I stammer my reply to Ripley. "No, honey. You already had ice cream, remember?"

Ripley looks from Max to me. "Why were you kissing Maxy?"

"Because we won the race. We were so happy we won the race, we gave each other a little kiss to celebrate."

"*Oh.*" Ripley looks disappointed.

Gigi quickly swoops in and grabs Ripley's hand. "Hey, honey. Guess what time it is? It's time for the Pony Parade!"

Ripley shrieks with excitement, and it's clear all thoughts of my kiss with Max have left her head.

"I'll take her with you," Dad says to Gigi. He flashes me a pointed look that tells me he's purposefully giving me the chance to speak to Max in private.

"I'm so sorry," Max says when the others are gone. "I don't know what came over me."

"It came over me, too. She'll forget about it, soon enough. She probably already has."

Max runs a hand through his hair. "I'm sorry, Marnie."

"I did it, as much as you did."

"Hellooo!" Mrs. Walters says, as she, her husband, and Max's boss, Scott, and his wife, approach. "Are you ready for the Pony Parade?"

"So ready!" I say, matching her energy.

"Don't tell anyone," Mrs. Walters says in a joking stage whisper, as she comes to a stop in front of Max and me. "But the very best place to watch the pony parade is over there. Care to join us?"

"Of course!" I chirp. I practically sprint to join Mr. and Mrs. Walters as they start walking toward the designated spot, leaving Max several steps behind me to chat with Scott and his wife. What was I thinking? Why didn't I pull back from that kiss? And the biggest question of all, did that kiss actually mean something to Max? Did he cross that line because he's developed feelings for me, or was it nothing but an impulsive mistake?

We get situated along the parade route on blankets provided by a friendly staffer. Wine, beer, and champagne are distributed, along with little baskets filled with crackers, cheese, and fruit. As we drink and nibble, I chat away with the Walters on the next blanket while Max chats with his boss on the blanket to our other side. In fact, besides Max and me clinking our glasses after Mrs. Walters says a sweet toast to "a great week and new friends," Max and I don't even look at each other, let alone speak. There's an elephant sitting on this blanket with Max and me. A pink, huge one that's plopped itself down between us and is now making me question everything.

After a while, Dad and Gigi join Max and me on our blanket, at which point we flag down a roaming server and get them drinks and a basket of goodies, too. They tell the group how excited Ripley was as her riding instructor for the week loaded her onto her designated pony—a sweet, gentle animal named Tootsie who's been carrying Ripley around all week.

After a few minutes, a man with a cowboy hat and microphone gleefully announces the pony parade will now begin.

We stand in anticipation of the kids being led past us in their sparkling helmets and scarves—accessories they decorated themselves in arts and crafts sessions all week. And a moment later, there she is. Our Ripley, looking as happy as I've ever seen her on Tootsie's back. Clearly, my sweet daughter has died and gone to heaven, and I couldn't be happier for her. At the sight of her beaming smile, tears of pride and joy flood me until I can barely see my grinning cowgirl through them.

On and on, my tears continue to flow, as Ripley slowly makes her way along the parade route with her designated staffer who's leading her pony carefully. I wish so badly this week didn't have to end. I wish it could go on forever. If only this fake engagement and love that feels so damned real for me could feel real for Max, too.

A high-pitched shriek of terror yanks me from my thoughts —and, suddenly, my brain realizes what I'm seeing. *Ripley is going down.* For reasons I can't fathom, she tried to twist on top of her pony, and wound up falling to the ground, as if in slow motion.

When Ripley's body reaches the grass, she bounces and crumples . . . *and then doesn't move*. It's an unnatural thing to behold her lying crumpled and still like that—and it instantly stops my heart. Did she break her neck? Is she still breathing? Oh, God, please let my baby be okay!

I scramble to leap off the blanket as fast as I can, but even before I'm fully vertical, Max is gone. Sprinting toward Ripley at full speed. I trail behind him, feeling nearly hysterical about what we're going to find when we get there, and then watch with wide, frantic eyes as Max dives in front of a staffer onto his knees in front of Ripley's motionless body.

"Don't move her, Max!" I shout. "Don't move her!"

By the time I reach Max, Ripley is moving, thank God, and Max is frantically patting down her tiny body down and inspecting every limb. As Ripley sits up, a woman arrives, shouting that she's a doctor. As a small crowd forms around us, Ripley says, "Mommy?"

"I'm here, baby. I'm right here." I dive down next to Max and burst into tears as the doctor examines my baby and quickly determines she's perfectly healthy and intact.

"Looks like she got the wind knocked out of her," the doctor declares. "That's all."

"I'm okay," Ripley says, standing up and dusting off her jeans. "Can I get back on Tootsie now?" The parade stopped when Ripley fell, and now everyone is looking at us for a sign of what to do next.

Still kneeling, I hug Ripley to me and cry with relief. "What on earth were you trying to do? You scared me to death."

"I saw you and Max crying, so I wanted to hug you, so you wouldn't be sad anymore," Ripley replies into my hair. "But den, it was a long way down and I went *boom*."

I laugh through my tears. "I was crying tears of joy because I'm so proud of you, peanut, not because I'm sad."

"Was Maxy crying tears of joy, too?" She looks expectantly at Max next to me.

Max looks at me, at a loss for words. When he returns to Ripley, he says, "I wasn't crying, honey. I think maybe I got some dust in my eye." His eyes meet mine again, but he quickly looks down.

"I'm so relieved she's okay," Mrs. Walters says on an exhale. She's crouching down next to me, looking pale. "I'm so sorry, Marnie."

"It's nobody's fault," I say. "Ripley suddenly thought she was six feet tall."

Ripley points at her nearby pony. "Can I finish da parade now?"

"No, honey," I say. "We've had enough excitement for one day."

"I want to finish the parade," Ripley insists. She puts her little hands on her hips and glares at me through her glasses for emphasis.

Max leans into me. "Let her get back on the horse, babe. Literally. There's a reason that's an age-old saying."

I look behind me, assuming my father is around here somewhere. He is. Right behind me with Gigi and Mr. Walters. When my eyes meet Dad's, he nods his agreement with Max.

"Okay, fine," I say. I tug on Ripley's arm. "But no wiggling this time. Stay put."

"I will!"

"I'll walk alongside you," Max says. "To make sure of it."

To my surprise, Ripley cheers. Apparently, Max tagging along won't cramp her cowgirl style at all. On the contrary, she's thrilled to have him as her personal escort.

"Come on, cowgirl," Max says. He scoops Ripley up and carries her in his strong arms to her vacated pony while the rest of us head back to our blankets.

As we walk, Mr. and Mrs. Walters apologize profusely. And again, I assure them it's nobody's fault but Ripley's. She's had careful riding instruction all week long. She knew to sit there and hold on. It was a total fluke.

When apologies have died down and everyone relaxes again, the group watches Max with Ripley. Mrs. Walters leans into me and says, "Max is so darling with Ripley. And Ripley obviously worships the ground he walks on."

My stomach tightens. "Yes, she does."

As promised, Max is walking protectively alongside Ripley on her pony as the parade slowly winds its way along its route, and the sight of his big hand gripping her tiny leg to make sure she remains steady and safe is doing crazy things to me.

"Ripley was right, by the way," Mrs. Walters says to me. "Max one hundred percent teared up when he saw her on that pony. Same as you. Wayne saw it before me. He's the one who nudged my arm and told me to look at Max's sweet facial expression. He definitely loves your little girl like his own. He's a keeper, for sure."

I feel sick. "Yes, he is."

"It's been a long time since Wayne and I have met a couple who reminds us of ourselves. Wayne and I believe in soulmates, and it's been such a joy to be around another pair of them this week."

My lower lip trembles, but I take a deep breath and stuff my rising emotion down. "Thank you so much. Max and I have loved being around you and Wayne this week, too." Shit. I'm crying. Big, soggy tears. Only this time, my tears are most definitely *not* borne of joy.

29
MAX

"Will you read me another one, Maxy-Milly?" Ripley whispers in the tiniest possible voice as she looks up at me from her pillow.

I look at Marnie for permission, and she shakes her head.

"Nah, Mommy says two is what you get tonight, cowgirl," I say. "And she's right. You've had a big day, and we've got a long travel day tomorrow. Time to get some sleep."

I've never helped put Ripley to bed before. Marnie has done it on her own every night this week after I've given Ripley a hug and goodnight kiss in the main room of our cabin. But after the scare we had earlier today during the pony parade, I found myself following Marnie and Ripley into the bedroom to get just a little more time with my little cowgirl—I guess, to convince my jangly nerves, once again, that she's truly okay. In fact, there's not a scratch on her other than a little bruise on her leg from where she fell. But knowing it could have been a whole lot worse has been wreaking havoc on my nervous system all day long.

"Will you both stay till I fall asleep?" Ripley asks. "Dat way, I won't have a nightmeero."

"Of course, we will," Marnie says, as I say, "You bet, sweetie pie."

Ripley closes her eyes, and my heart skips a beat at her adorableness in repose. Her little eyelashes set against her skin. Her rosebud mouth turning slack.

"I love you, Mommy," Ripley whispers, her voice already relaxed.

"I love you, too, peanut."

"I love you, Maxy."

I've never said it back to her. I've thanked her. Shucked and jived and figured out all sorts of deflections in reply. But this time, the words tumble out easily. "I love you, too, princess."

Ripley's eyes shoot open, and a wide smile splits her little face. Apparently, this being the first time I've said it back hasn't gone unnoticed. In fact, she's lit up. The opposite of what we want her to be while trying to get her to fall asleep.

"Mommy, are you and Maxy going to kiss again?"

I'm sure Marnie's freaking out every bit as much as me but she manages to smooth a lock of hair away from Ripley's cheek and calmly reply, "No, honey. That was a one-time thing."

"Naomi's parents kiss. I saw Grampy kiss Gigi, too."

Marnie looks at me, as if to say, "Now what?"

"Yeah, adults who really like each other sometimes kiss," I say.

"You really like Mommy?"

"I do. Yes."

"Do you really like Maxy?"

"I do," Marnie says stiffly. "Maxy is moving to another state —to California—for a really exciting job, though, so we won't get to see him very much when we get home. This week was a special time to get to spend with him, but this is all the time we're going to get, unfortunately."

"Is dat the same place where we went to Disneyland?"

"It is. The place Maxy is moving isn't close to Disneyland, but, yes, California is home to Disneyland."

Ripley considers that. "Can we move to California with Maxy, so we can see him every day and night, like at camp?"

My heart stops. And by the look on Marnie's face, her ticker is doing something similar.

"No, honey. We're going to stay in Seattle."

I feel the need to reassure Ripley of my affection for her. To make sure she understands I'm moving to make my professional dreams come true, but that doesn't mean I won't miss her. But my tongue is tied and my brain short-circuiting.

"Max is moving to California for a job he's wanted for a very long time," Marnie says. "So, let's be happy for him, instead of sad for ourselves because we'll miss him, okay?"

Ripley doesn't look convinced. But she manages a sweet little "okay," even through her obvious disappointment.

"Now, go to sleep, love muffin," Marnie says. "We've got a big travel day tomorrow."

"How come I have a mommy and a Grampy, but Naomi has a mommy and a daddy *and* a grampy and a grammy? Why can't I have a daddy and a grammy, like her?"

Marnie stifles a whimper. "Gigi is like a grammy now, don't you think? And not every family has a daddy. Some families, like ours, only have a mommy. Other families have *two* mommies. Some have two daddies or—"

"I only want one daddy," Ripley says. Her little chin is wobbling. "I want Maxy to be my daddy."

Marnie and I both have instant, palpable reactions. For her part, Marnie's breathing halts. Her body stiffens. On my end, tears spring into my eyes. This is exactly what Marnie *didn't* want to happen. Exactly the thing that made her say no in the beginning. And suddenly, I'm realizing I should have listened to her. I shouldn't have pushed and cajoled and begged. I should have put Ripley first, not my career ambitions. It's all so clear to me now. I've failed this little person, and I'm gutted about it.

When it's clear Marnie's at a loss for words, I take over. "I'm sorry," I say. "I just can't. But that doesn't mean I don't love you. Because I do. With all my heart."

Ripley sits up and hugs me, and it takes all my willpower not to break down and sob into her soft hair.

"I love you, Maxy-Milly," she whispers.

"I love you too, cowgirl. I've had the best week ever with you. Wasn't it fun?"

"It was da best week of my entire life."

"Mine too. I'm gonna miss you when I move to California."

"I'm gonna miss you, too."

"Excuse me," Marnie whispers hoarsely. "Max will stay with you till you fall asleep, honey. Mommy has to go to the bathroom."

My eyes are closed, and my face still buried in Ripley's hair, but from the sound of Marnie's voice and rapid footsteps, it's clear she's not merely walking out of the room. *She's fleeing.*

"Okay, bedtime," I say, after I've gathered myself, and Ripley lies back down.

"Will you tickle my face while I fall asleep?" she says. "Like dis." She flutters her fingertips over her cheeks and forehead.

"Sure."

With a satisfied little grin, Ripley closes her eyes while I run my fingertips along the planes and grooves of her perfect, angelic face, and when her breathing becomes rhythmic and her lips part, when I'm sure she's fast asleep, I creep out of the room and find Marnie sitting on the couch with her head in her hands.

I sit next to her. "I blew it. I shouldn't have pushed you to come here."

She drops her hands. "Are you kidding me? It was the best week of her life. Mine, too. I wouldn't have missed it for anything, no matter what happens next."

I'm floored. "Really?"

Marnie nods. "This week was magic for both of us."

"For me, too. Best week of my life."

She smiles weakly. "Nothing comes for free. I knew that

when I said yes." She swallows hard like she's physically stuffing down words on the tip of her tongue. And, suddenly, I can't wait a second longer to kiss her. I pull her to me and press my lips to hers, and Marnie slides into my lap and straddles me. We don't maul each other, though, like usual. There's no sense of urgency in our kiss. It's not primal, heated lust fueling our lips this time. It's affection. Emotion. Sadness. *This is a slow and tender goodbye kiss.*

I take Marnie's face in my palms as I continue to kiss her. To revel in her. As my tongue swirls with hers, I try to memorize everything about this moment, so I can remember it forever. Soon, though, I'm too aroused to continue doing this here. I get up, lifting her along with me, and carry her into the bedroom.

After laying her onto the bed, I get her clothes off, and then mine, and return to kissing her. After kissing her mouth, I kiss her cheek, her jawline, her neck, as my fingers gently stroke her slit. She's getting wetter and wetter with my touch, and her clit harder and more swollen. She's plainly aching for me, every bit as much as I'm aching for her; but since this might be the last time I'll ever get to fuck Marnie Long, I force myself to take my time. To memorize, revel, and prolong. I never want this moment, this night—this week—this *life*—to end. But end, it must. Which means it's time to fuck her farewell in a way that honors the time we've shared and hopefully creates a lasting memory.

Marnie is writhing and moaning now as I continue kissing and caressing her. She's so fucking wet, I'd sink into her like a knife in warm butter if I went in now. But it's too soon. If this is it for us, if this is all I'm ever gonna get of this goddess, then I want to draw this out as long as I can. I leave her mouth again and start kissing every inch of her, from her jawline to her breasts and belly, to her hips and thighs, and finally make my way between her legs. By the time I get to her clit and lick her bull's-eye—once, twice, three times—Marnie grips the sheet beneath us and comes with a loud groan, which she quickly stifles by shoving a pillow over her face.

When her pleasure subsides, she removes the pillow, and I kiss her again. As our kiss deepens, I slowly sink myself inside her—all the way—and the moment my full length is buried, it feels like a dam breaks inside me. Emotion surges inside me. Rightness. *This feels like home. Exactly where I'm supposed to be.*

A hurricane of deep-seated need and desire and yearning envelops me. As I move my pelvis, Marnie matches my movement, until we're a single, gyrating unit. I look into her blue eyes and feel certain I could die right now and not regret it.

"Max," Marnie whispers. She puts her palm on my cheek. "I . . . I'll never forget you. Never regret you."

I don't know what to say to that, so I simply kiss her again. And with each thrust of my body, each swirl of my tongue, my heart feels like it's expanding. Stretching. Reaching some breaking point as it hurtles toward decimation. I touch Marnie's gorgeous face again as I kiss her, fuck her, *claim* her, beg her not to hate me when I'm gone, and there's no mistaking the way her passion is surging along with mine.

I feel desperate to get deeper inside her. To get so fucking deep, I'm touching her very soul. I hitch her legs around me, folding her body underneath mine, and grind myself into her, impaling her with every inch of me, and she presses her forehead against mine and grips the back of my neck, shuddering and gasping for air.

"You're so fucking beautiful," I murmur, as my pelvis grinds into hers. "You're perfect."

Oh, fuck. I can't get enough. I'm always addicted to this woman, but right now, I feel something even more intense than that. Like I'll physically die if I don't get her to come while my cock is buried deep. I'm in a frenzy, out of my head with the insatiable need to make her come like she's never come with anyone else. I want to ruin her for anyone else. If I can't have her, then I don't want anyone else to have her, either. She's mine. *Mine.* Even if I can't be hers.

My thrusts are becoming increasingly intense, our movements together frenetic, our breathing labored and ragged and raw. I kiss her deeply, and then whisper into her ear that I can't get enough of her, that I've never wanted anyone the way I want her, until, finally, she grips my neck like she's holding onto a life preserver in stormy seas, grits out a tortured groan, and has a fucking seizure beneath me. I place my palm over her mouth to stifle her growls, as she twists and gyrates throughout her powerful orgasm.

Not surprisingly, her pleasure hurtles me into my own. I come so hard inside her I'm momentarily blinded by little white stars exploding in my vision.

After we've both stopped moving and the room is filled with nothing but our ragged breathing, I kiss Marnie's neck and suck on a nipple. I stroke her breast and nibble on her jawline, still not ready for whatever just happened to be over. When my lips finally meet Marnie's again, we kiss so passionately, I feel dizzy. My heart is pounding so hard against my sternum, I'm surprised it's not creating hairline fractures in it.

What was that? I wouldn't call it sex. It felt more like a spiritual awakening.

I slide off her and lie on my back, too overcome to speak. When silence persists, and neither of us has said a word, Marnie pads wordlessly into the bathroom. I hear the sound of the toilet flushing. The shower turning on. And through it all, I lie motionless and staring at the ceiling while trying to figure out what my body just confessed.

When Marnie returns to the bed, she's naked, and her hair is wet and combed back. She slides into bed next to me and snuggles close. But still, neither of us speaks for what feels like an eternity.

After a while, Marnie asks, "Have you ever been in love?"

My heart stops. "Why do you ask?"

"Your mother told me she hasn't seen you this happy in a long time. She said you were in love in college and suffered a broken heart and haven't been the same since."

"Thanks, Mom."

"That's all she said. No details provided. Will you tell me what happened?"

I take a deep breath. "I had a girlfriend the last two years of college. I told her I wanted to marry her after law school, and she said she wanted that, too, so we moved in together. The summer before law school started, I found out she'd been fucking my best friend for several months. I lost my girlfriend— the woman I thought would become my wife—and my lifelong best friend, all in one fell swoop."

"I'm so sorry. Talk about a double whammy."

"Losing my friend was the worst part. I got over her, relatively quickly. Never got over him doing that to me. I'd trusted him with my life."

"That's horrible."

"It's okay. Time heals all wounds."

"Are you sure about that?"

"Absolutely. Looking back, it was for the best. Without a relationship to worry about, or a best friend constantly telling me to stop studying and come have some fun, I was able to throw myself completely into my studies in law school, and even double up by getting an MBA. I graduated at the top of my class, which meant I could get a job at the best firm in Seattle. And now, here I am, with an offer to work for Wayne Walters' legal team, exactly the thing I've wanted since my earliest days of law school. If all that stuff hadn't happened in college, who knows if I'd be in this position now. I'm guessing no. So, it was all for the best."

Marnie looks skeptical. "I'd think getting betrayed by two people you trusted completely, at once, would leave a mark on a person."

"I'm fine."

"Are they still together?"

"No. They're both married to other people. He's got two kids. She's got one. Or so I've heard from Auggie. He's always got the scoop about everyone."

"Were you friends with that guy before college?"

"Since preschool."

"Oh my god, Max."

"He's the reason I don't really have a lot of friends now. I made some friends in law school and at my firm. But law school is a pretty cut-throat environment, and then people scatter afterwards for all their various jobs. And work friends come and go, you know? But whatever. I've got Grayson and Auggie, so that's good. I don't have time to have lots of friends, anyway, so it's all good." I scowl when I detect pity in Marnie's blue eyes. "Don't look at me like that. I'm not a puppy at a shelter."

"I feel bad that happened to you."

"Don't worry about it. It's made me a stronger person. I'm better for it."

Marnie shakes her head. "No wonder you have such a hard time letting down your guard and trusting people. I would, too, if that happened to me."

I frown. "Who says I have a hard time letting down my guard and trusting people?"

Marnie scoffs. "You dispute the characterization?"

I think about it for a moment. "Well, no. Not really." I scratch my chin. "I've just never thought of myself that way. And I've certainly never drawn a line from that incident to any current reluctance to trust."

"Well, it seems like a straight line to me," Marnie says. "Add the whole thing with your father at age fifteen, and I'm thoroughly impressed you're not a serial killer."

"That's thanks to my mother. If it weren't for her, I might have been the second coming of Ted Bundy."

Chuckling, Marnie rolls onto her side and scoots closer until her nose is mere inches from mine. "Speaking of your mom, do you dispute her statement that you've seemed happier this week than you've been in a long time?"

"Fuck yeah, I dispute it." Marnie's shoulders droop with disappointment, so I slide my fingertip underneath her chin and whisper, "I've never been this happy, ever. Period."

I'm expecting her face to light up, but she looks nothing but pissed now.

"What?" I ask.

"Nothing."

"Tell me."

"I think you know."

"I don't."

Marnie sits up and runs a hand through her wet hair. "It pains me to know we both had the best week of our lives, literally, and yet we're not going to keep this going when we get back home. It hurts to know I'm going to have to say goodbye to you."

I sit up. "We wouldn't have to say goodbye if you'd be fucking reasonable about your expectations. If you'd compromise a little bit."

"What would be the point?" she says. "If you're not sure after this week that Ripley and I are what you want for the long haul, then a long-distance relationship, one in which we try to keep this going while you're working yourself to the bone in a new job, in a new city, while I'm still juggling everything all by myself in Seattle, isn't going to make you change your mind or make me happy."

"How the fuck could I be sure right now?" I bellow.

"Quiet," she hisses.

I take a deep breath and whisper-shout, "Yes, this week was magical. Yes, it was the best week of my life. But that doesn't matter when my brain knows this week hasn't been real. We've been living in a fantasy—in a little Utopian bubble where we've been able to focus our undivided attention on each other without work or real life getting in the way."

"It felt real to me."

"It *felt* real, but it wasn't. The true test is what happens when we're in the real world again."

"I know exactly what happens in the real world. You'll be in California and Ripley and I will be in Seattle and this week will quickly become a distant memory."

"Why does it have to be black and white like that? Remember when you told Mr. and Mrs. Walters at the opening party you supported me moving wherever my career took me, because you can work in any city and Ripley's young enough to move without missing a beat? You said that, Marnie."

"*Not so loud.*"

"You said that."

"Yes, I did. About my *fiancé*. The fake version of you who'd put a ring on it and promised me a motherfucking happily ever after!"

"Not so loud."

Her nostrils flare. She exhales and gathers herself. "Don't you see the important context underlying me making that comment to Mrs. Walters? Can't you see the thing that existed then that doesn't exist now?"

I clench my jaw and grit out, "Why can't we date when we get back? Why isn't that on the table?"

"Long distance?"

"Yeah, unless you want to move to California and date me from there."

Marnie scoffs. "I'm not going to uproot Ripley and chase a man to another state without a firm commitment and a ring on my finger."

I glance at the ring on Marnie's finger—the fake one we picked out together a lifetime ago. "So, you're telling me, if I told you to keep wearing that ring, and never take it off, to wear it for real, you'd be down for that?"

She doesn't hesitate. "Yes."

"No. Seriously, Marnie."

"Seriously. Yes."

I can't believe my ears. I only said that to call her bluff. *And yet, she's serious?* How could Marnie possibly think it'd be reasonable to get engaged, for real, after spending only one week together—and inside a fantasy, no less? I can't believe she's serious, so I press further. "You're honestly saying you and Ripley would move to California with me, if I told you to keep wearing that ring and consider it a real commitment in the real world?"

"Yes."

I'm blown away. Flabbergasted beyond my ability to process. "And yet . . . you'd say no to dating me, long-distance?"

"Correct. I'm not looking for a long-distance relationship. You heard Ripley. She wants a fucking daddy. And daddies are *there.* In person." She exhales. "If it were just me, maybe I'd give a long-distance relationship a whirl. But even then, you're a workaholic, Max. And you're starting a new job where you're going to work harder than ever to impress everyone. How often would we even see each other? I wouldn't want to bring Ripley with me, when I came to visit you, so how often would *she* see you? I wouldn't expect you to make it to Seattle very often, given how hard you work. And if you came, how stressed would you be about work the whole time?" Something on my face concedes all her points. That's clear enough when she motions to my face and says, "You see my point." Marnie stares at me for a long moment, waiting for me to say something. When I don't, she takes my hand and says, with surprising tenderness, "I'm ready to build a life with someone. I want another baby, if I can have one. I want a home. A partner. A teammate. I want to know someone's got my back in good times and bad, no matter what, forever, and I've got theirs. For the first time in my life, I'm not only clear on all that, I'm also certain I'll be a fantastic wife or partner to some lucky man. If you're not going to be that man, then I'm going to look for him when we get back."

My heart is racing. My head swirling with panicked thoughts. "Okay," I whisper hoarsely.

Her jaw tightens. "Okay, *what?*"

"Okay. I understand where you're coming from. And I'm sorry I can't offer you what you want."

Marnie glares at me like I've insulted her. "It's not only what I *want*," she says. "It's also what I deserve. And Ripley, too."

"Of course, you do. Both of you. I didn't intend to imply otherwise."

Marnie takes a deep breath and exhales. "Good talk, Max. I'm glad we had this conversation. It'll save me from wasting my tears after we get home." She gets up. "Thanks for a great week. Congratulations on the new job." She takes off her fake diamond and tosses it onto the bed. "We're still within the return period," she mutters. "You should be able to get a full refund."

"I'm not gonna return the ring. Marnie, *wait*."

I try to shove it at her, but she waves me away.

"I don't want it," she says.

"Sell it, if you want," I counter. "But it's yours."

"I don't want it, Max. I don't want the ring or the money you spent on it."

"I bought it for you, remember? And it wasn't cheap."

Marnie shakes her head. "If I'd known when you bought that ring what an amazing week we'd have, I would have insisted you'd return the ring after family camp and get your money back."

I sigh. "Would you stop being such a fucking pain in the ass and take the goddamned ring? I'm not going to return it, and I don't need a fake diamond ring sitting in my desk drawer for the rest of my life."

She folds her arms over her chest. "And I don't want the fucking memory of how fun it was to wear it, okay?" She throws up her hands. "Give it to the next woman you ask to be your fake fiancée. Or your real one someday. It looks real enough. She'll never know the difference."

I grit my teeth. Why is she doing this? Only a nut job would make a lifelong commitment this quickly. For fuck's sake, if I were willing to slip this ring onto her finger again, and tell her it was for real this time, wouldn't that be a huge red flag? She's insane if she thinks any rational person would do that.

When my silence becomes deafening, Marnie turns and stomps out of the room, throwing over her shoulder, "Thanks for a great week."

When she's gone, I stare at the half-opened door—the space where Marnie stood a moment ago—feeling utterly incapable of commanding my limbs to move. My entire body is quaking with adrenaline. My heart squeezing painfully. I should go to her. But to say what? I've got nothing more to say than what I already have.

With a deep sigh, I slide into bed and tell myself Marnie is the crazy one, not me. She's asking too much. Being naïve. I tell myself these feelings I'm having for her will disappear when we get back to reality. That soon, this magical week—this alternate universe where I was Marnie's fiancé and future husband and Ripley's daddy—will fade from memory and feel like nothing but a beautiful dream.

30
MARNIE

Ten days later

"Aw, honey," Lucy says sympathetically. "I've never seen you so brokenhearted. I wish I could help."

My other friends at the table—Victoria, Selena, and Jasmine—chime in to say essentially the same thing in various forms and iterations.

"Nobody can help me," I murmur, staring blankly across the restaurant. "There's no way around this storm; I simply have to go straight through it and feel *all* the pain."

The five of us are sitting in our usual downtown spot for another monthly dinner. Luckily, nobody brought a plus-one this time, so I've felt comfortable baring the naked depths of my heartbreak without holding back. No sugarcoating. No putting on a brave face, like I usually do. My friends are getting Real and Raw Marnie tonight. And she ain't pretty. If only Max had felt even half of what I did by the time our last night of camp rolled around, he'd have *begged* me not to take that damned ring off.

My heartbreak and rejection feel that much worse, now that my period is three days late. I haven't taken a pregnancy test yet out of sheer terror, so I have no idea if I'm late due to stress or because I'm carrying Max's love child. I'll take a test within the week, I think, if my period doesn't come before then. Hopefully, that will give me enough time to push past this acute sadness, at least enough to handle whatever outcome without totally falling apart.

Another reason I'm not itching to take a pregnancy test just yet is that I'm admittedly still holding out hope Max will change his mind, track me down, and beg me to wear his ring, after all. In the unlikely event Max were to do all that, I'd want it to be for no other reason than he's realized he loves me madly and genuinely wants to make a lifelong commitment to me, rather than because Max now feels a sense of obligation to me, thanks to an unplanned pregnancy.

Victoria looks around the table as she says to the group, "What has that dastardly man done to our resident man-eater?" To me, specifically, she says, "Look, I know you probably don't want to hear this, but the reality is that Max is but one tiny gold-fish in a vast ocean. Take some time to mend your broken heart, yes, but then you'll get back out there, better than ever, and catch yourself a gigantic whale."

"That's right!" Lucy says punching the air. "If Max is too stupid to realize you're as good as it gets, the best he'll ever find by a long mile, then fuck him."

I wipe my eyes and reply weakly, "I don't want a whale. I want Max."

My friends share a look that conveys deep concern. And I don't blame them. I've never been this girl before—a lovesick, tearful, dejected mess. Tonight, the feeble Marnie sitting at this table bears no resemblance to the kick-ass, confident one they nicknamed Marnie the Man-Eater in college.

My friends suggest perhaps I should give in and try a long-distance relationship with Max, and I tell them all the same things I told Max in Wyoming. That the logistics wouldn't work out and the relationship would be doomed. That I know I wouldn't feel satisfied with Max's crumbs when I know I want the whole damned cookie. And in the end, my friends agree, regretfully, it's probably the right call, even without knowing about my potential bun in the oven. Whether it turns out I'm gestating Max's child or not, I want a partner who's going to be fully present in my life. A true partner who'll conquer the ups and downs of life at my side. If Max doesn't want to be that partner, then I'm not going to waste my time trying to convince him. And I'm certainly not going to reveal a possible pregnancy to him as a means of getting him to commit to me.

"Max hasn't been ghosting you, right?" Selena says. "So, there's still hope."

I've told my friends about my business-related communications with Max since we got back from Wyoming a week and a half ago. He's called me several times to convey good news regarding the prototype he's developing; but whenever we speak, Max is all-business, so I am too.

Jasmine, the quietest member of our group, says, "Selena's right. As you and Max continue to talk about business stuff, I'm sure he'll slowly realize he wants you. Absence makes the heart grow fonder. Give him a chance to realize what he's lost. Give him a chance to miss you and regret the choice he made."

"I can't let myself hope for that," I say, even though it's everything I'm hoping for. "I need to move on."

Selena places her hand on my arm as a gesture of sympathy, inadvertently showing off the dazzling engagement ring on her hand, and I suddenly realize how selfish I've been to monopolize the entire dinner conversation tonight.

"Enough about me and Max," I say, wiping my eyes with my napkin. "Selena, tell us about your trip to Costa Rica with Grayson."

Selena kindly asks if I'm sure I'm ready to change the subject. She says the group is here for me as long as I need it.

But when I insist I'm ready to move on and can't wait to hear her news, Selena enthusiastically regales the group with stories of her fabulous trip, including showing us a slew of happy, smiling photos with her new fiancé. And, of course, we all react with interest and excitement.

Our waiter comes by with the dessert menu, and the table's conversation shifts to which treats we're going to order for the table. As we're debating our options, my phone on the table buzzes with an incoming text, and I take a peek at my screen. In my fantasies, it's Max texting to say he's realized he's desperately in love with me. In reality, however, I'm sure it's my father saying Ripley wants to say goodnight to me.

"Oh my fucking god," I blurt, instantly halting the table's conversation. I look at the expectant faces staring back at me. "Ladies, I just got a text from motherfucking Mr. BDE."

Everyone gasps.

"As in Max's *father*?" Lucy asks. By now, the whole group knows the sordid story, so she's not giving me away.

"Yep," I say. "As in Alexander Vaughn—the cheating, lying sociopath himself. He's texted me from a new number, since the old one is blocked." I read Alexander's short text to the table: "'This is Alexander. Please call me, Marnie. I have something important to tell you.'"

Rapid-fire conversation ensues, culminating in Victoria asking, "Are you going to call him or block the new number?"

"Block him," I reply. "That's an easy one. Whatever that bastard wants to say to me, I don't care to hear it." I tap a few buttons on my screen and smirk. "*Done.*"

Jasmine says, "What if he's got something important to tell you about Max?"

I shake my head. "Max is estranged from his father. If there's something important going on with Max, Gigi would tell me about it. Or maybe she'd tell my father, and he'd tell me. Either way, Alexander is the last person who'd have important information about Max."

Victoria frowns. "I support your decision, but I can't deny I'm curious what that man wants to say to you after all this time."

"Me, too," Jasmine admits. "Has he found out you and Max aren't really engaged?"

"Probably. When we got back from camp, I told Gigi she could tell her closest family and inner circle the truth, so they won't keep asking her, 'So, when's the big wedding?'"

Jasmine taps her chin. "Let's think this through, Marnie Girl. Perhaps you could use Mr. BDE to light a fire under Max's ass." She cocks her head. "What if you could get a message to Max through his father? Even if they're estranged, I'm sure if you talk to Alexander and let it slip that you're madly in love with his son, that spicy nugget would somehow get back to Max."

Everyone expresses enthusiasm for the idea.

"You haven't told Max you're in love with him yet, right?" Lucy asks.

"No, not in those words."

"In what words?" Selena asks.

"I told Max at camp I wanted to wear his fake engagement ring for real. He has to know I wouldn't have said that to him if I didn't love him."

Everyone's suddenly got an opinion. They're all talking at once. Above the din, Selena says, "Marnie, there's nothing more powerful than a person saying the actual words. Maybe Max needs to hear them from you to realize the depths of his own feelings."

I scoff. "Why would I tell Max I love him, when I know for a fact he doesn't love me back? I'm not a glutton for punishment. If he loved me, he would've told me that night. Or since we got back. And he hasn't."

Selena says, "Sometimes, it takes time for a person to figure out their feelings. Grayson knew he loved me long before I knew I loved him back."

We all laugh and tease Selena that Grayson fell in love with her, sight unseen, over their first text exchange, so the example she's provided is meaningless.

Selena chuckles. "Okay, fair enough. But Max is a far more complicated and guarded person than Grayson. Maybe Max does love you, Marnie, but he simply doesn't *realize* it yet. Maybe he needs a fire lit under his ass, like Jasmine said."

Jasmine agrees and adds, "He could be sitting somewhere right now, missing you and yearning for you and slowly realizing he totally blew it. Hearing the news that you're in love with him might be the very thing he needs to realize he's feeling exactly the same way."

I think about it but ultimately shake my head and say, "Max knows how I feel. I'm not going to chase him." In truth, if my period weren't three days late, I might very well go along with this diabolical plan. But with the possibility of a little Vaughn growing inside me, I'm especially loath to make the first move in this situation. As far as I'm concerned, the ball's firmly in Maximillian's court.

"Now's not the time to be stubborn," Victoria insists. "You love the man? Well, then, go get your man, Man-Eater. Call Mr. BDE and tell him you're madly, wildly, irrevocably in love with his son and see what happens next. At the very least, you won't wonder 'what if' that way."

"And while you're at it, also tell Mr. BDE to fuck off," Jasmine adds. "You deserve to *finally* get to say that to him." As my friends know, when I found out Alexander was married, I texted him a screenshot of the social media post that had tipped me off and asked if it was the real deal. Instead of answering me, he immediately blocked me and then ghosted me forevermore. And that was that. I never heard from the man who supposedly loved me again. Not directly, anyway. I certainly got an earful, indirectly, from Alexander when he told all those horrible lies about me to his son.

My eyebrow quirks up. "I agree it might be worth calling Alexander to tell him to fuck off," I say. "But not for what he did to me. That's old news. The only thing I care about now is telling Alexander to fuck off for the horrible way he's treated Max." My friends know about the lies Alexander's told about me recently, the ones he told Max when he genuinely thought Max was engaged to me. But they don't know the story of poor fifteen-year-old Max finding out his father was cheating on his mother, so I tell them that story now. Of course, my friends are outraged that Alexander had the nerve to demand his young son remain quiet to keep the family together, so they bang the drum for me to agree to a phone call with Alexander, all the more.

Feeling emboldened, I grab my phone and tap out a text to Alexander:

> Me: I'm at dinner with friends. I'll call you tonight when we're done, at my earliest convenience.

Even before I've read my reply text to my friends, Alexander hits me back.

> Alexander: Are you downtown, by any chance? If so, let's meet for drinks after your dinner. What I need to say to you, I'd rather say to your face, anyway.

"Oh, jeez. What now, ladies?" I ask. I read my friends Alexander's text, and they all encourage me to suggest a meeting at Captain's, which is right down the street from us. "Only if you all come with me," I say. "Even in a public place, I don't want to be alone with that horrible man."

"Of course, we'll come," Victoria says. "We'll sit at a nearby table and watch you like hawks and rush over to take Mr. BDE down, if needed."

"Thanks. I think being in his presence might be physically painful for me. But it'll be worth it to get to tell him off for all the ways he's mistreated Max."

Everyone agrees with that assessment.

Jasmine says, "I'm excited to watch you rip him in a new one. When our beloved Fire really gets fired up, she's a sight to see."

As everyone agrees, Lucy says, "It's too bad Captain's doesn't have popcorn on its snack menu. I have a feeling this is going to be a popcorn-worthy take-down. I, for one, can't wait to see it."

Laughing, Victoria says, "Not to mention, I can't wait to *finally* get a look at the notorious Mr. BDE."

31

MAX

I'm sitting at my desk at work, staring blankly at my law school diploma on the wall. I've spent my supposed last day at my firm's Seattle office tying up loose ends and saying goodbye to colleagues. On Monday, I'm supposed to start my dream job—my new assignment as a member of Wayne Walters' core legal team in Silicon Valley. But I'm having second thoughts about that—feeling guilty about the lies I told Mr. and Mrs. Walters at family camp. I need to come clean with Mr. Walters before stepping foot in his office. That's the right thing to do. But since I haven't told my boss, Scott, the embarrassing truth about Marnie and me—and I also know for a fact Scott would disembowel me if I tanked my relationship with the firm's biggest client—I haven't yet picked up the phone to do the right thing. It's so unlike me to be dishonest. Totally out of character. And now, I'm feeling ravaged by guilt.

I'm also feeling ravaged by another feeling, too—something that can only be described as homesickness. I've tossed and turned every night this past week and a half, while telling myself that horrible ache in my heart isn't real. Or if it is, it'll pass soon. But with each sleepless night, it's becoming harder to deny the truth: *I miss my family, terribly. I want them back.* It's as simple as that. My brain knows they were my fake family, but my heart feels like they were as real as it gets. It makes no logical sense for me to miss them the way that I do. For fuck's sake, I miss Marnie and Ripley so much, I feel like I'm on the cusp of tears at all times.

With a sigh, I pull Marnie's fake diamond ring out of my pocket and stare at it with a heavy heart. Marnie told me to sell it, but I can't do that. Instead, I've decided to keep it as a memento of the happiest week of my life. Why wouldn't Marnie simply be rational and agree to a long-distance relationship with me?

My phone pings with a text, and I glance at my screen, hoping I'll see Marnie's name on it. Nope. It's my brother texting me.

Auggie: Ashley and Dad are kaput!

Me: What? Since when?

Auggie: Since four days ago, when she left Dad for her horseback riding instructor because she found out she's preggers with the instructor's baby. Bwahahahaha. I'm with Mom at her place now sipping champagne in celebration.

Me: Are you sure the intel is accurate?

Auggie: Yep. I found out through the friend of mine whose sister is besties with Ashley.

Me: Ha! Ain't karma a bitch, Dad? I wish I could have seen his face when Ashley told him the news and ditched his ass.

Auggie: Mom said the same thing. When she heard the news, she laughed so hard she peed her pants.

> Me: Well, Mom pees when she sneezes, so that's not saying much. Haha. Tell her big congrats from me.

> Auggie: Come join us for champagne and tell her yourself. Henry is babysitting his granddaughter tonight, so Mom and I are hanging out at her place all night.

My heart stops.

If Henry is babysitting Ripley, then that means Marnie is out tonight.

Is she with her girlfriends?

Working?

Or on a date?

The thought of Marnie on a date instantly makes the hairs on my neck and arms stand on end. What if Marnie's out with someone who's willing to give her everything she wanted from me? We've been back for a week and a half, after all. That's more than enough time for any man to fall head over heels in love with Marnie Long! *I should know.*

Wait, what?

Full clarity slams into me.

I'm head over heels in love with Marnie Long.

Oh, fuck.

What have I done?

Suddenly, I know for a fact I'll never be happy again, if I lose Marnie forever, especially because I was too chicken shit to follow my heart. I'll be tortured for life, if someone else gets to fuck that goddess every night. Hold her close and call her baby. Oh, fuck no. I can't let some other man take my place next to my woman!

And what about Ripley? I can't let some other dude play princesses with my girl. Or take my spot at the dinner table next to her and listen to her explaining all the reasons *purpole* is her favorite color. That's *my* seat next to Ripley. She's *my* little chatterbox. *I'm* her glitter-haired daddy, and nobody else!

> **Auggie:** Where'd you go? Are you coming to hang out with Mom and me or not?

> **Me:** Sorry, no. There's something urgent I need to do.

> **Auggie:** Do you need help packing this weekend?

> **Me:** Not sure yet. Gotta go.

Thankfully, Marnie and I gave each other access to view each other's locations during family camp, so we could always find each other on the sprawling property. Hopefully, Marnie didn't block my access when we got home, or I'm going to have to call Henry and beg him to tell me where his daughter has gone.

I swipe into my location finder app and jolt when I see Marnie's location. *She's at Captain's.* On a Thursday night, no less. Which means she's there for Singles Night. My skin bursts into flames of jealousy and regret. I've got to make things right with Marnie. Right fucking now. I've got to get my family back before it's too late.

My heart crashing, I shove the ring in my pocket, grab my wallet and keys from a desk drawer, and leap out of my chair, determined to race down to Captain's, confess my love to Marnie, and plead with her to put her ring back on. As soon as I lurch out of my chair, however, my boss, Scott, appears in my doorway.

"Oh, good, you're still here," Scott says. He ambles into my office with the urgency of a snail and takes the chair opposite my

desk, so I force myself to sit back down, even though I'm physically quaking with the need to get out of here and race to
Marnie.

"Guess where I just came from?" Scott says with a wink.
"*The partnership selection meeting.*" He leans forward. "I'm not
supposed to tell you this, but I think you're going to be *extremely*
happy about this year's selection."

By all rights, I should be ecstatic about what Scott is imply-
ing. I've wanted to make partner at this firm since I walked
through its doors almost seven years ago. And yet, the only thing
I truly care about in this moment is tracking down Marnie and
stopping her before she leaves that bar with someone else and
then falls madly in love with him and forgets all about me.

Scott leans back in his chair. "The vote was unanimous this
year, which is rare. But there was only one person who *finally*
showed me he's got what it takes to become one of the leaders of
this firm, rather than a simple cog in the machine. Finally, I was
able to throw my full support behind that person and convince
everyone his time had finally come."

I cock my head, feeling confused. For the past several years,
Scott has told me he went to bat for me relentlessly in the partnership committee meeting. Unfortunately, though, each and
every time, the committee wasn't convinced about me for one
reason or another, so the offer went to someone else. That's what
Scott has told me, anyway. Repeatedly.

"That's interesting," I say. "What qualities did this certain
someone show you this year, as opposed to prior years, that
made you feel comfortable finally throwing your full support
behind him? Are you referring to the fact that Wayne Walters
noticed him this year?"

"Well, yes, Wayne was part of it. But Wayne has different
priorities than we do as a firm, so he was only one factor. For
me and the committee as a whole, it mostly came down to my
newfound belief that this person has finally become as cut-
throat and ruthless as we need him to be. He's finally willing

to do *whatever* it takes to get ahead. It's a fantastic thing to see."

My heart is thumping. "You base this conclusion on what, exactly?"

Scott leans forward and smirks. "Based on what I saw you pull off at Wayne Walters' ranch." He chuckles. "That's when I knew you're finally willing to do whatever it takes to get ahead. Bravo, Max. *It's about time.*"

I'm baffled, and I'm sure my face shows it. I haven't told Scott the truth about Marnie and me yet. I haven't told anyone. I know Mom told her sisters and best friends so they'd stop pestering her about the wedding, but Scott isn't friends with Mom. Did Mom tell Scott's wife? I guess it's possible, but I can't fathom it, since they're not close friends.

Scott chuckles. "Come on, Max. You can cut the bullshit now." He leans forward again. "*I know.*"

My stomach tightens. "You know what?"

"The truth about you and your fake fiancée."

My breathing hitches. *Fuck.*

"It's okay, Max. I'll never tell Wayne the truth. Hell no. Like I said, his measuring stick is very different than mine, and I don't think he'd appreciate your brilliant maneuvering the way I do. I personally thought your fake engagement was a stroke of fucking brilliance—a sign you're finally willing to be ruthless. I think what you did was admirable; but I don't think Wayne, and especially his wife, would react quite the same way." Scott shakes his head and laughs. "All these years, I've watched you working your ass off, while everyone around you was working smarter, not harder. I've watched you picking up work for your colleagues when they wanted to go on a vacation or to their kid's soccer game. You even picked up the slack for Shelby last year when she went to Wayne Walters' ranch—when you should have been sabotaging her to get her slot!"

"*Sabotaging* her?" I breathe out. I can't believe my ears. This is my *boss* saying this shit? My *boss* is putting me down for being a diehard team player—for putting our clients' needs above my own ambitions? I'm beyond shell-shocked. I'm utterly stupefied.

Scott continues, "Year after year, I've watched you putting in the hours, and helping your friends, when what you should have been doing was stepping on a fucking neck." He smiles broadly, like a proud poppa. "And then, suddenly, there you were at family camp, lying your ass off and stepping on a neck like a goddamned assassin. *Good for you, Max. Good for you.*"

I feel like I'm going to barf. I hang my head and choke out, "How'd you figure me out?"

"Come on, son. I've known you for almost seven years. You overplayed your hand." When I look at him blankly, Scott adds, "The Max *I* know isn't capable of being as happy as you pretended to be at camp. Also, I've never once heard you talk about Marnie, or seen a photo of her on your desk or as the lock screen on your phone; and suddenly, you can't stop making googly eyes with your supposed fiancée and fawning all over your soon-to-be stepdaughter? Despite all that, I still wasn't positive my suspicions were correct the first few days. But then, you went overboard with that three-legged race, and I knew. That's when I was sure it couldn't be real. You're simply not capable of being *that* big a goofball for real."

I'm barely able to breathe, let alone speak, through the stampeding of my heart.

Scott continues, "Just to be sure, though, when we got back from Wyoming, I talked to your secretary, and she confirmed Marnie had never once called your office landline, looking for you. She confirmed you'd never once mentioned Marnie or asked her to send flowers. And that's when I knew, without a doubt, I'd figured you out." He chuckles. "But since I'm not a man who leaves anything to chance, I invited your father to drinks last night, and he confirmed what I already knew. It took a while for him to rat you out; I had to walk him through my entire thought process before he'd finally do it, but he finally gave you up." Laughing, Scott shakes his head. "I think the most impressive thing is that you knew my wife would see your mother's post and tell me about it, and that I'd then tell Wayne about it. I'm sure you felt like a family camp invitation was a long shot, but you pulled it off. Yes, you got a bit lucky, in terms of the dominoes falling right; but you *made* that luck. That's what I told the partnership committee, when they pushed back a bit. I said, 'The kid's a Machiavellian genius. A killer. He's one of us.' Finally, I was able to say that about you, with confidence, and recommend *your* name, above all others, for the first time. And in the end, they all agreed with me."

It's a gut punch to find out my boss has been lying to me for the past three years. And even worse, to find out my work ethic, integrity, and willingness to be a team player—the things I value most about myself—are the things that have made Scott think *less* of me in the past.

It's suddenly crystal clear to me I've spent the last seven years of my life busting my ass to climb a fallacious mountain with a summit that doesn't align with my core values. All this time, I've prioritized the cult of work and ambition above what really matters: my relationships with family and friends. Above searching for love and maybe even settling down and starting a family. For fuck's sake, I've worked myself to the bone to get myself into a club I'm suddenly realizing isn't even worthy of having me as a member.

In a flash, I feel enraged with myself for the time I've wasted. The hours I'll never get back. And most of all, for the week and a half I've spent sitting here at this desk when I should have been throwing myself at Marnie's feet and begging her to be mine forever. To wear my ring again—*only for real this time.*

I jerk to standing. "Sorry to disappoint you, Scott, but I wasn't faking a damned thing in Wyoming. You've never seen me that happy because I've never *been* that happy. Because you've never seen me in love before. Because you don't fucking know me at all."

Scott looks shocked. "Max, your father already told me—"

"I'm guessing *you're* the one who told my father the truth, actually, and he just went along with it, after what you said made perfect sense to him. But either way, even if he thought he knew the truth when he sat down with you, he was wrong about that. My father doesn't know Marnie and I fell in love for real during our week together. He doesn't know that every smile you saw on my face was genuine. That every moment of happiness was the real deal. I was a goofball that week because Marnie and Ripley bring that out of me. Because they make me remember who I really am. I looked so much like a man who was madly in love that whole fucking week, because I *became* one. *I am one.* So you can shove your fucking partnership up your ass. *I quit.*"

While Scott sputters in shock, I waltz past him toward the door of my office, bound and determined to right all my wrongs, once and for all.

"Is this a joke?" Scott shouts after me.

I stop in the doorway. "The only joke is that I ever gave a shit about impressing you and the rest of the soulless sharks at this firm. I'm not one of you, thank God, and I never will be."

Scott gets up and points an angry finger at me. "If you think you can quit this firm and still join Wayne's core team, think again. You need this firm, Max. Wayne never hires in-house counsel directly; he always hires from the pool of attorneys he's already worked with from outside firms."

"I don't care about my career right now, Scott. I'll figure out my next career move once I've got my family back by my side, where they belong. They're the only thing that matters to me now."

Scott calls me an idiot before launching into a tirade, but I don't have another second to waste on him. While he's still screaming at me, I stride with purpose down the long hallway and into the firm's expansive, marbled lobby, and then straight into the glittering elevator. Thankfully, it's pretty late in the evening now, so I only pass a few scattered people as I go, all of whom give me a wide berth as I march on by with an enraged scowl on my face.

Captain's is only a few blocks away from my office, so I forego the parking garage and head straight to street level. When the elevator doors open, I hurl myself into the crisp Seattle night air and start sprinting toward my destination, as fast as my legs will carry me. *God help me, please, don't let it be too late.*

32

MARNIE

"Here you go," Alexander says. He hands me a dirty martini and takes a seat next to me at our small corner table at Captain's.

I'm not going to drink this martini, obviously, given that my period is late, but I figured it might raise suspicion with Alexander or my friends across the bar to ask for a club soda instead of my usual drink. In my non-pregnant state, I'd never pass up the chance to enjoy a well-made martini, especially at Captain's, which is renowned for them.

As Alexander gets himself seated across from me, I can't help marveling at his uncanny resemblance to Max. How did I not realize when I first laid eyes on Max that he reminded me so much of a certain married man who'd recently dented my heart, not because Max's eyes happened to be the same ocean-blue color, not because Max's strong jaw line resembled Alexander's, but because the young, fit, dashing patent attorney in the designer suit had half Alexander's DNA inside his cells?

"Thank you for agreeing to meet me," Alexander says. He smiles, and my body recoils. No matter the physical similarity of the two men's smiles, I'm now fully aware that Alexander's is designed to hide his sinister, dark soul, whereas Max's is a window into the beauty of his.

"You're looking gorgeous, as usual," Alexander says, drawing me from my thoughts. "Better than ever."

"Get to the point," I snap on an exhale. "Say whatever you came to say."

Alexander smirks. "Can't you guess?"

I pretend to sip my martini. "No, I can't." It's a true statement, although, if I had to guess, I'd say Alexander is here to threaten me not to go to his wife with news of our past dalliance. I'm guessing when I gave Gigi permission last week to tell her closest inner circle the truth about my fake engagement to Max, Alexander was one of the people she told. Which likely means Alexander, having now realized he's got no leverage to keep Max from telling his wife about his philandering past with me, is now on a mission to threaten, cajole, charm, or otherwise convince *me* to keep quiet through any means necessary.

Alexander leans back in his chair. "I've discovered the truth about your supposed engagement to Max." He smiles. "I know why Max went ahead with the ruse. The only question is why *you* did." His smile widens. "Clearly, you wanted to make me jealous. To get my full attention. Well, good news, Marnie. Your plan worked."

My mouth hangs open. "What? No."

Alexander scoffs. "Come on, Marnie. It's just you and me here now. We can talk freely. I admit I was jealous as fuck when I saw Geraldine's post. In fact, the minute I saw it, I realized what I'd lost: the only woman I've ever truly loved."

I roll my eyes. "Oh, for fuck's sake."

"It's true. The thought of you becoming my daughter-in-law and fucking my son every night was pure torture for me. I swear, I've never been so tortured in all my life."

"First of all, you swearing to anything is meaningless. And second of all, I said yes to Geraldine making that post because you'd treated her horribly during your marriage, and she seemed amused by the idea. That's it. I was simply helping your ex-wife have a little fun. I promise you mean nothing to me." I pretend to sip my drink. "I honestly hate you. You're a truly despicable person."

Alexander chuckles. "You just gave yourself away, sweetheart. The opposite of love isn't hate. It's indifference. If I truly meant nothing to you, then you wouldn't have continued to go along with the ruse, once Geraldine had had her fun. You kept going with it to get my attention."

I can't quickly fashion a response to that accusation, since I agreed to go to family camp only after hearing about Alexander's horrific comments to Max. In that sense, I suppose I did, in fact, continue with the lie, at least in part, to piss off Alexander.

Alexander leans forward, his blue eyes blazing. "When I found out you and Max weren't actually a couple, I knew in that moment what I needed to do." He tries to take my hand on the table, but I yank it away. He says, "I've left my wife for you, Marnie. I've come here to tell you—"

"What?" I shout. "Oh, God."

"That I never stopped loving you. Wanting you. Thinking about you. And now, I'm finally free to—"

"Stop, Alexander. Don't say another word." My heart is lodged in my mouth. Clogging up my throat. Making my breathing erratic. "Let me be clear," I spit out. "I feel nothing for you, other than disgust. Not only for the way you've treated me, Geraldine, and your other two wives, but even more so for the way you've treated poor Max. When he was only fifteen years old, you had the vile audacity to tell him to keep his mouth shut about your unfaithfulness. And when you genuinely thought Max was engaged to me, you told him horrible lies about his fiancée, simply to save your own skin."

Alexander's blue eyes are a raging forest fire now. "Admit it," he spits out. "You targeted Max from the very beginning to get to me."

Feeling enraged, I glance at my friends across the bar to

steady myself, and when I see their kind faces staring at me, all of them ready to sprint over here to stand by me at the slightest signal, I feel emboldened. I return to Alexander and puff out my chest. "Go fuck yourself, Alexander. After I blocked your number, I promise I never thought of you again."

"Listen to me. Now that I know about your daughter, I know how to make this worth your while. I'll put you up in a luxury apartment near my office and bankroll a live-in nanny for you. I'll even send some high-end clients your way, if you'd like."

"You came here to make me your paid whore?" I bellow, much too loudly, but, luckily, my voice is swallowed by the loud din of the bar. I lower my voice and hiss, "We're done here." I jerk to standing, intending to bolt to my friends' table across the bar, but Alexander is quicker than me. He rises with astonishing speed and grips my arm like a vise before I'm able to stride away.

As I try unsuccessfully to jerk my arm away, Alexander grits out, "You're forty years old and you've got a small child, Marnie. Do you really think you're going to get a better offer than the one I'm making you? Take what I'm offering and be fucking grateful for it."

"Let go of her!" a male voice shouts as a blur of a figure descends upon Alexander.

I whip my head toward the source of the voice, and to my immense shock and relief, its owner is the man I love. The man of my dreams. *The one and only Maximillian Vaughn.*

33
MAX

As I sprint along the sidewalk toward Captain's, I check my phone to confirm Marnie's still there, and, thank God, she is. Although I suppose the term "thank God" is a relative thing when the woman of my dreams is at Captain's on fucking Singles Night.

When I reach the large, metal front door of the bar, I swing it open and barrel inside like a man possessed, and then stand immediately inside the door, surveying the place. It's packed tonight. Noisy as fuck. *Where's Marnie*? When I don't immediately see her, I head toward the tables in the back.

Is that Selena? It is! She's sitting with all Marnie's friends at a large table in a corner. My entire soul breathes a sigh of relief to realize Marnie came here on a girls' night out, and not specifically to meet a dude. But wait. No. False alarm. Marnie's not sitting with her friends. Did she go to the bathroom or to the bar to get the next round? Did she step out the back door to a quiet spot to say goodnight to Ripley? *Or has she already left with someone for the night*? Oh my fucking God. Has Marnie already "headed outside for a smoke" with some lucky guy?

My skin and lungs are on fire and my head is spinning. I turn around and scan the bar area frantically, but Marnie's not there.

Same thing when I peek out the back door. She certainly wasn't out front when I got here moments ago, so that means my only hope is that she's in the bathroom. Please, God, please. I start marching across the bar toward the short hallway leading to the bathrooms . . . and stop dead in my tracks when I spot her.

Marnie is sitting at a small table with my father.

How did this come about? Was she here with her friends, and she happened to run into Dad? Or did Dad call Marnie and ask her out the second Ashley dumped his ass? Or, shit, worst-case scenario, did *Marnie* somehow find out about my father's newly single status and immediately contact *him* to rekindle their romance? The thought makes me want to drop to my knees and weep. Either that or lurch across the bar, smash one of those martini glasses onto the table and use a jagged shard to slit my father's fucking throat.

As I'm still trying to process what I'm seeing and feeling, and how this travesty came about, Marnie jolts up, looking furious. In a flash, Dad jerks up from his chair and grabs Marnie's arm in a tight, angry grip. And that's it. My body flies into action, instinctively, whether or not my mind knows what to make of this situation.

In three bounding steps, I make it to my father and grab his arm. "Let go of her!" I shout.

There's a blur of commotion as a couple nearby figures leap into action to keep the peace. Two guys suddenly hold me back while someone else gets between my father and me. I'm vaguely aware of a swarm of activity surrounding us—Marnie and all her friends clustered around my father and me, shouting and screaming.

"He's my father," I say to whoever's holding me back. "I'm not gonna deck him. I just wanted to stop him from hurting her."

After a beat, my captors release me. As it turns out, one of them is a bouncer. A big one, at that. "No fighting at Captain's," he says in a deep baritone. "You fight, you're banned for life. One strike and you're out."

"He was violently grabbing my fiancée's arm."

The big guy shakes his head. "Rules are rules."

"She's not his fiancée," Dad spits out, smoothing his shirt from where I grabbed him.

"She is, as far as I'm concerned," I say. I turn to Marnie. "Unless I'm too late to make things right?" I motion to my father and Marnie by way of explanation, nonverbally asking if she's chosen him over me.

"Oh, God, no," Marnie chokes out. "Your father asked to talk to me, so I came to hear him out and then chew him out about the way he's treated you. That's all this is. I promise he repulses me."

One of Marnie's friends pipes in to say, "It's our fault she agreed to meet with him. She wanted to block and ignore him, but we convinced her to come down here and let him have it."

Relief and elation flood me. "Thank God. I love you, Marnie. That's what I came to tell you. I was a fool to let you go. I was a fool to think what we had wasn't real. I want you and Ripley. I want our family back. For real. Forever. Please, let's pick up where we left off."

Marnie throws herself at me, and as I hug her, I suddenly realize my father is still standing nearby, watching us. Rage floods me. His wife left him, and then he found out the truth about my so-called engagement—probably, from Scott last night —so the bastard figured he might as well take his shot with the sexiest woman alive today?

I break apart from Marnie and furiously address my father. "You're dead to me, Alexander Vaughn. The reasons are too many to list, but it's enough to know your wife left you for her riding instructor, so you immediately came after your son's woman."

"*His wife left him*?" Marnie bellows. She throws up her hands. "He told me he left his wife for me!"

"Typical," I mutter. I glare at my father again. "Stay away from me and my family. You got that? *They're mine.*"

Dad scoffs. "Fine with me. If you want my sloppy seconds, have at 'em."

Fucking hell. My fist connects with Dad's face before my brain even knows what's happening. And mere seconds later, I'm being dragged through the crowded bar toward the front door by a pair of exceedingly strong arms.

"I'll walk out!" I shout. But whoever's dragging me doesn't let go of me. In short order, the front door is flung open, and I'm suddenly thrown onto the sidewalk onto my ass. When I look up, it's that same big bouncer from before who's standing over me.

"You're banned," he grits out. "I actually don't blame you for decking him. I heard what he said. But I can't bend the rules for you."

"I understand. You won't see me again."

The big guy smiles. "I bet that felt good, eh?"

I return his smile. "Yeah, it felt fucking amazing."

As he turns to head back inside, Marnie and her friends barrel out the front door and straight to me on the sidewalk. When Marnie sees me sitting on the ground, she screams and drops down to me, her breathing labored. "Are you hurt?"

"Not at all. I feel great." I peek over Marnie's shoulder to find all her friends crowded around and staring down at me. But there's no sign of my father.

"Where's Alexander?"

"They dragged him out the back door," Selena says. "It was lovely."

"Was he hurt?"

"His nose was bleeding," the platinum blonde replies with a snicker. "That seemed to be the extent of it, though."

Marnie grabs my shoulder. "I'm sorry I came here to meet with him. I wanted to tell him to fuck off. Not for myself—but for you. But it was a mistake. He's not worth it."

"Thanks for wanting to go to bat for me, baby. But let's put him in the rearview mirror now, okay? It's full steam ahead for you and me."

Marnie bites her lip. "What kind of full steam ahead are you envisioning?"

I grin. "Stand up, and I'll tell you."

With a wary look on her face, Marnie slowly rises to standing, and while she does that, I grab the ring from my pocket and shift onto one knee before her. When the vignette I'm now striking becomes a dead giveaway of my intentions, Marnie and her friends collectively gasp and titter.

Marnie's got one hand over her mouth now, but I take her free hand in mine and say, "Marnie, my love, I've never been happier—and I mean that literally—than when you were wearing this ring on your finger and I was calling you my fiancée. I've never been happier than when you and Ripley were mine—my family. Baby, please, put this ring back on and become my fiancée again—only this time, for real and forever."

"Yes!" Marnie screams.

My heart bursting, I slide the ring onto her finger, where it belongs. "I'll get a replacement for this—the real thing—as soon as possible. But for now, this will have to do."

"You didn't actually ask her the question, Max!" one of Marnie's friends—the cute dirty blonde one—shouts.

"Well, let me do it now." I gaze up at Marnie, smiling. "Marnie Adele Long, will you make me the happiest man in the world and marry me?"

"Yes!" Marnie screams at top volume, making me, and all her friends, and several random onlookers, laugh and cheer.

I pop up and embrace my fiancée, as our audience cheers and applauds. "I love you," I whisper, before taking her face in my palms and kissing her. As our audience continues cheering, I dip Marnie low, making her giggle.

"I love you, too," she says. "So much."

When I finally release my new fiancée, I call out to her friends, "I'm banned from Captain's for life, ladies, so we'll need to find another bar for our *ad hoc* engagement celebration."

"The Pine Box is right down the street!" the cute dirty blonde shouts. She's Lucy, I think.

"Onward, to The Pine Box!" I shout, making everyone whoop and cheer. I add, "Drinks, shots, and the finest champagne are all on me!"

Our group starts walking down the sidewalk toward our destination, with Marnie and me holding hands and strolling behind.

"What made you change your mind?" Marnie asks.

"It's more like I came to my senses. I've been miserable. I really blew it, baby. I wish I could rewind the clock and get a do-over. I wish I would have said all this on the last night of camp."

Marnie's eyes prick with tears. "No, honey. This was perfect. As heartbroken as I felt, I only wanted you, if you were sure."

"I am. I've never been surer of anything in my life."

As we share a smile, Selena in front of us draws our attention by shouting, "Grayson!" When we turn to look, she's got her phone against her ear. She says, "Honey, get your hot ass downtown to The Pine Box. Max and Marnie just got engaged—for real this time—and we're going to celebrate." Selena turns back to Marnie and me. "Grayson says congratulations. He's on his way." After we reply with gratitude, Selena returns to her call. "Actually, we were just at Captain's, but we can't celebrate there because Max is now banned for life." Selena chuckles. "I'll let Max tell you the story."

Marnie nudges my arm. "If Grayson's coming, we should invite Auggie, too."

I nod enthusiastically. "He was having drinks with our mother earlier. Maybe they're still together, and she can come with him."

"That'd be awesome! It's too bad we can't invite my father, but he's watching Ripley for me tonight."

"We'll have a nice celebration dinner with our parents this weekend," I say with a wink. "I've been missing our family dinners."

Marnie beams a huge smile at me. "So have I. So much."

"And in the meantime," I add, "we'll get shitfaced at The Pine Box."

Marnie pats my arm. "You get shitfaced tonight, Boo. I'll be our designated driver."

"We can take an Uber."

"Nah. I'm happy being punch drunk on nothing but my love for you."

Laughing, I kiss her hand. "Let's play it by ear. If you change your mind, we'll take an Uber." I pause. "I should probably mention I'm unemployed, as of a half-hour ago. I hope that doesn't change your answer."

"Unemployed?"

"They offered me partnership tonight because I've supposedly proved myself ruthless and cut-throat, so I quit. Don't worry, it's the best thing I ever did. I'll tell you all about it later."

"What about Wayne Walters? Are you still going to work for him?"

"I doubt it. I'll figure that out later, though. As long as I've got my family with me, it doesn't matter what happens next in my career."

"Babe, what the fuck happened tonight?"

I chuckle. "I promise I'll tell you all about it later, my love. Right now, all you need to know is that quitting the firm and tanking my chances of working for Wayne Walters was the second-best decision of my life, topped only by my decision to beg the woman of my dreams, the amazing Marnie Long, to become my future wife."

34
MAX

"Hang on," I whisper after Marnie unlocks her front door. "I'll carry you across the threshold, babe."

Marnie giggles. "That's for the wedding night, honey; not the engagement night."

"It's so nice, why not do it twice?" Laughing, I scoop her up, and then creep with her in my arms through the dark, quiet house, taking great care not to wake Henry or Ripley as I go.

"I can't wait to fuck my beautiful fiancée," I whisper as we make it into Marnie's bedroom. "Oh, sorry. *Make love* to my beautiful fiancée."

Marnie snickers. "No, you can fuck me."

I'm a bit drunk, while Marnie is as sober as a judge. True to her word, she let me party tonight, and then she safely drove us home. As my steely boner attests, however, the alcohol in my bloodstream hasn't tamped down the white-hot lust I feel for this woman in the slightest.

I lay Marnie down on her bed, kissing her hungrily and pulling off her clothes. When I get her naked, I unzip my pants and rub my tip against her. I'm already wet with pre-cum, and she's already as wet as can be, too. Clearly, we're both raring to go.

"I've missed you," I whisper hoarsely as my fingers slip in and out of her warm wetness.

Marnie moans. "I practically had an orgasm when you punched your father. And then again when you pulled out the ring."

I trail kisses from her breasts over her belly and then lap and worship at the altar of her pussy till she's gripping the duvet underneath her and coming against my mouth.

"Fuck me, Max," she whispers. "I'm aching for you."

She doesn't need to ask me twice.

I roll her onto her side, lie flush behind her, and enter her slowly. As I fuck my woman, I've got one hand cupping her breast and the other rubbing her clit. As we move together, I kiss her neck and whisper into her ear about how good she feels, how I can't live without her—that I love her with all my heart and soul and everything I am—and, soon, we're both barreling toward ecstasy. I've never felt so certain about anything in my life. Now that I'm here, I can't believe I ever hesitated. Marnie's the home I've been aching for my whole life—the serenity and rightness I've always yearned for, without even realizing it. I feel whole now. Complete. Like my soul has met its match and my life has found its purpose.

Marnie's intimate muscles ripple around my cock with her orgasm. And a moment later, I'm hurtled into a kind of bliss I've never experienced before. It's physical pleasure mixed with spiritual serenity—and it's a fucking amazing combination.

"I love you," I choke out as I release forcefully inside her. "Oh my god, Marnie. I love you so much."

Marnie turns to face me. "I love you, too."

We kiss passionately for several minutes. When we break apart, we lie nose to nose, smiling broadly. All of a sudden, I'm zapped with a new realization. A new yearning. My guard is completely down now. My defenses decimated. And in this new state of being, I'm suddenly aware of a deep-seated desire exploding inside me.

"Max, I need to tell you something," Marnie says, just as I'm blurting, "Let's make a baby."

Marnie stares at me. "What did you say?"

"I said, 'Let's make a baby.'" When it's clear I've rendered her speechless, I forge ahead. "You said at camp you want another baby, if you can have one, and I haven't been able to get that comment out of my head. I want a baby, too, Marnie. With *you*. So, why wait?" When Marnie still says nothing, I add, "Babe, I swear I'm ready. As a matter of fact, I wish you weren't on the pill, so we could have made a baby just now."

I'm expecting Marnie to react with enthusiasm, but she looks like a deer in headlights.

"What's wrong?" I ask, my stomach tightening.

"Are you sure about that?" Marnie says slowly.

"I am. Let's do it. Statistically speaking, we don't have much time. So, come on, let's—"

"My period is three days late, Max. And that never happens to me."

My brain scrambles. My heart stops. "Are you telling me . . . you're pregnant?"

"I might be. I have to take a test to be sure."

"Holy shit. Take one now."

Marnie laughs. "I don't have one in the house."

I sit up. "Let's go get one."

She giggles. "Lie back down, honey. We'll get one in the morning."

"I don't think I can wait that long."

"You're not freaking out?"

"Not at all. Like I said, I'm ready."

"You weren't ready a mere week and a half ago."

"Well, I'm ready now, baby! I mean, other than the fact that I'm currently unemployed. That's some unfortunate timing, but we'll figure it out."

"What happened with that? Why'd you quit?"

I tell her the whole story without leaving a single detail out, and Marnie is one hundred percent supportive of my decision.

"I need to call Wayne Walters tomorrow and tell him everything," I say. "Not only because it's distinctly possible Scott will call him tomorrow and tell him everything to sabotage me, but also because I've been feeling guilty about the way we lied to him and his wife. They didn't deserve that. The ends didn't justify the means."

"I'm so glad you feel that way," Marnie says on an exhale. "I've been feeling sick to my stomach about the lies we told them. They're such nice people. I feel terrible about lying to them."

"I'm sure Mr. Walters will tell me to go to hell, once he finds out the truth," I say. "Either way, when he finds out I quit the firm, he'll revoke my offer, regardless. As he should. I wouldn't want to work for him based on deception, anyway. If I couldn't get onto his team honestly, then I don't deserve to be there at all."

Marnie hugs me. "Hopefully, he'll forgive you and ask you to join his team."

"I highly doubt that."

"If not, you're a brilliant lawyer. I'm sure there are a thousand ways you can make a good living."

"There are. Don't worry about that. We'll be fine."

"Of course, we will. We're a family now. We're in this crazy thing called life together." She smiles. "If it makes you feel any better, my father told me tonight he's moving in with your mother, for good, and giving me this house. That means we can live here, and you can sell your place or rent it out while you figure out your next career move. That takes the pressure off, right?"

"It does. I think I'll sell my place and invest a whole lot of money in our little start-up."

Marnie gasps. "You really think my little doodles could lead to us having an actual, profitable business?"

"I'm sure of it. In fact, my buddy is so gung-ho about your ideas, he suggested we develop another three of them, out of the gate." I smile. "And now, we've got the funds to do it."

"Oh my gosh. My father unwittingly has impeccable timing."

I nod. "My mom didn't tell me about your dad moving in with her. That's big news."

"They just decided today. Dad said they're both sure they want to be together forever, no matter what. He said they can't stand being apart, even for a night."

"Aw, they're so cute."

"He said they'll be more comfortable living in Gigi's place, rather than the house my dad shared with my mother. So, this place is mine now." She smiles. "Ours."

I sigh with relief and hug her again. "I love you more than I knew was possible. And Ripley, too." I touch Marnie's belly. "And you, too, my little baby-to-be, if you're in there."

Marnie beams a beautiful smile at me. "I hope I'm pregnant. I'd love to have a baby that looks just like you."

"Hey, don't wish that on the poor kid, when they've got a face like yours they could inherit."

We kiss and kiss, overwhelmed with joy and relief and love.

When we manage to release each other's lips, we cuddle and revel in our happiness.

Marnie says, "Ripley's going to be so happy when we tell her in the morning."

I inhale sharply. "Let's tell her now."

Marnie giggles. "She's fast asleep."

"She'll fall right back asleep. She's a kid. Come on, baby. I can't wait till morning."

Marnie pauses, her blue eyes sparkling as she looks down at my face. But finally, she laughs and says, "Okay, let's do it."

With a whoop, I leap out of bed and throw on my clothes while Marnie throws on some pajamas from her drawer. When we're both dressed, we creep down the hallway and into Ripley's dark bedroom, where her cherubic, sleeping face is softly illuminated by her Moana nightlight.

Marnie takes a seat on the edge of the tiny bed, closest to Ripley's face, while I sit near Ripley's feet.

"Ripley," Marnie whispers. "Honey, wake up."

After a few more tries, Ripley's eyes finally flutter open. She looks from her mother's face to mine. "Am I dreaming?"

"No, you're awake," I whisper. "I couldn't wait till morning to ask you something, sweetie pie. Something super important." I pause for dramatic effect. "Can I be your daddy—*please*?"

Ripley gasps. "When?"

"Starting now. We'll have a wedding and a party later with friends and family, but if you say yes now, then I'll start being your daddy right this very second, and I'll keep being your daddy forever and ever."

Ripley bursts into tears. She sits up and throws up her little arms. "Dat's all I ever wanted my whole entire life!"

Marnie stands to make way for me, and I scoop Ripley into my arms and hug her to me. "I love you so much, cutie pie," I coo softly.

"I love you, too, Maxy. *Daddy*."

My heart explodes as the sacred, magical word leaves Ripley's mouth. Marnie joins our hug, making this a three-way family hug, at which point I choke out, "I promise to be the best husband and daddy, ever. I love you both so much, with all my heart, and I promise I always will."

EPILOGUE
MARNIE

"Do you, Maximillian, take Marnie to be your partner in life, your beloved wife, for better or worse, through good times and bad, through sickness and health, and all the ups and downs life has to offer and everything in between?"

Max squeezes my two hands as he continues looking deeply into my eyes. "I do, with all my heart." He smiles and adds something we agreed he'd say at this special moment: "I also take Ripley to be my beloved daughter, for better or worse, through good times and bad, through sickness and health, and all the ups and downs life has to offer and everything in between."

After Ripley tossed her flower petals down the aisle earlier, she took a seat in the front row with Grampy and Gigi. And since we didn't tell her Max was going to make that promise to her in front of the world, she lets out a little gasp and squeal that make our entire audience giggle. Some of them, through tears of joy.

Our audience is small for today's festivities—my father, Gigi, Augustus, all my friends and Grayson, a handful of close extended family members, and, of course, our hosts for this dream wedding, Wayne and Jenny Walters. There are also a few clients of mine whom I consider good friends. A friend of Max's from his old firm, Shelby, and her family, and a few friends Max has made the past months working for his hero, Wayne Walters. But that's it. Less than thirty people are here to witness our intimate nuptials on this glorious afternoon at the Walters' sprawling Wyoming ranch, which is exactly the way Max and I wanted it.

Now that Max has finished his vows, I turn my attention to our officiant—Wayne Walters himself—since it's time for him to ask me the same question he's just asked Max. To my surprise, however, before Wayne addresses me, Max leans down and kisses my small baby bump, making everyone in the audience coo some version of "awwwwww." When he stands upright again, Max places his palm on my belly and says, "And I promise to be the best daddy I can possibly be to you, too, little peanut."

Well, damn. I can't help getting teary-eyed at that. I look at my best friends in the audience through my tears, and we all simultaneously swoon. From there, my eyes drift to Dad, Gigi, and Ripley, and we all share huge smiles.

"Ready, Marnie?" Wayne says.

I return to Max. And then Wayne's smiling face. "Ready."

Wayne and his wife, Jenny, have quickly become family to Max and me. So much so, when we told them about our bun in the oven after the first trimester had passed, and we also mentioned our plan to get married at City Hall before the baby's birth, they *insisted* on hosting an intimate wedding for us at their ranch—in a meadow right outside their personal home on the property. Of course, Max and I couldn't resist accepting their generous offer. The Walters' ranch is the place were Max and I fell in love, after all. The chance to seal our eternal love here, and also bring everyone we love to this magical place for a fun-filled week of celebration afterward, was too good an offer to pass up.

The morning after Max quit his firm and proposed to me, he called Wayne to tell him the whole truth without holding back.

He also told him he'd proposed to me the night before with the ring I'd worn throughout camp and that he'd quit the law firm for reasons he detailed with honesty.

During the call, Wayne didn't say much. He's a quiet man who generally thinks first and speaks second. But after he hung up with Max, he talked to his wife, Jenny, and relayed the details of his surprising conversation. From what Jenny's since told me, the couple talked at length about the situation, and when Wayne finally called Max back, he offered him the same position on his core team in Silicon Valley that he'd offered at family camp; except, of course, in this new iteration, Max would now be working directly for Wayne's tech firm, as one of his in-house attorneys in his legal department.

From what Jenny's told me, it was she who said to her husband, "Honey, nobody could fake the kind of love we saw between Max and Marnie and Max and Ripley that week. Even if Max didn't realize it himself until later, Max and Marnie are soul mates and it's written in the stars for him to be Ripley's daddy. Everyone makes mistakes. Max wasn't the one who posted about his engagement in the first place; his mother did. Can we blame him for rolling with it before he fully realized the implications? He thought the cover story would be a harmless way to finally meet you. When he realized the ruse went too far, he told you the truth. I vote you give Max a do-over. I have a feeling you'll be very glad you did."

Thankfully, Wayne took his beloved wife's advice, because ever since Max started working for Wayne, he's been kicking ass, right and left, for the company. Also, from a personal standpoint, he's exactly where he belongs. Finally, Max feels like a valued member of a team. Finally, he feels like everyone he works with is working toward a common goal. As a result, genuine friendships have been formed quickly; mutual respect abounds; and Max has never been happier plying his trade.

When Max comes home at night to Ripley and me and our beautiful new home overlooking the San Francisco Bay, he's practically floating on air. No matter how long a day he's had or what particular problems might have arisen throughout his long workday, Max always seems *energized* when he walks through our front door and straight into my waiting arms. And I'm always pretty damned energized myself.

I don't cook for clients in our new hometown. I've left my private chef days behind me for now, though I still love cooking for my family and devising new recipes for the line of cookbooks Max and I are developing to compliment the vast assortment of cooking gadgets and kitchen tools we've recently brought to market with astounding success.

Holy hell, some of those doodles in my notebook turned out to be solid gold. We've only just gotten started, but sales of our first batch of products have smashed all sales projections. I've got a lot to juggle these days between Ripley, the new business, and our baby on the way. I'm sure life will be even more chaotic when Baby Marcus arrives, but it'll be a labor of love all around, so I can't wait.

Marcus. That's the name we've chosen for our son. Full name: Marcus Henry Vaughn.

Initially, I suggested the name as a tribute to my late mother, Marcia. But when Max and I realized Marcus Aurelius was a famous Roman Emperor, we were doubly sold. We weren't motivated to continue the Vaughn family tradition of naming baby boys after famous rulers. We certainly didn't intend our son's name as any kind of a nod to Alexander. But we also didn't want Alexander to spoil our fun. Gigi shares her given name, Geraldine, with some famous Albanian queen, after all. Plus, my father, Henry, shares his name with history's most notorious English king. Therefore, giving our son a famous emperor's name didn't feel as much like a tribute to Max's father, but, instead, as the continuance of a tradition shared by our baby boy's entire family on both sides—a tribute to Daddy, Uncle Auggie, Gigi, and Grampy.

I'm a tiny bit freaked out to have a newborn in a new city,

away from all our family and friends back home. But the flight between San Francisco and Seattle is only two hours, so we've already been able to see everyone quite a bit since the move, and everyone has assured us they'll come to visit so often after Marcus arrives, we'll get sick of seeing them and beg them to leave.

"Marnie," our darling officiant, Wayne, says with a huge smile. "Do you take Maximillian to be your partner in life, your beloved husband, for better or worse, through good times and bad, through sickness and health, and all the ups and downs life has to offer and everything in between?"

"I do," I say, looking into Max's blue eyes. "With all my heart and soul."

"Ripley, can you bring us the rings now, honey?"

My father carefully hands Ripley the wedding bands, and she walks with them in her upturned palms toward us like she's walking on a tightrope stretched across two skyscrapers.

We know it's customary for the best man to hold the rings. But I couldn't pick a maid of honor out of my best friends, even though we all know Lucy and I are especially close. Plus, at such a small wedding, making my best friends stand alongside me in matching gowns didn't feel right to me. And so, Max opted to let his best man, Auggie, sit next to his mother in the front row and observe the ceremony holding her hand, rather than standing alongside Max. It feels right to me, poetic, to stand up here with Max and nobody else. We've got the best family and friends in the world, and we love them dearly; but Max and I are excited to face the world together, as an unbreakable pair, just me and him against the world.

When Ripley reaches Wayne, Max, and me, she carefully holds up her palms to Wayne, who takes the rings and compliments her on a job well done.

"Stay up here with me, peanut," I say. "That way, you can walk down the aisle with Daddy and me when we're officially husband and wife."

Ripley visibly vibrates with excitement at that suggestion. She scurries behind me to the spot I've indicated, the flowing skirt of her purple dress swinging as she goes. It was no surprise when Ripley asked if she could wear her favorite color for today's wedding. Also, no surprise when she asked to wear the little diamond necklace Max gave her for her fifth birthday. The big surprise was that when Ripley asked to wear purple, she pronounced the word expertly, with no extra "o" sound to be heard. It was a sad day for us all, Dad and Gigi included. We'd all grown quite fond of Ripley's adorable pronunciation of purple—*purpole*—and had even started using it ourselves as an inside joke.

Wayne hands Max the gorgeous wedding ring he'll slip onto my finger to seal our fate—a simple diamond band I'll wear alongside the fake diamond ring I wore at family camp. Many times after slipping that fake ring onto my finger outside Captain's, Max has expressed his intention to get me the whopper of a diamond ring Fake Marnie picked out online for Fake Max to give her. But I've explained to Max repeatedly I only picked out that ridiculously expensive ring when I didn't know Real Max would one day propose in earnest. If I'd known things would turn out the way they have, I never would have suggested Max spend the equivalent of a Ferrari and then some on an engagement ring.

Also, as I've told Max many times, the ring I wore at family camp while falling in love with him has sentimental value for me. Plus, it looks the same, basically, as the real thing, so why spend a huge sum on essentially the same exact thing, only with real diamonds, when we could invest that same amount in our new business? Max has repeatedly pushed back on my reasoning, but in the end, he agreed to let me keep wearing my fake ring alongside my new band.

"Max, repeat after me," Wayne says after handing the sparkling band to Max. "This ring is a circle that never ends. As is my love. With this ring, I promise to become the best husband to you I can possibly be." After Max repeats Wayne's words with tears in his eyes, Wayne continues, "Every time you look down at this ring on your finger, please remember how much I love you and our family."

Max repeats the rest, but before sliding the band onto my finger, he says, "Hold on." With a wicked smile, he reaches into an inside pocket of his suit jacket and pulls out a second ring to go along with my new band—a jaw-dropping sparkler I instantly recognize as the jaw-dropping *real* engagement ring I selected for Fake Max to give Fake Marnie.

"Oh my god," I blurt. "No, Max. It's too much."

"No, my love, it's not even close to enough." Max slides my wedding band onto my shaking hand first, followed by the Ferrari of a sparkler after it. And the minute I see both rings on my finger, I can't deny it: there's a difference—a massive one—between the costume diamonds I've been wearing for months now and the stunning ones practically blinding me now. I throw my arms around Max's neck and thank him, and we embrace for a long moment.

"I'd never marry you with fake diamonds," Max whispers into my hair. "*Please*."

Wayne says, "Marnie? Ready to seal this marriage and kick off the party?"

I laugh. "Absolutely."

I break free of my embrace with Max and do my side of the ring ceremony. After Max's platinum band is firmly secured on his third finger, we kiss jubilantly to seal the deal.

Wayne bellows, "I now present to you: Mr. and Mrs. Maximillian and Marnie Vaughn!"

As the crowd cheers, Max takes my hand and deftly scoops Ripley up with his free arm. As a threesome, we bound down the center aisle, surrounded by cheers and applause, all of us feeling like we're floating on air.

Max turns to me wearing the biggest smile I've ever seen on his handsome face. "I love you, Mrs. Vaughn!" he shouts. After

I've returned his sentiment, he turns to Ripley. "Who's your daddy?" Ripley giggles and pokes her daddy's broad shoulder. "That's right!" Max shouts exuberantly. "And don't you ever forget it!" He returns to me. "We're a family, baby. Forever. I love you both so much—and I promise I'll never let either of you forget it."

THE END

Do you want to find out how Grayson, a quintessential golden retriever hero, won over Selena, the sophisticated older woman/single mother he meets through a wrong-number text and calls "Hot Teacher"? Get your copy of their spicy, swoony, funny romance with a happily ever after, **Textual Relations**.

Or maybe you'd like to read about Auggie? His spicy, funny, swoony romantic comedy will keep you turning the pages fanning yourself and laughing out loud all the way to Auggie and Charlotte's Happily Ever After! Get your copy of My Neighbors Secret!

If you prefer, feel free to check out any of the romance titles in Lauren's catalogue, described below. **All books by Lauren Rowe are available in ebook, paperback, and audiobook formats.**

BOOKS BY LAUREN ROWE

STANDALONE Romantic Comedy Series

Who's Your Daddy?

When thirty-year-old patent attorney, Maximillian Vaughn, meets a sassy, charismatic older woman in a bar, he invites her back to his place for one night of no-strings fun. It's all Max can offer, given his busy career; but, luckily, it's all Marnie wants, too. But when Max's

chemistry with Marnie is so combustible, it threatens to burn down his bedroom, he does the unthinkable the next morning: he asks Marnie out on a dinner date.

Mere minutes after saying yes, however, Marnie bolts like her hair is on fire with no explanation. What happened? Max doesn't know, but he's determined to find out and convince Marnie to pick up where they left off.

Textual Relations

When Grayson McKnight unknowingly gets a fake number from a woman in a bar, he winds up embroiled in a sexy text exchange with the actual owner of the number—a confident, sensual older woman who knows exactly who she is . . . and what she wants.

No strings attached.

But as sparks fly and real feelings develop, will Grayson get his way and tempt her to give him more than their original bargain?

My Neighbors Secret

When Charlotte gets into her new dilapidated condo to start fixing it up for resale, she finds out the infuriating stranger who's thoroughly messed up her life is her new next-door neighbor.

Also, that he's got a big secret.

She confronts him and proposes they work together to get themselves out of their respective jams, even though they both admittedly can't stand each other. Yes, he's let it slip he thinks she's pretty. And, okay, she begrudgingly thinks he's kind of cute. But whatever. They hate each other and this is nothing but a business partnership. What could go wrong?

The Secret Note (A Novella)

He's a hot Aussie. I'm a girl who isn't shy about getting what she wants. The problem? Ben is my little brother's best friend. An exchange student who's heading back Down Under any day now. But I can't help myself. He's too hot to resist.

Dive into Lauren's universe of interconnected trilogies and duets, all books available individually and as a bundle, in any order.

A full suggested reading order can be found here!

The Josh & Kat Trilogy

It's a war of wills between stubborn and sexy Josh Faraday and Kat Morgan. A fight to the bed. Arrogant, wealthy playboy Josh is used to getting what he wants. And what he wants is Kat Morgan. The books are to be read in order:

Infatuation

Revelation

Consummation

The Club Trilogy

When wealthy playboy Jonas Faraday receives an anonymous note from Sarah Cruz, a law student working part-time processing online applications for an exclusive club, he becomes obsessed with hunting her down and giving her the satisfaction she claims has always eluded her. Thus begins a sweeping tale of obsession, passion, desperation, and ultimately, everlasting love and individual redemption. Find out why scores of readers all over the world, in multiple languages, call The Club Trilogy "my favorite trilogy ever" and "the greatest love story I've ever read." As Jonas Faraday says to Sarah Cruz: "There's never been a love like ours and there never will be again… Our love is so pure and true, we're the amazement of the gods."

The Club: Obsession

The Club: Reclamation

The Club: Redemption

The fourth book for Jonas and Sarah is a full-length epilogue with incredible heart-stopping twists and turns and feels. Read The Club: Culmination (A Full-Length Epilogue Novel) after finishing The Club Trilogy or, if you prefer, after reading The Josh and Kat Trilogy.

The Reed Rivers Trilogy

Reed Rivers has met his match in the most unlikely of women—aspiring journalist and spitfire, Georgina Ricci. She's much younger than the women Reed normally pursues, but he can't resist her fiery personality and drop-dead gorgeous looks. But in this game of cat and mouse, who's chasing whom? With each passing day of this wild ride, Reed's not so sure. The books of this trilogy are to be read in order:

Bad Liar

Beautiful Liar

Beloved Liar

The Hate Love Duet

An addicting, enemies-to-lovers romance with humor, heat, angst, and banter. Music artists Savage of Fugitive Summer and Laila Fitzgerald are stuck together on tour. And convinced they can't stand each other. What they don't know is that they're absolutely made for each other, whether they realize it or not. The books of this duet are to be read in order:

Falling Out of Hate with You

Falling Into Love with You

Interconnected Standalones within the same universe as above

Hacker in Love

When world-class hacker Peter "Henn" Hennessey meets Hannah Milliken, he moves heaven and earth, including doing some questionable things, to win his dream girl over. But when catastrophe strikes, will Henn lose Hannah forever, or is there still a chance for him to chase their happily ever after? *Hacker in Love* is a steamy, funny, heart-pounding, **standalone** contemporary romance with a whole lot of feels, laughs, spice, and swoons.

Smitten

When aspiring singer-songwriter, Alessandra, meets Fish, the funny, adorable bass player of 22 Goats, sparks fly between the awkward pair. Fish tells Alessandra he's a "Goat called Fish who's hung like a bull. But not really. I'm actually really average." And Alessandra tells Fish, "There's nothing like a girl's first love." Alessandra thinks she's talking about a song when she makes her comment to Fish—the first song she'd ever heard by 22 Goats, in fact. As she'll later find out, though, her "first love" was actually Fish. The Goat called Fish who, after that night, vowed to do anything to win her heart. SMITTEN is a true standalone romance.

Swoon

When Colin Beretta, the drummer of 22 Goats, is a groomsman at the wedding of his childhood best friend, Logan, he discovers Logan's kid sister, Amy, is all grown up. Colin tries to resist his attraction to Amy, but after a drunken kiss at the wedding reception, that's easier said than done. Swoon is a true standalone romance.

The Morgan Brothers

Read these standalones in any order about the brothers of Kat Morgan. Chronological reading order is below, but they are all complete stories. Note: you do not need to read any other books or series before jumping straight into reading about the Morgan boys.

Hero

The story of heroic firefighter, Colby Morgan. When catastrophe strikes Colby Morgan, will physical therapist Lydia save him . . . or will he save her?

Captain

The insta-love-to-enemies-to-lovers story of tattooed sex god, Ryan Morgan, and the woman he'd move heaven and earth to claim.

Ball Peen Hammer

A steamy, hilarious, friends-to-lovers romantic comedy about cocky-as-hell male stripper, Keane Morgan, and the sassy, smart young woman who brings him to his knees during a road trip.

Mister Bodyguard

The Morgans' beloved honorary brother, Zander Shaw, meets his match in the feisty pop star he's assigned to protect on tour.

ROCKSTAR

When the youngest Morgan brother, Dax Morgan, meets a mysterious woman who rocks his world, he must decide if pursuing her is worth risking it all. Be sure to check out four of Dax's original songs from ROCKSTAR, written and produced by Lauren, along with full music videos for the songs, on her website (www.laurenrowebooks.com) under the tab MUSIC FROM ROCKSTAR.

***Misadventures Standalones* (unrelated standalones not within the above universe):**

- ***Misadventures on the Night Shift*** –A hotel night shift clerk encounters her teenage fantasy: rock star Lucas Ford. And combustion ensues.

- ***Misadventures of a College Girl***—A spunky, virginal theater major meets a cocky football player at her first college party . . . and absolutely nothing goes according to plan for either of them.

- ***Misadventures on the Rebound***—A spunky woman on the rebound meets a hot, mysterious stranger in a bar on her way to her five-year high school reunion in Las Vegas and what follows is a misadventure neither of them ever imagined.

Lauren's Dark Comedy/Psych Thriller Standalone

Countdown to Killing Kurtis

A young woman with big dreams and skeletons in her closet decides her porno-king husband must die in exactly a year. This is not a traditional romance, but it will most definitely keep you turning the pages and saying "WTF?" If you're looking for something a bit outside the box, with twists and turns, suspense, and dark humor, this is the book for you: a standalone psychological thriller/dark comedy with romantic elements.

AUTHOR BIOGRAPHY

Once you enter interconnected standalone romances of USA Today and internationally bestselling author Lauren Rowe's beloved and page-turning "Rowe-verse," you'll never want to leave. Find out why readers around the globe have fallen in love with all the characters in this world, including the Faradays, the Morgans and their besties, alpha mogul Reed Rivers and the artists signed to his record label, River Records.

Be sure to explore all the incredible spoiler-free bonus materials, including original music from the books, music videos, magazine covers and interviews, plus exclusive bonus scenes, all featured on Lauren's website at www.laurenrowebooks.com

To find out about Lauren's upcoming releases and giveaways, sign up for Lauren's emails here!

Lauren loves to hear from readers! Send Lauren an email from her website, say hi on Twitter, Instagram, or Facebook.

Made in the USA
Las Vegas, NV
16 November 2023